SECOND
SIGHT

SECOND SIGHT

A Novel

ELIZABETH COOKE
WRITING AS ELIZABETH McGREGOR

Copyright © 1999 by Elizabeth McGregor

Cover design by Kat JK Lee

ISBN: 978-1-5040-1939-2

Distributed in 2015 by Open Road Distribution
345 Hudson Street
New York, NY 10014
www.openroadmedia.com

SECOND
SIGHT

ONE

$\mathscr{S}$HE HAD LEFT THE MAGAZINES AND BOOKS on the table the previous evening. She had been reading the small paperback before she went to bed, and she knew that she had left it open, face down, to mark her page.

But now it lay centre stage, closed, neatly on top of Kieran's journals. Next to it lay the hardback on Masada, and the dig reports from Syria bound in their pale yellow matt with black spiral spine. Three very correct inches separated each pile. And they were all the same three inches or so from the edge of the table. They faced her in a mute, accusatory grid.

Her first thought had been safety. *Ruth could get in at night.*

That morning, an hour before, she had turned at the first sight of those neatened books, fury slamming through her along with fear. She had run upstairs in a blind panic, this intrusion one too much, the manipulation one too many, the whole forming one heavy block in her head. She knew then what people meant by the straw that broke the camel's back. Such a very slight thing bearing down so suddenly and so hard. She had packed as quickly as she could, dropping things unfolded into the suitcases, stuffing them haphazardly into free spaces. Some of her choices were bizarre. A thick sweater patterned with marguerites—she had never even liked it. Deck shoes with worn rope soles that wouldn't see out another summer.

Every few moments, she had glanced out of the window, to where her four-year-old son lay perfectly still under the trees. Theo was stretched on the ground at the edge of the lawn, as if lying in wait, his gaze fixed on the roots of the beech hedge, his small arm extended, wrist bent, palm upwards as though clasping another invisible hand. The spring morning was dry and cold, and a scouring wind blew straight down the valley, shaking the trees.

Lin had looked up at the hill that rose steeply behind the garden. It was ridged until its very top, a green chalk mound with an indentation at the summit. Beyond that summit rose a higher one, the heathland of the Hamble monument with its crowning white-stone tower. She had stared at it, and then back at the boy. There had been no noise in the valley other than the distant sound of a van toiling up the long gradient of the lane that wound round the eastern slope of the hill. The world was quite deserted, dead.

Lin had glanced at the bedroom clock. Ten thirty. It would be past midday now in Pedhoulas. Kieran would probably ring her at midday, and she had become abruptly afraid of being there for the call, of being plunged into going over the same ground again. She was tired of the ritual: explaining what Ruth had done; listening to his amused dismissals.

She had once believed that he still loved his ex-wife. Now she thought that it wasn't love but habit and sloth. He liked Ruth's attention just as an indulged son loves to be stroked by his mother. He did all but curl up in Ruth's lap and let her smooth his hair. It was Ruth this, Ruth that, Ruth who was so respected, Ruth so sensible, Ruth so kind.

Lin knew that his voice could keep her in the house. And, as she had thought of Kieran, a crazy pattern interrupted her line of sight: the tool-worked leather at the edge of his desk, the reflection of sunlight on a stone path cut by an irregular fence. Castellated blocks danced across the light, and she had closed her eyes and pressed her hand to the side of her head. The piercing image had flashed and subsided.

She had zipped the last case, and run into Theo's room. The floor was filled with toys: massed ranks of tin soldiers, Star Wars ships, grotesque little plastic aliens. Her son was halfway through a battle that had already lasted several weeks. Each night the lines were moved, the tactics changed, new ranks murdered, the dead resurrected. It was an intensely crowded, complicated world, and she knew with a sinking heart that she was about to destroy it. Biting her lip, she had snatched up two of the largest toys, and filled a carrier bag with some of the figures.

Then, minutes ago, something had stopped her. Some last regret, some steadying hand. She had paused, staring at the wall, then looking out again at Theo still oblivious on his stomach by the hedge. She tried to imagine what Ruth would say, how she would twist this absence.

She had gone downstairs for another look.

Imagine it. To come in at night, with Lin and Theo asleep upstairs. Come in at night, and do nothing at all but walk through to the sitting room and correct whatever traces there were of Lin's presence. In Lin's own house. In Kieran's own house.

In the house that used to be Ruth's.

So like Ruth not to do more. Another disenchanted, discarded wife might have slashed the seats, ripped the books apart. Or worse: set fire to the house while they slept obliviously on.

Ruth had stood back and taken her exile well. Behaved in such a civilized fashion. There had been no hysterics from Ruth, no accusations, no scenes. Oh . . . perhaps a little at first. Raised voices in these rooms. Followed by fury of a quieter, more long-lasting kind. Phone calls . . . there were always phone calls, even now. Ruth needing Kieran in the evening. Kieran going over to her flat to talk.

But then . . . this.

Lin had changed the lock on the front door, the great Georgian wood door that faced down the drive. She had assumed, a month or so ago, that that was where Ruth came in. Straight through the front door.

But Ruth must have more than one key. She must have the keys to the whole house.

Lin stared now at the table.

'No,' she whispered. 'No more.' Her fingers closed over the piece of paper in her pocket: the address in Hampton, her old student flat.

She went back to the hall, not running this time but walking with a confirmed purpose, her face set. She picked up the first case and went out to the car. Then, with the car loaded, she went around the side of the house and out onto the long, sloping lawn that ran down to the river. The grass was bumpy, yellowed in places, patched with moss. The chestnut trees hung over it, splattering uneven shadows, their rustling, whispering and swaying filling the air.

'Theo!' she called. He didn't move.

She walked over to him. She took several deep breaths, the pain in her head squeezing the last to a sharply drawn sigh. Theo didn't look up, and she lay down full-length at his side, resting her head on her folded arms. The salt marks of that morning's tears felt like paint on her face.

Her son's small fist clenched suddenly on her arm.

'Look,' he said. He had managed to prise the last upside-down flowerpot from the mound, and gave a little cry of triumph. 'Nest!'

She turned her head and looked at him.

'What are you doing?'

'Waking them up.' He had a pointed stick, and was prodding the cone-shaped patch of earth.

'They're already awake,' she said. She gazed at the ants feverishly scouring the upturned ground, by turns caressing and dragging the disturbed pupae back to the dark.

'Look . . . they running.'

'Yes. They're frightened,' she told him.

The wingless females toiled in the earth, the smallest frantically circling the storehouses, driven by the need to maintain the salivary secretions of the bodies of their young. Lin glanced at Theo's preoccupied profile, his four-year-old absorption in their task, the inner darker red of his parted lip, the smoothness of his face, the curious forked crease at the corner of each eye, the fair lashes under dark brows that gave him such a surprised look.

'Theo,' she said. 'We've got to go.'

'In a minute.'

She got up, smoothed down her clothes, and looked back at the house. It was lovely. The vast square flint-and-cob building dominated the small rise above the village, set in its own half-acre of lawn.

A prickle of sensation ran down one side of her head, slightly behind her ear, from below the crown to the edge of her jaw. She put up her hand to feel the path of the pain: a curious, blunt blow of electricity.

She held out her hand to him. 'Time to go.'

He rolled on his back. 'Where we going?'

She pulled him to his feet, stroked the grass from his sweatshirt. Even in the racing shadows of the branches, the wind tasted of the chalk blown from the hills above them. She held him to her, resisting his squirming, and pressed her lips to his hair.

'Away,' she murmured. 'We're going away.'

TWO

*R*UTH CARMICHAEL WAS LISTENING.

Her face was turned away from her patient as she pressed the stethoscope against Caroline Devlin's back. She found the other woman's proximity, if not unpleasant, certainly unappealing.

As she looked to one side, she could see the ordered neatness of her own desk, the peace lily with its naked white bloom, the uncurtained white blind drawn across the window. Her surgery office had a view of the Victorian street below, and the park across the way. Directly opposite, a giant copper beech had just begun to darken on the long journey to its bloodied summer black. She glanced at it, then beyond to the clock tower beyond the trees. It was midday. The surgery was running late. Caroline Devlin was her last patient.

'What can you hear?' the woman asked anxiously. 'You can't hear anything unusual?'

Ruth took the instrument away from her ear. 'I can't hear anything at all if you continue talking,' she observed mildly.

'I'm sorry,' Caroline replied.

The skin of the woman's exposed back was very pale. It was mottled with tiny threadlike moles: an example, if ever Ruth had seen one, of a body replicating a personality. Caroline Devlin was a marriage-guidance counsellor: a thin, wispy woman with a frayed manner, as if on the edge of an anxiety attack. A long ponytail of greying brown hair was twisted into an artfully untidy pleat whose strands hung down her neck. The knot of hair was secured with a wooden pin four inches from Ruth's face. The hair smelled of talcum powder.

Ruth closed her eyes and listened to the echoes of the heart.

She admired this rhythm more than any other. She had found it mysterious from being a child, lying with her head fastened with pressure against her own pillow. The relentless opening and closing, the perfection, the immediacy of response. The human heart pumped five litres of blood a minute, beating ninety thousand times a day, more than thirty million times every year. A large muscular fist, tethered in the chest by its arteries and veins, and protected by a double-walled sac attached to the breastbone and diaphragm, its beating—the dull and sharp double contraction—controlled by the autonomic nervous system originated in the brain. Ruth always thought of this superior operator of the system, the brain, rather than the slave heart itself when she listened to that blunt-peaked thud in the chest. Behind every beat, an imperative. And she was also deeply fascinated by the sound of a heart fractured and labouring.

Which she could not hear now.

She took the stethoscope away and looked at Caroline Devlin.

'Tell me again what happened,' she said.

Caroline laced her fingers together in her lap. 'It was very curious,' she said, 'very sudden. I was simply reviewing my caseload before work. I had drunk a cup of coffee, taken a phone call . . . and felt this sensation as if I was been pressed between two closing walls . . .' She looked up at Ruth. 'I really think it's nothing,' she added hastily. 'If it hadn't been for my colleagues overreacting—'

'And your arm felt strange, you said?'

'Just the merest numbness, a little tingling. It went away very quickly.'

'Which arm?'

'The left.'

'And where exactly was the tingling?'

9

Caroline spread her hand. 'Here in my finger. Just one finger, the third.'

'Any other symptoms?'

'No.'

'Have you experienced this before?'

'Never.' A rigorous shaking of the head.

'Any history of heart disease in your family?'

A silence while Caroline Devlin paled. 'None.'

'Have you had a blood cholesterol test recently?'

'Not recently. Five years ago. The reading was about seven.'

'Did you feel nauseous when this happened, this morning?'

'No.'

Ruth nodded at Caroline's clothes folded on the chair next to the couch. 'You can dress again now,' she said, moving away to her desk, where she sat down and began to make notes.

From the other side of the curtain came Caroline's voice. 'I really think this is due to stress, you know,' she said. 'We've been terribly busy. One of our office staff told me this morning that there's this enormous nerve running down your chest, and when it clamps up, it feels just like a heart attack.'

Ruth did not look up. 'Does it?' she murmured. 'How interesting.'

Caroline Devlin emerged and sat down on a nearby chair.

Ruth was not a particularly popular GP. She was not effusive, friendly, or necessarily approachable, although she was perfectly capable of such reactions if they were needed. Yet she did have an impressive, unhurried calm. Patients often said that she had time to listen to them. Either that or the other side of the coin: that she would not be rushed.

Now she put down her pen and gazed at her notes in silence for some time. Then she glanced back to Caroline.

'We've got a portable ECG in the nurse's room,' she said. 'I'd like you to have a check on that.'

'I see,' Caroline said. 'I'll make an appointment.'

'There's no need,' Ruth replied. 'The nurse will have finished her list, so I'll pop through now and get it organized.'

'Now?' Caroline echoed. 'I can't possibly do that. I have clients this afternoon.'

Ruth smiled as she stood up. 'Just a check. Nothing to worry about.'

She left the room and walked along the corridor to the short flight of stairs. As she reached the top, she heard the receptionist call her. The woman was leaning out from the counter, looking up the stairs.

'Dr Carmichael?' she shouted. 'Are you there?'

Ruth came slowly down the stairs. The woman's confusion cleared.

'Ah . . . must have just missed you. Call for you. Outside line.'

'I'm just coming for Antonia. Where is she?'

'Finishing a vaccination,' said the other receptionist, from behind a wall of records: hundreds of bunched yellow envelopes kept on bulging shelves.

'Call her for me,' Ruth said. She picked up the phone irritatedly. 'Who is it?'

'They didn't say.'

Ruth looked at the receptionist coldly. She put the phone to her ear. 'Yes?'

'Ruth . . . it's Lin.'

Ruth's face did not alter. She continued staring expressionlessly into a space beyond the counter, between the two women facing her.

'Can you hear me?'

'I can,' Ruth said.

There was a pause. Lin sounded frayed, shadowy, her voice almost drowned by the noise of traffic.

'Keep away from me,' Lin said.

'I'm sorry?'

Another crackling, booming pause.

'You heard me, Ruth. Keep away. Just keep away.' Lin hung up.

Ruth listened for a moment to the buzz of the disconnection, then replaced the receiver on its rest below the counter. She allowed herself the faintest, briefest of smiles.

'OK?' the receptionist asked, looking over her shoulder.

'Chris, come here,' Ruth said.

The woman took a couple of steps towards her, eyebrows raised.

Ruth lowered her voice and leaned towards her.

'Don't ever shout for me like that,' she said. 'Do you understand?

11

There's absolutely no need to shout up the stairs. No need at all to raise your voice.'

The other woman blinked.

'Do I make myself clear?' Ruth asked.

'Yes,' the receptionist replied. A flush of embarrassment crept up her face.

'Tell Antonia to stack up the ECG and call me when it's ready,' Ruth said.

Utterly composed, she turned and walked away.

THREE

*T*HE PHONE RANG AT PRECISELY MIDNIGHT.

'Lin . . . is that you?'

'Yes.'

She heard Kieran try to control his voice. 'Where's Theo?'

'Right here.'

She glanced over at the open door leading to the only bedroom, a tiny eight-by-six room under the eaves, where Theo was now soundly asleep. They had a bedroom, sitting room, and a bathroom down on the half-landing. Sometimes, in the darkness, Lin could hear the slow, muffled bleep of the alarm on the front door of the shop far below.

'Is he all right?' Kieran asked.

'Of course he is.'

A pause.

'I've warned you, Kieran,' Lin said softly. 'Dozens of times.'

'Where are you exactly?'

'We're in Hampton.'

He gave a deep, impatient sigh. 'When did you get there?'

'Yesterday.'

Another silence, then, 'This about beats all.'

13

'Maybe now you'll take me seriously,' she said quietly.

'I spoke to Ruth last month—you know that.'

'You told her not to come to the house any more?'

'Yes,' he replied. 'She denied it, Lin, as I could have told you.'

She stared around the living room. The phone was next to the sofa where she slept. There were no curtains on the window. No need so high above everyone else, with a view of roofs and the winding hill and the river.

Kieran's voice came back softly. 'I just got in and found this message,' he said.

'I rang you at noon.'

'We've been filming up the coast from here,' he said.

'Is it hot?'

'No, it's raining.'

She said nothing. Filming was misery in rain. *She* ought to know. She could hear other voices, a great many, but far back from the phone he was using.

Two thousand miles away, Kieran glanced about himself. He was in a small Cypriot hotel in a mountain village. The reception desk was a counter four feet from a door that had probably been propped open for a hundred years. The floor was a lurid green linoleum, the steps from the door bright blue. Calor Gas cylinders lined the steps and the pavement outside. And beyond the door the rain sheeted down in one solid curtain, straight and heavy. There was no breath of wind. The temperature was stuck at sixty-five.

'How is Harry?' Lin asked.

'Never mind him. Lin . . .'

She felt his exasperation. 'This is your doing,' she told him. 'She still comes around, Kee. She was there on Monday.'

'Look, I accept it's something of a pain,' he said. 'You know what she is. Needs to be in there. Can't you just tolerate her? It's not as if she's malicious—just the opposite.'

Lin stared in exasperation at the ceiling, knotting her fist on the lumped-up blankets that covered her.

'I wonder how much *you* would stand of it if you were here more often.'

'I'd be glad to see her. I like Ruth.'

'Yes,' she agreed. 'You obviously do.'

'You're letting this get out of proportion, Lin.'

'She comes in at *night*! What more do I have to say to convince you? She comes at night, for God's sake!'

'To do what?' he demanded.

'Nothing. That's it, don't you see? She just sits there, rearranges magazines . . .'

'She rearranges magazines?' His tone was now incredulous. 'You've left home because my ex-wife rearranges your magazines?'

'Yes!' Lin retorted. She felt tears beginning to block her throat. 'She has a set of keys and comes into our house at night, Kieran. Or when I'm out during the day. I know she's been there.'

'Have you asked her about it?'

'What?' Lin said.

'Have you asked her if she's doing it?'

'Of course not!'

'Then how do you know it's Ruth?'

'Oh, God.' For a moment, Lin put the receiver down, then lifted it again to her ear. 'If it isn't her, I'm in even worse trouble,' she said almost tonelessly. 'I've got a stranger coming into my house at night and fumbling around, moving things. Never taking things. Never destroying things. Just moving stuff around. Can't you see how crazy it is?'

'It's crazy all right,' he murmured.

She caught his meaning. 'You mean Ruth can't be crazy, so *I* must be?'

'Now—'

'I'm the ridiculous one. She's the one constantly ringing up and coming round here. But *I'm* the ridiculous one. I'm crazy. I'm . . . what? Overreacting? Of course. It's me—that's right, I forgot.'

She closed her eyes. The room suddenly felt cold. She had a sensation of being cast away, isolated. There was a sudden violent thump from Theo's room.

'Wait a minute,' she said into the phone.

'What is it?'

'It's Theo. Wait a minute.' She dropped the phone and swung her legs down off the couch. In the dark she ran over to look into his room. But her son was lying perfectly still, on his back, the bed coverings still tucked tightly around him. She leaned down, checked his breathing, the sweet warm smell of him.

Lin went back to the living-room couch and picked up the discarded receiver. 'It was nothing,' she said.

Kieran had obviously taken the time to gather himself for their next flurry. 'I've only been away six weeks.'

'I know that.'

'And you say she's escalated to this in six weeks?'

'I'm telling you—' Lin began.

'This is such a petty thing to do, Lin.'

'Aren't you afraid?' she asked.

'About what?'

'Afraid for me. Someone's coming into our house—'

'But not breaking in? And then doing what? Do you really think Ruth would come in and just sit there? Just fiddle about with the furniture? Why? What's the purpose?'

'I don't know,' Lin said miserably.

'Do you see how utterly fantastic this sounds? I'm more afraid for you there now, wherever you are.'

'I'm not imagining it.'

'I didn't say so.'

'I can hear it in your voice.'

'Well,' he said, smiling to himself. 'You do have a wonderful imagination.'

She didn't reply. She couldn't. She fisted one hand and put it to the side of her head. If he had been present in the room, she might have hit him. She sat with her knees now pulled up to her chest, her free arm wrapped around them, her breath coming in short, progressively laboured gasps.

'Kieran,' she said slowly, 'don't belittle me.'

For some time there was nothing but the background voices on his end of the line. She heard someone loudly ordering drinks. She could even hear the whispering slush of the rain.

'I'm all right here,' she said finally. 'It's a little flat, over a shop in the Liddles.' That was a warren of market streets just out of the centre of Hampton: a mixture of delicatessens, bookshops, secondhand-clothes stores. 'Don't you remember Edith Channon? With the shop? She lives below me. She—'

'I can't believe it,' he said, as if he had heard nothing of the last few sentences. 'To leave home over this—leave our beautiful home—'

'Your home,' she corrected him. 'Yours and Ruth's.'

'No, no . . .'

'Yes, *yes*. She still thinks it's hers. It's like . . .' Lin finally broke down, much to her own disgust after all her attempts to seem rational. She wanted to play this trump card calmly. *Ruth or me. Choose Ruth or me.* And instead she could hear herself weeping, gasping.

'Darling,' he said.

'I don't *want* to have to leave the house,' she said. 'Oh God,' she murmured, a private plea that was barely audible.

'How are you feeling?' he asked.

She fumbled for a tissue on the table alongside the sofa. She found nothing, and wiped her free hand over her face. 'What?'

'Your headaches.'

'Oh . . . OK.' This was a lie. Something in her head, something in the way she looked at the world, the messages she processed through, was awry. She couldn't determine the exact difference. It was as if the world were made of some subtly altered substance: the same and not the same.

Another long pause. 'Are you working?' he asked.

She stared at the phone helplessly. 'Frightened I won't finish your script?'

'Don't be funny.'

'Or the editing?'

'Lin, please.'

She made a grudging face to herself. 'I'm working,' she told him. Working in the moments—sometimes no more than fifteen minutes at a time—that Theo would allow her. Her bursts of sharpened, irregular concentration had also changed, heightened and distorted. Sometimes, as she sat down to write, the page seemed to lie at the end of a kaleidoscopic tube. Then, closing her eyes, reopening them, this image would vanish.

She was so very tired.

'You know what this is?' Kieran asked. He sounded closer now, as if he had cupped his hand over the receiver. 'This is blackmail.'

'What can I do if you take her word over mine?'

'I don't take her word over yours. I'm simply . . .' Another selection of the correct phrase. 'I'm simply astonished,' he said finally. 'And disappointed.'

Her heart went cold. She tightened her grip on the phone.

'Just tell her,' she said very evenly, 'to stay away. Leave us alone. Have her own life. Not mine. Not yours.'

'All right,' he conceded at last. 'All right. I'll phone her tomorrow. But, if I do, you must promise me one thing.'

'What is it?'

'Go back to the house.'

'No.'

'Oh, really!'

'No,' she repeated.

She started to put the phone down, then rapidly pressed it back to her ear. 'Don't tell her where I am, Kieran,' she said.

'Why should I?'

'Promise me.'

He laughed to himself. 'Hope to die.'

Exasperated, she gave in to a childish impulse and hung up on him. She listened to the street, the silence.

'You don't know,' she murmured. 'You don't know.'

On the other side of Europe, he put down the receiver.

'What is it?' Harry asked him.

'Sometimes I wonder,' Kieran said.

Harry handed him a drink. Kieran's agent had been holding ready two thumb-smeared glasses, a quart of Scotch tucked under one arm. Harry was a short man, carrying much more weight than he could afford, who looked older than his forty years, with a heavily greying beard and a rumpled, battered look. Kieran allowed himself an amused moment of pity.

Ever the concerned agent, Harry had arrived only two days before, scenting trouble and trying to avert it. Kieran was already enmeshed in another running battle with the crew over locations, changing his mind, altering the script, scorching the telephone lines between here and London. Ben Lazenby had already gone home, and left the last half-episode to his assistant.

Harry felt like the original fish out of water. He had spent barely two hours, on first arrival, in his pre-booked hotel; for the rest of the time he had been accompanying Kieran on bumpy, sweaty, dank journeys along tracks whose overstated scent of thyme and breathtaking views did nothing at all to ease Harry's mood. They had spent last night here, where Harry had grumbled for a full hour about the stacks of empty Beck's crates and a 1930s bathroom of peeling, verdigris grandeur.

'Why are we here anyway?' he had demanded. 'There's a beautiful hotel just down the road.'

'Not with this view,' Kieran had told him.

They had been sitting outside, looking over the white church in the valley, while a thin Cypriot girl swept the path and the empty road.

Harry put a hand on his arm now. 'You want to tell me what's going on?'

'She left the house.'

'Lin? Why?'

'Because of Ruth.'

Harry put down his glass, looked at his feet.

'That's what she says—but it's not true.'

Harry glanced at him. 'How do you know?'

'Because it's too absurd.'

'Oh, *absurd*. Right. What exactly?'

Kieran considered for a moment, then shrugged. 'It doesn't matter. She'll come back.'

'You are having a great month. Anyone left to insult?'

Kieran waved his hand. 'She often goes away for a couple of days to do research. She always has. This is just that, dressed up—dramatized. She'll be all right by the time I get back.'

Harry was staring at him. 'And that's it?'

'That's it.'

Harry bent his knees to look up into Kieran's downturned face. 'You're a piss-poor liar.'

Kieran ran his hand through his hair, but made no reply. Then, with a grudging smile, he extended his own hand, flat, and pushed Harry's face away.

Harry went back to the bar.

In the corner, an elderly couple were staring at Kieran, both with the bemused smile reserved for the unknown confronting the famous, as if Kieran were an illusion capable of vanishing at any moment.

And Kieran possessed, Harry had to admit, a perfect television face.

They had altered the graphics on *The History House* this year. The programme was impressive, no longer giving off that made-in-the-provinces aura. It was immensely slick now, with a cellophane-wrapped quality. Some of the original quirkiness had gone, of course, ironed and airbrushed away. Hand-held cameras, with their choppy style, had edged out the static frames of the first episodes. But that had suited Kieran all the more—made a good partner to his casual charm.

Kieran was in his mid-thirties, dark, tall and lean, with a lazy sexual smile that rattled the screen. Since *The History House* began two years ago, he had become a national name.

The opening credits of the programme were imposing: a packed sequence of ramparts, Elizabethan courtyards, country houses, bones in burial ditches, air-shots of the Thames, causeways, and vast Neolithic rings bleaching through downland. Stone eagles transmuted to Byzantine horses, each image bordered with the red-and-gold of the programme logo. The horses in turn melted into flags, swords, crowns and crests, with Kieran's smile miraculously and handsomely appearing between the familiar faces of politicians, newscasters, actresses, and sports stars. All to a throbbing and insistent tune written specially by a knighted West End composer.

The final episode of the previous series had been particularly well done. In the opening shots Kieran was revealed standing on a small headland overlooking a Welsh estuary. Next to him was another television face: a game-show celebrity known for his quick wits and bordering-on-the-offensive grin.

They had looked rather a comic couple, each vying for the camera's attention: Kieran with his laid-back air, his faint but seamless tan, his trademark black shirt and black leather jacket; the older man as pale as Kieran was dark, and dressed sadly in a golfing sweater and sparkle-patterned tie. He rapidly lost the battle, poor man, standing in a cow rut while Kieran lounged on a nearby wall.

'Tell me how you came to buy such a marvellous place,' had been Kieran's opening line.

The comedian had laughed. 'Well, it's a funny story . . .'

Not a very funny story, as it had turned out. Kieran had listened, smiling, then taken the other man's arm, as if guiding an invalid down the grassy slope. A nice touch, Harry had to admit. 'And now let's look at the Bronze Age evidence . . .'

Of course, Kieran had not always been such a household name.

When he and Ruth first met, she had just taken up partnership in the town medical practice, and he had been doing a postgraduate course at the university. Three years later he had his teaching post: History, of course. Roman history. The Punic Wars. He had once lovingly described his old flat to Harry: filled with Latin and Greek texts, a bachelor's flat on campus—before Ruth had reorganized him. She was older than him by five years. Kieran admitted that he had not then possessed a grain of ambition, so after their marriage it had been Ruth who had manoeuvred him towards a better job, Ruth who had thrown the discreet little dinner parties, Ruth who had fitted them both so well into the university hierarchy. She was the perfect hostess, Kieran had told him. Utterly charming. He had been promoted by the time he was twenty-eight.

Harry studied the same man now. Lin had also wrought a complete change in his career. Kieran was a lucky man, the kind who always fell soundly on his feet, the kind nurtured by one clever woman after another, nurtured and mothered for his good looks and his charm, and his air of being the naughtiest boy in the school. A lazy, smiling

Flashman. Nevertheless, Harry was sure that Kieran was at heart an academic, not a television personality. Television was not his meat at all; to Kieran it was just a passing game.

'Hell, poor old Lin,' Harry said out loud. Several feet away, Kieran glanced up. Harry rejoined him. He liked Lin. She was an original, a one-off, and more of a contrast to Ruth Harry could not imagine. He switched the whisky bottle from palm to palm.

'Another glass?'

'No,' said Kieran. 'I'm going to bed.' He walked to the stairs.

As Harry watched him go, he drained his glass, a thoughtful expression on his face. Then he turned and leaned over the counter behind him. There was a litter of paper there, an ancient switchboard, a safe lurking underneath it, the ubiquitous plate of little oranges. Oranges everywhere out here. No crisp packets in the roads, no cigarette packets, just orange skins squashed every hundred yards. Oranges in the road, orange trees at the side of the roads. He picked one off the plate and began peeling it, thinking, speculating.

Kieran's passing games.

Sucking on the fruit, moving the sweet pith around his mouth, Harry looked hard along the counter. The girl who had attended it an hour before was now behind the bar across the damp hall, taking no notice of the reception area.

There was a sheet of lined paper beside the phone, and Harry turned it around with his fingertips. On the paper was a UK telephone number.

Lobbing the orange peel out into the rainy street, Harry swiftly wrote down the number. Then, taking the whisky bottle with him, he went up to his room.

FOUR

THE EYES COULD BE DIFFICULT.

It took time, that was all. Time and infinite patience. Gripping the body between her knees, Edith Channon pulled the head away from the neck socket, and slipped the stringing hook under the loop, keeping tension on the elastic. She bent over the placid face, gently working it away from her—twisting it. There was a head hook in here somewhere.

She picked up the holding stick. Just as she did so, the tension in the line slackened and slipped.

'No,' she whispered. But it was too late. The line was gone.

At her side, Theo's small face almost rested on her shoulder.

'Look what I've done,' the old woman murmured.

'What?'

'Lost my line. Now I'll have to re-string her.'

'Is it a bad doll?'

Edith laughed. 'No, not a bad doll. Just me. Just my fingers.' She held up the auburn-haired head. The body lay on her towel, flesh-pink arms, yellowed torso, jointed shoulders, hips and knees. 'What do you think?' she asked. 'Is she pretty?'

Theo considered the bisque socket head, eerily detached from its shoulders.

'She got staring eyes.'

'She won't have when I'm done,' Edith said. 'They'll open and close like a real baby. She needs something called a rocker unit.' She turned the head upside-down so that he could see. 'Look inside,' she said.

'Wire and paper.'

'Not paper. Cork. Old cork. I'll take that away and put new cork there.'

'Inside her chin?'

'Inside her chin.' Edith put the head down. Theo stroked the auburn hair.

'A man made that doll,' Edith said. 'Ninety years ago.'

'Why?'

Edith thought. 'For little girls to hold.'

Theo made a dismissive noise in his throat.

'Look up on the shelf,' Edith said. 'Look at the Japanese ones.' She pointed across the dim shop. 'You know what they call him? Shoki, the Devil Chaser. He protected boys. Fathers—daddies, you know—bought them as presents for their boys. And look at the one on the horse. See him? On a lovely horse. He's a samurai. A warrior.'

Theo looked, but made no move towards them. 'Got lots of old stuff,' he observed.

Edith smiled, and returned to the repair. 'Yes,' she said. 'To match me.'

Theo got down from the seat and went to the window.

'She won't be long,' Edith said.

He was silent, one thumb and index finger twisting the seam line on his cotton shorts.

As she worked, occasionally he looked back at the shop, at the three walls crammed floor to ceiling with shelves, and every shelf in turn crammed with bodies, hands, dresses, faces. Theo dare not look at the shelf nearest to him, alongside the window, where a horrible female doll, six inches high, stood in a glass case. She had a wrinkled black face, an open mouth, yellowed teeth and glass-bead eyes, and she carried a basket of threads and ribbons and combs. It was the first thing he had noticed when he came into the shop two days ago, and while Lin had been exclaiming, 'Oh, my goodness, look at the dolls! More than ever!' he had been gripping her hand, ignoring the soldiers, the stuffed Sunny Jim, the disgusting Struwwelpeter with his long nails, and had been staring transfixed at the apple-head pedlar.

'Look, Theo,' Lin had said, 'Russian dolls. They go one inside the other.'

'I do wish someone would buy them,' Edith had said, glancing from the shelves to Theo's stricken face and back again. 'It's all the presidents, you see? Brezhnev . . . Stalin . . .'

'How clever,' Lin had murmured.

'I suppose so,' Edith had said.

She had taken a step forward and kneeled in front of Theo. 'Are you coming to live upstairs?' she asked.

Theo didn't reply. He liked the old lady's face, but held up his hand to his cheek, flat and pointing outwards, so that it shielded from him the sight of the pedlar.

'I don't like her,' he had said.

'Theo!' Lin had objected.

Edith had merely smiled. 'It's not me. It's Nanny,' she had said, nodding to the glass box. 'Disgusting old thing, isn't she? They pickled apples until they got hard, and then carved the face. I wouldn't buy a thing off her, would you?'

'No,' Theo had retorted vehemently.

Edith had straightened up. 'There's no dolls upstairs,' she told him. 'It's all nice and white. I painted it myself. You can see up and down the street.' She had gone to the door to the stairs, then turned back to him. 'Do you like fudge?' she asked.

'No,' he said.

'Cake?'

'Yes.'

'Sponge or with raisins?'

'Raisins,' said Theo.

'Well, I don't cook them,' Edith said. 'But I eat them all right. With a cup of tea.'

'Yeth,' Theo had said, not sure of her, gripping Lin's hand and retreating behind her legs.

'How old is he?' Edith had asked.

'Four.'

'On holiday?'

'Sort of . . . a bit of a holiday.'

Edith had smiled. 'You know, you haven't changed. Maybe a bit thinner, though you can't afford to be. Here long?'

Lin had paused. 'Maybe,' she had said.

'That's OK,' Edith replied. She took down the keys of the upstairs from a hook inside the stairwell, and then followed her up.

Now, this following morning, Theo turned back to look at Edith. 'What you doing now?' he asked.

'Well, I shall wash her head inside and out,' Edith replied. 'I shall take off her hair and clean it. Then I'll make her eyes right. And she'll go to sleep when she's put back together.'

'Going to wash her head,' Theo repeated.

'Come and help,' Edith said.

'Noooo . . .'

The door opened.

It was Lin.

He ran over to her, and she picked him up at once, as he wound his arms around her neck. 'Hi,' she said, kissing his cheek. 'Been good?'

'Waiting for you rather anxiously,' Edith said. 'Did you find my GP OK?'

'Yes.'

'Fix you up all right?'

Lin tried to prise Theo's head from the crook of her shoulder. She looked over him at Edith. 'Thank you for looking after him.'

'It's no trouble.'

'I think I'll take us both for a walk,' she said. 'Can I get you anything from the shops?'

'No, no,' Edith said. 'I'm perfectly all right.'

'Is the man in every day?' Lin asked.

Edith looked up. 'Which man?'

'The one downstairs.'

There was a floor between them; Edith had the rooms behind the shop.

'Which man downstairs?'

Lin frowned. 'I can hear him walking about, running the water,' she said.

Edith looked at her for some moments. 'Oh, him,' she said. 'He's in and out. Sometimes I don't hear him for weeks.'

Lin hesitated, then smiled. 'I'll leave you in peace,' she said.

Holding her son's hand, she went out of the shop. She paused for a moment, then turned left. Her expression, Edith noted, was pinched, closed, her eyes squinting against the morning sun.

'Headache,' Edith murmured to herself. 'Yes . . . terrible headache.'

FIVE

*I*T HAD BEEN A SUMMER'S DAY, beyond the doors: too hot by far, humidity pressing sweat from every pore. The sun had long ago retreated behind a thundery yellow cloud.

Ruth's attention had been caught by a sudden movement outside.

All those summers ago, the woman had come running across the car park towards the hospital. Ruth could see that her arms were held rigidly in front of her a few seconds before she actually saw what the woman was carrying. She ran in an ungainly, staggering fashion, much too heavy to be running at all, her mouth dropped open with the effort. She must have weighed eighteen stone.

The child sagged in her outstretched grasp, its head curled inwards, only the white nape of the neck visible. Inwards against the mother's chest. The child wore a red T-shirt and red-and-white striped shorts; the mother an orange shift, home-made, stained under the arms, too short for her. Wide, mottled, white legs pumping. Hair shorn close to her head.

For a moment, Ruth was reminded of a shot she had seen in news coverage of a war: stricken mother; injured, unconscious child, and the shock and panic in the parent's face.

Ruth blinked.

The doors swung open.

They were not automatic doors and, as a result, there was that fleeting impression of surprise. The doors could not open on their own, but there was no one near them. They opened and the mother rushed in, and abruptly, in the disjointed remembered images, the scene changed from one of complete silence—the dash across the car park nothing more than a mime—into a crash of noise. The mother was keening: a primitive noise way back in her throat, one of complete horror.

'Help me!' she shouted. 'Help me!'

Ruth went forward.

Strange, no other nurses. No other doctor. There must have been, of course. There must have been.

'What happened?'

Ruth looked down at the child: a little girl of about seven, red-haired, freckle-skinned, small bony arms curled into a foetal helplessness, small bony legs with skinned knees. There were bruises on the arms, a long healing cut on the forehead.

'She just . . . she just . . .' The mother was having trouble breathing.

All at once, the doors crashed open again, and two men and a boy in his teens rushed in, all shouting at once.

Ruth tried to take the child. The mother resisted.

'Let me look at her. Bring her through,' Ruth said.

Where had everyone on Casualty been that day? They were in a barren, unpeopled landscape of grey walls, lacquered, overpolished floors. An abandoned trolley. A bed with a single green-paper sheet.

She put the child down.

Nothing more than a little lightweight sack of flesh. What did she weigh? Not more than four stone.

'She was in the garden,' the mother was saying.

'What's the matter? What's the matter?' asked one of the men.

Ruth tried desperately to ignore him. *Pull the curtain.*

She turned the child's head to left and right. The skin was swollen, puffy. The cut on her head was masking a deeper, more penetrating bruise that would surely show black in a day or two.

'What caused this?' Ruth demanded.

'She fell off the swing in the back yard. On to concrete,' the mother said, eyes wide with fright. Every time she took a breath, it was with an agonized, grinding gasp. Smoker. Heavy smoker.

'When?'

'Yesterday.'

Ruth felt around the child's head for fracture.

'She was all right . . . she was all right . . .' the mother gabbled.

'She was running round the garden half an hour ago,' one man said. Presumably the father. Also overweight. Grey-faced, unshaven, the bloodshot eyes of a drinker. 'Took my eyes off her one minute, then she's lying down by the fence, like this.'

'There was nothing to trip over,' the woman said.

'Any other injuries?' Ruth asked.

'Injuries?' the mother echoed.

Ruth turned on her. She waved her hand pointedly at the head wound. 'You see this—is there anything else?'

'What?'

'I am asking you if I might find any other injuries,' Ruth repeated.

The parents glanced at each other.

'You . . . ?' the man exclaimed. 'What d'you mean?'

'I haven't got time,' Ruth said.

She called for X-ray.

Too late, she called the consultant paediatrician.

And the doors swung, with the woman running behind them . . . and the green sheet, and the raised red skin under the curly hair . . . all in silence now, everything silent and slow, warped out of line . . .

With a jolt, Ruth woke up.

Her heart was pounding. She had a choking sensation in her throat. And then it passed: the doors receded, the child, the mother, the paper sheet, the phone on the wall, her own slick palms, her sense of righteous indignation.

She had fallen forward a little in the car seat, her chin tucked almost on her throat. As she straightened, her neck complained. She put her hand up to massage it, arched her back, and took several long, deep breaths.

Ruth could not sleep.

This was not a temporary condition.

She often dozed in the car, only for five or ten minutes. Or just before morning surgery, or listening to music at night. Just five or ten minutes. Whenever she slept, however briefly, she would immediately be dreaming vividly, picking up threads from the last dream, sometimes the same dream, sometimes this one. More often than not this one: this old one.

She was not a natural insomniac. As a child, a teenager, she had slept as soundly as the next person. Her sleeplessness had begun as a medical student, and been reinforced by the hours as a junior doctor in hospital. And now her day, instead of being comfortably split into night-and-day segments, was an irregular pattern, sleeping where she could and never for more than four hours at night. She could stop the car when out on call, if she were early for an appointment—which was rare, but possible—and fall asleep there and then, waking again to disorientation.

There was a rhythm, if you were sufficiently sensitive to perceive it, of waking and movement, of ebb and flow in the world. Rhythms of wakefulness and occupation—patterns. But insomniacs like her obeyed no rhythm, no pattern. They put their heads down and lay awake, eyes wide open, body exhausted, brain racing.

Kieran had always been amazed at how long Ruth could continue without needing to go to bed. It came in useful in her line of work, she always maintained. 'You're some kind of saint,' he would reply.

They had been the perfect couple. *They still were.*

Ruth started the engine of the car, put it into gear, and pulled slowly out of the lay-by at the top of the hill. Down the narrow lane, the village could be clearly seen, its green valley.

Reaching the Priory at eleven o'clock, she was surprised not to see Lin's car in the drive. Ruth got out, perfectly composed, and walked to the front door, noticing the unkempt shrubs on either side of the steps.

She had always kept the elaeagnus trimmed, pruning out the green shoots so that the plant remained variegated. As she waited for the ringing of the Victorian bell-pull to subside, she saw that there was plenty of green in the plant. The creeping willow, with its grey-yellow catkins, was also overgrown, allowed to fall over the coping stones closest to the door. *Untidy. Much too untidy.* But just the sort of thing that Lin allowed, even encouraged. It was so damned irritating that Lin was allowed to do this to Ruth's own house.

Lin thought that there was some sort of strange merit in letting life take its course. Even the euphorbia, so elegant, so unusual if treated carefully, were out of their assigned plot—and in the sunlight where they would not flourish. There was some advantage, Ruth could accept, in a little loose rein from time to time. But if you let that rein slacken completely, anything living was liable to choke itself, out-run itself, push into the sunlight where it was not wanted.

That was what was wrong with Theo.

Too much light and too little restraint.

From the day he was born.

Ruth considered that she had done remarkably well that same day. So bloody well, in fact, that the moment she got home she had poured herself a large brandy, toasted herself wordlessly, and swallowed it in one go. The scorching in her throat was nothing to the dry heat in her heart, the furnace burning with a blank roar. Kieran had rung her at six-thirty in the morning, waking her from an hour's blessed unconsciousness.

'Ruth?' he had said, his voice wary.

'Yes.'

'I'm sorry it's so early . . .'

'What is it?' she had asked.

A pause. His inordinate pride in the reply. 'A boy.'

Oh God. Oh God.

'Congratulations. How is Lin?'

'Wonderful. Four hours of labour!'

'What weight?'

'Ten pounds.'

'Amazing.'

'Isn't it?'

There had been a long silence.

'Oh, Ruth,' he had said. 'It's only because I didn't want you to hear it from someone else. You know so many people here, and would maybe think I'd kept it from you.'

'I know,' she had said. 'Thank you.'

'I don't expect you to be happy. You don't have to pretend you are.'

'I *am* happy,' she had lied, her voice smooth. 'You wanted a son.'

'Yes,' he had said. His tone had been full of tears.

It was that, above everything else, that she remembered—that haunted her still.

She had gone in to visit that same morning, after surgery. As she paused at the door of the maternity ward, she had seen Kieran and Lin sitting on the same bed, gazing into the cot alongside. It had been a perfect family picture. She had taken a deep breath, then walked straight over to them, smiling.

'I'm sorry I've brought no flowers,' she said.

Lin did not reply.

'Look at this boy,' Kieran said. 'Look at the size of him! And he's got red in that blond. You see?'

'His grandmother was Irish,' Lin had commented. 'It's a throwback.'

Ruth and Kieran had glanced at one another. The subject of Lin's mother was fragile even then.

'What are you calling him?' Ruth had asked. She had leaned down and looked at their son, lying on his side with two round fists close to his face.

'Some godawful classical thing,' Lin said.

'It's a good name,' Kieran replied equably. He was not about to be swayed from a decision that apparently he had made entirely alone.

'Do you know what it is?' Lin asked Ruth. 'You won't believe this. Theophilus.'

Ruth had bitten down a smile. 'Ah,' she said. 'Distinctive.'

'You can't lumber him with that at playschool,' Lin had muttered. 'Can you imagine it?' She had snorted, running one hand down her cropped hair and pulling at the fronds on her neck, a gesture that Ruth knew well. 'He can't play football with a name like that. You can't call it out in Tesco's. It can't be whispered in his ear by his girlfriend without her falling about laughing.'

Kieran had listened expressionlessly. 'My son isn't going to play-school,' he had said. 'He won't be running around Tesco's either.'

Ruth had looked at the pair of them: the girl still so young-looking—she looked not a day over sixteen, especially without make-up—and Kieran fourteen years her senior, and carrying today—as he was wont to do when crossed—an air of world-weary superiority.

'Look,' Ruth said, 'what about Philip, or Paul? Or Mark Anthony?' The suggestion had been swallowed by the silence around the bed. 'They're classical, too, aren't they?'

'Marcus,' Lin said with a touch of triumph.

'No,' Kieran said.

'I can't believe that the two of you hadn't settled on a name before this,' Ruth had remarked. 'Why not call him Albert or Fred?' She had sat down on the chair at Lin's side. 'Old-fashioned names are coming back, you know. Someone here called their daughter Lily the other week. I thought that was rather pretty.'

'I want to call him Theophilus,' Kieran repeated. 'It's a good strong name.'

Ruth had pretended not to hear. 'Something plain. Something he can carry about without embarrassment. Sam? John?'

'Every time we talked about it, it ended like this,' Lin had muttered. 'I thought it was a joke. Honestly I did. I don't see what's wrong with Doran. It's Celtic—Irish. You've got a Celtic name yourself,' she added pointedly to Kieran.

He had begun to laugh. 'Darren . . .'

To Ruth's knowledge, Lin had never once called her son by his full name. The next time she had seen her, three weeks later, their son was 'Theo'.

She pushed the thought of the child to one side, closed her eyes briefly, then rang the doorbell again.

At once she heard footsteps along the flagged hall. The door opened on Mrs Sawyer, dressed in her usual ancient overall.

'Oh, Mrs . . . Miss Carmichael,' she said.

'Hello, Meg.' Ruth stepped over the doorstep.

The cleaner fluttered with consternation, a reaction that Ruth had purposely ignored from the day Lin had installed herself at the Priory.

'Is Lin here?'

'No . . . no, she isn't,' Meg Sawyer said, closing the door. 'I've been down the laundry room, I didn't hear you.'

'Where is she?'

'I don't know. Not at all.'

'When did she go out?' Ruth asked.

'Well, I . . .'

Meg Sawyer stood wringing her hands. Ruth tried not to smile. Meg was a willing, loyal soul, completely overwhelmed by serving two wives in the same house. Ruth knew that she liked Lin—after all, Lin was the same age as Meg's daughter. There was something rather similar in their looks, too. Short dyed hair with a long fringe, rather better done in Lin—she was forced to admit—than in Meg's Diane, who must have bleached it herself since she was twelve. There was the same thin, boyish look to them, too. Thin and nervy and undernourished. Pale-skinned. Large, mobile mouths. Something unpleasantly sensual.

'I'll wait for her,' Ruth said. She put her bag down in the hall. 'A cup of tea would be wonderful, Meg.'

'I don't think she's coming back today,' Meg said. The expression on the poor woman's face was almost agonized at this evident breach of confidence.

'Oh?' Ruth asked.

'She's been away two days. I didn't know until this morning.'

'She left a note?'

Meg didn't reply. She looked stricken.

Ruth let her off the hook. 'How long is she gone for?'

'I don't know,' Meg replied. 'Really I don't.'

'Spur of the moment, I expect,' Ruth murmured sweetly.

'Yes,' the other woman agreed.

'I should still love that cup of tea,' Ruth said.

Meg struggled with a rebuff, then abandoned it gladly. 'So would I,' she admitted. 'I've been doing the house since eight.'

They walked towards the kitchen, through the beautifully proportioned Georgian hall, then a long wood-panelled corridor right to the back of the house.

'It's a good bit hot for April,' Meg said, as Ruth sat down in the kitchen armchair which she herself, five years ago, had re-covered in navy linen. It seemed, as she lowered herself into it, to cling to her with a cold memory: Kieran weeping by the far window, herself tracing the design of fleurs-de-lys in the heavy cotton. Sleet against the glass. The table laid for a supper which was never eaten. The claret glass which had already been emptied before she came home.

Ruth now smoothed down her skirt. 'And where do you suppose she's gone?' she asked.

'I don't know,' Meg said, too quickly.

'To one of those specialist libraries of hers,' Ruth murmured.

Meg didn't reply. She opened the cupboard and brought out Lin's cups, yellow and blue, huge garish lemons and pears on a cream background.

'I'm surprised she took Theo,' Ruth said.

'She took his toys,' Meg said. The woman's hands froze for a second as she filled the kettle. It overflowed from the tap. She fussed over it while Ruth stared levelly at her.

'His toys?'

'Yes, some of them.'

'She took Theo's toys?' Ruth repeated.

Meg looked out of the window. 'I think we'll have a good summer,' she said.

Ruth got up. She went back out into the hall, and up the stairs.

On the landing, she turned right, and walked down to Theo's bedroom. In it, she opened his wardrobe doors. Nothing especially seemed to be missing: there was plenty left on the hangers, all stuffed in together. Ruth bit her lip. She went back down the landing to the master bedroom. This was tidy, bearing Meg Sawyer's hallmarks of army-neat sheets and coverlet stretched to a perfect tension, the pillows lined up mathematically edge to edge.

Ruth took a deep breath. She could smell Lin: Lin's tennis-teas flowery cologne, Lin's books on the bedside shelf, those thick volumes of physics and philosophy. Ruth walked over to them with a wry grimace. If it fooled Kieran, it did not fool her.

All Lin's reputed cleverness had disintegrated in the first year at university. Becoming pregnant had dissolved her supposed genius—

the books, the work that Lin did now, did not convince Ruth in the smallest way. Her intelligence was a flashy, momentary flare in the dark. Careers, reputations, achievements were not built on leaps and vaults. Now Lin laboured in Kieran's shadow, sucking from him. Ruth was not to be fooled, not for a moment—not for a fraction of a second. Lin was a type, and Kieran had been snared by a type, a coloured picture.

She regretted his stupidity. But the damage it had done was not beyond repair. Lin's presence here was merely as a tenant. Everything here, by right, was Ruth's. She had a right to stand here and survey the stolen bedroom. She had a right to come in whenever she liked.

She went into the ensuite bathroom.

There were no cosmetics on the shelves, no toothbrush or paste. No hairbrush.

Ruth went back to the bedroom, and into the small dressing room where all Kieran's and Lin's clothes were hung, Lin's on one side, Kieran's on the other. Ruth stopped dead in her tracks. There were obvious absences and gaps. On the shelf above the racks there was only one suitcase, matching the single case on Kieran's opposite shelf. They had more than two suitcases between them.

She came back out, and walked slowly down the stairs.

Meg Sawyer was standing at the bottom.

'Has anyone rung here?' Ruth asked her.

'Rung?'

'Rung. On the telephone.'

'No . . . but the fax machine . . .' Meg's words trailed away as Ruth strode over towards the study. 'I don't think . . .'

Ruth closed the door behind her.

Meg Sawyer stood looking at it for some time, alone in the still hallway, listening to paper being torn from the fax in the study, listening to Ruth picking up the phone. She took one step towards the door, then thought better of it, turning rapidly away, brushing her hands over her hair as if to rid herself of the responsibility of Lin's secrets.

'Oh dear,' she murmured, as she went back to the kitchen. 'Oh dear, oh dear.'

SIX

$\mathscr{I}$T WAS TWO IN THE AFTERNOON of the following day that Edith Channon called up the stairs.

'Lin! You have a visitor!'

Four flights above, the door opened, and Lin's footsteps could be heard on the landing. 'Who is it?' she replied.

'She asks who it is, the bitch,' Ben Lazenby said.

The elderly woman recoiled, frowning at him.

'She's done it deliberately,' he muttered, then walked up the first flight. 'Is there any bloody end to this?' he shouted.

Edith could hear Lin laughing. 'Oh, it's you,' she said. 'I'll come down.'

'No, no, no,' Ben muttered. 'I'm halfway to a heart attack, so why stop me now?'

Edith watched the enormous frame of Lazenby retreat upwards. Clicking her tongue in disapproval, she went back into the shop and closed the connecting door.

Emerging on the landing by the entrance to Lin's flat, Lazenby did in fact look as if he were in danger of a seizure. He was six foot three, on the downside of sixty, florid-faced, and with the expression of an exhausted bulldog. Lin stepped forward to kiss him.

'For God's sake, a seat and a drink,' he said.

They went into Lin's flat.

'What is it, half a mile up that hill?' he rumbled on. 'No bloody place to park, I'm coming down with something, I've got sinus trouble or something, like a band around my fucking head, and I have to walk four miles from a car park—two pounds an hour, two pounds an *hour*—up a hill and then sixteen flights of stairs in the Hammer House of Horrors. What d'you call this? Who's she downstairs? Place out of the fourteenth-century, dolls looking at you. Do you know what she's doing down there? Putting in a tongue. A fucking *tongue!*'

Lin was laughing. Lazenby had flopped onto her only armchair.

'Tea?' she asked. She went to the sink in the corner and ran the water. The pipes clanged briefly in the wall.

'Horrors,' Lazenby repeated. 'Where is he?'

'Where is who?'

'Theophilus the mighty.'

She cocked her head towards the bedroom. 'He sleeps for an hour in the afternoon.'

Lazenby looked around at the floor littered with toys, a large jigsaw on a coffee table under the window, and Lin's laptop on the dining table, with a view from the window of the slate roofs across the narrow street.

'My sweet girl,' he said. 'What in God's name are you doing here? You look like death.'

Lin didn't reply for a moment. Then she smiled, murmuring, 'Thanks.' Carefully and slowly, she laid a tray with cups and saucers. 'I've only got malt loaf,' she said.

'Ah, God.'

'I'm sorry. Theo loves it.'

'Never mind, darling. I had lunch at the Gill. Do you know it? Just outside town.'

Lin turned back to him, smiling. 'How do you find the best restaurants when you've never lived here?'

He raised an admonishing finger. 'Ah, but I have,' he said. 'In another life I spent eight months here doing costume design.'

She was genuinely surprised. 'You did?'

'When I was young and fit, in another century,' he said. 'It had no hills then.'

She laughed again. She brought the tray over, and handed him a cup of tea. 'Where is Marianne?' she asked.

'Forty miles away, receiving the sympathy of her father.'

Lin wasn't surprised. Ben always had young girlfriends, and he never got on with their parents. Lazenby watched Lin pour, his face set in a concentrated expression of concern.

'Lindsay,' he said at last, 'what are you doing here?'

She sat back on her heels and looked up at him.

'Have you left the great man?' he asked.

'No.'

'What, then? A sabbatical? Do they allow that in marriage? Time off for bad behaviour?'

'No, no. I . . .' She adjusted herself to sit cross-legged. 'Harry rang me last night. How did he know where I was?'

Lazenby shrugged.

Lin sighed. 'I couldn't stay in the house another day,' she said. She picked at a thread on her skirt. 'I suppose that makes me certifiable.'

Lazenby put the cup down. 'Well, you know my theory on country houses,' he said. 'One goes there to die for the WI.' He sat back, lacing his hands across an ample stomach. 'The people I've known buy a longhouse in Suffolk, then come screaming back to London within six months. Tractors! I mean, one knows they're necessary . . .'

'It wasn't the country,' Lin said. 'And it wasn't the house.'

Lazenby stared at her.

'How is he?' she asked.

'As usual,' Lazenby said.

'When did you leave Cyprus?'

'A week ago. I had things to do.'

'Was he all right?'

Lazenby momentarily closed his eyes. '*Chérie*, you and I, you and I . . .' He opened his eyes again. 'I wonder what we did in our last life to deserve him.'

To say that Lazenby did not like Kieran would have been a massive understatement. Ben hated Kieran's good looks—those of a weary, slightly soiled angel. He resented the air of knowingness that Kieran made his own. Ben also, unfortunately for the theme of the programme, hated academia being stuffed in his face when he only had two CSEs to parry with. Most of all he hated the photograph of Kieran that hung in Channel 12's foyer. He had never been more thrilled than when, at a party just before Christmas, he had heard Kieran described as possessing 'fading chambray allure'. Despite being the producer of Kieran's programme, he had rung Harry immediately to tell him that. More than once he had asked Harry to persuade Lin to come in on one or two scenes, citing her looks, her off-the-wall humour.

Lin watched his face. 'Is it that bad?'

'Bloody pre-menstrual vindictiveness. He treated Malcolm on the crew as if he were something that had adhered to his shoe.'

'Oh, God,' Lin sighed.

'No good here, won't stand there, this slope too steep, this not the right ambience, this not indicative of period—this whitewash too fucking white, if you please . . .'

'He's a perfectionist,' she murmured.

Lazenby sat forward. 'No,' he said, 'that's not it. I've worked with perfectionists all my life. Shall I tell you what's at the heart of this? Anxiety. He's not sure—for all his star status.'

Lin looked down, away.

'What *is* it with the two of you?'

'He's so remote,' Lin replied. 'I don't think he likes television, Ben.'

'He was damned enthusiastic enough four years ago.'

'Well . . . times change. Maybe I pushed him. He seemed so much in a rut.' She bit her lip. 'But maybe he liked his oblivion with Ruth. Maybe that's what's happening now—wanting to go back.'

'What do they say about him at the university?' Lazenby asked.

Lin said nothing.

'Besides their hating him, naturally.'

With deliberate slowness, Lin lifted her cup and drank.

'You *are* a loyal girl,' Lazenby said.

'He's very clever,' she responded.

'Like shit,' Lazenby said.

She flashed him a look, saw he was smiling rather sadly at her.

'Lin, how old are you?' he asked.

'What is that to do with anything?' she asked, smiling too, with something of the same slightly mournful quality. 'I'm a hundred and six.'

'How old?'

'Why?'

'Stuck up here with *his* son.'

'I'm twenty-four.'

'If you hadn't met him, what would you be doing now?'

'Oh, Christ . . . a postgraduate course.' She put down her cup. 'No, I wouldn't,' she contradicted herself. 'I'd be in Nepal, or a chicken-gutting factory, or prison.'

'Of course. And how do you suppose that would happen?'

'Because I don't stick at anything,' she said.

'Except Mr Gallagher.'

'Ah . . . yes.'

'You have a brilliant mind,' Ben said, 'an analytical mind, a creative mind. You can write, you do his research, you see the most extraordinary tangents. I have climbed this medieval Everest to tell you I would much prefer to have you on the screen than your husband. I come, in fact, upon a white charger—you don't see him? I have a sword in my hand—'

'Ben . . .'

'Actually a chequebook. Actually a contract.'

'What?'

'Actually no. I have no chequebook and I have no contract, but I will. I could. I shall. I am tired of the star, darling. This comet with his cloud of dust. And if you are leaving him, you must not leave *me*, my clever girl—'

'I'm not leaving him,' she said.

'Are you not?' he replied.

They stared at each other.

'Dear girl,' Ben said.

She shifted backwards on the carpet, to take herself out of his reach. 'Please don't be kind,' she said. 'I'll start crying, and you'll be sorry.'

He looked at her with compassion. 'That's true,' he said. 'Why now? Why this?'

'Ruth,' she murmured, taking his offered handkerchief. She blew her nose, and offered it back.

'Keep it.'

'Oh, I'm sorry . . .'

'No, darling, please do hawk into my possessions freely.'

She actually managed to laugh.

'And Ruth?' he asked.

'She comes into the house. She thinks it's still hers.'

'Oh, lovely. There's normal for you.'

'Kieran is very fond of her.'

'Is he having an affair with her?'

'No, no . . . but he's . . . they never quite broke that bond. I am the interloper.'

'You are his wife.'

'I'm . . .' She paused. 'What am I? The second one. The younger one.'

'And she comes around uninvited?'

'She rings, too, more and more often. For nothing. Almost like a raincheck. These strange, going-nowhere conversations. What am I doing with Theo? Is Theo well? The weather . . .'

'Is she lonely?'

Lin eyed him acutely. 'I don't know. She's frantically busy, supposedly.'

'Isn't she older than you both?'

'Yes, much. Years older than me.'

There was a pause. For all his concern for Lin, Lazenby found it hard to stray from the subject of work, which was his main preoccupation. 'You know that he's threatening not to do another series?'

'Yes, I do.'

'Has he told you why?'

'No. He just criticizes the scripts.'

'Which *you* prepare, for no payment.'

'I'm happy to help him.'

Lazenby leant forward, and pointed a finger at her. 'That's a very unprofessional attitude. You are wickedly naïve. It's a fault. A flaw.'

She said nothing.

In the bedroom, Theo began to stir. Lin stood up, looking towards the door.

Lazenby caught hold of her wrist. 'Get back to your house and change the locks. Drive the mad old bag away,' he said.

'I can't do any of that without Kieran's support,' she told him. 'I was hoping this would shock him into doing something.'

'And will it?'

'I don't know,' she said. 'I didn't really rationalize. I just had to get out that day, and I thought he would—'

'Get on a plane? Send in the SWAT team? Hang her out to dry?'

'Yes. Something dramatic like that. Some big gesture—this once.'

'Listen,' Lazenby said. 'Get back to the house. You *are* entitled to half of it. Start thinking about your career. And I don't mean a career as Gallagher's skivvy.'

She eyed him steadily. 'Does he ever talk to you about Ruth?' she asked. 'When he's away from home?'

Lazenby returned her look. 'He doesn't confide in me, love.'

'That's it,' she murmured, turning away. '*Love.*'

He watched her weary walk to the bedroom door. 'Blind,' he replied. 'So they say.'

SEVEN

$\mathcal{B}$ y Friday, they were at the Tombs of the Kings. There was a hotel close by, with a view of the sea and—to Harry's relief—clean towels, room service and fresh air. It was the last stop before the flight home.

Early on Friday morning, Kieran went down to Reception alone. He retrieved the package that had been sent by overnight courier from the States, and took it out onto the long terrace overlooking the sea. With a cup of coffee at his side, he opened it, tearing the Private and Confidential sticker, glanced over the pages of manuscript, and then read the covering letter. Once he had finished, he sat for some time staring out at the ocean, his foot tapping absentmindedly.

Ruth had rung him last night. He had taken the call in his room.

She was always good at reading his mind, and at no time was that more obvious than now, as he sat preparing himself to deliver Lin's reproach.

'Kieran, I've been up to the house,' she said, 'and I can't find Lin. You do set me the most impossible tasks.'

He found himself smiling. 'When I ask you to keep an eye on her, I don't mean like a bloody bull mastiff,' he said.

'What on earth do you mean?'

He paused, smiling a little, looking down at his feet. 'Look, I know this was my idea, but you'd better stay away for a while.'

'Is there a problem?'

'Yes. Look, you *know* Lin.'

'What is it?'

'She claims you have a set of keys.'

Ruth's laughter was slow in coming, light in tone. 'Well, of course I have keys.'

'Since when?'

'Kieran . . .'

'All right. But don't use them.'

'I shouldn't dream of it.'

'You haven't let yourself in with them?'

'Of course not! Kieran, what on earth is this about? I don't mind dropping in to see if Lin's OK while you're away—I know I promised you that—but, really, I have other things to do.'

'Yes, I appreciate that.'

'I went there this morning and found Theo's clothes and toys are missing. Quite a few, anyway. It seemed odd, that's all. If you know all about it, naturally it's none of my business.'

'I know all about it.'

'Fine.'

'Look, she's got a bit concerned—'

Ruth audibly sighed. 'Kieran, I think I've been rather good about this, you know.'

'Yes,' he agreed, 'you have.'

Five years since he had first seen Lin.

Since Lin had first come between them.

After he had placed the advertisement requesting an assistant, she had turned up early one morning in his campus room, seeming about twelve years old, swamped in an enormous coat.

She had been nineteen, very thin, medium height, short reddish hair, with a strand of plaited blue and black cotton around some longer strands at the front. He had been very surprised to see her, knowing her already by reputation as an awkward, shy, brilliant girl studying in another discipline. Mathematics was so far removed from history that she might as well have come from another planet.

Yet he recalled, during the first five minutes of interviewing her, that she had been at his last lecture. He remembered how she had drawn his eye by her fidgeting in the second row. She had twitched, she had sighed, she had even whispered to herself. Towards the end, she had sat forward and rested her head in both hands, elbows supported on knees, running her fingers constantly through her hair. It had occurred to him that she had listened to him exactly as if he were on radio and not ten feet in front of her in the flesh.

At the interview he had asked, 'What did you think of my lecture?'

She had shrugged a self-conscious shrug that belonged to adolescence.

'Do you have a particular interest in Hasdrubal?'

'Brothers.'

'Sibling rivalry, all that?'

'Yes.'

'Do you have brothers?'

That brought a flash of contact: a wry, self-deprecatory smile. 'Oh yes,' she replied. 'Three.'

'Younger or older?'

'Older. A lot older.' She glanced at the window. 'I'm the cuckoo in the nest.'

'Sorry?'

She looked back at him, waved her hand. 'No . . . nothing, nothing. It's a kind of joke.'

She had a Liverpudlian accent. Its faint Celtic charm suited her; he guessed at an Irish connection from the reddish hair. His eyes had ranged over her as she sat with her hands tucked between her knees:. the most unprepossessing of candidates, her self-consciousness revealing the crown of her head more often than her face. He found himself looking hard at the clean, white parting in her hair, at the small bunch of hair that stood upright at the crown.

The coat which drowned her was Persian lamb, a charity-shop

reject. Under it she wore boots, jeans and sweater. In the warmth of his office, the coat smelled. She saw his eyes stray to it.

'Did they pay you to take it away?' he asked.

She didn't reply; but she smiled.

'I hear good things about you,' he continued. 'Tell me about your article.'

He already knew that, at seventeen, she had written a piece about the nature of time, which had won an award. Matthew French, her personal tutor, had been to see him only that morning. As they talked about her coming for this interview, French had worn an expression of rebuff.

'Why is she applying to *your* department? She's nothing to do with history.'

'Perhaps she wants a break from you.'

French had smiled coldly: they were adversaries, not friends. Kieran knew the man well enough—and his arrogance—to realize that this particular student, with her strange brilliance, was a totem, a talisman. Lin had not looked impressive—impressive was the last adjective he could apply—but she was a thing to impress with, a badge, a password.

Kieran had studied her hard that morning. She had returned an occasional intense glance. She had made no comment on her article, but asked instead what he was paying for the four-week vacation work. She had, to his amazement, gone on to calculate his reply on her fingers.

'Aren't you going home for Christmas?' he had asked.

'Just for a couple of days,' she said.

'It's a large manuscript. There are graphics,' he had explained. 'I write longhand, you ought to know. I've had complaints from other secretaries.'

'I don't mind.'

Then he had hired her. Not because he had much faith in her ability to type. Instead it was something, most irrationally, to do with her hair: the white parting at the centre, and the paleness of the face under it. It had touched him with its frailty.

Fatal. Fatal.

Lin had worked hard for him, arriving early on the first morning of the vacation. He had given her the four box-files containing the final draft of *Carthaginian Kings*. He would go in to see her at nine, then leave her while he got on with his other work. He had quickly formed an opinion of her: he thought her rather dull, as clever people often are. And then, one day in the second week—it had been four days before Christmas—he had come back at lunchtime to find her laughing.

'Hello,' he had said, closing the door behind him.

'Oh God, oh God,' she said, both laughing and groaning.

He had walked over to the table where she was sitting at the computer. 'What is it?' he had asked.

She had shaken her head, sat back, dropped her hands from the keyboard. She wiped the corner of one eye, before letting out an enormous sigh. 'It just annoyed me at first, but this morning it struck me as so . . .'

'So what?'

She shook her head. 'No . . . no, I'm sorry. It doesn't matter.'

He had sat down. He had a vast sheaf of paper with him, and he settled it carefully on the desk between them.

She had examined him, staring him full in the face, her eyes ranging over him.

'How many copies do you sell?' she asked.

'Quite sufficient.'

'Sufficient,' she had repeated. 'Look, this is—' She had stopped. 'Don't you know what this is?' she continued. She picked up the last page she had been typing. 'You know, it's so clogged. It's so heavy . . .'

He had been writing textbooks for three years. Being an authority on a very narrow field, its very narrowness, perhaps even its impenetrability, satisfied him.

She was still holding up the page. 'I mean, look at this. The way you phrase things. You've got four clauses—look at that, four clauses in that one sentence alone. You've lost the thread—and all these men, these men bigger than life, they've shrunk. They were so big, and you've shrunk them into these dreary sentences . . .'

Kieran had opened his mouth. He had felt absurdly hurt—hurt to his core. He was the departmental head, the academic, the published author.

'*The prevarication of the elder members of the governing Senate had an adverse effect upon military operations . . .*' She put down the page, temporarily exhausted by her outburst. Then, quite suddenly, she blushed. 'Don't take any notice of me,' she said.

He stared at the abandoned page as she pushed back her chair. 'I'm going for a walk,' she said. She had stood up, pulled on the terrible coat, and looked down at him. 'I'm sorry,' she added. 'Maybe that was rude.'

He had nothing to say. The criticism had been so unexpected, it completely erased his ability to speak.

Still standing by the desk, she continued, 'I had to type some verse this summer—by an American making a tour of Europe. He'd written poetry about every city he visited.' She started to laugh. 'I've never read anything so bad in all my life. It was *my shrivelling orbs, they light upon thy wrinkled hills, thou God-given bed blanket of green-swamp sward . . .*'

He smiled.

'It's true, honestly—absolutely true. I thought it was some kind of parody, a joke. And he was all classical references, Latin phrases . . .' Kieran thought of his own classical references. 'And he had a publisher in the USA, can you believe it? They *published* him!'

'And I remind you of him?' Kieran said.

'Oh,' she said. She bit her lip, then grinned.

Of course, he could have fired her. He should have fired her.

But he took her to lunch.

They had walked across the suspension bridge at the height of the midday traffic, in the middle of the Christmas rush. Halfway across, turning away from the concertinaed bedlam of cars beside them, Lin had leaned over the rail to look at the three-hundred-foot drop. Kieran had never been afraid of heights until that moment, but the sight of her thin frame outlined in its outrageous mothballed coat against the sky, and the winding brown mud ribbon of the river below, sent an electric charge through him. He was abruptly convinced that she intended to throw herself off, that at any second she would hoist herself up.

'Don't go any further,' he said.

She seemed not to hear him but, after gazing at the river, looked from side to side.

'Do you know that the man who designed this bridge also patented a knitting machine?' she asked. 'And a sheaf-making machine, and a pocket copying press, and a process for making leather tougher?'

He was still watching her feet, convinced that she was about to spring.

'He made bridges and docks and tunnels . . . Do you know how he got his idea for the Rotherhithe tunnel?'

'No,' he said. 'Industrial history isn't my field.'

She sucked in her breath—like a teacher annoyed at an intransigent child. 'It was the ship worm,' she said. 'The head of the *Teredo navalis* is protected by two boring shells. They can gradually grind wood—even the hardest oak—into a kind of flour. Behind these shells the worm makes a tunnel of its own excreta.'

'Lovely,' he said. 'Now get down off the guard rail.'

She had looked at him in surprise. 'I'm only resting one foot.'

'Don't,' he insisted.

He had taken her to a very trendy Italian restaurant. As they entered, she commented that she passed it every day but could never afford to go inside. He suddenly felt that his stock had risen, that he had some sort of value at last.

She had ordered pasta, and he fish, with a bottle of wine. He sat back while they waited for their food.

'Tell me about yourself,' he said.

'Do I have to?'

'Sorry?'

'Is it a part of my contract?'

He laughed. 'Of course not.'

'You're married, aren't you?' she asked. 'To a doctor?'

'Yes. A GP.'

'What's she like?'

'Oh—very organized. Very calm in a crisis, as you might expect.'

'Is she pretty?'

'She's rather beautiful, in fact.'

Lin had drunk half the first glass of wine. There followed a long silence.

The food arrived. She ate with relish, then asked for a dessert. He indulgently watched her work through a huge slice of sherry-laden cake while he drank his coffee. He ought to have had control of this situation, but felt that he did not. She had the most unsettling, almost dangerous aura. Even now he still expected her suddenly to leap up, or faint, or scream. She constantly fiddled with things—the cruet, the cutlery, the cloth. She stared around at other customers with a gaze that was too frank. The coat lay folded on the chair next to her, and seemed more pungent by the minute. He had seized on it as—he hoped—a neutral topic of conversation. And to distract her from inspecting the painting above their heads.

'You don't see Persian lamb anywhere these days.'

She looked back at him. 'No. Out of fashion, I expect.'

'My mother used to have a coat like that.'

She seemed interested. 'Did she? Is she still alive?'

'No. Is yours?'

A strange expression, rather browbeaten, crossed her face. 'Yes, very alive.'

'Your father?'

'I don't know.'

'Why is that?' he asked.

She picked up the coat, blushing hard. 'Could we go?' she said.

They lunched again before Christmas Eve, when she went home armed with his gift to her, a small Roman amulet. She had been astonished to receive it, and he even more astonished to give it. Clearing through his desk early that morning, he had found it. Bought from a tourist stall on a trip to Israel: a green copper band decorated with two curved snakes. He had wrapped it in tissue paper and presented it to her.

'But I haven't got you anything,' she had protested.

'It doesn't matter in the least. This is . . . well, hardly a tremendous gift.'

To his complete surprise, she had lifted her face from her inspection of the band, and shown him eyes filled with tears.

'Are you looking forward to going home?' He was suddenly rather desperate to change the subject.

'Oh,' she said. 'I don't know if looking forward is a good description.' She had carefully rewrapped the amulet, folding the tissue precisely over it before putting it away in her bag.

'When will you be back?' he had asked.

'In three days.'

On the day after Boxing Day, he had gone into the refectory closest to his department, and found her eating breakfast. For some reason the sight of her hunched over a bowl of cornflakes, looking so cold, had struck him to the heart.

He had walked over to her. 'Did you have a nice time?'

She put down the spoon and pulled the cup of tea towards her. Her hand on the cup was frail, blue-veined, almost transparent.

'Are you all right?'

'I think I've got flu.'

'Have you seen a doctor?'

She had not. They walked to his office together, but it became apparent as the morning wore on that she was not well.

'I'll take you home,' he had said.

'There's no need.'

'I'll walk you halfway, at least.'

In the event, he went with her to her room. It was in one of the residential blocks, a Victorian house that had been renovated. She had walked up the stairs very wearily, and opened the door without a word. He couldn't hear anyone else in the house, and presumed that most of the occupants were still away.

'My God, it's freezing in here,' he said.

She lay down on the bed, still wrapped in her coat. 'I used to have a nice top flat with a dotty landlady called Edith,' she whispered, shivering. 'Then the girls here persuaded me to share.' A pause. 'I wish I hadn't come. It's always cold.'

'Why isn't the heating on?'

'There's a meter.'

He went over to look. There was no money in it. Glancing back at her, he saw that she had closed her eyes. He put several pound coins into the slot.

'Have you got any food?'

'Yes,' she murmured. 'In the kitchen.'

He had gone down the corridor, found the kitchen, and looked in the fridge. On her shelf—marked with her name on a Post-it note—were two tubs of yoghurt and a carton of milk. He looked in the cupboards. Another personal shelf, marked with another Post-it note. Three cans: soup, tinned fruit, tuna. He went back to her.

'There isn't very much.'

She didn't reply. He walked to the bed.

On the table next to it was a small photograph in a wooden frame. He was surprised to see that it wasn't of a person, but showed clouds of gases, points of blue light, a formation in the foreground that contained blooms of white, an explosion of heat.

'Lin,' he said.

She seemed to be asleep. He leaned down and looked hard at the narrow, pale face, the hands drawn up to her chin. He felt a rush of compassion so strong that it unnerved him—and he had drawn back.

It would have been quite natural to tell Ruth that same night that the girl was ill and that he had taken her home. But, for a reason that he didn't quite understand, he did not.

EIGHT

$\mathscr{L}$IN WOKE AT ONE IN THE MORNING in a state of complete terror.

She thought that she was being smothered, that the room was full of voices. When she opened her eyes, for a moment she saw nothing at all, only felt an oppressive, blanketing pressure on her mouth and eyes. There was no air and no light, and she was convinced that there was someone else in the room. *More than one person.* There was that cramped feeling of a crowd, the murmur of moving bodies, the whispering crush of other people's backs, hands, hips. More and more were coming in, shifting irritably as they met the resistance of those already there.

Still half asleep, Lin stood up.

Abruptly the pressure vanished. She lifted her hand to one side of her head, where the skin felt tight and curiously numb as if carrying the invisible imprint of fingers. She massaged the spot, and opened her mouth, rotating her jaw. The right hand side of her face was dead.

Her head was full of the past.

She had been dreaming about Irma.

Poor, plain Irma, so old-fashioned, the kind of girl who was always overlooked. Irma seven years ago, plain from her plain brown hair in its plain brown style, looped to the side and secured with a brown slide, right down through her plain face and brown eyes, her plain sensible jumpers and skirts, her plain flat shoes. Irma had been at least thirty, never married—never likely to be.

Irma used to sing *When My Little Girl Is Smiling* over and over and over. Irma singing in the Hunting Dog's kitchen, where they both worked Sundays. Irma wore 4711, and the kitchen was full of that sickly scent, and of the cooking dinners. Irma would be singing when Lin arrived at ten; the back windows open, more often than not rain blowing off the sea in a horizontal curtain, fine and billowing; the Hunting Dog's sign blowing slowly backwards and forwards, bright red in the grey street.

A lot of mist came off the bay, even on hot days: coating the shops, coating the pink, the acid green, the bright blue, the orange, the plastic sandals and buckets and spades and rafts and sunglasses and hats and pretend spiders. Souvenir shops and fortune tellers, their doors open to the fog-laden, humid street.

Lin screwed her eyes shut now. Past and present were lividly alive in this same room.

In the palmist's seafront booth, on the very last weekend of the summer, the woman had told Irma's fortune—all kiddies and mother and pools wins—and then had picked up Lin's hand. She had laid it flat on her own palm, and said nothing at all, nothing—until she dropped it again and pushed Lin's pound coin back towards her across the pewter-topped table.

'I can't take your money,' she'd said.

'Why not?' Irma had demanded in the face of Lin's puzzlement. 'Hasn't she got a future?'

They had both thought that tremendously funny, and had gone screeching out of the booth into the Bank Holiday crowds.

On the last night, just a fortnight before Lin went to university, she and Irma had gone down and listened to the tide. It had surged right up to the steps under the promenade, and they could hear a faint tinkling noise, strange and rhythmic and attractive. Then they had realized it was the tin cans, the beach rubbish, caught up in the weed at the bottom of the sea wall, being dragged backwards and forwards with every wave. That had set them off laughing all over again.

'S'real picture postcard here, innit?' Irma had said . . .

Lin stood up now, hands to both sides of her head. She wanted to wake up properly, but seemed unable to.

. . . Irma had gripped Lin's hand in her own. 'Listen,' she had told her, in the dark, on that last night, her face barely a line or two of grey. 'You forget everything that's happened. You go off and forget that bloody Michael—selfish git, what is he? A mistake. Two hours' mistake. You don't think of anything else. You forget this road, you forget all those people, you forget you ever worked weekends here, and then you never will have come here at all. You go to college and be brainy, and you forget your mam, you forget . . .'

Then, in an instant, Irma and the painted seaside rail against which they stood were gone.

Awake. At last.

Lin went to the window, and looked down at the town. There was nothing much to be seen in the dark now except for the yellow lights on the main road below the market lane, and one long vast drop of angular roofs. No Georgian crescents visible now: usually a curved yellow rim at the bottom of the hill, behind the tops of the trees of the park. Just the navy-blue sky, flat-box extensions on the back of houses, and the neat and regular stepped rungs of chimneys.

The air was close. She opened the window, hand fumbling on the looped Victorian catch.

She could still taste and smell the meals in the Hunting Dog. 'You have little hands—look—little hands!' That was Irma's voice, in the din of the kitchen at one o'clock, as they slopped the Sunday Special—three slices of beef, one Yorkshire pudding, two tablespoons of swede and carrot, and a slice of stand-up gravy—onto yet more plates. Regular Sunday lunch at the Hunting Dog on Askethwaite seafront. A Babycham with a cherry on a stick waited on a shelf above her head, her reward from Michael. She never did tell him how much she loathed Babycham.

And he would be wiping glasses with slow, slow precision, watching her as she threaded her way through tables, plonking down the customers' dinners: the fish and the beef and the shepherd's pie.

Michael had taken her to a café in the Lakes—as a treat, amid warnings and shakings of the head from Irma. He had been a pale man, very thin: pale hair, very pale hands with translucent fingernails and very short fingers. He must have been twenty-five. Unmarried. His own car. Very quiet, with a fixed look. She had never been taken anywhere in a car by a man—she was so criminally naïve—and she had thought of the afternoon as a jaunt, a joke. And, besides, if Michael thought . . . she could handle Michael. You could push him over with one thumb—spit in his eye. Not that it would ever come to that. He was too shy, too slow; he just had a car.

She had sat in the leather passenger seat, her handbag in the glove compartment, pretending to be entirely adult, even bored, while the trees sped by and the hot air-heater grilled the flesh of her legs. It had come as a terrible shock when, later in the day, Michael had tried to kiss her. He expected to kiss her, and more. All for a trip in his car, and a stale scone and a cup of tea on the side of Windermere.

No one outside in the street now. One in the morning.

Lin went over to the stove and felt the kettle. It was still faintly warm from the last drink. She didn't want to light the gas for fear of waking Theo. She took down a cup, spooned coffee into it, squinting in the shadows, and poured the lukewarm water onto the granules.

Ruth?

Ruth . . .

Coffee in a department store, the worst place of all, tables set just three feet away from the clothes racks. Sitting wedged helplessly into a corner—with Ruth facing her. Lin had been reading a newspaper, submerged in it, one foot propped on the adjacent chair, when someone had sat down opposite her, placing a cup carefully between them. Lin had looked up.

Ruth!

How had she found her? Even now, years later, Lin didn't know. Lin had been waiting there for Kieran. He had been giving a lecture in the Guildhall across the street, card-holders only, the Fabreith Society. Summer, five years ago. Kieran had left his wife. They were not yet in the Priory. Ruth had left it, Kieran had left it too. He was living in rooms in the university while they argued over the division of ownership. It was a time of transition, a confused time, a hiatus for them all. Ruth had bought herself a flat in town, the beautiful flat that Kieran had described to Lin as being Ruth's ivory tower.

Lin had been so sure of him then.

It was a hot day. Lin wore a sleeveless T-shirt, cycle shorts. She had let her hair grow. She was twisting a strand of it in her hand as she read, and on seeing Ruth, on staring at her sudden materialization, the strand had become fixed around Lin's fist. Unknowingly she clutched it for comfort as Ruth calmly stirred her coffee, ran her eyes over Lin's scanty clothes, her bare feet. Ruth herself was dressed in a plain silk shift dress; her legs were tanned and smooth. She looked a little tired: the only crack in her armour.

'How are you, Lin?' she had asked.

It was the first thing Ruth had ever said to her.

Lin knew about her. Of course, she knew about her. Ruth was a constant invisible third presence. Kieran even kept a photograph of her on his desk at work. But Lin had never actually met her before. Never spoken to her until now.

'I'm all right,' she said, convinced that her own voice sounded reedy, nervous, ashamed.

Ruth had smiled.

'Are you going to live at the Priory?'

'No,' Lin had replied, thinking, *This is quite mad. Mad. Why is she here?*

She had meant it, though, about the Priory. Lin was only too well aware of Ruth's imprint on the place, the past history of Kieran-and-Ruth screaming from its every surface. Besides, it was too big. Not *her*. Too lords-of-the-manor. Embarrassing. Embarrassing to draw up there and pretend to be lady of the house. No, no, Lin had sworn at the time. *Never.* Little flat somewhere, little terraced house, little make-do-and-mend, orange boxes, creaky bed, Belfast sink, that was her. That was like home, back-to-back in Liverpool, redbrick street, donkeystoned step, twitchy net curtains, mass on Sunday. She was comfortable in her tiny room with her books on planks over bricks and a ropy cassette player. She had seen Kieran's study in the Priory, with its high-tech desk. She had seen the immense hallway, the Aga range, the high-ceilinged bedroom with its American heritage quilt, its rag-rolled walls. She hadn't wanted it at all.

Ruth had sat there with her hands folded in her lap, never taking her eyes off Lin's face. Her expression had been perfectly composed.

'What are your plans?' she asked.

Lin had finally managed to release the fist of hair. Conscious of her own bitten fingernails, her hands discoloured from leaky carbon paper, she had tucked her hands into her armpits, hugging herself. 'I've got no plans,' she had said at last.

'Free spirit,' Ruth replied. Just the merest, faintest touch of sarcasm. She drank her coffee as Lin had looked from side to side. There was no way out unless she pushed past, forcibly lifted Ruth's chair with the woman still sitting on it.

'I wanted to tell you something,' Ruth said.

She had looked in her bag, taken out a tissue, and slowly wiped her fingers. For the first time, Lin noticed the fine lines around her eyes. She wondered if Ruth had been crying and thought that perhaps she had. There was a rim of red at each corner, inside the lid.

Ruth put the tissue back, snapped the handbag shut, leaned forward across the table. Across the way, behind Ruth, an overweight woman, puffing and blowing in the summer heat, fumbled through the rails of clothes, hissing and tut-tutting at the price tags.

'I wanted to tell you,' Ruth murmured, 'that I shall get him back.'

'What?' Lin said.

'You heard me.'

Lin had never told Kieran. He would not have believed her.

Ruth had been so very good . . . oh, so very good, so very controlled and civilized about the whole thing. She had been faultless.

Michael was stacking the bar shelves. Lin could see his scalp, baby pink though his hair. It made her skin crawl, her stomach heave.

He had looked up. She turned at once and ran out of the pub, and crossed over the road. The promenade ran straight as a die to left and right, a long black string bordered with runners of lawn. The Council had planted wallflowers in the beds, but they looked wrinkled and sad.

The irony of the wallflowers had struck her as she paused at the rail. Michael hadn't even danced with her. She had never even been taken to a dance. She had only been taken out in his car.

She had then gone down the concrete steps to the wet sand. The tide was out, and there were mudflats stretching for a mile into the bay. There were no shells nearby, no seaweed, only litter: tin cans, bread wrappings, condoms, plastic bags. She had walked under the pier, and sat down on one of the stone blocks into which the iron supports of the pier were embedded. Soon she had seen Michael running down the beach. She watched him, seeing clearly what a misfit he was: wrong clothes, wrong face. An old face on a man of twenty-five. His silly loping walk. That chain, like the chain for a pair of spectacles, that he wore snapped to his belt, its other end snaking into his pocket where it clipped to his door keys. He lived with his mother in Hemmelwyke, one of the towns further up the coast that thought itself better than this resort with its bait shops and funfair and bed-and-breakfasts. He had been her only son.

Lin had looked down at the muddy, gritty sand. By the time that Michael got to her, he had been damp from the sea mist, the foggy air. He didn't even ask her what the matter was. Perhaps he had already known from her face. She had been just eighteen. One stupid eighteen-year-old.

She had hit him, slapped him full in the face, just as he had opened his mouth to speak. He had tripped backwards, managed not to fall over, holding his face in amazement.

She had never again gone back into the pub. She had only gone near it that one Bank Holiday to say goodbye to Irma—two months before Lin had left for good.

'On our way,' said a voice. 'Coming through!'

A burst of laughter.

Lin froze in the dark.

Pressure slammed against either side of her head. She dropped the cup into the sink, put both hands to her ears. The force of it was vivid, piercing—the hum of deep water, the aching compression of space—and the pain violent.

And then it was gone.

She looked around her, expecting to see the owner of that voice.

But there was no one in the room. She walked over to the open door and looked down at Theo.

Her son was curled on his bed, his thumb in his mouth.

She dropped to her knees at his side, stroked his hair, and finally laid her head next to his. Fear was lodged in a tight small ball in her chest.

'I love you,' she whispered.

In the darkness, she took his loose, warm hand in her own.

NINE

$\mathcal{K}$IERAN REMEMBERED the exact moment when he had fallen in love with Lin. It was etched deep in his brain.

He and Ruth had always thrown a party on New Year's Eve, and that year was no different. They had moved into the Priory in August, and this was the first time they would have room to move, room for Kieran to be the expansive host he had always fondly imagined himself to be.

The Priory matched a picture in his head that he seemed to have carried with him since childhood. The village itself had something of a schizophrenic character. At the eastern end there was a long row of council houses facing scrubby fields. But, as you then descended the hill, the road curved round to reveal a main street, and down there was a common and a stream, and several beech trees, and a spectacularly ugly village hall roofed in black corrugated iron. It was a place of miniatures: thin pavements, small windows, low eaves. On his first visit he had found the sign for the Priory propped up in an overgrown hedge, and had driven through the broken gate to see the house looking blandly golden against its backdrop of green.

It was a low, square house in an acre of lawn and woodland, sitting at the flat bottom of the valley. Behind the house were a couple of pasture fields, and then the rapidly rising slope of the hill beyond, pale and treeless except for its ancient circle of chalk. The Droddin, as it was called, was four concentric circles cut into the hill's gradient, but only one still remained clear: the central one, about a hundred feet across. The remaining circles spread away from it rather like ripples on water, only just visible under the soil. All down the slope the hill was ridged from soil slippage, so the whole effect was of one giant green pool into which a prehistoric stone had been thrown. Behind that rose the stocky white finger of the Hamble stone tower, a Victorian memorial. When Ruth first came to see the house, she had paused in the driveway, looked up at the hill and said ironically, 'Oh, how nice. Its own halo and candle.'

Kieran had painted such a glowing picture before her visit that she told him it ought to be called the Shrine and not the Priory. It was far too expensive for them and, once they moved in, they found out that all its appealing little idiosyncrasies were of the expensive kind, too. The back stairs, for instance, that he had so loved on first sight—a crooked flight that ran from a back bathroom down to the kitchen—proved to have dry rot in the panelling. The water came out of all the taps rust-red at times. The heating boiler expired in the first month, and there was a leak in the roof. The whole place, with the onset of winter, smelled terribly of damp.

But Kieran loved it. One morning, coming downstairs wrapped against the cold in his old plaid dressing gown, he had emerged into the hallway at the exact moment that a wintry sun touched the floor through the opaque glass panels on either side of the door. Silhouetted on the glass itself, like a Japanese painting, was a bird. It was perfectly outlined and still. He had felt this was some sort of subtle gift: a good omen, a blessing.

Although Ruth didn't share his passion for the place—he wondered fondly if she had ever experienced such an emotion—she nevertheless did not complain at either the costs or the cold. They kept the dining room, drawing room and music room empty that winter, because they couldn't afford to furnish them; but she made sensibly tough covers for the kitchen chairs and table, and turned the little study into their sitting room where the patched leather couch from his campus office sat looking very much like a poor relation. Ruth refused to buy cheaper furniture or carpets just to fill the rooms. 'We'll do one room at a time, as we can afford it,' she insisted.

For the party she had performed a miracle.

The empty rooms all lay at the front of the house and, instead of trying to hide them, Ruth made a feature of the echoing space there. On Christmas Eve they had bought three huge trees. They had put one in the flagstoned hall, one in the drawing room, and one in the dining room. Ruth put candles ready on the bare sills, fireplaces and floors. They had then decorated the trees with silver foil and heavily berried holly from the village hedges. Candles lit the trees in the side rooms, and a massive log fire glowed on the one in the hall. When it got dark, the effect was magical. The vast dark green aura of the trees in the high-ceilinged empty rooms was otherworldly—almost primitive—as if earth spirits had invaded them.

He and Ruth had toasted each other. 'You're a genius,' he told her.

She had smiled in that brisk way of hers. 'I have my moments, I think.'

On New Year's Eve morning he asked her, over breakfast, 'Shall I invite Lin Harris?'

'If you like.'

He had buttered his toast. 'She seems to be all alone at the moment. She might be grateful.'

Ruth didn't answer. She finished her coffee and began working on the crossword. He looked up and saw her head bent over the newspaper. She had a birthmark just below her ear on the right-hand side of her face, a curiosity that he found touching, as if she were showing a fault, a fracture, in her orderliness. Probably, his pity for her, for the composed woman with such a central flaw, was at the heart of his love for her. And, although he did not know it yet, it was this same sympathy for the flawed that drew him to Lin. Lin's defencelessness despite all her brilliance. Ruth's infertility in the centre of all her abundant accomplishment.

'Perhaps I *won't* ask her,' he said.

But he did.

He was driving into work that morning, only two days after seeing Lin back to the cold room in which she lived, and he glimpsed her in the street just before the university buildings. She had been sitting by herself on a seat, reading, though it was freezing cold. He had pulled the car over immediately, and run back towards her.

'Lin,' he had said, 'what are you doing?'

She had waved the book at him. 'Reading.'

'Are you feeling better?'

'Yes.'

'Are you waiting for someone?'

'Yes,' she said.

He had felt ridiculously disappointed at this, and it must have shown in his face.

'I'll come into work this afternoon,' she continued.

'I wasn't thinking of that,' he told her.

She had closed the book, smiling a little with her head bowed.

'Would you like to come to a party?' he asked.

'When?'

'Tonight.'

She had pursed her lips.

'My wife would like you to come,' he added. Why had he mentioned that? To give his invitation an air of respectability, he supposed.

She wrote down his address in pencil on the flyleaf of the book.

He had then got back into his car, and, just as he drove off, he saw her being met by a boy of her own age. The boy took her hand, and she danced down the row of benches, the hem of her coat held up in one hand. That image remained with him for hours, days: her small, thin form revealed by the open coat, her fingers gracefully splayed, her toes pointed.

She came to the party.

The invitation said eight o'clock, and most guests dutifully arrived on the hour. By the time Lin knocked on the door two hours later, the party had moved back to the kitchen, where Ruth had laid out the food. There were only two couples in the candlelit hallway. Kieran had gone to open the door and found Lin standing there, looking nervous and lonely, clutching a bottle of red wine to her chest. She was wreathed in the coat.

It was desperately cold outside.

'Come in,' he said.

'I couldn't see any lights from the lane,' she said. She stepped over the threshold. The people still in the hall stopped talking and gazed at her.

'Can I take your coat?' he asked.

He eased her arms out of the velvet-cuffed sleeves, reduced to that damp-scrub feel at the cuffs, and took the bottle of wine from her. She was wearing a black T-shirt and a short black skirt. Her neck and arms were thin and bony-white in the candle's light. He noticed that her shoes were muddy.

'You haven't walked?' he asked.

'Only from the bus stop.'

He stared at her. The nearest stop was on the main road over the hill. It was at least a mile and a half away along narrow, unlit roads. It had never crossed his mind that she wouldn't get a taxi or a lift.

'Where's your friend?' he had asked, looking past her into the darkness.

'What friend?' she said.

'You came all on your own?'

'Why not?'

He led her down the hall. 'We're just eating,' he said. Falsely cheerful, his voice boomed along the empty space. 'Come along and meet Ruth.'

She had followed him into the kitchen, where there was a crush. He couldn't see his wife, so instead grabbed a plate from the table and forced it into Lin's hands.

'Help yourself,' he said. 'What do you want to drink?'

'Anything.'

'Well . . . give me a clue at least.'

'Anything.' She had lowered her voice, and her head, and her gaze was fixed on the table. There were bowls of salad and pasta in front of her, but the serving spoons had disappeared—moved further up the line. The woman directly in front of Lin was talking at the top of her voice about the parish council and some boundary dispute.

In the line ahead, two men were calling at each other across other people's heads.

'Venison sausage! Four quid a pound—makes them himself—shoots the bloody things himself—you go along the road—on the left . . .'

Kieran saw Lin begin pulling at the hem of her skirt. She was trying to pull it further down over her bare knees.

He elbowed his way through the crowd, glimpsing Ruth in the pantry, talking to several other women as they dished up food. All of their guests were people Ruth knew. Many of them already wore that blurred expression of swiftly consumed drinks. When Kieran brought Lin's drink back to her, she was standing in the same place, with her plate still empty.

At that moment the woman next to her turned round and gave her a look of frank astonishment.

'And who do you belong to?' she asked.

Kieran gave Lin her glass. 'Lin is my assistant at the university,' he said. 'Lin—this is Angela Wadham.'

'Assistant?' Angela said, laughing. 'My God, I thought you were someone's daughter!'

That was possible. Lin was at least fifteen years younger than anyone else in the room, and had that hangdog, bruised and embarrassed look of a teenager dragged to a parents' party.

'Lin is preparing my manuscript for the publisher,' he explained.

Angela peered down at Lin. 'So you're studying history?'

'No,' Lin said.

'My son's at Sussex,' Angela turned to Kieran. 'Politics, you know— I ask you!'

'Lin is very clever,' Kieran said. 'She has had several things published herself already.'

Angela Wadham ignored his reference to Lin. 'What do you think of this appraisal?'

'I'm sorry?' Kieran asked.

'This appraisal committee. They want to do a survey of the village.'

'I'm afraid I don't know anything about it,' he admitted.

'It's an invasion of the parish function,' she said. 'We can't persuade you to stand for the parish council?'

'I leave all that sort of thing to Ruth,' Kieran said. Out of the corner of his eye, he saw Lin put down her still-empty plate and turn away.

'Do you think I *could* ask Ruth?' Angela Wadham persisted. 'She must work awfully long hours already. She's a consultant for the nursing home, isn't she?'

'Yes, I . . .' His gaze wandered away. Lin was nowhere to be seen.

'So would she have the time?'

He smiled. 'Would you excuse me just a second?'

He had walked away briskly, back down the hall—into the gloom. Putting his head around the dining—room and drawing-room doors, he saw that she was not in either place. He went to the front door.

She was already halfway down the drive.

'Lin!'

She neither stopped nor looked back.

'Lin!'

He stepped outside. It was icy cold, and the grass had a sheen that promised frost. His breath floated in clouds in front of him. He began to jog along the drive, past the row of parked cars. He caught her up underneath the trees by the entrance.

'What are you doing?' he said.

'Going home.'

'But you only just got here!'

'It was a mistake,' she said.

He pulled her arm. 'What do you mean? What's a mistake?'

She wriggled away from him. 'Coming here—all this.' She nodded in the direction of the cars.

'But why? Lin, you've only been here two minutes. Where are you going?'

'Back to the bus.'

'It's over a mile from here.'

They were out in the lane now, edged on both sides with ten-foot hedges that bowed slightly towards the road. 'More like two.' She smiled.

He stepped in front of her. 'You can't walk that.'

'Why not?'

'Well—something might happen to you.'

'What?' She seemed amused.

'An accident, anything . . .'

'You mean I might get raped?'

'It's possible.'

'Out here in Never-Never Land?'

'What are you talking about?'

'The land of the venison sausage.'

'Sorry?'

She turned away, shaking her head.

'Let me at least get the car,' he said. 'I'll drive you to the stop.'

'I'm fine.'

'Oh, for God's sake,' he said. 'Stay here a minute.'

Exasperated, he ran back to the house. His car keys were in his jacket pocket. It took him a full five minutes to negotiate his way out, and by the time he got to the lane she was nowhere to be seen. He accelerated through the dark, cursing her under his breath. At the village centre, he saw her standing by the little parish hall, staring up at the flat-topped hill with its prehistoric patterns. He stopped the car and opened the door.

'Get in,' he said.

She hesitated a moment, then did so.

He started to pull away. 'I don't understand you,' he said.

'Parish appraisal,' she said. 'What's that?'

'How the hell should I know?'

'Politics—I ask you!' she mimicked.

'Look, I barely know the woman. I don't know what the hell she was on about.'

They drove in silence. It took barely five minutes to get to the main road. The bus stop—a solitary post on the very summit of another hill, and exposed to every element—stood in its lay-by ahead of them. He tried to work out, as he drove, why he was so unreasonably, chokingly angry with her.

She put her hand on the door handle.

'Wait until the bus comes,' he told her. 'You'll see it coming, miles away from here.'

They waited.

The night was pitch dark, and very still.

'Didn't you ever have parties, at home?' he asked.

'Sometimes.'

'Well, then . . . ?'

'Not like yours,' she said. 'Not that kind.'

'What kind, then?'

She laughed softly, and leaned her head against the window.

'Tell me,' he said.

She was silent for some time, her breath forming an opaque outline to her profile on the glass. He thought that she wasn't going to reply. And then, very quietly, she began to speak.

'I'm not ashamed of where I come from,' she said.

'Why should you be?'

'Just to let you know,' she said. 'I'm not.'

'What is that to do with anything?'

She gave a laboured sigh.

There was no sign of the bus. He tapped his fingers on the steering wheel. 'Tell me about your brothers,' he said.

'Why?'

'To fill in the time. Your mother, then? Your father?'

'I told you, I don't know him. He left home before I was born.'

'You've never seen your father at all?'

'I've never seen either of them.'

He looked hard at her. 'Either of them?'

She smiled crookedly. 'My brothers have one father, and I've got another. Because of mine, theirs left home.'

He worked it out for a moment. 'Your mother had an affair?'

She laughed softly. 'My mother met a man, she never asked his name, he was Italian, she fell pregnant . . .'

'With you.'

'With me. On hearing the happy news, her husband left.'

'Ah . . .'

Another silence.

'Ah,' she finally mimicked. 'Ah.' She stretched out her legs, crossed her arms, leaned her head on the headrest. She took a deep breath and began to speak rapidly in her slightly lilting tone. 'And my brothers, Patrick, Michael, Roy, such awful good boys they are, twenty-five, twenty-four, twenty-two, spanking jobs too, mechanic, tool fitter, cast-iron pan company, hoping their mother is long past having sex, as any good God-fearing Catholic woman ought to be, if she ever was on it, which God pray she wasn't . . .' She paused a second, laughing at her own speed and turn of phrase. 'And then there is Lindsay bawl-ing her head off in the front room, and the kid hasn't even the grace to look like her mother—Jesus have mercy!—let alone any of the rest of them. The shame! The disgrace! And one day along the street, a woman stops my mother with the pram, and Patrick is along with her, and this woman looks in and she says, "Holy Mary, mother of God, whose child is that?" And my mother gives the pram to Patrick, and "Mine," she says, and she gives her hat to Patrick, and she bunches her fist, and she lays the woman flat out in Scotland Road.'

By now, Kieran too was laughing.

Lin stopped smiling, bit the side of her lip. 'My mother is Irish,' she said. 'She is not a woman to be crossed.'

'Are your brothers married?' Kieran asked.

'Yes, all married.'

'Were they, even then?'

'No, they all lived at home until they were thirty.' She laughed softly. 'Genetic programming. Twenty-nine, you give your mam your wages. Thirty, you give your wife your wages. Thirtieth birthday, housing list, engagement party down the club.'

'They didn't leave home until their thirties?'

'My mother wouldn't let them.'

Kieran, again laughing, shook his head. 'It must have been quite something, having three older brothers to defend you.'

She looked at him aghast. 'You think they defended me?' she asked. 'They hated me.'

She turned away from him and stared out of the window.

She thought of the street: redbrick terraced houses with a foot of concrete under the window, and a big stone sill. There was a mile of terraces lined up in rows. Named for flowers and First World War bat-tles and prime ministers. Violet Street, Primrose Street, Ypres Street, Perceval Street. Rows of red brick, with a white nameplate high on each end-house wall. Shiny in the rain. Twenty streets on their side of the road, a road that led down to Bootle docks.

'Roy was the worst,' she murmured. 'He was usually left to look after me. He would say that the Social were coming to get me, nobody wanted me, they were throwing me out. He used to say I stank. He used to say I smelled of my father. I had the front bedroom, so I used to run upstairs and look out to see if the people coming to get me were walking down the street. I hid under the bed until it suddenly dawned on me, when I was about twelve, that no one would ever come. And when I told Roy, he said, Nobody *will* ever come—especially not your dad.'

She turned her head towards him. 'So you see,' she said, 'I've lived on another planet to you—and everyone down there in your house.'

In the cold dark silence, Kieran leaned forward and kissed her.

She was strange to the taste: not unpleasant, but dry and cold. Her mouth made no response. He had the sudden and dreadful sensation, as his face touched hers, that he was actually kissing a thin anxious child of ten or twelve. He drew back and saw her eyes fixed on his.

'Will you look after me?' she asked.

'Yes,' he heard himself say.

While they had been sitting in the car, the old year had passed.

TEN

*T*HEO,' RUTH SAID.

The child looked up, although he could not possibly have heard her voice from across the river. Even from this distance, Ruth could make out his blond hair, his stocky little body. He was wearing bright blue shorts and a blue striped top, not unlike the doll now carefully wrapped in the bag at her side.

Ruth had been into Edith's shop that morning, after standing for some time on the pavement across the narrow street, judging the run-down atmosphere of the place, the cracked road surface, the iron rail alongside the pavement on the rapidly rising incline, the open windows at the top of the house, above the shop: they were attic windows just beneath the Flemish lipped roof. What a place to bring a child, she had thought. So typical of Lin. A crowded market street of second-hand shops, furniture restorers, and dusty jewellery behind security-screened windows. Indian fabric hung from rails. A delicatessen on the corner. The market abutting the road.

Ruth had bought a Lenci doll from Edith Channon.

In fact, it looked rather like Theo with its tightlipped, wary, sideways glance. The rag doll had real little black rubber boots on its feet,

74

and a Twenties-style Christopher Robin mop of hair. The fabric of the face was very pleasant, smooth, almost like suede.

Edith had never taken her eyes from Ruth. 'Do you collect?' she asked.

'I've never bought a doll in my life,' Ruth had replied truthfully, 'but it looks like someone I know.'

'A present?'

'Yes.'

'Shall I wrap it?'

'It's for a boy.'

'A boy,' Edith had repeated, still glancing up repeatedly at Ruth as she wrapped, a puzzled expression on her face. 'Not many boys like dolls.'

Theo was climbing the playground ladder now, not very successfully. Lin was standing at the bottom of the ropewalk, holding out both arms.

Between them, the river that sliced through the centre of the town ran swiftly between its concrete banks. Ruth glanced to her left. It was a much-photographed bridge, with shops across its entire length. A fan-shaped basin of deceptively slow water spread out under it. Then came the broad, shallow-stepped weir. After that, the water was pushed into a narrower channel and began running more quickly, with a green stretch of park on either side. Ruth turned and, keeping the playground in sight, walked up to the bridge and began to cross it.

Her first reaction to Theo had been savage. She remembered it in pinpoint, brightly lit detail.

Kieran standing on the back step of the house, half in and half out of the kitchen door. Ruth had been sitting at the table.

'What did you say?' she asked him.

'Lindsay Harris,' he had repeated, not looking at her but at some distant point beyond the edge of the garden.

It had been spring, and the light that came into the room that morning was touched with acid green. There had been an interminably long silence, in which she tried to piece together the neatly tilled landscape of her life that had just broken bluntly in two. 'But she's only nineteen,' Ruth had said. That was all she could think of. Lindsay Harris was no more than a child.

'I . . .' Kieran hadn't got any further, for Ruth had risen to her feet.

'And she's one of your students.'

'She's not mine. Not in my department.'

'She's a student at the university.' Ruth felt a rising tide of disgust constricting her throat. 'How could you be so stupid.'

'This isn't—'

'You'll lose your job—your living.'

'She's leaving.'

'Lose your reputation, everything . . . for what?'

'She's leaving the university.'

'Why?'

Already she knew the answer. She knew in the moment he at last turned around to face her.

'She's pregnant.'

Said. It was said.

The sharpest of knives could not have made a deeper cut. The thought of a surgical knife slicing through flesh actually flashed, for a second, in Ruth's mind.

'I see,' she had murmured.

He had put his head in his hands. 'I'm so sorry,' he told her. 'I don't even know how this happened.'

'You don't know how she became pregnant?' Ruth had echoed. 'For heaven's sake, don't insult me.'

'No, no . . . this whole thing, I don't know how it's happened.'

She stared at him, his last few words resonating in her head. Flat, dead notes: *I don't know, I don't know . . .*

'You're sick,' she said.

And it had been true. He really had been sick, infected with Lin and her child. And all the things he had told Ruth, all the reassurances that he had given her since they had first met, that he was not in the least paternal, that he had never wanted children, that her inability to have them meant nothing at all to him, less than nothing, that he had never liked children or felt the smallest interest in them . . . all that had vanished overnight.

Lin was pregnant with his child.

At nineteen.

Spring, five years ago.

A judgement on her, Ruth had thought at the time. For past sins. For the child in the ward lying limply in her mother's arms.

Spring. A day like this, in fact, she considered, as she walked across the bridge. Very like this. She looked into the shoulder bag, and her hand closed familiarly around the shape of the doll.

Theo saw her first.

He was standing at the top of the ladder, when his gaze fixed on her. He became very still, other children pushing him from behind.

'Come on, Theo,' Lin was saying. 'You're holding everyone up. Come on, step down, I can catch you . . .'

She noticed the direction of his gaze, and turned. Ruth was ten yards away. The colour drained out of Lin's face.

'Hello,' Ruth said. 'Hello, Theo.'

Lin turned back to Theo, lifted him bodily from the top of the small slide and into her arms. Quickly, without another glance at Ruth, she began to walk away, Theo with his arms tightly about her neck and staring back in Ruth's direction.

'Lin,' Ruth called. She saw the way that Lin was going, down the path that ran alongside the river, to a gate at the farthest corner where there was another small footbridge. There were steps to negotiate on the way, and Ruth began running parallel to the path, downhill across the grass.

'Lin!'

She saw Lin hesitate on the steps, as if trying to retain her balance. Slowly, Lin took the steps one at a time, feet pausing together on each one. By the time she got to the bottom, Ruth was almost alongside her.

'I've only come to see if you're all right,' she said, trying to block Lin's way.

Lin looked her full in the face for a second, then skirted around her, brushing her arm. Theo shrank back in Lin's arms as if he had been touched by an electric charge.

'Don't be silly,' Ruth said. 'Just talk to me. I've got a present for Theo.'

Lin walked on.

Annoyed now, Ruth rapidly strode after her, taking hold of her arm.

'Lin,' she commanded.

At last, Lin stopped. 'Don't you understand English?' she demanded. Ruth noticed that her face was extremely pale, almost uniformly white. 'I told you to keep away from us. What are you doing here?'

Ruth tried to stroke Theo's arm. 'I want to help you,' she said.

Lin started to laugh, then abruptly stopped. 'Help?' she echoed. She looked at the ground for a second, shaking her head in disbelief. Then she stared back into Ruth's face. 'I *know* what you want,' she said.

Suddenly she turned and began to run.

'Lin!' Ruth shouted.

Lin had reached the bottom gate. Another mother was standing close to it, trying to negotiate her way through its narrow space with a pushchair and an older child clinging to its handle. At the side of the gate, the river roared and sped along its thin channel, white water now, an entirely different animal to the sluggish green pond closer to the town. Lin bent down and helped the other woman lift the wheels of the buggy over a step, glancing repeatedly over her shoulder at Ruth who was walking purposefully towards them.

Theo began to cry, picking up Lin's distress. Almost absentmindedly, Lin kissed him, smoothing his hair with an agitated gesture. The other mother was saying something to her. Her toddler looked up at Theo and made a face of sympathetic anxiety. Lin tried to get through the kissing gate with its large, rounded fence. Theo, crying and struggling, caught hold of the swinging doorway, and Lin put him down. He slipped through, and, propelled by Lin's communicated fear, ran straight ahead towards the water.

Lin let out a scream.

Ruth, too, began to run. It seemed like a very long time, a time of disconnected pictures . . . of the stranger's face, and her child's, turned and looking back at Theo . . . of Lin frozen half in and half out of the gate . . . and of Theo, arms spread straight on either side, as if he were balancing across a wire, teetering on the edge of the river, a white backdrop to his own blue-and-white outline. As Ruth reached the gate, Lin pushed through to the other side.

Ruth saw her ghostly face in profile. Then suddenly Lin seemed to freeze, as if she had come up against an invisible wall. Her gaze rolled away from Theo and upwards, until her head pitched backwards at an angle.

It was just as though Lin had been shot, suddenly pierced by a bullet, stopped in her tracks. One hand strayed to her throat, the other hung loosely at her side. Her back stiffened and her whole torso became rigid, crucified.

Then soundlessly, smoothly, she dropped to the ground.

ELEVEN

*I*T WAS ONE-FIFTEEN IN THE MORNING IN CYPRUS, and as hot as it had been the previous afternoon. Even inside the airport terminal, Kieran could feel the humidity subtly adhering to his skin, the legacy of a sudden evening thunderstorm.

He looked up at the departures board. Green digital lettering flickered: *01:15 Gatwick. Delayed.*

His gaze passed around the airport lounge. Families slumped around him in almost every possible combination: grandparents, parents, couples with babies in strollers, teenagers lolling asleep with Walkmans still clamped to their heads. Occasionally people would stare at Kieran, then glance away . . . glance back . . . venture a smile that he had made a rule not to return. Around his feet swilled a seemingly perpetual stream of wandering, fractious toddlers. A two-year-old passed him now, one fist comfort-clutching a knot of his hair, the other smearing a wet biscuit along the empty seats.

Kieran shut his eyes, blocking out the airport, recalling Theo's voice. His son had sounded furious and exhausted, gabbling distorted syllables between weeping coughs. Then Ruth had come on, soothing and impenetrably calm.

'He's all right,' she had said. 'Just worn out.'

Kieran had rested his head on his hands, staring at the sea beyond the hotel-room balcony, seeing and not seeing the colour: unfractured blue stretching for miles.

'And Lin is . . . ?' He had glanced down to the hospital name scribbled on the piece of paper. At the ward number, and the name of a consultant. Despite Ruth's soothing tone, the shock of the call had disorientated him. He had tried, while she talked, to untangle why Ruth was in Hampton at all.

'She collapsed. I called an ambulance.'

He still stared at the words on the paper. 'She fainted?' he said. 'Outside in the street?'

Interference on the line buckled Ruth's tone. He couldn't tell her emotion.

'Why were you there?' he asked at last.

'She wanted me to come.'

He frowned. 'She . . . ?' He couldn't work it out. 'Is it serious?'

'It could be any number of things. Something as simple as hysteria . . .'

'What was she hysterical about?' he asked, dumbfounded.

'Not in that way.'

'You think this is an emotional thing?'

'I can't say, Kieran. You know . . .' Her voice trailed away.

'What?' he asked.

'It's not for me to say.'

'What exactly?'

'Let's not go into that now. Plenty of time when you get home.'

He had closed his eyes, pinched the skin between his brows in an effort to focus his thoughts. 'You think she's unstable?' he said.

'Let's talk about it when you get home.'

He could hear Theo's complaining monotone, but not his words. He tried to imagine Ruth's expression, but failed.

Then Theo gave one high-pitched, violent scream.

'What happened?'

'Nothing,' Ruth murmured. 'He's just very tired.'

'Where are you?'

'At home, of course.'

'Your own home?'

'Yes, Kieran.'

'Thank you for looking after him.'

There was a pause. 'It's my pleasure,' she said. Then the buzz of disconnection.

He had placed the call to the hospital straight away, and was put through to the consultant neurologist, Werth.

'Do you know if your wife suffers from migraine?' the man had asked.

'Migraine? She's had some headaches.'

'Has she complained of any specific, disabling pain in the last few days?'

'I haven't been home in weeks,' Kieran told him. Down the phone, Kieran could hear the clack of feet along a polished floor, and the shunting of a metal trolley.

'Has she had any contact with mumps?'

Kieran laughed shortly. 'I've no idea.'

'Any disturbances to her balance, her vision, memory?'

'Why don't you ask her?'

'I can't do that reliably just now.'

Kieran had thought about that, considered its implications.

'Does she wear spectacles?' Werth persisted.

'No. What's wrong with her?'

'We have to do a few more tests. But there are a number of things we're looking at.'

'What did you ask about mumps for?'

'There's a strain of meningitis from the Coxsackie virus—'

'Meningitis,' Kieran repeated, not a question.

'That might explain the abruptness, the suddenness of the illness. But then, so would a lot of other things.'

'Which you're testing for.'

'Quite.'

The last light of the day had been fading.

'I'll try to get back by tomorrow morning,' Kieran had promised.

Harry came walking back now towards Kieran's seat in the airport, interrupting his thoughts. 'Some woman over there wants to know if you're the man on the telly.' He grinned, sitting down beside him.

Kieran turned to look at him. 'How did Ruth know where Lin was?'

'How should I know?'

'Did you tell her?'

Harry looked wounded. 'I hardly know Ruth. I don't even know where she lives. I've only ever met her once.'

Kieran looked up again at the impassive face of the departures board.

'I didn't tell her,' Harry insisted.

'Somebody did,' Kieran said.

Harry snorted derisively. 'May I make a tiny suggestion?' he muttered, picking up the polystyrene cup of coffee he had brought with him and blowing on it noisily. 'For everybody's sake, Kieran, sort your bloody life out.'

TWELVE

*T*HEO HAD BEEN SINGING.

In the back of the car he was producing the same phrase over and over. The song had no name—it was one of his own—and Lin had the feeling that this one piece of melody, those few formless notes, had become lodged in her head. They were physical. They had shape. And the shape was long and blunt, forcing upwards from the base of her neck into the centre of her brain.

She remembered putting her hands flat on the steering wheel. It was during the journey from the Priory to Hampton. Resting her head on her hands had given only a temporary respite. The sun had been shining across the dashboard. Through the cracks between her fingers, Lin could see white rectangles, orange stripes, oblique blossoms of hard colour. Her head had felt unbelievably heavy.

She had taken a wrong turning more than once. And yet she knew this road so well. Crossing the river for the second time, she had seen that the water's surface looked unnaturally metallic, the reflections painful and piercing, the sun-refracted ripples filling the interior of the car as she had crossed the bridge.

'Theo,' she had whispered. 'Don't sing that any more now.'

He had obeyed. In the silence that followed, she turned her head—so weighty, so slow, feeling every interaction of cartilage and muscle and bone—and looked at the place where he had been sitting.

He was not there.

She opened her eyes.

It was blessedly, blessedly dark. No orange, no white, no ripples.

She turned her head a little now, and saw a small patch of light from an open door. Wincing, she looked away, closing her eyes again, and pressing her head into the pillow. It was night. Late at night.

She had been brought here in an ambulance. She remembered the paramedic; remembered his name badge, his grey hair, his grey shirt. Remembered the blunt shape of pain becoming a block. Stone liquefying and pouring into her skull, and re-forming into granite, filling every last cell, every scrap, every contour, until her head was all stone.

She must have been dreaming for hours, a dream that had been alarmingly real.

'Nearly there,' a voice had said.

The dreams had marched through the room, across her, through her body.

'Awake?' a woman's voice asked.

She forced herself to look into the room. A nurse was standing at her bedside.

'What time is it?' Lin asked.

'Three o'clock. How are you feeling?'

'Where's my son?'

The nurse lifted her wrist, feeling for the pulse. 'Don't worry about that for a moment. He's quite safe.'

'Is he here?'

Someone passed by the door: a shadow, no sound.

She had been dreaming before Theo's song: a great pressure of vivid, pelting image. There had been streets full of people, noise laced with the sound of water.

Water by a gate. Ruth at the gate. Water rushing in drains and sewers, in public fountains. No gate. No Ruth. Water boiling and staining the purple-dyed robes in the yard vats. Sawdust obscuring the site of sacrifices made on the stone, on the doorsteps of houses, to appease the gods. There were new gods in Rome every day—conquered gods accommodated.

She had been walking in the streets of the tanneries, and the smell had been overpowering. The sound of the water, the long slow slope of the street down to the river . . . she had passed through a labyrinth of jostling houses into a thoroughfare of bookbinders, leather binding, sandal-makers. Somewhere deep in her brain, her reasoning ability tried to take control. She, too, carried a book in her hands and, looking down, she had seen that it was a pile of modern manuscript.

'Are you thirsty?'

She tried to think, to come back to her body, to remember its needs. She was out of her flesh. Somewhere else.

She had paused at the door of a bookbinder's shop, staring at her feet. She had known that she must not enter with her left foot first: it was bad luck. She must put her right foot forward. The smell had been getting worse, the sewage from the houses running in clay pipes just under the neatly arranged cobbles, emerging as twin open channels between the cobbles and the stone house-steps. Birds had fluttered in cages over her head. In a fit of panic she had crouched, scattering the pages to left and right. Feet trampled them. They had split into fragments and dissolved. All the words had gone running away down the street, mixing with the stench of the Argiletum.

'I have to know where he is,' she murmured.

'Mrs Gallagher,' the nurse said, 'don't fall asleep on me now. Can you hear me?'

The scenes had mixed.

She had been in Carthage. In Suk al-Khamis. In Zama. At Lake Trasimenus. She had not been on the road any more: that long humpbacked rolling road rising to the hot blue sky. Not in the Priory. Not in the flat any more. Not at the side of the river.

'All the time in the world,' they had said. Anonymous voices populating her body. She had shrunk far down inside her own flesh, and found a horde of strangers there: all Kieran's text sprung into three dimensional emphasis.

She had been behind the eyes of Gaius Flaminius leading his troops round the stony outcrop of the lakeside. There had been a fitful, streaming mist. Hannibal had concealed his troops in the mountains above him—to the side of him. She had felt their breath, heard their blood, saw their thoughts, in one clear realizing second just before she saw them. Fifteen thousand had been about to be slaughtered. And it was not yesterday, not a year ago, not two thousand years ago, but *now*. No past, no future, just one vast extended living moment in which all experience was sunk. *There is all the time in the world.* The Roman army had borne their wounds on their faces, anxious to die quickly and well, because the shame of defeat meant that they could never go home or be admitted into their families again. They had gone forward almost in haste, turning themselves so that the blows of the enemy would fall on their chests and necks and shoulders.

Lin wondered idly if she were dying now. She had looked back to where the paper had fallen in the Argiletum, in the stench and the sun. Somewhere, if she were dying, Kieran would have written it down for her. Kieran wrote every death down, great or small. His preoccupation with the way men died was one of the gory appeals of the programme. She had copied out deaths onto screens or transparencies, and made them vivid. Somewhere on those shreds, she had thought, her own name would now be written.

Across the Roman street through which she had come, crowds pushed their way over the public passage. The filthy insulae reached five or six storeys into the Italian sky, higher than all the respectable houses and villas nearby. The walls of the insulae were wattle and daub, and the only air admitted to them was through clay grilles on dark landings. Crowds swarmed the basements and every floor right up to the sixth, where the roof was a layer of tile and the walls were open to the elements. She had been part of the shuddering, collapsing towers of the past. She had lived there once . . . now . . . tomorrow. She would come crashing down with them. She would be buried alive.

'Mrs Gallagher,' said a voice a hundred miles away.

The lights, the crush, the smell of the city, the fluttering paper pages, Theo's unbearable repeated song, the orange-and-white glare, all mingled.

Lin opened her eyes. The nurse was still there.

'Back with me?' the nurse asked. She lifted Lin's arm and put a blood-pressure cuff around it, at the same time switching on the small nightlight by the bed, momentarily scorching Lin's sight.

'Everything's mixed up,' Lin said.

She looked past the nurse's shoulder and then, for the first time, she noticed the faces.

There was a whole host of people looking in at her through the window. *It's three in the morning*, she thought. The nurse inflated the pressure cuff, and the flesh on Lin's arm tightened. There came the comforting descending tick of the meter.

But there were still people outside, looking in at her.

She shifted her head very slightly on the pillow. This sent a smooth rocket of pain out through the top of her head—so very intense that it was almost beautiful, unlike any other pain, so shocking and full in its perfect power. She waited till it subsided to rhythms of electricity that permeated down her face and descended, at last, on her heart. The nurse had not even noticed. She began to take off the cuff.

The people at the window hadn't moved. Lin saw that their faces were lit by a gentle, nightlight glow. Each one had a rosy and pleasant gleam. They stood in a polite row beyond the glass, some smiling. Women, men, children: occasionally they looked in at Lin as if checking whether she was awake, whether she could see them.

They must be cold out there, Lin thought. Why don't they come inside? What are they waiting for? Why are they *allowed* outside this ward? She closed her eyes momentarily. She badly wanted to lift her hand to her face, to cover it—she would like a little privacy. But the effort—which she could clearly see compartmentalized into separate actions in her mind: tense the muscle in the shoulder, raise the forearm, bend the elbow—proved unbearably complicated. She couldn't visualize the final result—the hand on her face, the fingers across her eyes.

'How is your back?' the nurse asked. She was leaning down almost level with Lin's face, and had a slight West Country accent. She had a round, dark-eyed, dark-browed face. 'Can you hear me, Mrs Gallagher?'

Lin had decided that she must still be asleep. Even the nurse was part of her dream. She was walking through images that were being randomly thrown at her: thousands of fluttering images, shuffling packs of cards drifting soundlessly down and covering her. *There is no one outside. It's three in the morning.*

And here was a woman sitting opposite her, in the dark.

The nurse was gone. The woman placed a hand, melodramatically, in the centre of her own chest. 'Me,' she said conversationally, 'I've been here twelve years.'

'Here?' Lin asked. 'In here?'

'Myocardial infarction.'

Lin was too tired to ask what that meant. The woman started to smile.

'You know what it is? Fancy word for a heart attack.'

Heart attack. Whose? Lin thought.

'Mine.' The woman glanced out of the window, as if to confirm her audience.

'Are you visiting me?' Lin asked. This time she did open her mouth, and real words came out. They reverberated around the private room like little discs of noise, bouncing back and forth.

Her visitor got up—or at least she made a movement that put her higher in Lin's vision. She held a handbag very properly in front of her, clasped with both hands. She wore a hat. Her suit—what Lin could discern of it in the shadows, and she ought not to have been able to discern anything of it, but she could see quite clearly the weave in the cloth; in fact she could see the whole intimate texture of the thread, the wool, the cotton mixed together, the way that the strands locked in place, and were bruised by the knitting machine, and were fixed and solid—she could see quite clearly, was a deep pink.

It's a very nice suit.

'It *is* nice. It ought to be nice, the price I paid. I bought it for my Mark's wedding. Do you like it?'

Lin made a tremendous effort to raise herself. She wanted to find the bell. A noise would break this dream. A movement would break this dream. A dream of hallucinogenic clarity. There was a sudden pain in Lin's back: a point of needle-like discomfort.

'That's your back, remember?'

Lin couldn't find the bell for the nurse. She flopped back, sighing, wincing.

'How does it feel?'

Someone held my hand, she thought.

Was it you?

She slipped away, drifting horizontally from the room. It was surprisingly easy, so easy that it puzzled her why she had never done it before. The corridor outside was mercifully empty. Floor-to-ceiling windows looked out onto a courtyard. There was a white wall on the other side. Far away down the echoing, polished tube of empty space was a little seating area, with green hard-backed chairs, and a coffee table, and someone was sitting watching all-night television.

Lin made a tremendous effort to right herself, to turn herself upright so that she could stand on her feet. It appeared to be disproportionately difficult, like standing vertically in a swimming pool with an enormous inflated cushion strapped to her chest. She wanted constantly to tip backwards so that she faced the ceiling with its recessed, blinding lights.

There had been a team of three people: two women, one man. They had carried some sort of surgical kit, and the moment that they came into her room—earlier today? when precisely today?—she could feel the tension rolling from them. The man had said, 'I shall need a slightly lower chair.' He had been concerned about the chair—in fact she had heard him actually thinking about the exact position he ought to be in, and worrying that he would make a mistake. He had done very few lumbar punctures. He had told no one about his anxiety, but she could see in his mind a picture of the needle slipping from the proposed point, puncturing the skin and sharding in the vertebrae. It wasn't possible, he had told himself. But he hadn't been able to rid himself of this image of the needle, just under the skin, splitting into two pieces. She had seen her own back, bared, and the knotted line of the spine.

She had slept while he fumbled with the needle.

She felt her feet lifting. Damn, it was so difficult to lie down in the air. She *was* lying down, of course—lying on the bed in the darkened room, and there was the nurse, and there was no woman in pink, and the nurse was making notes on the chart at the end of the bed.

'I think I'm going to be sick,' Lin said.

'No, no,' the nurse soothed. 'Don't try to get up. Lie flat. You won't be sick now, not after a lumbar puncture. You'll feel a bit better, as long as you don't try to get up.'

'I'm going to be sick.'

The nurse put a steel dish on the bedside. It felt extraordinarily cold against Lin's arm. 'Shall I wait?'

'Yes . . .'

Long seconds of silence.

'Better now?'

In the dark, Lin smiled. 'Can I see my little boy?' she asked. 'Do you know where he is?'

'In the morning, I expect.'

'Where is he? What happened to me?'

The nurse went out, and Lin looked at the space where she had been.

Did she hear me speak at all?

Did I ask?

'Come back,' she called. 'Please.'

Far, far away she heard Theo crying. Felt him crying. Felt his pain in the centre of her chest, the constriction in his throat. Felt his confusion and terror.

She began to call his name.

THIRTEEN

$\mathscr{R}$UTH WOKE AT THREE-THIRTY.

For a moment she was completely disorientated, seeing the wall of bookshelves opposite her, the white rugs on the polished wood floor, the heavy sitting-room drapes still tied back and letting in the distant glow of the town lights. Then she remembered that Theo was occupying her own bed. She propped herself on one elbow.

The noise that had roused her was soft. She got up from the couch, and pulled her dressing gown around her. Going down the hall, the sound increased until, as she opened the bedroom door, it became a continuous sobbing.

The bed was empty.

'Theo,' she whispered, 'where are you?'

She switched on the light. The brocade spread was almost off the bed. The sheets were tangled into a knot. She saw, with a fleeting moment of annoyance, that the boy had been moving the books on the bedside table, and that her clock was face-down on the floor.

Walking to the end of the bed, she saw him. Theo was sitting on the floor, in a tiny gap between the bed and the wall. He had pulled the spread over his head, and his face peeped out. His thumb was firmly plugged in his mouth, but the sobs still escaped him.

'Whatever's the matter?' Ruth asked. She kneeled down in front of him. 'Hmmm? Why aren't you asleep?'

His round eyes were full of fear. Clicking her tongue against her teeth, she stood up and tried to hook her hands under his arms to lift him. He responded with a primal screech of terror.

'All right, all right,' she said, dropping her hands immediately. She sat back on her heels.

'All sorts of people,' he said.

'There's no people at all,' she told him. 'Just you and me. You've been dreaming.'

His sobs increased.

'I shall make some chocolate,' she said. 'You'd like that, wouldn't you? Some nice hot chocolate to drink? Daddy's coming all the way in a plane to see you. He's on the plane right now, this minute, and he's expecting to see a nice little boy in the morning . . .'

'Mumma,' Theo muttered.

'Mama's in hospital, darling.'

She looked at the boy. His hair was quite dark, like his father's, and its colour touched a nerve in her, a reservoir of need that squeezed her heart dry. The eyes, however—secretive and piercing—were Lin's.

'Come on,' she said. 'You can't stay there all night.' She made a determined effort this time to lift him. He began kicking out at her.

'Don't do that. Be a good boy.' With brute force she pulled him clear of the bed, and took the brocade rug away from him.

He opened his mouth, as if about to scream, and then looked at her intently. It was as if he had read her thoughts, seen into her. She ventured a smile at him. She had never had any feeling for children, never known how to speak to them, but she would try now. She would learn for Kieran's sake.

'Wouldn't you like to live here all the time?' she asked.

She reached out to stroke him, and he suddenly punched her away. Annoyed, she caught hold of his arm. He squirmed and fought.

She tried to lay him on the bed and pin his arms to his side, and was rewarded with several thrashing kicks at her stomach.

Finally she gave up. He immediately slid from the bed and crawled into the same corner from which she had just retrieved him. There he sat in a ball, arms clasped across his knees.

'Stay there, then,' Ruth said, getting up. She looked down at him for a moment, with her hands on her hips, and then turned to leave. 'I don't expect you'll die.'

As she went out, she turned off the light, and slammed the door.

Bitterly and softly, Theo began to cry.

FOURTEEN

THE NIGHT-SHIFT HANDED OVER AT HALF PAST SEVEN. The new nurse on duty came in to see Lin, and looked at her casually from the end of the bed.

'How are you feeling?' she asked.

'I've been dreaming.'

'That's good.' The nurse took the chart from the bottom of the bed and looked at it. 'You've had a nice sleep after your tablet.'

Lin could barely remember the medication. But she remembered the nightmare, if that was what it was. Theo had been in her bed. She had felt his wet hands, wet face. The nurse moved alongside her.

'I feel as if I've run a long way,' Lin said.

'You have, in a manner of speaking.' The nurse lifted Lin's hand and chafed it momentarily.

'Have there been people here?' Lin asked.

'Where?'

'Here, last night.'

'Oh, I should think so.' The nurse put her hand on Lin's wrist, feeling for the pulse.

'I don't think I've got one,' Lin murmured. 'I think I died.'

The nurse smiled and continued. Her touch was very cool, and Lin felt a prickling sensation run along her arm.

'Was there a woman visiting anyone?' she asked.

'Probably.'

'In a pink suit?'

'I don't know. Do you think you could eat?'

'My head . . .' Lin tried to conjure the words. There was a whole vocabulary back there, resisting her attempts to retrieve it. 'I've got a crawling feeling like ants, lots of ants, under my skull.'

'Mmm . . .' It was a throwaway, noncommittal noise. For the first time, the nurse looked at her intently.

'I want to see my little boy,' Lin said. 'Where is he?'

'I shall find out for you.'

The effort to speak was excruciatingly slow: Lin's tongue was tied to the roof of her mouth. Her body was foreign, transmitting messages that she knew she ought to understand. They came from a great distance, the gnawing tingling in the skin of her neck, the bracelet of tension in her upper arm, the coldness of her feet.

The nurse took her temperature.

There was so much noise in this place, it was hard to concentrate on the small, routine movements of the person in front of her. Lin could hear the murmuring voices of a large crowd in the corridor; she could hear their shuffling feet, softly whispering, fold over fold of sound. Hundreds of slippered feet moving slowly along the narrow space outside the door. She turned her head to the doorway, expecting to see them, a crowd of students, or visitors. Some kind of official visit. At any moment a head—or several heads—would appear around the frame, looking enquiringly at her, smiling encouragement.

'Is it busy today?' she asked the nurse.

'Oh yes . . . always busy.'

'Do they come this early?'

'Who?'

'The people.'

The nurse pressed her hand to Lin's forehead. 'Would you like some analgesic for your headache? Shall I ask Doctor?'

There was a rush. The hundreds pressed in, all talking at once.

Lin saw shapes, faint colours. The air temperature plummeted. And through the nurse's hand, refracting along the fingers, came a bright light.

'I can't hear what they're saying,' Lin said. 'Too much at once. I can't hear.'

The nurse took her hand away, and the light smoothed to a vibrating line, a cord between them.

To Lin's complete astonishment, she could suddenly see the nurse in her house that morning. She saw two teenage children standing at the foot of the stairs; they were arguing. The nurse, buttoning herself into her uniform dress, came down the steps, taking no notice of them at all, flicking the red jacket from the banister and pulling it on in one fluid movement. She looked at a clock above the door, then back to the kitchen.

Her husband had died last year.

Subdural haematoma.

Lin could hear his voice. Hear him saying, softly and repeatedly, that it had been the damnedest thing. Lin could see the mist-dank park, the clothes piled on the ground, the other men in the makeshift Sunday-afternoon football team. She could see a pair of driving shoes, brown brogues—she could see the fence, the concrete post between the wood panels . . .

He had reached for the ball, and someone had barged him from behind. She could feel the impact of the fence post on his skull, hear the bantered swearing, the conversation, the resumed game . . .

She stared at the nurse, astonished. She was filled with a sudden and completely overwhelming grief. My God, it had been so stupid, such a small thing, no pain at all really, no more than an ordinary hangover. The husband was close to her, his features indistinct, but the shoulders, arms and hands very clear . . . he had felt suddenly very tired when he had got home. He had gone up to bed, aware of dragging his feet through mud, through slime, to the blessed comfort of the bed. It was so outrageous, so stupid, that he was dead. She felt his complete frustration: outrageous to be so dislocated, to speak constantly, as he did, and never be heard at all. He had stayed at the side of the bed for hours, while the nurse who was his wife had tried to wake him. It had been getting dark, and the ambulance came, and they carried him out. *Christ!* . . . so stupid, such a small thing, no pain at all really, no more than an ordinary hangover. He had felt suddenly tired . . .

She was in his body, seeing what he wanted desperately to show her, moving again up the steep stairway where the red jacket had hung a moment before, turning the right-angled corner at the top, walking along the green-carpeted landing, opening the bedroom door, falling asleep, waking, standing at the side of the bed while the paramedics lifted him, while his children stood in the crack of the door like two statues, watching the drama played out in the bedroom.

It was so stupid, such a small thing, no pain at all really, no more than an ordinary hangover. He had felt tired . . .

'Stop,' Lin said. 'Stop, stop, stop . . .'

She was genuinely frightened, unable to see the nurse any longer, her whole vision and hearing filled with the man, over and over and over. He had never moved from the side of the bed. He played it repeatedly, stuck in the never-ending three-hour groove of the afternoon.

'What is it?' the nurse asked.

Lin's hand was locked to the back of her head, scratching at the weeds growing.

'It was so stupid, such a small thing, no pain at all really,' she muttered. 'No more than an ordinary hangover . . .'

The nurse took her hand away, pressed the button above the bed, made soothing noises, brushed the sheet flat and then brushed her fingers along Lin's face.

'What is it?' someone asked: another nurse at the door. The ward sister.

'I think she had a petit mal.'

The sister came in. 'Shall I ring for Werth?'

'Is he here yet?'

'No.'

They both paused.

'I think we probably should.'

The sister looked at Lin over the nurse's shoulder.

Lin began to shake uncontrollably.

'Now, now . . .'

'Can't you take them away?' Lin begged. 'The footsteps. The whispering. Their *noise!*'

The sister patted the nurse's shoulder. 'I won't be long. Stay here.'

Making an agonized effort, Lin raised both hands to her face. She tasted metal—the sterile metal of a dental probe, that same dead sensation in her mouth. She thought of Theo: pushing him on the swing, or sidestepping his trike on the path as she hung out the washing, or his little hands helplessly fumbling, bending and breaking the stem of the runner-bean plant that he had grown and that they were planting . . . a hundred small, inconsequential, everyday tasks that now seemed forfeited for ever.

'They have to go away,' she said, through the interlocked fingers pressed to her face, her mask of defence. 'Oh, please, oh God. I don't want them. They must all go away . . .'

FIFTEEN

KIERAN HIRED A CAR AT THE AIRPORT.

The drive down to Ruth's through the winding green lanes was a slice of paradise. It was seven a.m. and there was little traffic; the sunlight stretched in broad flat bands over the hills, a breathtaking rose-gold overlying the pale-green downland. As Kieran came off the tops and into the valleys, growing wheat of an almost consistent acid green bordered the road. He could see the small Dorset town now, a full five miles away still, sitting centrally in the fertile valley: a flint circle with a few lights still blazing in the early sunlight.

At Frome Abbott he stopped the car by the water and got out. The air smelled quintessentially English: green and damp and sweet. The river was already wide here, rushing at a good pace through the fields.

He was only a mile or two from the Priory. Lin often brought Theo along these lanes for a walk. Theo had told him that there were herons here, although Kieran had never seen one. It must be months now since Kieran had even walked to the edge of the Priory garden and looked at the river there, at the thick green coating of weeds in the chalk bed.

Last summer Lin had organized a duck race for the village fete, which it had ended in their garden. She had told him that the finishing post was at their own wooden planks across the water, and Theo, eyes shining, had confided that a man in long rubber boots had come to fish the netted plastic ducks out of the water. Kieran remembered listening to them both with tired bemusement. He didn't know then what a duck race was.

He still didn't.

Lin had tried hard. Tried to fit into Ruth's place. Tried to be a good member of the community. Everywhere she went, they eyed her suspiciously, staring down her youth, looking from her to Theo and back again. Kieran knew that the village was polite to her, but not friendly— and there was an ocean in that difference. Lin did not fit in, with her long and shapeless skirts, her Doc Marten's boots, her occasionally vividly hennaed hair. She had felt the exclusion keenly, he knew. And, although she had been born and bred in a city, she determinedly walked the lanes, taking Theo to and from the local playgroup, going to the village shop, gritting her teeth against the whispered comments, the sideways glances. She was so persistently cheerful about it all, Kieran mused. 'You're just a little bloody ray of sunshine, aren't you?' he had said to her once.

She had given him a wry smile. 'Irritating, huh?'

Theo took after her.

'We saw birds in the field!' Theo's reedy, lisping voice last year.

Lin's amused addition. 'Forty or so little pheasants, little chicks, in the bottom field. Where have they all come from?'

He had been reading at his desk, and page-scrolling the computer screen with his free hand. 'What field?' he had asked, without looking up.

When? November . . . March? When?

Lin, at Christmas, cursing the fairy lights. 'Where has the frilly bit gone?' Her fractured, helpless laughter. 'Look for it, Theo—a frilly bit . . .'

Kieran hadn't helped her. He had been too busy.

He turned away from the river, and got back into the car.

He reached Ruth's flat at a quarter to eight. The apartment was in an Edwardian building just out of the town centre, on a leafy and quiet street. When Ruth opened the door to him, she was already dressed. She paused a second, then stepped forward and kissed him very lightly and very fleetingly on the cheek.

'Hello,' she said, stepping back to let him in. 'Go through. Theo's in the sitting room.'

Kieran threw his car keys on the hall table, and walked to where his son, propped in the corner of the couch, sat with a piece of toast halfway to his mouth, his eyes glued to the television.

'Look who it is,' Ruth said.

The boy made no movement at all. Kieran switched off the set and placed his face, at eye level, directly opposite his son.

'Hey,' he said.

Theo's lower lip protruded in an expression of defiance.

'I came back,' Kieran said. He reached forward and tried to hug him. Grudgingly, Theo lowered his head to his father's shoulder.

'You miss me?' Kieran tried to lift Theo's head. 'Hmmm? Miss me?'

Ruth came to his side. 'He hasn't said much this morning,' she murmured.

Kieran looked up. 'What time do you have to go to work?'

'Half an hour.' She smiled down at Theo. 'We've been getting on well, haven't we, sweetheart?' She bent down and stroked the boy's hand where it lay over Kieran's shoulder. 'Haven't we?'

Theo didn't respond.

'I'll make some coffee,' Ruth said, straightening up and leaving the room.

Kieran followed her out to the kitchen where—although he suddenly felt extraordinarily tired, as if he could sleep with his head on the breakfast counter—he sat down at the table. He made a concession to his fatigue by propping his head on one hand.

'He had some sort of nightmare last night,' Ruth said, with her back to him.

'Thanks for taking him in.'

'I don't think I had much choice.'

Watching her, Kieran bit one side of his lip. As she turned back to him, he rearranged his face. 'Why were you there?' he asked.

She raised her eyebrows. 'Sorry?'

'In Hampton.'

Ruth pulled out a chair, and sat down opposite him. 'Do you know where she was living?' she asked. 'Some student flat she used to have way back, when she first came to university. Long before that house near the campus.'

'Ruth . . .'

'It's over a shop. You know those little back streets where all the secondhand furniture places are? There are drug addicts in that area, you know.' Ruth frowned, shaking her head and fixing her gaze on the table in front of her. 'I can't understand the two of you,' she said. 'Taking Theo to a place like that.'

'I had no idea she was going there,' he said.

She looked up. 'No idea?'

'She went away suddenly,' he explained.

'Why?'

'It doesn't matter.'

'Had you two fallen out?'

'No, not exactly.'

'What, then?'

He held up his hand. 'Ruth,' he repeated, 'why were you there? Who told you where she was? I just can't believe that Lin rang you yourself.'

She smiled. Behind her, the kettle switched itself off. She made a move to get up to make the coffee, but he put a hand flat on the table by way of stopping her. It made a dull, resounding thud.

'Am I the wicked witch again?' she asked.

'This is perfectly serious.'

'Yes, you're right. It is serious. What am I supposed to have done now, besides break into the Priory on a regular basis?'

'That's just it.'

She started to laugh. 'You're telling me she went away to avoid me?' Still laughing in astonishment, she shook her head. 'Really, this gets worse.' She leaned forward. 'She rang me and asked me to go there,' she said.

Kieran stared at her.

'It's the truth,' she said.

Ruth returned his look, then got up and fixed the coffee, returning to the table with a pot and two cups. She watched his face carefully. 'Have you spoken to the hospital this morning?'

He gave a prolonged sigh. 'No.' In a desultory fashion, he began stirring sugar into the black liquid.

'I have. Ten minutes ago. They seem to think that Lin has had some kind of seizure.'

'Seizure?' Kieran paled. 'What do they mean?'

'The lumbar-puncture results aren't back yet. They think it's probably viral, if it's meningitis.'

'Do you get seizures with meningitis?'

'I don't know, Kieran. I've never seen a case of meningitis. Most doctors haven't.'

'What do they mean . . . a seizure?'

'It was like a mild form of epilepsy.'

'But she hasn't got epilepsy.'

'No.'

They looked at each other.

'I have to go to work,' she said, rising.

He looked down for a moment, then he also stood up. 'I'll take Theo back home later. Mrs Sawyer will be there today. He can stay with her while I go to the hospital.'

'When do you plan to go?'

He ran his hand through his hair. 'I don't know . . . I'll try to get an hour or two's sleep before I drive again. Then have a shower, breakfast. Maybe midday . . .'

'If you wait until one, I'll come with you,' she said. 'I won't have to be back again at the hospital until four.'

He was surprised. 'No, no. That's OK.'

She smiled at him, going to the sink with her cup, then picking up her case from the side of the door. 'I'll drive you there,' she said. 'I won't go in and see Lin if you prefer me not to.'

'It's OK really,' he said.

'It is not OK,' she told him. 'You're far too exhausted to drive any more.' She waved her hand, a brief inclination of the wrist. 'Be a good boy,' she said.

SIXTEEN

$\mathcal{T}$HE NEUROLOGIST CAME TO SEE LIN AT TEN O'CLOCK; he brought six students with him. Lin was lying on her side, with a single pillow under her head, staring at the same space outside the window where the people had congregated during the night to look in at her. As it got lighter, she had realized that her room was on the third or fourth floor, level with the roof of some lower block. There were two trees beyond that: two tall, elegantly thin limes. She had been watching their untiring movement for some time.

'Good morning,' said a man's voice.

She thought it better to say nothing at all. She waited for him to come round her side of the bed, to look in her face.

He was young—perhaps not forty—and was very neat and clean. Brown hair with grey, precise-looking hands, a very charming smile.

'My name is Mark Werth,' he said. 'I hope you don't mind me bringing along this crowd of dissolutes. I'm afraid you're a curiosity.'

He drew up a chair and sat down.

She would have liked very much to be able to move. Instead of which, a smothering shroud of fatigue forced her to lie still. There was no conceivable way that she could lift her hand, or roll her body to another side. She was tired of the view of the trees.

'How are you feeling?' Werth asked.

'Like a two-headed dog,' she murmured.

They all laughed politely.

'Can you tell me what day it is?'

She looked carefully at his face, wondering how many times he would come and see her and introduce himself, and ask that same question. Over and over—like those people out in the corridor, endlessly moving from room to room, searching in continual circles for the selves they had left behind.

'The first?' she murmured.

He crossed his legs slowly, then placed his hands, crossed also, on top of his leg. 'The first of what?'

'The first day. Just the first.'

'And the month?'

She looked back to yesterday, which hung like a stone weight in her head. 'It was April.'

He smiled. 'That's right. It's still April. Do you feel that a long time has passed?'

'Yes.'

'Can you tell me your address?'

There was a pause. 'Ruth's house,' she whispered.

'I see. Mrs Gallagher, when were you born?'

'I was born in a thunderstorm. The lights went out.' A small, sighing laugh escaped her. 'My mother told me that.'

'Do you mind if I examine you?' Werth stood up.

Lin closed her eyes, exasperated. It was a three-dimensional puzzle of the most complicated kind, trying to find which sensation belonged to which finger, which patch of skin.

Very gently he lifted the sheet and blanket.

'I've got a pin in my hand,' he said. 'I just want you to tell me when you feel me touch you.'

She felt the pin.

'Good, good,' he murmured. He came back to his previous position, and lifted her nearest hand. 'And this?'

'Yes,' she responded.

'That's fine. And your eyes . . .'

He shone a light into her eyes. It was like an almost solid thing: she felt it probing on her retina. The white sheet below her hand lit up with a fretwork of blood vessels. When he had finished, he sat down again, and put his hand over hers.

'What do you think might be wrong with you?'

She tried to understand. She felt like laughing. What might be wrong with her?

'I'm a pain in the neck,' she said.

'You have a pain in your neck?'

'No, no . . .'

Werth sat back, frowning.

'Who are those people?' she murmured.

He watched her for another second, then turned away. The ward sister came to his side; he said something to her. They both looked back at her.

'Do you remember feeling ill this morning?' he asked.

She said nothing.

'Do you remember any unusual tastes, smells . . . sounds, perhaps, before you felt ill? Did you feel afraid, for instance?'

Lin shook her head. She raised her hand at last on its own, and was amazed to see its infinite complexity. The operation of nerve, muscle, cartilage and bone; the compacted messages leaping from one synapse to another. Her hand, and everything beyond it, including the neurologist's face, and the faces of those alongside and behind him, were similarly detailed.

'Do you remember any unusual tastes or sounds, Mrs Gallagher?'

As she lowered her hand, still watching its movement, she saw that it left a short-lived trail of luminescence.

'If I'm not dead,' she said, 'are you?'

She closed her eyes after Werth had gone.

For a very long time she felt as if she were travelling slowly along a soft, smooth tunnel whose walls hummed with subdued light, and whose colours altered continually. Time ceased to have any significance.

She woke from this dream with a start, a sense of coldness, to see Kieran looking down at her.

'Hello,' he said.

'Hello,' she murmured.

He looked around critically at the sparse room.

'You look very tired,' she said. 'What time did your flight get in?'

He glanced down to her. 'It doesn't matter about me,' he said. 'How are *you*?'

To her chagrin, Lin immediately started to cry. 'I want to go home,' she whispered.

He smiled, bringing a chair next to her bed, and taking her hand into the clasp of his own. 'I'm glad to hear it,' he replied, as he sat down.

'There are strange people here,' she continued, sobbing now. 'Strange things are happening.'

'What kind of strange things?'

'People coming in the middle of the night—ordinary people, not nurses—and talking to me . . . Then they vanish . . .'

'Coming in here, into this room?' he echoed, frowning. 'But this is a private ward.'

'And I keep hearing and seeing . . .' Her voice trailed away. He saw that her gaze was now fixed on their linked hands, and an expression of horror was dawning in her face.

'What is it?' he asked. 'What's the matter?'

The horror became fully fledged, vivid and all-encompassing, as he continued to watch Lin's expression. Her mouth dropped open a little, her eyes rounded in shock; what little colour had been in her face rapidly drained from it. Kieran squeezed her hand harder by way of reassurance. Her look flew from their hands up to his face—where her eyes ranged over him as if she were reading some terrible message in his features. Then, she pulled her hand away with a little moan of despair.

'What is it?' he repeated. 'What?'

'My God,' she murmured. 'No, no . . .' She squeezed her eyes shut, and tears edged from under her lids and ran down her face.

'Lin,' he said, genuinely disturbed now. 'Lin, talk to me.' Kieran leaned forward in an instinctive reaction, to kiss her face, but her response was sudden and violent. She opened her eyes and turned her head away and, with a fumbling struggle, pushed her hands under the sheet.

'Don't,' she said. 'Don't touch me.'

He sat back as if he had been stung. 'Why not?' he asked.

She looked in misery away from him, to the far wall.

'Because I don't want to hear how you feel,' she whispered.

SEVENTEEN

$\mathcal{R}$UTH WAITED until Mark Werth's morning clinic was finally over.

He occupied a suite of rooms—all ficus trees, Japanese pools and pebble waterfalls, she wryly noted as she sat in a chair directly opposite his office. Werth came out hurriedly at half past one, carrying a briefcase, his jacket slung over one shoulder.

She got up and went over to him.

'Mr Werth? My name is Ruth Carmichael. I'm a friend of Lin Gallagher.'

He took her hand. 'How do you do,' he said.

'I'm also a GP. I wonder if I might have a word?'

He hesitated a moment, then smiled. 'I'm just going to the canteen,' he said. 'If you can bear to watch me eat, you're very welcome.'

She followed him to the fourth floor, and a view of the town that showed its crooked main street and the black parish church on the hill. Ruth selected a table, sat down, and waited, shading her eyes against the sun while Werth stood in line. When he came back with his tray, he handed her a cup of tea he had bought for her.

'I didn't know which,' he said, 'tea or coffee.'

'This is fine,' she said. 'Thank you.'

He sat down and began eating hurriedly.

'How often do you have your clinic?' Ruth asked.

'Every week.'

'You must see quite a few patients.'

'No shortage of clients for either of us, I guess,' he said.

She sipped her tea. 'I'm worried about Lin, Mr Werth. I wonder if you've made a diagnosis.'

'I don't make a diagnosis without all the facts.'

'Did you think Lin's state indicative of temporal-lobe dysfunction?'

He ate in silence, then lowered his fork. 'Why don't you tell me what *you* think?'

'I wonder if you are considering temporal-lobe epilepsy.'

'And *you* are?'

She shook her head. 'No, I don't consider it at all. Have you spoken to her GP?'

'No. To be frank, I was more interested in the meningitis. Chances to observe it are so rare.'

'I see . . .'

'Why epilepsy, necessarily?' Werth asked.

'The ward sister told me this morning that she thought Lin might have suffered a petit mal.'

'Ah.'

Ruth waited, but Werth offered nothing else.

'Mr Werth,' she said. 'I ought to tell you that Lin isn't always the most balanced of people. She has a bit of a history of mental disorder.' Not entirely to Ruth's surprise, he did not answer. 'Emotional problems,' she added.

'And you're here to tell me what they are.'

'Only in as far as they might help you.'

Mark Werth returned to his plate, cutting his food into precise, equally sized squares.

'Eighteen months ago,' Ruth said, 'Lin spent a fortnight in psychiatric care.'

'Voluntarily?'

'Yes.'

'I see.' He finished his meal, and pushed the plate away.

'Would you like to know why?'

He considered. 'I think I would prefer Lin to tell me herself, if she thinks it's relevant.'

His expression was absolutely noncommittal. He didn't know what to make of the woman sitting opposite him, and found himself unwilling to guess her motives in coming here. Nothing much, however, shocked him. He was used to the most bizarre confessions.

Only that morning, a patient had described having a sensation of such profound religious intensity that he felt he had spoken to God. The man had produced several exercise books, all closely written, describing his days in minutes, sometimes seconds, of experience. The pages were full of repetition, underscoring and red-ink capitals. He had told Mark Werth that he knew when things would happen; he walked through the world with a constant sense of *déjà vu*. He *knew*. He *knew* with certainty, with intensity, what the world was made of, the nature of man—with a sense of otherness, of significance.

The patient's whole experience, however, was neurological. All the assaulting knowledge, the predictions, the intrusion of God, real as they seemed, were simply fragments of dreams. Heaven had not opened itself to this patient. No divine light had descended on him. He had merely experienced a spike pattern; the electroencephalogram had revealed slow waves and a bi-temporal emphasis more pronounced on the left-hand side.

It wasn't God at all. In fact, God might disappear entirely after the prescription of primidone.

Werth's gaze, which had been momentarily fixed on the view beyond the window, returned to Ruth. She met it with a smile.

'She's married, of course,' Werth said, 'to the rather famous Kieran Gallagher.'

'Yes.'

'And she has a small child.'

'Yes.'

'How old is he?'

'Four.'

'Did she suffer from postnatal depression?'

Ruth's glance dropped temporarily. 'I wouldn't know.'

'Has the child suffered in any way?'

'No. At least—'

'You feel he's affected?'

'Yes, exactly. He is affected by her emotionally. Of course he is.'

There was a silence. 'Excuse me a moment,' Werth said. He went back to the counter and returned with a second cup of tea. Sitting down, he stirred it for some time. 'Is Mr Gallagher here?' he asked her eventually.

'Yes, he's in seeing Lin now. I gave him a lift in,' she said.

'I see.' His fingers lightly tapped the table. 'I wonder why he didn't ask to come and see me.'

'I offered to come while he visited Lin.'

'To tell me your conclusions.'

'No,' Ruth replied equably. 'I don't have any conclusions. I haven't seen her. We simply wanted to help you with the background.'

'Mr Gallagher—her husband—wanted you to tell me that his wife had an emotional crisis last year?'

'Yes.'

'And you thought that this might help.'

'Doesn't it?'

He looked down at the table. 'Yes, of course, it might help. Especially if I think she's presenting with temporal lobe—and you think there's a chance she's completely deluded?'

'You've misunderstood me,' Ruth said. 'Not deluded, just under strain. Prone to stress.'

'Ah, yes,' he murmured, 'stress. You must see a lot of it.'

There was a silence during which a girl dragging a trolley came to clear away the plate and cups. They watched her through a laborious wiping-down of the surface between them. When she had finally gone, Ruth spoke again.

'This is terribly difficult for me,' she murmured. 'I'm so fond of Lin, and she's suffered so much. It's quite desperate to think there may be some new problem, so . . .' She looked up at him frankly, and smiled. 'I suppose I prefer to think this is a recurrence of something old, an emotional failing, if you like, rather than anything serious physically.'

'And yet you're here to suggest temporal-lobe epilepsy.'

'No, no,' she objected, 'quite the reverse. I'm sorry if I haven't made myself clear. I thought it sounded like TLE. I'd be so relieved if it weren't.'

Werth returned her smile. 'Well, we shall have to keep our fingers crossed.'

Ruth's gaze lingered on him. 'Lin is a lovely girl, but very fragile. She has to be sheltered, protected from . . .' She looked away for a moment, showing a little flicker of distress. 'Protected from hurting herself with her wild fantasies.'

This last phrase checked Werth; he stared for a while in complete surprise. Then Ruth sighed, and gathered up her handbag from alongside her seat. 'Will Lin be kept in for long?'

'We'll see.'

Ruth inclined her head, with a wry expression, recognizing the kind of dismissal she often employed with her own patients. She stood up, and extended her hand to him. 'Thank you very much for your time. I'm glad to have met you.'

Mark Werth watched her walk out of the canteen. That is a very beautiful woman, he thought. He put her age around thirty-five, but that was purely down to her complete composure and the give-aways of the throat and eyes. From the back, she looked ten years younger— her walk springy, her figure slim. He wondered acutely for some moments how long Ruth Carmichael had known Kieran Gallagher. He wondered about the conversations in the car between them today.

With friends like that . . . he thought.

But, as if to censure this train of thought, his bleeper sounded.

EIGHTEEN

HARRY HAD GONE STRAIGHT HOME from the airport, but not stayed there long. After a shower and change of clothes, he had set out to walk two miles across London, to visit Ben Lazenby.

Lazenby lived in Edwardian splendour in central London. His flat was in a claustrophobic square populated by politicians and media freaks. Harry had not the least hesitation in cataloguing the lot of them as freaks; after all, he represented most of them.

Marianne answered the door.

'Hello,' Harry said, slinging his coat down on the chair in the hall. He gazed upwards at an enormous wind-chime over his head. Two carpet fitters were busy laying a bright red carpet up the stairs. He looked at Marianne, and raised a questioning eyebrow.

'Don't ask,' she said. She was a tall, aristocratic-looking girl, hardly twenty, long in the face and with a chin-length sheaf of white-blonde hair. She looked wearily as if her life had already passed before her.

'What happened to the Pollock?' Harry asked, meaning the enormously expensive painting that had graced the hallway on his last visit.

'Too angular,' she drawled, shutting the door. 'Cutting chis. Too black. Not auspicious.'

'Cutting what?'

She walked to the back of the house, and Harry followed her. In the huge kitchen, Lazenby sat in an armchair, muffled up as if against Siberian cold. He was shouting into a phone. Paper littered every inch of the six-foot table, and was spread liberally on the chairs and the floor. 'Mahler,' Lazenby was saying. 'Ta . . . da . . . tadada . . .'

Harry propped himself against a worktop.

'A drink?' Marianne asked.

'Coffee.'

'Decaff, Café Direct . . . ?'

'Marianne, just put something in a cup.'

Ben had already waved at him to sit down. Harry did so, resting his head in his hands. A cat came and lay at his feet, stretching itself to full length on its back. He nudged it away with the tip of his shoe.

Lazenby came off the phone. 'Don't come near me,' he said. 'I've got this flu. What do you think of the hall? Feng shui. Releases the energies, gets everything flowing.'

'What did you get for the Pollock?'

'Nothing. It's in the bank.' Ben took out a handkerchief, and wiped his nose. 'I had this chap round last month—went through the whole house. We had a little shrine up here, we had him clapping like a maniac in every room, we had bells, we had Chopin, we had holy water, we had fucking anemones—don't ask—we changed the carpet because of the colour, I've got these crystals, I had to take the wrought iron out of the balcony, I had to put a fish tank in, he said we had to move the bathroom out of the fortunate bloody blessings—'

'Ben,' Harry interrupted.

'Do you know what it cost me?'

'No.'

'Thousands! Do you know what it's done for me?'

'Ben . . .'

'Nothing. Got this flu—worst flu I've ever had. I've been in bed, I've had her there blowing horse pills down my neck with a funnel, I've had Bellamys cancel the contract, I've had Lin Gallagher disappear into exile, I've had a musicians' strike, I've had a burst pipe in the cellar, I've got fucking chilblains, I mean! I said, what the hell is a chilblain, for Christ's sake. Williams said, "It's either that or gout," and bloody well smirked! I've had Elizabeth refusing to work Lotus . . .' He paused. Marianne was laughing softly from the other side of the room. 'And I've got this bitch laughing,' he said.

'Ben,' Harry murmured, 'it's about Lin.'

'What about her?'

'She's been taken into hospital.'

Ben stared at him for a moment. 'When?'

'Yesterday. Kieran and I caught a flight back this morning. He's gone to see her now.'

'Is it serious?'

'No one knows.'

'But . . .' Ben paused. 'I went to see her at the beginning of the week. She was fine then.'

'It was very sudden.'

'With what?'

'They think maybe meningitis, but they don't know yet.'

'God,' Marianne said.

'Jesus,' Ben echoed. He looked up. 'This is *his* fault,' he said. 'Kieran's.'

'How do you figure that out?'

'Leaving her to the mercy of that ex-wife of his.'

Marianne delivered the drinks. Harry took his cup gratefully.

'Get him something to eat,' Lazenby said.

'I'm all right,' Harry replied.

'Get *me* something to eat, then.' He made a face of supplication at Marianne, who stuck her tongue out at him and turned away.

Harry looked down at his feet.

'You know his trouble?' Ben said. 'He believes his own publicity. What did you get out of him? The trouble we had filming.'

'I know,' Harry said. 'I've heard it all from the crew these last few days.'

'What the hell is the matter with him?'

Harry sighed. 'I don't know. He's restless. Something isn't right.'

Marianne had given Lazenby a slice of toast, which Lazenby promptly stuffed, folded, into his mouth. After a couple of chews, he spoke with his mouth full. 'Lin thinks he prefers the ex-wife. She thinks he's sick of TV and wants to go back, rewind, give it all up. Give her up.'

Harry frowned. 'She said that?'

'Reading between the lines.'

'I don't think it's as bad as that.'

Ben leaned forward, pointing at him. 'I don't care what it is, frankly,' he said. 'I'm sick to death of him. If he's prevaricating over this next contract, I'll have him dropped. It doesn't make good film. Now, I'll tell you what I want.'

Harry sat back, and crossed him arms.

'I want Lin,' Ben went on. 'I've got something in mind for her. Something along the same lines, but perkier. He labours those celebrities, deflates them. She'll perk 'em up. *Big Breakfast, Don't Forget Your Toothbrush*. In-your-face stuff. I'm cogitating, and if Gallagher doesn't fall in line, I swear to you, Harry, it's no go. I'll sink *The History House*. I'll put Lin in a new vehicle.' Lazenby's gaze drifted to one side. 'What hospital is she in, poor cow? I'll send her something.'

Harry told him. Lazenby scribbled the address on the nearest piece of paper. Then he looked up. 'I don't want to make your life difficult,' he said almost kindly. 'But that's the size of it.'

Harry sighed, finally getting sick of the cat and forcibly pushing it away from his feet. 'I don't like the sound of this Ruth business,' he said. 'She was there when Lin was taken ill, you know.'

Ben had picked up a file and now glanced at Harry from over its open pages. 'There's something going on there,' he said. 'Mark my words.'

'Not according to Kieran.'

Ben snorted, but said nothing. It brought on a coughing fit.

'I'll leave you in peace,' Harry said, trying not to echo Marianne's almost malicious grin as she showered several wads of tissue into Ben's lap.

'Go and see Lin,' Ben said. 'Go and tell her what I said. Cheer her up.'

'I might,' Harry murmured, turning for the door. 'I might.'

NINETEEN

$\mathcal{L}$IN LAY LOOKING AT THE DOOR of her hospital room, her fists clenched on the top of the sheet, her body rigid.

It was mid-morning. She was deep in a thickly gathering web: a space filling, inch by prolonged inch, with steadily thickening sound. It had a physical texture, a corrugated, wave-like motion, lapping inexorably closer to the bed, voice over voice, whisper over whisper, echo over echo, no tremor ever entirely finishing, but leaving the ghost of its remains in the air. It was like being inside a sound box, an amplifier, where the initial sound was forever multiplied.

She tried to make out individual words, but couldn't. Some voices, muffled and repetitive, sounded insistent, instructive. Their impatient authority coated every syllable, but she couldn't match the notes together to make sentences. Other voices drifted far in the background, ethereal and plaintive, occasionally breaking into hopeless soft sobbing and weeping. In between, the crowds mingled and rippled.

'Lin?'

She stared at the doorway. She knew this person's sound. Another voice replied. Lin forced herself to focus, terrified she would lose this one intelligible coupling of words. Her knuckles whitened with the concentration. 'Please God,' she murmured, 'make it stop.'

Edith Channon's face appeared. She nodded a couple of times, looked back along the corridor as if to reply to the invisible other party, and then bustled into the room.

'Now then, dear,' she said, smiling broadly. 'What on earth are you doing here?'

Lin stared at her.

'Can you hear me?' Edith asked. She stroked Lin's face briefly.

'Yes,' Lin whispered.

Edith rummaged in her straw bag and brought out a crushed bag of fruit. She looked in the locker, pulled out a dish, tutted over it, and took it over to wash in the sink. 'Dusty,' she said. 'You see, a nurse would have done this automatically once.' She turned, brought the dish back, and began to fill it. 'Do you know what they're all doing down there at that desk? Filling out forms. Discussing who's going to some counselling seminar.' She clicked her tongue disapprovingly against her teeth, gave a nod of satisfaction at the filled bowl, then sat down at Lin's side.

'You've got a high colour, dear,' she said. 'How are you feeling?'

'Strange,' Lin murmured.

'A headache?'

'No . . . not that.'

Edith's eyes ranged over Lin's face. She leaned forward, arms crossed and balanced on the bed. 'I had such a shock when that woman came racing back with Theo,' she said.

Lin's glance trailed away, trying to fix on the source of the noise.

'What is it?' Edith asked.

'You'll think I'm mad,' Lin said.

'Why should I?'

'Voices.'

'Oh?'

'Hundreds.' Lin's mouth trembled.

'Well, tell them to go away.'

Lin's eyes fixed on the old woman's. 'What?'

'They don't know you can hear them, probably. They talk all the time you know, trying to get someone to listen. When someone does, they just pile in, like water rushing through a crack in a pipe. Tell them to buzz off.'

Lin stared at her silently.

'No,' Edith said, 'you're not crazy, and neither am I.' She sat back, and looked around her. 'I believe in them. I sense them, and I see them occasionally, but I can never hear them.' She looked back at Lin. 'How long have you heard them? Just today?'

'Yesterday . . .'

'And before?'

'Before what?' Lin was struggling to make sense of the conversation.

'Before you felt so ill.'

'No, no . . .'

'Never heard noises in houses, people talking to you?'

'No.' Lin was frowning deeply.

'Not in the flat?'

'No.'

Edith smiled. She stroked Lin's arm once, very gently. The sweetness of the gesture, and the fact that Edith had turned up at all, suddenly made Lin want to cry. She bit the inside of her cheek, willing herself not to start again. She was not the crying kind, but these last few hours seemed to have rewritten that particular character trait. The tears came pouring out for no reason. Unless this constant apprehension was a reason. The fear that something uncontrollable was happening. Something inside. Something outside. Something in her perception, her ability to order and understand the world.

'I don't understand. I can't fathom it,' Lin said. 'It frightens me . . .'

'What do the doctors say it is?'

Lin brought one hand to her forehead. 'They tested for meningitis, but it isn't that. They just told me so, an hour ago: no traces at all.'

'I see.'

'They're talking about a scan.'

'To try to find where the noise is coming from, the pictures?'

Lin looked hard at her. 'Yes.'

Edith seemed to consider for a second. 'What do *you* think it is?'

Lin bit down hard, her mouth in a wrinkled line of self-pity that she hated and willed herself to eradicate. These tears, these feelings: they were like clutching, dragging hands. 'I had postnatal depression last year,' she said. 'I had it for a long time. Maybe this is a mental problem. I don't know anything about schizophrenia . . .'

To her surprise, Edith began to laugh. 'Schizophrenia?' she echoed. 'What makes you think you've got schizophrenia?'

A flicker of anger at Edith's rebuff swept the threatening tears away. 'Because I can hear bloody voices,' Lin retorted. Raising herself onto one elbow brought on a sharp spike of pain. She immediately dropped back onto her pillow. 'I'm sorry,' she said.

Edith wasn't in the least ruffled. 'You think far too much,' she said.

Lin opened her tightly shut eyes. 'What?'

'Far too much—always did.'

Her air of disapproval made Lin, for the first time that day, smile. 'I *think* too much?' she repeated.

'Bad, bad thing.'

Lin shook her head slightly.

'I'll tell you why,' Edith said. 'Because we think too much, we rationalize, we pretend we're kings of the world, we reduce everything to an equation.'

'Edith,' Lin said, quietly. 'I'm a maths student.'

'Are you?'

'Don't you remember?'

'No,' Edith said firmly, 'but it proves my point. We forget to feel. To *feel*. We don't trust our feelings. Feelings are all that count, and yet we want chapter and verse. We've lost the art of faith. Then we start to wobble, like *you're* wobbling.'

Lin looked at her with a subdued, weary affection. 'Some wobble,' she said.

'Exactly. One heck of a wobble.' She smiled at Lin with a smart glint in her eye.

Lin started to laugh; it lasted moments. She flattened her palm against the top of her head.

'Pain?'

'Yes.'

'Can you hear the voices?'

Lin listened. 'Drum . . . drum . . . drum . . .'

'It's the spirit world,' Edith said.

'It's what?'

'Spirit.'

There was a silence. Lin took several long, deep breaths. 'You think I'm seeing dead people?' she said.

'And hearing them. Don't you think so, too?'

'I wondered.'

'There you are, then.'

Lin sighed deeply. 'I said I wondered. I didn't say I thought so.'

'I see,' Edith responded.

'Edith,' Lin said. 'I don't believe in ghosts.'

'That's all right, dear,' Edith told her. 'They believe in you.'

'Oh God,' Lin murmured.

Edith continued regardless. 'I've been going to my church for twenty-two years, and I can tell you they are as real as you or I. More real, in fact. We live at the bottom of a murky pond. When we go back to spirit, we explode back into light. These voices come from the light, like soundings, like sonar.'

'What church?' Lin asked.

'My spiritualist church.'

'Oh, those places,' Lin said.

'Now there's something *you* forgot.'

'What?'

'I used to attend when you first lived in the flat. I used to tell you I went there.'

'You're right,' Lin said, 'I forgot.' She shook her head a little. 'Edith, those aren't churches. They're a trick—magic tricks.'

'And your voices are a trick, I suppose? Not real?'

Lin paused. 'They must be.' She frowned helplessly. 'It's a chemical somewhere, an imbalance . . .'

'Have they given you anything for it?'

'They gave me something this morning. An anti-epilepsy drug.'

'Did it help?'

Lin swallowed hard. 'No.'

'You see?'

'It's an illness,' Lin replied tonelessly and almost inaudibly. 'I don't know what it is. Something in my head. Some virus. I don't know.' She paused, looked away, turned her head towards the window. 'I want to see Theo,' she said, grief in her voice.

'Ruth took him home,' Edith said.

'Kieran came, but he didn't bring him. He said he thought it was better if Theo stayed at home yesterday—so as not to upset him.' Her tone was jagged with unease. 'He mustn't be with Ruth,' she said. 'Not at all. Not for a minute.'

Edith looked down at the bed and momentarily closed her eyes.

Ruth had come storming back into the shop yesterday afternoon, Theo wailing in her arms. She told Edith that Lin had been taken ill, taken to hospital in an ambulance, and that Lin had asked her to pack his things.

'Where are you going with him?' Edith had asked, following up the steep stairs at half Ruth's pace.

'To my flat,' Ruth had replied.

As she ascended, Edith could hear Ruth pulling out drawers in the room upstairs, then lifting the suitcase down from the top of the shaky wardrobe. Theo had begun to scream in earnest, a one-note torrent of anguish and panic.

'Shut up,' Edith heard Ruth say, as she finally reached the head of the stairs.

Theo had been standing in the centre of the room, rigid, paralysed, tears streaming down his reddened face. Edith had rushed towards him.

'Come on, now,' she had said, trying to soothe him, stroking his face. 'Mummy is going to be all right. You'll see. You can go and see her right now. She's only been taken to a bed for a lie-down. We'll take you right now . . .'

Ruth had turned on her, grabbing Theo's hand, her other hand still occupied with the hastily filled case. 'He's coming back with me. I shall ring his father,' she said.

Edith had stood up from her crouching position at Theo's side. 'You're not going to the hospital?'

Ruth had lowered her voice. 'Do you really think that's any place for a child?' she had whispered savagely.

Edith had stared at her as Ruth shouldered her way past. It was on the tip of her tongue to ask what was wrong with Lin, what could be so terribly wrong that her son wasn't allowed to see her. All kinds of visions flashed through her mind. Lin bloodied and lying still. Lin in pain and alone. She had no idea what had happened, only that there had been some sort of accident, some sort of collapse. God only knew what nightmares flitted through the child's mind at the same moment.

'You'll see Mummy tomorrow . . . very soon . . .' Edith tried to say, as Ruth bundled him down the stairs. By this time Theo had stopped screaming and had gone white with horror, silent with shock.

'Don't worry about Mummy,' Edith called after him. 'I shall go and see her. I shall see she's all right.'

Theo glanced at her, just once, as they turned the corner of the stairs. It was a look of helpless terror that struck her to the core.

'Be careful with him,' she had called to Ruth.

There had been no reply.

Edith looked up now at Lin, not knowing what to say. Certainly not the truth. She looked in Lin's eyes, mentally crossed her fingers, and said, 'I'm sure she's looked after him wonderfully. I'm sure he was all right.'

Lin looked back at her. Silence fell between them.

TWENTY

*L*ATE THAT SAME AFTERNOON, Mark Werth sat with Lin while she slept.

When she finally woke, it was almost dark.

'Hello,' Lin murmured. Her hand was lying on the outside of the sheet, and she made a slight waving motion with her fingers.

'How are you feeling?' he asked.

She smiled. 'You must get fed up of asking that question,' she said quietly. 'Don't you ever want to tell people how *you're* feeling?'

'All the time.'

'I've got a headache,' she said.

'That's really not surprising. I'll get you some medication.'

'Not yet,' she said. She glanced towards the window.

He watched her. She seemed calm.

'Are they real,' she asked, 'the things I see?'

'Tell me what they are.' He leaned forward, crossing both arms in front of him, resting them on the bed.

She frowned, her gaze trailing about the room. 'I see people,' she said, looking very slowly about her, just as one would look at a crowd gathering. Her eyes wandered from head height to the floor, and back again. As she spoke—and it was such a sane and reasonable voice—he felt a prickle of unease at the back of his neck.

'What made you ask if I were dead?' he asked.

She smiled slowly. 'Because this is not like life.'

'In what way?'

'Sounds. The things I see. It's almost like dreaming. Or death, perhaps. I feel very strange—as if I'd stepped out of the world.' She gazed at him with an almost blank stare. 'I want to come back,' she said quietly.

'Do you feel very depressed, Lin?'

'No, doctor,' she sighed. 'I do not feel very depressed. I do not feel at all depressed. Confused, yes . . . frightened, frustrated.'

'But you feel very tired.'

'Tired is . . . not the word for it.'

'Exhausted.'

'You know those old-fashioned wringers, that they used for squeezing water out of washing?'

'Yes.'

'Right through one of those—flat as a pancake.'

'Tell me about these people you see,' he said.

'They are different . . . all kinds,' she said slowly. 'The lady in pink, she isn't here now, but she's been here last night, this morning. And there's a little boy of about six or eight. He's very lost. He cries. And there are two men, boys, I suppose, of about seventeen or eighteen. They're waiting. They ask the nurses questions, and no one answers them. We're in this waiting room, this room, an anteroom. We wait . . .' She sighed, twin lines of concentration marked on her forehead. 'Who are they all?' she murmured. 'If I knew them . . . but I don't know them.'

'Perhaps they're people you've seen on television.'

She stared at him.

'Think of your memories like holograms,' he said. 'The brain records your memories in infinite detail . . .'

'That's not it,' she said.

'Hold on, let me explain,' he told her. 'What, to the eye, is the difference between a manufactured image and an actual image?'

'OK. But *you* can't see them.'

He glanced behind—to where she had nodded her head. 'No, Lin,' he said, 'I can't see anyone.'

She closed her eyes. 'Oh God,' she said softly.

'Lin,' he said. 'Are you able to concentrate on what I'm saying?'

'Yes,' she said.

'It's possible you have some kind of brain disorder. It may be having neurological effects,' he told her. 'With epilepsy—for instance a kind called temporal-lobe epilepsy—patients can report strange effects. They might hear or see something they had forgotten long ago—anything at all, like a railway station, a taste of their mother's cooking, a smell from their childhood home, even an emotion. Lots of people think they see God, for instance. They have a sense of knowing the universe and all its secrets. Or they might feel very afraid, or have sexual feelings, or be angry.'

She had opened her eyes, and was staring at him.

'And they might attribute the effects they sense to some very odd causes. They might feel that the sunlight—or the darkness, or one particular sound—makes odd repercussions, odd connections, in their head. And sometimes it does. The brain is a complicated network; it has functions we don't grasp. In the hypothalamus, for example . . .'

'This is a side effect?' she asked. 'Like an itch under the plaster of a broken arm?'

'Yes, you could say that. That would be a fairly good analogy.'

'These people . . . they are itches to scratch?'

'Maybe, yes.'

'But they talk,' she objected.

'That is possible.'

'They say things I don't know about—I've *never* heard about. Things I don't understand at all.'

'It will be something you have indeed heard and stored away,' he replied equably. 'There's no need for us to understand the things we memorize. And we memorize all the time unconsciously: everything we see and do and feel.' He smiled at her kindly, taking his time, speaking slowly, waiting to see that she had understood him. 'The brain is a limitless hard disc constantly processing,' he went on, 'and when we injure the brain, or it's subjected to illness—and perhaps you've had a viral inflammation that has suddenly aggravated this, like a particularly high temperature in a computer, threatening to burn out or short-circuit, subjecting those billion cells to unbearably high pressure—'

'Mr Werth,' she interrupted, 'they are real.'

'They will seem extraordinarily real, yes.'

'No. Not *seem*.' She put her hand to her head, tracing a line across her forehead. 'I'll tell you what's the strangest thing of all about it,' she said, looking at him without turning her head. 'Want to know?'

'Of course.'

'I was never convinced before that I was really alive.'

'What do you mean?'

'Like ordinary people. I always felt alone.'

He frowned a little. 'You'll have to elaborate for me,' he said.

She hesitated for a moment. 'I've always been the odd one out,' she said softly. 'At home: the youngest, a girl, the *clever* one . . .' She made a little self-conscious face. 'Or so they always said. Also I looked like no one else in my family, and I had a head full of odd thoughts . . .'

'Odd in what way?'

Again she waved her hand briefly. 'Oh, nothing too extreme, but I felt . . .' She tried to find the right words. 'I felt different to everyone around me.'

'Did you see and hear anything unusual then?'

'No,' she replied firmly. 'I'm just saying that I've always felt out on a limb, different, alone.'

'Well, we *are* alone,' he told her. 'At the most important times of our life we are alone.'

'But I felt that all the time. I felt that I wasn't connected to the world,' she murmured. 'I wanted to be physically bigger. I never knew how to make small talk. I just could never *understand* . . .'

'That isn't uncommon. The psychiatrists even have a word for it.'

'Oh, I know that,' she said.

'Well, then?'

She gazed at him for a long time. 'Maybe you're a memory hologram, too.'

'I can assure you'—he pinched his arm—'I'm really here.'

She lifted her head. 'Like the man in the boat.'

His smile faded and he sat back, crossing his arms over his chest. He realized that her gaze had settled on a point behind him, somewhere a little below the ceiling. She was suddenly transfixed.

'Don't you know anyone who died of drowning?' she asked in a low-key, lilting tone. 'He had a small sailboat, and he died quite close to land.'

Werth said nothing.

'It infuriated him, you know,' she said, 'to be that close—he could see the harbour, he could see the headland, and—damn, that wave. Just like that. So very quick. Damn . . . that wave.' Her voice was tender and low. 'Just went away so quickly. He saw you and your mother loading the car, putting in that green slick-covered coat, the basket, his boots . . .' She gave a great, laboured sigh. 'Oh well,' she said. 'That's the way it goes. My little boat with the blue paint. One damn wave. Oh boy . . . oh boy.'

She managed, very slowly, to sit up. She rubbed her hands over her face. 'What time is it?' she asked.

Werth looked at his watch. It took him some moments to register the time, and tell her. 'It's . . . almost six.'

'There's a kind of fog,' she murmured.

He leaned forward and looked intently in her face. 'Lin, do you remember what you've just said to me?' he asked.

She seemed to be half asleep. 'Sorry?'

'Do you remember what you just said to me?'

'The boat,' she murmured.

He stood back, utterly perplexed. As he did so, she seemed to rouse a little. 'They won't go away, once they've come,' she said. 'That's what's driving me mad. They just won't go.' She turned her head, to look at the trees beyond the window. 'Where did I remember the boat from?'

Werth shook his head.

She looked around at her locker. 'I'm thirsty,' she said.

He poured her a drink of water.

'I have to drink a glass an hour,' she said. 'I wish there was gin in it. Can't you please get me some nice Gordon's?'

He smiled, and watched her empty the glass. He put it back on the locker for her. She slumped back on the pillow.

He walked over and looked out of the window at the last fading light.

'Can you tell me what the man in the boat looks like?' he asked.

'About sixty-five . . . white-haired. Burly, not tall, muscular.'

Werth turned and looked at her, arms again crossed. 'Do you always see such detail?'

'Yes.'

'So you're seeing a lot of pictures: moving images of people?'

'Yes.'

'And they speak to you? They move in relation to you—you see them in specific places, moving through doors, along floors, and so on?'

'Some of them do. Others just come. They materialize—and they vanish.'

'You see concrete images and blurred images?'

'Yes.'

'And tell me again. Sounds?'

'Yes. Voices.'

'Speaking like . . . like this man?'

'Yes.'

'All the time?'

'Not all the time.'

'How often? Every hour? Every few hours?'

'Oh no. Sometimes I see nothing unusual for a few minutes.'

'So you are seeing these strange images every few minutes?'

She closed her eyes, frowned, and lifted her hand very slowly to her throat, as if speaking was an increasing effort. 'There are crowds and crowds of people,' she said, 'and those I can't see, I can hear—outside.'

'And all this has only happened since you were admitted to the hospital?'

'Yes.' She seemed to be getting very tired. He thought she might have drifted into sleep, so long was the next pause. As he stepped towards the bed, she rolled onto her side and clamped one hand to the side of her head.

'Lin,' Werth said, 'what do you see now?'

She did not reply, so he lifted her wrist, felt the pulse racing.

'Oh, for God's sake,' she said. 'All right, all right.'

She opened her eyes. He felt a curious friction under his fingers.

'He says,' Lin told him, 'to call you Tunny.'

Slowly, Werth put her hand back down to the bed. Equally methodically, he lifted the sheet over it and smoothed it down.

'Am I still scratching an itch?' she asked.

He said nothing.

'Damage beyond the primary visual cortex,' she murmured.

Just for a moment, he swayed a little backwards. 'What?'

She narrowed her eyes as she looked at him. 'It just came into my head. You thought it just now, as you were touching me.'

He made no comment at all. Instead, he stepped away and leaned against the window, watching her silently. There was a very long pause.

'I was in hospital last year,' she said at last. 'Not like this one. It was a psychiatric ward. My husband said that I needed help.'

'And did you?' Werth asked.

She laughed quietly. 'Oh, yes.'

'Why was that?'

'Because I tried to kill him.'

In the silence, they both could hear the visitor's bell sounding along the corridor. Werth pulled up the chair and sat down again next to the bed.

'He's quite a famous man,' Lin continued. 'He writes books. Perhaps you've heard of him.'

'Yes, I know. Kieran Gallagher: *Christ's Wife*.'

'That was published two years ago. He wrote *Forbidden Fruit* this year.'

'I saw *Christ's Wife* on television. Your husband presented it.'

'Yes,' she said. 'That was my idea.'

'And the house thing.'

'I was hired as his assistant, to type out his manuscript. He was writing history books for schools then.' She rested her head on the pillow, and looked at the ceiling. 'When you saw him lecture, he was creative and clever; everyone wanted to listen to him. But when he put pen to paper, he dried out. So, for that manuscript—it was

Hannibal—I rewrote some of the chapters in the style that I had heard him speak. All the black jokes, the comparisons with modern leaders.'

'Those are considered his trademarks.'

'Yes, the politics.'

'You wrote his books? And the TV adaptations?'

'No . . . no. I just rewrote, edited. But I write the scripts for the . . .' She smiled at him. 'The house thing.'

'You're a busy woman. And when you met him, you were a student yourself?'

'I was, but I gave it up after I had known him for eighteen months.'

'Why was that?'

'I became pregnant.'

'He was already married?'

'Yes. He was married to Ruth Carmichael.'

'I see . . .' Werth stared at her, almost hearing the pieces clicking into place, rather ominously, in his own mind. 'And last year? What happened last year?'

She paused as if trying to marshal her thoughts. 'I went a little crazy. He had always told me that I was mad.'

'Why?'

She shrugged. 'Have you ever been married?'

'Yes. Some time ago now.'

'He wanted me to be more like Ruth—that's the bottom line.'

'In what way?'

She sighed. 'Ruth is very calm and ordered. She's very single-minded, dedicated. I'm not. I get bored, antsy. I don't plan. I have all these ideas: a head full of ideas rocketing around. Or I get preoccupied with doing something with Theo, perhaps . . . I'm difficult to live with.'

'Does your husband say that?'

'Oh, yes. He feels I ought to calm down.'

'And the ideas that rocket around?'

She lifted her hand from under the sheet and placed it softly on his. 'I'm not a manic depressive, if that's what you think. They don't rocket round *that* much.' For the first time, he heard her laugh, and was surprised and pleased at the genuine warmth in it.

She smiled. 'Am I an interesting case, Mr Werth?' she asked almost plaintively.

He smiled at her in the encroaching darkness. 'Yes,' he said. 'You are indeed a most fascinating case.'

It was past ten when Mark Werth finally got home that night.

As soon as he got in, he rang Directory Enquiries to find Ruth's number.

She sounded tired.

'I'm sorry to disturb you,' he said, 'but I wanted to ask something about Lin Gallagher.'

'All right.' Ruth gave a very long sigh.

'Has she ever been to Ireland?'

There was a pause. 'Ireland? No, I don't think so . . . oh, yes, of course. She went with Kieran to promote his book last year.'

'What part did she visit?'

'I can't remember. Is it important?'

'Did they go to Galway at all?'

'I really can't say. Why?'

Werth paused, drumming his fingers on the table at his side.

'Nothing. It's a long shot—a very long shot. I'm sorry to have bothered you.'

'It's no bother.'

They spoke briefly about Lin herself—no more than pleasantries. Ruth Carmichael sounded too weary to be very interested.

He put down the phone and walked several times around his living room, picking up items and putting them down again absentmindedly. Eventually he went upstairs, showered, and got into bed.

Where he lay awake for over an hour.

Mark Werth's grandfather, who had always insisted on calling him Tunny, had drowned off Galway's Abbeyhead peninsula in a little sailing boat four years ago. It had a peeling blue-paint hull—and it had been sunk in seconds by a single wave.

TWENTY-ONE

$\mathscr{R}$UTH'S PHONE RANG AGAIN TWO HOURS LATER.

She was in the depths of sleep, dreaming of the day she had left the Priory. Except it was not at all as it had been in real life, with Kieran and she silently packing boxes, then sitting down together, as if at a wake, to drink a final cup of tea. She hadn't—as might have been expected—hated him that morning. No, rather, throughout that whole insidiously encroaching nightmare she had felt a growing realization that their separation would only be temporary, that their link was too strong. He would come back, even if it took years. He would come back to her. She would draw him back by pure force of will.

And she had believed that ever since, with absolute certainty.

In this dream, however, Lin was exerting a power she did not possess in life. She stood in the hall of the Priory, throwing Ruth's belongings out into the drive. Ludicrously she wore a wedding dress, a mountainous confection of satin and chiffon, with a great trailing veil ten feet long. She was bedecked in flowers—in her hair, on the shoulders of her dress and sewn into its folds.

Ruth saw her lovely spelter statue of greyhounds fly past, the dogs incredibly and actually running, released from their immobility, charging headlong, as real dogs might, towards the light. She saw the wildness and joy in their eyes as they passed her, just an inch from her, at shoulder height. But, as they hit the steps, they changed to metal again, clanging in an ugly fashion as they tumbled down the stone.

The note altered. It became a buzz: the subdued trill of the phone. Still half asleep, she picked it up from the bedside table.

'Yes?'

'Ruth. It's Caroline—Caroline Devlin. Can you come out?'

Ruth blinked, trying to orientate herself. She glanced at the clock: it was five minutes past two.

'Caroline?' she echoed. 'I'm not on call tonight.'

'I know. Please . . .'

The strangled, gasping sound finally broke Ruth fully awake.

'What's the matter?'

'Please come . . .'

'Are you ill? What is it?'

There was no reply. She heard the receiver on the other end hit something hard, then it was picked up.

'Is that Dr Carmichael?'

'Yes. Who is this?'

'Martin Devlin.' It was Caroline's teenage son, sounding fumbled, aggressive. As Ruth propped herself up on one elbow she realized that the boy was drunk. 'She's got a chest pain. It's bad . . .'

Ruth heard Caroline's voice, objecting incoherently, in the background. At that point Martin obviously turned his head away from the phone. 'What do you want to do?' Ruth heard him shout. 'You want to die while she's thinking about it?'

Ruth swung her legs out of bed. 'Call the emergency number now,' she said loudly, for him to hear. 'And tell your mother I'm on my way.'

She had to get him to give her the address. It was two miles away, on the outskirts of town. Ruth drove there in the sweatshirt and jog pants she had pulled on; she was not in the least cold, as the night was surprisingly warm. There was a full moon that clearly lit their street, picking out detail on windows, cars, doors, even the colours of flowers. As she had turned into the street, she at once spotted Martin Devlin standing in the doorway. The borders of the lawn in front of him were a moonlit fringe of daffodils and hundreds of densely planted narcissi. Ruth had a sudden and uncharacteristic feeling that they were all already ghosts moving in a phantom landscape.

She pulled up and got out of the car.

'Where is she?'

He led her through to the sitting room, cursing under his breath as he collided with the door frame. As soon as she went through, Ruth realized there must have been quite an argument: books and magazines were scattered and up-ended across the floor. A plant lay on the carpet, its soil spread around it. A plate, that had evidently held a meal, was in two pieces near Caroline's feet.

Caroline herself was seated on the couch, her face very pale, her skin sheened with sweat. One hand was pressed into her left shoulder.

'Have you phoned the ambulance?' Ruth asked the boy. He had slumped full-length in a chair.

'She won't let me.'

Ruth stared at him. 'What?'

'No, no,' Caroline murmured.

Ruth went over to her, and dropped to her knees.

'Where is the pain . . . your chest, your shoulder?'

Caroline slightly inclined her head, her expression frozen into one of fear. Ruth knew that look: she had seen it before on those in the final stages of terminal illness, or in the eyes of road-accident victims trapped but still conscious. It was as if they could see a picture not visible to anyone else—their eyes fixed on a spot before them as though confronting the bodily spectre of their distress, seeing it in comprehensive detail. In such moments, those in pain experienced a different reality to their audience at the bedside. Ruth opened her bag, took out the stethoscope and listened to the woman's heart. She placed her fingers on Caroline's wrist. The pulse was rapid, fluttering. Ruth looked down and saw that the couch was stained.

'She was sick,' Martin said.

'How long has this been going on?'

'Dunno . . .'

'Ring the ambulance,' Ruth said.

'She just wanted you.'

'Dial nine-nine-nine.'

The boy muttered something, but did as he was told. Ruth noticed that Caroline's gaze followed his every movement. When she did finally look at Ruth, it was with a glance of such grief, such desolation, that it momentarily stopped Ruth in her tracks.

She took the cannula from her bag. 'Caroline, I'm going to give you an injection. Can you hear me?'

Caroline closed her eyes, and her colour seemed, quite suddenly, to fade from its already ghastly grey to white.

'Shit,' Ruth muttered. She injected the anistreplase and, in the very moment of administering it, suddenly realized that she carried no monitoring equipment. Normally, on call, she would carry a portable ECG, but everything was in the surgery. Martin was still on the phone.

'How long are they going to be?' Ruth said.

'How long will it be?' the boy repeated to the operator.

'Tell them this is extremely urgent,' Ruth said. 'Say that I'm here, and I say so. Very urgent.'

She was still holding Caroline's hand, and felt it go limp. She turned back to look at her, and both saw and heard one terrible gasp for breath. The fingers, now unresponsive, were cold. Ruth felt for a pulse, but there was none.

'God,' she murmured.

Martin had replaced the phone, and was standing on the opposite side of the room. He was staring at Ruth, twisting one corner of his sweater in his fingers, the other hand wiping his nose.

'Help me get her to the floor,' Ruth said.

He did not move.

'Martin, help me get her to the floor.'

At last he stepped forward. They laid Caroline down, and Ruth began heart massage. Her son said nothing. As Ruth worked, she heard him go out of the room. After both massage and mouth-to-mouth, Ruth checked the pupils of the eyes, and saw that they were enlarged.

'Caroline,' she said. 'The ambulance will be here very soon.' She stared down at her patient, abruptly feeling extremely irritated. This whole situation struck her as needless: the lack of any phone call to an emergency number, Caroline's own intractability, her son's drunken fog. Needless and stupid. Now Ruth had a dying woman to cope with, where she might have had a live patient in the Coronary care unit. She fought down her angry impatience.

Martin came back with a dustpan and brush. He knelt down a few feet from his mother, averting his gaze from her, and began sweeping up the soil from the carpet, making great black arcs on its pile. None of the soil went into the pan.

'Only a bloody plant,' he muttered.

Ruth had no time to pay attention to him. The fact that he did not seem to grasp the urgency of the situation didn't surprise her. She accepted this with the same angry feeling choked down far inside her. She had known even sober relatives walk away from the dying, too shocked and frightened to be able to face them. She had seen women in the last stage of labour fight to get off the hospital bed, insisting that they were going home and would come back at another time—as if the agony could be put away, or as if they could willingly leave their bodies and return at will. And besides all of which, the boy was desperately drunk, his eyes glazed, his colour ashen.

'Tell me if the ambulance is coming yet,' Ruth said. 'Go and look at the door.'

He continued to fumble with the dustpan.

'Get on your bloody feet and go to the door,' Ruth snapped.

They heard the siren.

Moments later, the paramedics came through the door. Ruth stepped aside, telling them what she had already done. At the mention of the anistreplase, the senior man looked up but said nothing. The ECG and defibrillator were attached. All three of them stared at the green trace-line.

'She's in VF. Stand back.' They gave Caroline the first shock.

There was no response. Nothing at all. The line was flat.

The paddles were replaced. Another shock.

Flat line.

Another shock.

Ruth looked away. She looked at the house plant, its leaves flattened and torn. It had been hurled to the floor and then trampled on.

Very slowly she lifted it up, smoothed the soil from the white ceramic rim, and replaced it on the coffee table.

'She's in asystole,' one paramedic commented.

Another shock.

'How many minutes of massage?' they asked.

'About five,' Ruth said.

'Try another ten.'

They gave adrenalin, and oxygen. The mask obscured Caroline's face. All Ruth could see now was the woman's thick early-greying hair with its naturally silver streaks.

'She's only fifty-two,' Ruth said.

No one replied.

It was then that Ruth realized that Martin had gone. The door of the sitting room and the front door of the house were both wide open. She slipped out of the room, trying not to look at Caroline's bare feet.

The boy was leaning by the garage. He had vomited.

Ruth put her hand on his back. 'Take some deep breaths,' she said.

He stood up. 'It's not my fault,' he told her.

'No, it's not.'

'No use getting fuckin' annoyed with me.'

'I'm not annoyed,' Ruth lied.

'*She* lost her temper . . . She . . .'

'OK, never mind that now. Come back inside.'

He followed her grudgingly, weaving as he walked.

'Where have you been?' Ruth asked.

'Flyers.'

'In town?'

'Yeah . . . mate's birthday.'

'Come and sit with her,' she said.

They went in.

By now the paramedics had Caroline on a stretcher.

'We had output,' one said.

'Where's she going?' Martin said, as the trolley went past.

Ruth lifted her bag from the floor, and put her equipment into it. When she straightened up, Martin was still staring through the open door. Beyond, the ambulance was just pulling out of the drive.

Ruth watched it go. To her surprise, she looked down and saw her own hands were trembling. She bit down hard on the inside of her cheek. There were tears somewhere, a rising and rolling sensation of fear. She breathed deeply, instructing herself silently to stop. Stop whatever that feeling meant. Stop the foreign feeling: the feeling of escalating panic.

She turned to Martin and gripped his arm. 'Come with me,' she said.

He remained frozen where he was.

She took his elbow. 'Martin,' she said, yanking him savagely in the direction of her car. 'We're going to the hospital. Pull yourself together and come with me.'

TWENTY-TWO

$\mathcal{K}$IERAN WATCHED THEO run down the Priory's long garden. Dressed in a faded red T-shirt, cut-off jeans and too-large Timberland boots, the boy left a dark trail in the dew of the early-morning grass. Ahead of him scooted one of the village cats, tail raised in alarm. Kieran, standing at the kitchen door, looked up at the sunlight on the east-facing hill of the valley, marking its slope in spectacular green-and-white ridges. Hamble monument was a brilliant chalk-white.

Theo ran down to the hedge gate and climbed it. His back was revealed as a patch of exposed white between shorts and shirt, as the boy leaned over the top of the gate and spread his arms, still calling to the cat. Beyond the gate, two dirty-looking little horses with matted manes and tails grazed the field. Theo tipped his head back and stared at the sky in a posture of unencumbered freedom and curiosity.

Kieran looked away. He had been trying to get Theo to eat breakfast. He hadn't known what to do when his son refused, scrambled down from his seat, tore open the door and ran outside. When Kieran had called him, Theo did not even look back.

He ought to go after him, he supposed. Kieran turned back to the kitchen and searched for his shoes; then a feeling of unfocused grief came over him. Sitting down, he stared at the floor.

Yesterday he had stopped in town to buy Theo a present. It was something that had been mercilessly advertised on TV, something Kieran actually disapproved of, but Lin had told him Theo coveted it. As soon as he got home, he had given him the parcel. Theo had unwrapped it slowly and carefully, but when he saw what was in the box his attitude had changed, and a huge smile came over his face.

'Like it?' Kieran had asked.

'Yea-y!'

Theo had started wrestling with the toy.

'Here,' Kieran said, taking it from him. 'Give it to me and I'll put it together. You'll smash it like that.'

'Launch it, launch it,' Theo demanded.

Kieran did his best. It was a dragon that flew by itself when cranked up. He wound the clockwork, and quite suddenly it soared up in the air, landing heavily on the opposite side of the room. *Fifteen pounds for that?* he thought.

'Again, again.'

They let it fly a dozen times, then he tried to get Theo to sit in his lap.

'Listen,' he said.

'Whirrr . . .' Theo was opening and closing the dragon's wings.

'Theo, listen to me.' Kieran took the toy away from him and hid it behind the chair. 'Theo, Mummy might not come home for a while. She's sick in the hospital.'

Theo said nothing.

'Theo,' he continued. 'What did Mummy say about going to live in Hampton?'

The boy didn't respond.

'Is she cross with me?'

Theo stuck out his lower lip.

'Why is she cross?'

Theo shook his head.

Kieran sighed. 'I have to do some work now,' he said. 'Maybe Ruth will come and see you this afternoon.'

The violence of the child's reaction surprised him. His son had struggled down from his grasp and stood in front of him, legs planted full-square, all defiance.

'She *not*!'

Kieran tried to take hold of his hand, but Theo's face was red with suffused fury. Then the boy had reached out.

For a second, Kieran had thought he wanted to be picked up and held or carried. He had started to hold out his own arms, smiling. Theo's fist had connected with Kieran's chest, and he felt a small pricking sensation. Kieran glanced down in surprise, and saw that the spear belonging to the toy dragon—a tiny ineffectual plastic spear only an inch long—was stuck in the weave of his sweater. He had looked back up at his son and saw Theo with his fist in his mouth, chewing on his knuckles.

Kieran now sat staring into space, thinking about this boy he hardly knew. He could count his mornings spent with Theo this year on the fingers of one hand. He never took him to school these days. He never even got round to playing cricket with him any more, having once vowed that he would teach him properly as soon as the boy was old enough. The life that Lin and Theo shared was a private thing, and Kieran was excluded from it.

Mother and son seemed unnervingly alike. Coming back after a long absence last year—he had been to Syria for five weeks—Kieran had found, instead of the welcoming committee he hoped for, no answer to his greetings shouted from the hallway. Offended, he had eventually found them out in the garden, curled up on a bench, barefooted, bare-legged, interestedly inspecting stones they had fished up from the gravelly shallows of the river. Kieran had paused in the shelter of the trees, watching them.

Lin was wearing a cloth dressing gown over her swimsuit, Theo nothing at all. They were prising sticky, colourless worms from the underside of each stone.

'What do they feel like, Theo?' he had heard Lin ask.

'Yucky.'

She had laughed. 'They are. They're awful yucky.'

The colour of her hair with its reddish tones, the faded pinks of the cloth on her shoulders, the small dark brown head at her shoulder and the pink rim of Theo's open mouth in its unconscious expression of complete fascination, all of this scene imprinted itself on Kieran's memory. He had hardly wanted to step forward and ruin the picture. When he did so, making his voice purposefully light and without a trace of the exclusion he felt, he was dismayed to see how accurately he had forecast his effect on them both. They stiffened and straightened and leapt up, as if he had caught them in some crime.

'What's all this?' he had asked.

'Nothing,' Theo immediately retorted.

Lin had ruffled their son's hair, raising her eyebrows in mock exasperation. She stepped forward and kissed Kieran lightly on the cheek. But he still felt that he had spoiled the afternoon, the hour.

All the time, he wanted to say how much he loved Theo. That ought to be easy to say—Lin said it easily. 'Oh, Theo, I love you,' she would say to him at night as she put him to bed, snuggling her face into the child's neck, while he squealed with delight and threw his arms around her. 'I love you *more*—right out into the sky.' 'I love you more—more than all the stars there are.'

Theo would desperately try to out-do her. 'I love you tons, sixteen elephants, big tall buildings, Ray Bolt's coal lorry. I love you wide, this wide, wider than the football pitch, as wide as this. I love you lions and tigers.'

That time Lin had sat back on her heels, laughing. 'I love you lions and tigers? Oh, Theo.'

It had only been last January, and she had come downstairs still laughing, folding Theo's clothes over one arm. 'Do you know what he just said?' she asked Kieran, putting her head around the door of his study. 'He said, "I love you lions and tigers." He said . . .'

She had stopped then. Kieran was aware of her standing there, but he had a marker on the page and wanted to put a footnote on it while he remembered his point. He had already heard them, anyway, even from the bottom of the stairs.

'Kee,' she had said after a moment. 'Kee . . . ?'

He had looked up, finally. 'Yes?'

'Why don't you go up and say goodnight to him?'

'I will,' he had told her. He couldn't remember now if he had done. On the kitchen wall, the phone began to ring.

He brought himself back from the past, and picked it up.

'Hello?'

'Mr Gallagher?'

'Yes.'

'Sorry to disturb you so early in the day. This is Mark Werth, Mrs Gallagher's consultant.'

'Good morning.'

'Mr Gallagher . . . I have a slight problem here.'

'Is Lin all right?'

'Yes. There's been no major setback. But I would like her to see a colleague of mine.'

'Why's that?'

There was a pause. 'Can I ask, are you intending to come down here?'

'Today?'

'I wonder if a visit from your son might do her some good.'

From the open door, Kieran could see Theo hanging upside-down on the fence gate, kicking the slats of wood. 'I think it would upset him,' he said. He turned back towards the room, shifting the phone to his other hand. 'Who is this other colleague?'

'Alan Carlisle. He's a psychiatrist.'

'I see.'

'Purely for an initial examination. To clear my own mind as much as anything.'

Kieran made a fist of his free hand, waiting while the bone bloomed white under the skin. His nails dug into his palm.

'Mr Gallagher . . . are you there?'

'You must do what you think fit,' he said. 'But I'm not taking Theo there if Lin needs a psychiatrist. He's been upset enough.'

'She would like to see Theo, I know.'

'Maybe in a few days.'

There was a pause. 'Could I just ask one other question? Is your wife psychic?'

Kieran laughed outright. 'What? No, of course not.'

'Has she ever said she sees images, people and so on?'

Kieran let out a sound of exasperation. 'Do you want my advice, Mr Werth?' he said.

'I want anything that will help me.'

'Lin was ill last year. She had a . . . a kind of breakdown, I suppose. Her doctor here said it was postnatal depression. I have to tell you I didn't quite believe that so long after Theo was born—almost three years. I love my wife, Mr Werth,' he continued, 'but she is very young, very brilliant, and rather . . . highly strung.'

'I see,' said Werth. 'Thank you for telling me.' There was a pause. 'But actually I don't think this is a mental problem.'

'But you want her to see a psychiatrist.'

'Just as a long shot. I'm doing other tests myself today.'

'I will try to come over. But I shan't bring Theo.'

They said their goodbyes. Kieran hung up the receiver, put his hands to his face, and held them there for what seemed like minutes. Eventually he lowered himself onto a kitchen chair, rested his elbows on his knees, and sat with his fingers pressed hard to his closed eyes.

Life with Lin had always been a whirlwind.

This was just another trip: another trip for which he was woefully unprepared.

He had first made love to Lin in his office, on his desk. The manuscript had been forgotten. He, and it, were swept away. As the weeks passed, he had found it impossible to concentrate. He had fouled up his seminars and lectures; he was called in to see Arthur Caldwell. Word spread round the department, and Kieran had made no effort even to conceal it.

In college they had called her one thing only—never her name. They called her the 'Gee-Gee'—the men with a lewd note in their voices, the women more subtly. It stood for the Ghastly Girl. It had been said first at some drinks party, and it had stuck. Lin had thenceforward been—she still was—that ghastly girl. Thin, young, clever. To all the middle-aged women and the old men . . . that *ghastly* girl. 'Oh, poor Ruth,' they all said. 'Poor Ruth! What did she do to deserve the *ghastly* girl?'

They were establishment snobs, stuffed shirts, traditionalists. To lust after the students was one thing, accepted as a necessary *frisson* that came with the job. Remarks about women were passed all the time, chauvinistic naturally. But to step over the borderline and actually have an affair with one, that was not done. It was humiliating, unforgivable. Kieran fell at once below the salt, and stayed there.

But he hadn't been able to rid his mind of her. Sometimes, driving in, he would prepare a speech. He would prepare to dismiss her. The four weeks he had originally employed her for had long passed. Now he went on paying her for doing nothing. Still agonizing over it, he would get into his room, and without a word she would calmly sit down on the couch where his students were due to sit in not more than five minutes—she would not even suggest he locked the door—and she would lift up her skirt and, naked underneath, open her legs. He would find himself instantly on the floor, on his knees.

There is nothing so stupid as a man besotted with a younger woman. No grotesque shape he won't bend himself into. He had let the deadline for his book slip. The phone calls had bounced around the air like echoes from another planet. Only when he was two months overdue, did she one day—she, not him—sit down and redraft the whole book, sketching out those fantastic, mind-numbing chapters.

It was so easy for her. So easy. She was so incisive, so neat and quick . . .

The moment he told Ruth of Lin's pregnancy, Ruth got ready to leave him. No scene, nothing ugly, nothing violent. She bought herself a flat in town, and then moved out. It took less than three weeks. Ruth's frigid, self-contained reaction had stunned him. Also, more to the point, it had made him feel a complete shitheel. Ruth had barely even wept—just a few tears one evening when she was feeling particularly tired. But there was no going back. Absolutely not unless he could swear never—*never*—to see or speak to Lin again.

What else could he do? Could he have abandoned Lin? Could he survive without Ruth? He had needed them both, wanted them both.

His life had been smooth before Lin came along. He had been promoted to his present post at thirty and had an excellent reputation. He was married to an accomplished older woman and they had a beautiful period home, always immaculate. His life had been level and even till then. He had worked dutifully on his books. Ruth had entered into the medical partnership at Gideon Street. Children were not an issue, as Ruth had honestly admitted her infertility to him, and he could never anyway imagine himself as a father. They had been a favoured couple then, in a summer landscape of compatible ease.

And then came Lin.

Swift, sexy, loving Lin. She was so unpredictable.

He grew rapidly to respect Lin's opinions on his work, though she attacked it surgically, cruelly, cutting it to pieces and sewing it back-to-front. His thoughts now fragmented, pursuing marginal theories for the first time in his life. She had encouraged him. She would help do research for him, and find the most oblique notions wildly engrossing. It was as if he was being pushed, physically, mentally and emotionally, down a plunging rollercoaster—he could almost hear his own shrieks. He never knew her as a person but as a kind of phantom, a wraith that had sprung from a sexual fantasy straight into his arms. She was lithe and careless where Ruth was calculating and controlled. She was young and she blasted him with life. She was raw where Ruth was refined. Lin was addictive.

And she was so funny. She was perfectly capable of renewing her little dance alongside the benches in public places—the image that had so painfully first nailed him. And she was fond of elaborate, dreadful shaggy-dog stories, and she loved to watch the worst of the soap operas, and she was a fund of seemingly useless facts . . . and she spent hours meticulously correcting his manuscripts at the cost of her own work . . .

And she adored him. She would tell him that over and over again. Ruth had never been so demonstrative, and it bathed his ego in warmth and light. Lin was alive.

Alive, alive. So alive.

Two days after Ruth left home, he took Lin to the Priory.

'I don't want to live here,' she had told him.

He had been amazed. 'This is a wonderful house.'

'It's not mine, though,' she said. 'It belongs to you and Ruth.'

He had sat her down: she on the bottom step of the stairs in the hall, he squatting in front of her. 'I can't afford to take another house anywhere,' he had said. 'This house is part of my divorce settlement. It all had to be worked out. After the divorce, I suppose I'll have to sell, as I don't make enough money to pay the mortgage on my own.'

'I'll move in with you once you find somewhere else.'

This remark, so casual, had cut him to the quick. He had actually felt something pierce him: a kind of fear. He was sure to lose her. 'You can't live in that room on campus,' he said.

'Of course I can. What would the department say if I lived here with you?'

'The department? Nothing. What's it to do with them?' He was really not naïve. He simply sounded so then—for interminable months on end. 'You *must* live here. You're pregnant.'

She had laughed. 'It's not an illness.' She glanced around her. 'All her things are here.'

'They aren't. Her clothes, her books—everything's gone.'

'I don't mean those things. I mean the bed, the plates you eat from, the cups, the furniture. You bought them together. They belong to her.'

'I'll get her to take away whatever furniture you don't like.'

'Don't be silly,' Lin said.

She did sleep in the bed, though. She slept between the sheets that Ruth had bought and embroidered. She put her head on the pillow-cases decorated with Ruth's intertwined acidanthera, their white faces outlined in red, framing Lin's own white face and scribble of uncombed hair.

It dragged on for several weeks.

Sometimes Lin would stay for days, especially if she was working on a paper. He would come home and find some room—the kitchen, the bedroom—littered with pages.

'What's all this?' he would ask.

'I'm thinking about something.'

Her stays became longer. He became inured to the mess she created, though he disliked it. He tried to tidy away after her. There was never a meal on the table even if she had been home all day.

'Are we going to eat anything?'

She would look up, grinning. 'I don't know. Are we?'

His publishers came down from London to see him. His editor was bemused by the changes in style in his latest book. They sat in the garden and talked about his future presentation. Lin was not in the house. Kieran had never mentioned her contribution to the manuscript. They offered him—after lengthy discussions—a new contract. Just before publication, he had been approached by Harry Marks.

Harry, in contrast, realized about Lin the first time he came down to visit; he was not easily fooled. She was there and, for once, she had cooked dinner—a wonderful dinner—and looked ravishing, fertile and earthy, then in her fourth month. And somehow, by the end of the first evening, without either of them referring to it, Harry knew that Lin was as much the driving force of the latest books as Kieran. He recognized something . . . saw something between them. He knew its value.

And of course he was impressed by Lin's sharp, strange, innovative mind. He thought her sexy, too. He told Kieran so, and congratulated him. Kieran explained to Harry about Ruth, but the other man had only shrugged. 'Happens all the time,' he had said.

When Lin came back into the room, carrying the tray of coffee, his appreciative eye ranged over her again.

As she spent more and more time at the house, Ruth was obliterated by inches under the chaos Lin brought with her.

One morning, about eight weeks after Ruth had left, Kieran walked into the bedroom from the shower and stopped to look at her. Lin was sitting upright in bed, wearing her same shirt from the day before, her arms crossed over her stomach. She wore an expression of fright.

'What is it?' he asked.

Lin said nothing. She was frozen.

He came to sit down on the bed. 'What is it?'

She shook her head.

'Forgotten something? Not feeling right?'

'Not feeling right,' she murmured.

He had felt the first pale touch of fear. 'Where? The baby?'

She gave him a lingering, sorrowful look. 'I can't tell you.'

'Can't tell me? Why not? What is it?'

She had put her head down on her knees. 'I just can't tell you,' she whispered.

He had lifted her head. 'If there's something worrying you, I want to know.'

She said nothing.

But she had wept for days, on and off. He would find her lying on the floor, or curled on a seat outside, or in the bath with the water cold around her, sobbing bitterly.

'Don't you want a child?' he had finally asked, exasperated.

'Yes, yes . . .'

'Then what's the matter?'

She still wouldn't say.

She seemed to be labouring with an inner, secret grief. He tried once or twice to penetrate it again, but without success.

'You'll hate me,' she told him.

'Hate you? Never.'

'You will,' she had moaned. 'You will.'

He sensed a new self-destructiveness in her that worried him. He wanted to be close to her, to forge a deeper relationship. He now missed Ruth and their comfortable conversations, and had thought that at this time, while Lin necessarily slowed down, he might be able to enjoy something similar with her. But Lin eluded him, even when in his arms. She was far away now, in communion with someone else— the other person inside her.

It came to a head one evening when she was five months pregnant. It was February and the temperature had plummeted. Because the Priory was so cold, she had refused to stay there. He went to see her in the rented room he so hated, and was furious to find that it, too, was icy. She was sitting at her desk, wrapped in several layers of clothes, reading and making notes. The door was unlocked.

'What are you doing?' he asked.

'What does it look like? This has to be in tomorrow.'

'I want you to stop.'

She gazed at him, put down her pen and laughed. 'You what?'

'Stop.'

'Stop this essay?'

'Stop, and come and live with me.'

She rested her head on one hand, perfectly at ease. 'Come live with me and be my love,' she had murmured. 'And we shall all the pleasures prove.'

He put a hand under her arm and pulled. 'Now,' he insisted.

Dragged to her feet, she pulled away from him. 'What's the matter?'

He had looked around, almost speechless with impotent fury. Lin had promptly sat down again.

'I paid off Ruth's portion of the mortgage,' he said.

'Oh?' she replied tonelessly, staring at him, her legs crossed, one foot tapping mid-air.

'I took out a bank loan,' he said.

'Is that good?'

'Lin,' he said, 'I want us to get married.'

Their wedding—almost eight months to the day after he had told Ruth of the affair; she had, with her customary efficiency, filed for divorce on the grounds of his adultery—was very quiet.

It was a bright June day. They went to that same Italian restaurant, and he ordered champagne. When they got home, Lin, standing on the steps of the Priory, had flung her arms around his neck and kissed him. He held her at arm's length and stared at her.

'Will I ever know what to make of you?' he had asked.

'No,' she said.

As they came into the Priory's hall, he had picked up the morning mail from the floor.

'I'm going upstairs,' she said.

'I'll bring you some tea,' he told her, sifting through the letters while watching her slow ascent out of the corner of his eye.

'Lovely.' She was almost at the top of the stairs.

'There's a letter for you.'

She paused and looked back at him as he turned it over in his hands. It had been forwarded from the lodging house she had left the week before.

'Who's it from?' she said.

'How do I know?'

'Maybe that man who's always chasing me,' she said. 'The one called Bill.' She continued on up, laughing at her own joke, and singing, 'Bill oh Bill oh Bill . . .'

As Kieran waited in the kitchen for the kettle to boil, it suddenly occurred to him that it could be her rent demand. It would soon be the beginning of the summer vac, and she would not have written to tell them she was vacating her room. He opened the envelope to check.

But it wasn't from the lodging house. It was from an address in Liverpool: a single sheet of handwritten paper, dated five days earlier.

Dear Lindsay,
    Not that you will be interested—but. Mum had a stroke two days ago. She is in Assen Street hospital, ward 4.
    Things don't look very good.

Robert

Kieran had folded it slowly and put it on the tray. He poured the tea and stood for some seconds looking blankly at the cups. Then he went upstairs.

Lin was lying on the bed, still wearing all her clothes. He put down the tray, picked up the letter and gave it to her. As she unfolded it, he asked, 'Who is Robert?'

She read it, still lying on her back.

'Who's Robert?' he repeated.

She sat up slowly.

'My brother.'

Kieran sat down on the end of the bed and stared at her. It struck him all at once—and with the force of a thunderbolt—that he really knew nothing at all about this shining girl that he had so quickly and wilfully married. She had put the letter down and was drinking her tea. He was amazed at her apparent calm.

'We must go and see your mother,' he said.

'No,' she replied. 'I haven't seen any of them for five years.'

'That doesn't matter now. They've written to you. This is important.'

'I don't have to see her,' she said. 'She wouldn't know me anyway, if it's that bad. What good would it do?'

The coldness of her reply astounded him.

'She's your mother!'

She got up from the bed and walked to the window. 'You don't know anything about it,' she said.

'No, I don't. Not surprising, really.'

She crossed her arms, staring out at the view. 'Not everyone lives like you,' she said.

'What does that mean?'

She mimed two blinkers on either side of her head. 'Like this—in your fairy grotto.'

He was staring at her in shock. 'What are you talking about?'

She shook her head. 'Taking people at face value. You don't see things, you don't look under the surface, you're not curious, you . . .' She turned to face him. 'You slip over the top, do you know? Slip over the top, scootering along like a cat on a wet roof. You accept things, you regurgitate them, you don't question them . . . you trust people.'

She delivered the final line as if condemning him. He couldn't believe that the conversation had become a catalogue of his own faults. He stood up.

'You must go and see your mother,' he insisted. 'Pack a bag. I'll drive you to Liverpool.'

'No.'

He turned on his heel, went to the wardrobe and took a case down from the top shelf. She came up behind him, wrenched it from his hands and threw it down on the floor.

'Can't you hear me?' she demanded. 'I said no!'

'Pack the case, Lin. You haven't got much time.'

'I don't care if there's no time at all.'

He picked the case up. 'I'll pack it for you.'

And he did so. She retreated to the bed.

'Kieran,' she said, after a minute or more, 'I can't.'

'Don't be ridiculous.'

'I can't. You don't know.'

'Pack your case,' he said, turning for the door.

'Where are you going?'

'I'm going to ring the hospital,' he said, without looking back, 'to see if your mother is still alive.'

TWENTY-THREE

*W*HEN LIN WOKE UP THE FOLLOWING MORNING, she knew at once that something was different. With her eyes still closed, her head buried deep in the pillow, she tried to work out what it was. And then it came to her: there was no more noise. There were no more people.

Immediately she turned on her back, opened her eyes and propped herself up on one elbow. Her hospital room was empty and there was no sound from the corridor. The incessant whispering and shuffling of feet had gone. There was nothing beyond the window but the now-still lime trees, outlined by the first faint light of dawn. No one at all . . . an empty world. She could feel the clarity of the space, the vacuum left by their absence.

They have slipped . . .

She swung her legs out of bed.

At once, her fingers and feet seemed abnormally large. She held out her hands and looked at them, lifted her feet and inspected them. Both hands and feet felt twice their normal size. She edged herself to the side of the bed and put her feet on the floor. The room swayed a little as she stood up, then righted itself. For the first time, she inched towards the window.

There was a quadrangle of grass three floors below, and a pathway, and beyond that a car park. There was no one visible on the paths, or in the car park.

'Hello,' said a voice behind her.

It was the nurse who had been there the first day, the nurse whose hands reeked of her husband and his last afternoon.

'Hello,' Lin replied. 'You're back again.'

'I've been on duty all night. You look better.'

'I feel better.'

The woman walked in. She glanced at the chart at the end of the bed, but didn't pick it up. 'Can you walk OK?'

'I don't know.'

'Do you want to try?'

'Yes.'

'See if you can walk a little on your own.'

Lin picked up her dressing gown from the chair. She was not dizzy, but the huge-feeling feet and hands remained a problem. The nurse headed back to the door, and Lin followed her, feeling for the wall. She realized that things had a heightened quality, more so than on any day since the illness began. The wall paint beneath her outstretched fingers was very smooth and thick, like cold fondant icing; almost as though, if she pressed hard on it, it would depress to form the shape of her hand.

'Would you like a drink?' the nurse asked.

'I would, yes.'

'Come down to the lounge, then. Take your time. I'll make a cup of tea and leave it there. You can have a shower, too, if you feel up to it. But don't lock the door—so I can keep an eye on you.'

Luxury! Lin thought. A shower and hot water and a toothbrush, and a comb through her hair. She felt as if she had been asleep for weeks. Her body ached mildly all over, as if she had been pushed and pummelled in some rotating machine. The nurse left, and Lin eventually stepped out of the door after her, looking down the corridor. She could see herself in the reflection of the window opposite. She was suddenly overcome with a need to see Theo, or at least speak to him.

ELIZABETH COOKE

She had no money, and did not know where her handbag was. Still, she could phone him. She could reverse the charges. She pushed open the swing door and looked around the square landing beyond. There was a lift and a stairway, but no phone. As Lin stood indeterminately in the half-open door, a light above the lift registered, and the doors opened. A hospital cleaner stepped out, carrying a box of detergent.

'You all right?' the woman asked.

'I wanted the phone,' Lin said.

'Downstairs. Ground floor.' She held the lift doors open with one foot. 'You OK to get down there?'

'Yes,' Lin said. 'Fine, thanks.'

Once inside, she pressed the button for Ground. The doors shut.

They have slipped, for a moment, into another wheel . . .

She knew what she had been dreaming of now. She knew who had told her that. The lift bumped, then dropped smoothly away. Lin rested her head on the slippery wall.

She had been waiting for a train going in the opposite direction to his when she had met the boy who talked about time. And it had been him she had been dreaming of: dreaming that she was still standing on that station while the soft rain blew in.

Lin had finished working at the Hunting Dog; she couldn't face Michael. And she no longer lived at home. For the whole of the last summer she had worked for a holiday-chalet company, starting at eight, finishing at six, cleaning out rooms. Social Services had placed her in a bedsit. She was very lucky to have it. It was only a fifteen-minute train journey from the chalets.

He, too, had been waiting for a train. Lin had bought a bar of chocolate from the vending machine and sat down on a bench. She hadn't eaten since breakfast. After a while, she had glanced over to see that the boy sitting nearby was drawing a complicated pattern on an exercise book lying open on his knees.

Fine rain, fine August rain, floated gently in on them, fanning and folding as people moved past. Other local trains came, but still not hers. Then, no trains came at all. The crowds on the platforms increased. Over the tannoy came a long, rambling announcement.

The boy on the bench had looked up.

'Please—what is that message?' he asked her. He sounded French. 'I don't hear what they say.'

She had noticed a round globe in the drawing on his lap—intersected by some kind of grid.

'There's been an accident,' she told him. 'On the track back there. So there are no trains.'

'No trains? For how long?'

'They don't know. It's a cow.'

'I am sorry—a what?'

She had started laughing. 'A cow's dead on the track. Stopping the trains.'

He had smiled. 'How can that happen?'

'I don't know,' she had said. 'Ask the cow.'

His eyes dropped to—and remained fixed on—the page. She had considered him for some time: the very neatly cut hair, the smooth face, the long-fingered hands. He seemed utterly unperturbed by the delay.

'Will you miss any connection?' she had asked finally.

'I don't know.' He carried on drawing.

'Where are you going?'

'London. St Katharine's Dock.'

'Why St Katharine's Dock?'

He glanced up at her. 'There is a kind of clock there that I want to see.'

'A clock?'

He continued drawing. At last her curiosity overcame her. 'What are you doing?' she asked.

He sighed and put down the pen. For the first time he really looked her over. 'You are at school?' he asked.

'Yes. Sixth form.'

'And what do you do in this school?'

'English,' she said, and he had smiled. 'What's wrong with that?'

'You stretch your mind, I suppose.'

'Maybe.'

Their eyes met. She waved at the page in his lap. 'And what's this?'

'This? For past time.'

'You mean a hobby.'

'Yes, hobby.'

'You do this at college?'

'At university, yes.' She had been surprised: he didn't look old enough. 'I do physics, mathematics,' he added.

'So what's this?'

'Dials. You know dials—like clocks?'

'Dials . . . you mean sundials?'

'Yes, I do dials.'

She had been completely floored. 'You design sundials?'

'No,' he replied. 'Not design. Not make. I learn.' He waved a textbook at her, which he had been resting on to draw. 'That is why I go to London, to see an upper equinoctial dial.'

She flopped against the back of the bench, grinning. 'Sounds like fun.'

'I have been here looking at another dial on a church. I am taking . . . the course, the work . . .'

'An option?'

'Yes, an option at university. An option to do time.'

She began to laugh. 'Oh, you're going to do time?'

He didn't pick up the joke. 'I work on mathematics and time.'

She had shaken her head. 'Well.'

'It is interesting, the way we look at time.'

'Oh?'

'This month is Fructidor, you know that?'

'It's August.'

'Yes, in French Revolutionary months, Fructidor. Do you know they divide the day into ten hours? They made decimal time, a new calendar. All the dials were changed.' He sat forward towards her.

'Revolutions attack time. There is nothing more important. Time rules us, rules everyone. After the revolution in Russia, they make five days in a week: the days with numbers, not names.'

'I know the Anglo-Saxon name for August,' she said. 'Weodmonath—the month of weeds.'

His face had changed: enthusiasm had wiped away the closed, private expression of an hour before.

'I don't like Fructidor,' she added. 'It sounds like a canned drink.'

'Vendemaire is next.'

'Better.' Then she said, 'I'm doing Anglo-Saxon poetry . . . my name is Lin.'

'Emile,' he said. Solemnly they shook hands.

For a while they fell silent. A hundred yards down the line, the sun was trying to shine through a veil-like haze.

'And you—you're on holiday?'

'No, I'm working the summer. Where do you live?' she asked.

'Paris.'

'With your parents?'

'My father. My mother lives in Milan with another husband.'

'Oh,' she said. 'My mother . . .' But she didn't finish the sentence.

They had eventually walked along the seafront to a café. There were only a few resolute walkers about—elderly couples for the most part. This resort, in contrast to the home of the Hunting Dog five miles further along the coast, was quiet—alive only in having a few fortune tellers and fish and chip shops. As they got closer to the cafe, they passed the big concrete pool of the boating lake. Boys balanced along its knobbly, encrusted rim.

Emile had leaned on the railings, and looked down. 'It's a funny place,' he said.

'Yes,' she said. 'It used to be fashionable here, in the Thirties. Now they don't quite know what to do with themselves.'

He bought her supper at the café. People at the bar of the pub afterwards turned to look at him when he ordered drinks, listening to his pronounced accent. When they came out later, it was dark.

'I'll walk you back to the station,' she had said.

It was half past ten. The only train running by then was the boat train to Ireland.

'I don't want to go to Ireland,' he said.

'I don't put people up,' she told him.

'You don't do . . . ?'

'Put people up. I don't have anyone to stay—in my room.'

'I see.' He regarded her very seriously.

'Look—you know what I mean.'

'You don't put people up, yes.'

She almost hit him in exasperation. 'I mean, I'm not sleeping with you.'

He had shrugged.

It was with some embarrassment that she led him down the street to a terrace of flats where she had the very top room. They had to climb eight flights of stairs. At last she had opened the door to reveal the couch, chair, wardrobe, table and sink. The room was twelve feet square. She didn't put on the overhead light because it made the place look bleaker than ever. Instead, in the dark, she walked across to the table to turn on the lamp.

'No—don't do that,' he said from the doorway.

'Why?'

He had walked in, closed the door and gone straight to the window. So high above the surrounding houses, Lin had a clear view of the sea. Down below were the backs of small hotels: their dustbins, yards. At night she would hear cats crying in those alleys and yards: sometimes, in high winds, their voices sounded like babies. In the last four weeks she had heard them crying all the time.

'You have glass in the roof,' he said.

'It's called a skylight.'

'Skylight . . . skylight, yes,' he repeated. 'Pretty word.' He stood looking up at it in the dark, then glanced at her. 'You are all right?'

'Yes,' she said.

'You are crying.'

'No, I'm not.'

He had looked at her. 'You are ill?'

'No. Just . . . a bit sad sometimes.'

He said nothing, but his hand brushed her face, down the length of her cheek. He looked up again at the dark night sky and the stars. 'There is the hunter.'

'Where?'

'There—in the stars.'

She looked. 'Do you know the names?'

'No, just some. There is Cassiopeia, I think. But I don't know which. And the Great Bear . . .'

'I'd have thought you'd learn them by heart. For the sundials and time thing.'

'I will,' he said. 'I will learn.'

Together they stared upwards.

'You look up at them when you sleep?' he asked. There was no curtain on the skylight, and it was directly over her bed.

'No,' she replied. She was still thinking about babies, and there were tears in her throat, in her mouth. She put her hand to her mouth to stop it trembling. 'I don't like looking at them,' she said. 'They make me feel funny.'

He had laughed. 'I think *you* are funny. Everyone likes stars.'

'They make me feel small.'

'But we *are* small—just cells. Just like . . . when you close your eyes quickly . . .'

'Blinks?'

'Yes, blinks of the eye.'

'That's why I don't like them,' she said. 'I'm not a blink of the eye.'

'But it doesn't matter if we are blinks. We come again a million times.'

She had turned to look at him, at the shadows and the planes of his face in the half-light. 'What do you mean?'

'We live all those lives . . . a million lives.'

'Are you Hindu or Buddhist or something?' she had asked.

He had laughed. 'No. My father is Catholic.'

'Like my mother,' she said. 'And these lives we all have, you think . . . but that isn't Christian.'

'No. Just sense.'

She sat down on her only chair, and rested her arm along the table.

'One life is a waste,' he said. 'Where do we go, all the people that die? We stack up, maybe—like on shelves, endless shelves of the soul . . . that is right? With a million dying every day. Another shelf in heaven. It gets overcrowded, don't you think?'

She had smiled. 'Yes.'

'There is no sense. But to recycle us, to use us again, that makes sense. To try again. And then I think . . .'

'What?'

He looked back again at the stars. 'I think maybe, sometimes, that outside of us there is no time at all, or that it is all the same time, all these lives . . .'

The room fell silent while she tried to work out what he meant. 'We live a million lives all at the same time?' she asked, incredulous.

He sat down opposite her, on the edge of the bed. 'I don't know,' he said, 'but it would explain how people say they see the future.'

'How would it?'

'Each thing that happens, it has a place,' he said thoughtfully.

'Like you and me, we sit in this place. In this place, maybe a hundred years ago, there is no house. Maybe five hundred years ago, no road. It is a field by the sea—yes?'

'Yes . . .'

'OK. Five hundred years ago, in a field by the sea, a man is walking. He is walking in a turning wheel. That is *time*. That is the century. Alongside him, but he does not see, are other wheels that turn—other centuries and lives. They all belong to this place. And then suddenly the man, he sees something different. Not the field, but a house, very tall. Or he sees what is outside now, a car coming towards him. What does the man think? He thinks he has seen a devil, maybe. And the man driving the car—'

'He sees a ghost.'

'That is right. A ghost. Just for a moment, the wheels slip together. The man in the field and the man in the car, they have slipped, for a moment, into another wheel. A wheel that is turning at the same time over the same place.'

She leaned forward towards him. 'I read about someone who was driving along a road in the south of England somewhere, and he saw a man riding a horse bareback, parallel with his car. He was shouting and screaming, staring at him, galloping full-pelt to keep up with the car. The driver didn't know what to make of it, and then he saw that the man on the horse was wearing skins. He had a spear in his hand. He was staring at him, as if he were terrified, shaking the spear in his hand, shouting, and then the car came to a turn in the road, and the horse and its rider vanished . . .'

She paused, smiling at him. Sometimes, as a small child, she had imagined herself as being much greater than she physically felt: as if the inner person were capable of stretching and popping out from the body and becoming immensely linear.

At Theo's age, she hadn't been able to put words to it, but she had seen herself curled around the world like a strand of wool reeling round a ball, going on and on for ever. Sometimes, looking at the stars, this feeling had blossomed uncontrollably, so she had always looked away, as she still looked away, with a sense of dropping into infinity, and of being invisible, strung out, lost. It had been that way all her life. She was alone—and the outsider. Never sure of having been loved, only tolerated.

'And you think it's possible that we are all living a million lives, all at once, in different wheels?' she asked.

'Yes. I don't know . . . it's a theory.' He reached forward, and took her hand. 'Time is in the middle, where we stand. It goes out, making ripples. We touch others—more ripples. We do things—more ripples. Soon you don't see the centre any more, only the ripples. On the ground under this house, on this very place, is what others have done. What we do, what others will do, we are all connected—all one. One time.'

'Ripples,' she said.

'This is what I think of.'

'And we could learn to see the other wheels?' she asked.

He smiled, squeezing her hand. 'That I don't know about,' he said.

They have slipped, for a moment, into another wheel . . .

She took him back to the station in the morning. He gave her his address in Paris. She wrote to it a month later, when she hadn't heard from him. But he never replied.

She had never forgotten their conversation.

The lift doors opened.

Lin stepped out now, looking to left and right for the phone. A large foyer stretched in front of her, with a central display of flowers. On the far side were the main entrance doors to the hospital, and to their left a reception area where two uniformed security guards had their backs to her, talking. She looked up at the clock: it was twenty minutes past six.

She walked over to the flowers, which were raised up in a large circular bed with a seat running all the way round. Their colours, she thought, were more vibrant than she could ever remember: in fact they had a kind of frequency that was almost vocal.

She could smell the geraniums . . . Lin stopped. No, that wasn't true. It wasn't only them. It was the grey-leaved cotton lavender underneath them, and the ageratum and verbena. Their wiry little stalks were almost bitter, like cumin, or cloves . . . She could smell their colours. Her heart began a prolonged beat, heavy with anticipation of something she could not name.

All their colours: the pink with hardly any depth at all, and the weight and complexity of the darker blues. She could smell the difference between the flower and the leaf. She could smell the soil underneath them. She could smell the brick that surrounded them—it had a flat, gritty contour—and the flowers themselves were a knotted mass of fruit, bruised even by the stakes that the stems were tied to. She stood for a long moment, dazed.

She sat down on the seat and placed her hands, for balance, on either side of her.

There was a connection.

There was a connection between the brick and the flower and the floor, and the flesh of her hand. There was a connection between the construction of the room and the building. There was a connection between the building and the flower and her hand. Connections everywhere. All around her. All around everyone.

She looked over at the two men standing at the desk, and saw with sudden and certain clarity the link between them. It was a kind of current. She saw it leap backwards and forwards. She heard it, to a lesser extent, in the way the desk faced the door, in the relationship between the door and the desk. It was universal, it ran like an urgent message through every fabric. Every object, moving or still. Everything living or dead.

Except that nothing was dead. Down through her hands, she felt the vibration shuddering through different tones and notes. The foundations under the floor: the cabling, the ventilation, the steel frame— even the ground under the lowest layer of concrete. Connected like links in a chain. Connected, like long strings of chemical or mathematical formulae, not static or lifeless at all but weaving perpetually to and fro, subtly altering.

Inside the most silent of objects, matter convulsed in wild patterns. The sand inside the brick that held the flowerbed writhed with the memory of its original flowing shape. Millennia echoed in the sand and in the genetic code of the plants, and in her own endlessly rewoven body. And the thing that held them together pulsed with a permanent imperative.

Life. It must fulfil life.

Life . . .

Lin stood up.

She could hear the motor engine before it came close. A vehicle was roaring up the long drive. *A connection.* Another important connection growing more intense every second. She started to run.

As she passed the desk, she felt the friction of a pulse—that urging, unbreachable command—arc between her and the guards on the desk.

'Where are you going?' one called.

'Out,' she called over her shoulder.

She heard, then instantly forgot, their reply.

The ambulance was accelerating towards one wing of the building which extended at right angles to the entrance. It disappeared for a moment behind trees—the same lime trees, she realized, that she could see from her window. She then saw its roof apparently floating between their leaves. She took off across the forecourt, tying the belt of her dressing gown as she ran. The paving stones were slippery with dew. As she rounded the grass bank that formed a barrier between Admissions and Casualty, a great wave of fear rolled over her. It was pinpointed, like a beam of light, on the back of the ambulance, where a paramedic was already pulling open the doors.

I can hear that sound, she thought. I can hear the thing he hit. The thing that hit him. I can see it. I can see the last flash before it impacted.

Oh God! The car!

I can hear him.

The roses clamoured as she passed, filtering the different fluctuations of air that carried a thousand existing messages. She could feel the roses turned in wholly on themselves, trying to decipher the possible threat in the changes of temperature and sound.

Two nurses had come out from Casualty. Between them and the paramedic, they were taking out a stretcher and looking down at the teenage boy. A woman was in the ambulance, frantically talking at the top of her voice. As they tried to lower the stretcher she tried to hold onto it.

Lin stopped behind the group.

'Put him down,' she said.

The nurses looked back at her. The mother, half in and half out of the ambulance, gaped in confusion.

Lin shouldered her way through, pulling the paramedic's hands from the neck collar. The boy's face above the white band was livid. A series of thin, deep lines had already closed one eye. He looked as if he had been hurled along a pavement on his face. Blood soaked his hair. But that was only the minor injury; the worse one was to his chest. She felt the force of the injury, and gasped. She felt the jumbled circuitry in the shocked, labouring heart.

She put her hands flat on the boy's chest. There was a moment of stunned silence, then one of the nurses hauled on her arm.

'You can't do that. Step back now. Come on—'

'Who the hell is this?' the paramedic demanded.

The other nurse was pulling at the foot of the stretcher. 'For God's sake, move her away,' she said.

The link was twisted, wrenched. But it wasn't broken.

'Nothing ever breaks,' Lin said. 'You just . . . make the shape straight. It can't break. Nothing ever does.' She took away her hands.

At that moment, with a renewed and increasing charge, she thought of Caroline Devlin, her counsellor last year. The image was so intense, and so unexpected, that for a second Lin shut her eyes tightly. She felt this other heart, so much older than the boy's, bending like cracked wood, wood weakened and warped by rain; felt the bridge that had been made between them weigh under the pressure. She had not seen Caroline for months, but she sensed her now, as if Lin were standing on one side of a glass wall and Caroline were on the other, and she could see the other woman's flattened hands pressed to the pane, see the lines on her skin, the flesh crushed to the barrier.

The paramedic grasped her wrist. 'Jesus!' he muttered.

Lin opened her eyes, gasping.

They swept the boy past. At the door of the hospital, a doctor was standing waiting. He was already questioning the nurse. His voice peaked, raw at the edge, acidtoned.

'Who are you?' the paramedic said.

'No one,' Lin replied.

Both Caroline and the boy receded, swept away.

She listened.

The sun was warmer now.

Under the grouped green regiment of trees, the garden was blissfully singing.

TWENTY-FOUR

$\mathcal{R}$UTH FOUND THE PRIORY'S FRONT DOOR UNLOCKED when she called later that morning. She paused on the step to put her keys back into her pocket, then stepped inside.

She found Kieran sitting in the drawing room. He was next to a coffee table piled with papers, a laptop and two cold cups of coffee. His legs were propped up on the couch, and he had Theo's new toy dragon on his lap, absorbed in a laborious attempt to fix it. He looked up as she came in.

'I didn't hear you drive in,' he said.

'Too busy playing with that thing,' she observed wryly.

He smiled. She leaned down and kissed him briefly on the cheek.

'You look utterly shattered,' she said, picked up the two cups, and took them away into the kitchen. Water could be heard running briefly. Then she came back and stood in the doorway.

Kieran put down the toy. 'And how are you sleeping these days?' he asked.

She leaned on the door frame. 'A couple of hours last night, before I was called out,' she said.

'Poor Ruth.'

She shrugged. 'Has Theo gone to playgroup?'

'Yes. Hell of a job it was, too.'

'Why?'

He sighed deeply. 'Do you know what he said? At the door of the village hall? I mean, right on the doorstep, with a dozen mothers trying to get in past me?'

'No. What?'

'He shoved this at me,' Kieran said, showing her the toy. 'I only bought it for him yesterday. He told me to break it—just like that.' He mimicked Theo's voice: 'Break it! Break it!' Kieran shook his head. 'I don't know what to do with him.'

Ruth sat down next to him. 'He was just playing,' she said.

He put the dragon on the coffee table. 'He thinks I've taken Lin away,' he said. 'He hates me.'

'I'm sure you're wrong.'

He looked at her steadily. 'I'm not,' he replied.

Theo had wrenched the toy into two pieces as Kieran was squatting down trying to placate him. They had already fought all the way down the street, wrestled at the gate of the village hall, and then sunk to a pitched battle in the doorway itself. Theo had seemed genuinely panicked, drumming his heels on the cement floor, smashing the two broken pieces into Kieran's chest. 'I don't want you. I don't want you,' he had wept. 'Break it . . . break it!'

'Don't say that, Theo,' he had said, trying to hold the boy's arms to his sides.

The playgroup leader had helped them both through the door. Once inside the room, Theo had run away, coat flapping behind him, and thrown himself on a pile of beanbags in one corner.

The woman at his side had patted Kieran's arm. 'Don't worry about him,' she said. 'He'll be fine in two minutes. You wouldn't believe some of the scenes we have, and then, once you're gone—'

'It's his mother,' Kieran said.

'Yes,' she replied. 'I did hear.'

'I just thought . . . something normal, something routine, for a couple of hours . . .'

'Yes, absolutely. Quite right.'

He had taken a last look at his son, whose face was turned away from him, buried in the beanbag.

Ruth's hand stroked his shoulder. 'Have you rung the hospital today?'

'That's the other thing. The consultant says he's bringing in a psychiatrist.'

'Ah,' Ruth murmured.

'You're not surprised, I take it.'

'No. Not in the least.'

'You think this is all emotional . . . psychological?'

'Well . . .'

'Do you know what he asked? He asked if Lin were psychic.'

'Psychic?' Ruth started to laugh. 'What on earth has she been saying?'

'I don't know. I don't like to imagine.'

Ruth's eyes widened by way of expressing ironic amazement. They exchanged glances, then Kieran took her hand affectionately, and kissed it.

'You are a little oasis of sanity,' he said.

Ruth smiled. 'What did you make of her yesterday?'

He shrugged. 'She was very quiet, hardly said a word.'

Ruth sat down at his side. 'It is possible to fake petit mal, you know,' she said. 'And headaches—or visions.'

'I can't see the purpose,' he said. 'What has she to gain?'

'Oh, Kieran, she has everything to gain. Your more regular attendance here, for one thing. Her dominance over you, if she feels that's slipping.' Ruth gave him a sideways glance. She stroked his hand, taking it carefully between both her own. 'You are far too trusting,' she said. 'None of this move to Hampton was serious, you know. It's a kind of refined tantrum, an attention-seeking.' She frowned. 'I must say, Kieran, I think it's quite unforgivable to prey on your feelings like this. To drag you away from your work, hold you to emotional ransom.'

'You really don't believe she's ill at all, do you?'

She paused. 'I hope this isn't what I suspect. I really do.'

'Tell me why.'

'Because if she's faking all this, it's very serious, you know. You're back to last year again—or worse.'

He flinched, then rested his elbows on his knees, putting his head in his hands. 'I can't work it out,' he said.

'You're exhausted,' she told him. 'This is what she does to you, Kieran.'

'I don't know what to do,' he said. 'I just don't know what to do.'

'Have you eaten anything today?' she asked. She made a move as if to get up. 'I'll make you something.'

He stopped her. 'No,' he said. 'I don't want to eat.'

He leaned back on the couch, and stared at the ceiling.

'I do hope I'm wrong,' Ruth said. 'Not for her sake, but for yours.'

He looked at her, as she reached out and brushed his hair from his forehead. 'And I hate to think what this is doing to Theo,' she murmured.

He hadn't taken his eyes from her face. He took her hand as she began to draw it away, and held it tightly; then he pulled her towards him. She leaned forwards and pressed her lips lingeringly to his mouth. For a moment their joined hands hovered mid-air; then she pulled his palm to cover her breast. He relaxed backwards, caught in the drowning pressure of her embrace as she put her arms around his neck. She smelled wonderful. For a moment he submitted to the infinite luxury of her well-remembered calm, her unhurriedness with him.

Then Lin's image sprung into his mind. He pulled away abruptly.

'Relax,' she whispered, smiling.

Across the room, he could see their heads and shoulders in the mirror. His tan looked unnatural; he saw yellow in his colour, a sick shade, a kind of jaundice in his expression. He saw a bulge across his stomach, where he was putting on weight. He looked weary, unfit. His face, without the camera smile, was dull, he thought—bland. He wondered where the lens picked up the colour, and wondered too what would happen when it didn't any longer, when the television screen looked as the mirror did now. He felt that time was coming fast—heard the breathing of some other favourite on his neck.

He looked again in the mirror—and saw Lin.

She was standing quite still.

'Christ!' he said. He sat up, pushing Ruth away.

'What's the matter with you?' she said.

'Lin.'

'What do you mean?'

'Lin—there.'

Ruth got up and walked over to where he was pointing.

'Lin was standing just there,' he said. 'She had her hands out like this.' He showed her. 'She was there . . .'

'OK.' Slowly, Ruth rearranged her hair in the mirror's reflection.

'Oh God,' he said. 'I really saw her.'

'Yes, I know.'

He watched her for a second, then sprang to his feet. 'Don't give me any sort of . . .' He floundered for the right words. 'Don't give me some sort of bloody psychological verdict now, for God's sake, please.'

'I wasn't about to,' she murmured evenly. 'I'm not a psychologist.'

'Look, I . . .' He sat down with a thump, pulling one hand through his hair despairingly. 'Oh, Christ in heaven.'

'Do you want to go and see Lin?' she asked.

'No!'

'Perhaps you want her back here with you.'

'Of course I . . . no . . . yes . . .' He pressed both hands to his eyes.

'I'm going to make us both some tea,' Ruth said.

As she passed him, he gripped her by the wrist. 'I wasn't thinking of her just then,' he said. 'I swear to you.'

'All right.'

'Don't humour me.'

'What would you like me to do—scream?'

He smiled. 'Yes. I'd like you to scream.'

'Would it do any good?'

'Yes. Then I could scream too.'

She laughed. 'Scream away.' She went outside.

After a few moments, he followed her. As he came into the kitchen, she set a cup of tea for him on the table. 'Sit down,' she said. 'I want to talk to you.'

'What about?'

'Lin.'

He waited for her to begin.

'Do you love her, Kieran?' she asked.

'I . . . yes, I do.'

She stirred her own tea. 'Are you sure?'

He sighed. 'It's not the same.'

'As what?'

'As you and I.'

She sipped her tea, set the cup smoothly back in the saucer, and looked at him directly. 'Do you love me, Kieran?' she asked.

He didn't answer. He sat looking hard at his hands clasped on the table top between them.

The phone began to ring.

He turned to look at it, gave Ruth an apologetic smile, and went over to it. 'Yes?' he said, as he picked it up.

'Is that Kieran Gallagher?' yelled a man's voice.

'Yes.' Kieran moved the phone away from his ear, wincing. 'Who's that?'

'The *Echo*, Mr Gallagher. I'm talking to *the* Kieran Gallagher?'

'What do you want?'

'Married to Lindsay Gallagher, right?'

'Yes. Look—'

'I understand your wife's been ill, Kieran.'

The use of his first name always irritated him. 'Yes. And I hope you'll respect her privacy.'

There was a pause on the other end. Kieran's last sentence was obviously being relayed to some third party. The man's voice returned, a smirk in his tone. 'Is privacy what she's after, then?'

'I'm sorry?'

'What was she doing this morning, then?'

'Do you mind telling me what you're talking about?'

'This morning, Kieran,' the voice bellowed. 'This morning when she brought the dead to life. Is it for your TV series, Kieran? We had a bet on this one. You reissuing the book, yeah? Publicity for the book, yeah? Can she turn water into wine?'

'What the hell are you talking about? What bloody book?'

The man began to laugh. 'Your book, Kieran. Your book: *Christ's Wife.*'

TWENTY-FIVE

*W*HEN HARRY GOT TO THE HOSPITAL at lunchtime, he went immediately to Mark Werth's office. Lin had called him at half past nine that
morning; Werth himself called ten minutes later.

As he opened the door, he saw Lin sitting stony-faced next to
Werth's desk. Harry introduced himself to Werth, then bent to kiss
Lin's cheek. Her gaze flickered over him.

'Mind telling me what all this is about?' he asked. 'What the hell are
you doing out of bed?'

'Just take me home,' she said.

Harry looked at Werth. 'How is she?'

'Don't act as if I weren't in the room,' Lin said.

'OK, OK . . . have you rung Kieran?'

'Yes,' she said. 'I rang Kieran, but Ruth answered.'

Harry winced. 'I see,' he murmured. He lowered himself to a seat,
looking at Werth, who still offered no comment at all, but nevertheless
never took his eyes from Lin.

Lin's expression was equally unreadable, but she reached up and
touched his arm. 'Harry, I've got to see Theo,' she said. 'He won't bring
him here. You have to take me home. You're the only person I can turn to.'

Harry put up two hands in a warding-off gesture. 'Hold on, hold on,' he said. He looked up at Werth. 'This is all right?'

'No,' Werth replied. 'But I can't stop Mrs Gallagher discharging herself if she insists on it.'

'You mean she's still ill.'

'I need to do more tests.' Werth looked back at Lin.

'Don't start again,' she muttered. 'I never rang anyone: only Harry and Kieran. She rang them. I didn't want her to. She never consulted me.'

Harry looked from one to the other. Werth leaned forward on the desk.

'Several local newspapers have been calling Mrs Gallagher's ward. There are two reporters there now. An hour ago a national paper contacted me. It's not a situation I like. It's not good for the hospital.'

'It's not good for me either,' Lin protested. 'I never rang anyone!'

Harry pulled up a chair next to Lin. '*Who* never consulted you?' he asked. He didn't like her colour: she was deathly pale.

'A woman whose son was brought in this morning rang the local newspaper,' Werth explained.

'She recognized me,' Lin said wearily. 'She came back out and she ran after me. She told the security guard from Reception who I was. She said she'd seen me in photographs with Kieran.'

'What was wrong with the son?' Harry asked.

'I don't know,' Lin said.

'You don't . . .' Harry looked hard at her. She rested her elbows on her knees, settling her head in her hands in a gesture of despair. Harry turned back to Werth.

'The boy was brought in with multiple injuries following a traffic accident,' Werth said. 'He stopped breathing in the ambulance. He'd been crushed by a delivery van. His mother was with him.'

'And she made the phone calls,' said Harry. 'OK, finally the mist clears.' He gave a short sigh, and got up to sit down opposite Werth. 'So Lin is there when the ambulance comes in . . .' He glanced over at her. 'What were you doing outside, Lin? Never mind—don't answer that,' he added quickly. 'So Lin was there, and the ambulance comes in, and . . .'

'I don't know what happened. I know no more than you,' Werth said.

'I just touched him,' Lin murmured, through her hands.

'You touched him, and then what?' Harry asked.

'I don't know,' she said. 'The paramedic pulled me away, the nurse was complaining, the woman was screaming. They took the boy inside . . . I only touched him.'

'But why? Why touch him?' Harry asked.

'Because . . .' She looked up. 'Oh God, no one believes me. I can't make anyone understand.'

Harry took her hand in his. 'Tell me,' he said. 'I believe you.'

She smiled vaguely at him. 'I heard him. It was just a matter of connection.'

'Heard him say what?'

'Not *say* anything. I heard what was wrong with him. I heard him as the ambulance was coming up the drive, and when I touched him I knew what was wrong with him.' She looked over at Werth, who was frowning hard. 'I didn't set out to save his life or anything,' she said. 'I just touched him—just for a second.'

Harry enclosed her hand between both of his. 'And this connection? What connection is that?'

She looked at him. There was a protracted silence. 'Please take me home,' she said. 'If you don't take me home, I'll ring for a taxi. I have to get home. Something is wrong with Theo.'

'Wrong?' Harry repeated. 'What's wrong?'

She shook her head slowly from side to side. 'I don't know. I just feel it . . . I feel it.'

He tried to read her face, but failed. He could see only exhaustion there. 'You ought to speak to Kieran,' he said. 'Why don't you try ringing him again? He ought to come and fetch you.'

She gave him a crooked smile. 'He was here before,' she murmured, tears forming in her eyes. 'I've lost him.'

'Lost?' Harry echoed, his heart sinking. *What have you done now, Kieran?* he thought. *You stupid son-of-a-bitch.*

Werth stood up. 'Could I have a word with you outside?' he asked Harry. He opened the door and they went out into the corridor.

Werth began talking at once in a rapid, even monotone.

'I want you to disregard any hysteria on the injured boy's mother's part,' he said, 'because I'm quite convinced that's all it is. She sees a famous face, her son isn't as badly injured as she thought, she claims some irrational miracle . . .'

'The boy was all right? Not injured?'

'Yes, yes. He was injured, but evidently not as seriously as anyone thought.'

'And that happens often, does it? An ambulance crew gets it completely wrong?'

'No, I—'

'I thought you said that he had multiple injuries and had stopped breathing.'

'That was one report. There'll be an investigation. Since the papers got hold of this, you can imagine how hard it's been to get a decent version. There's a meeting this afternoon. But . . .' Werth put a hand to his head, his fist loosely clenched, a reflex of frustration. 'Look, that's actually irrelevant to Lin's health, what state the boy was in. It's completely clouding the main point.'

'Which is?'

'The hallucinations she's suffering.'

'Hallucinations?' Harry echoed, horrified.

'The conviction of extrasensory power, the sensation of knowing things that are impossible to know, are all symptoms of a physical disorder.'

'What . . . ?' Harry tried to get a grip of the situation. 'Look, the last I heard was she had meningitis or something.'

'There's no meningitis.'

'What is it, then?'

Werth took a long, deep breath. 'I feel quite sure that Mrs Gallagher does have a problem—perhaps even a problem that predated her illness, and which the recent inflammation has exacerbated.'

Harry felt his temper begin to fray. 'But what kind of bloody illness? You've lost me, doctor. I don't know what the hell's going on here.'

'An illness with a neurological origin. Perhaps temporal-lobe epilepsy. Perhaps something far rarer,' Werth told him. 'Perhaps an old injury to a specific lobe. It might only involve an extremely small area. I would like to do an MRI scan—we could even have a bleed in there. It's important to find out what it is we're dealing with.'

Harry looked back towards the door. 'She doesn't want to stay here.'

'No.'

'So what do you want me to do—hold her down while you tie her up?'

Werth gave a grimace. 'No. I was hoping you could persuade her to at least take the test.'

'Does it have to be done today?

'Well . . .'

'Because,' Harry said. 'I've known Lin for five years, and she's a good girl, she's a very intelligent person, she's creative, she's original, she's warm-hearted, she's all those things, but she can be as stubborn as hell. Especially where Theo is concerned.'

'I see.'

Each man exchanged a ghost of a smile.

'Can I bring her back?' Harry asked. 'Can I take her home to see her son—set her mind at rest? Bring her back tonight, or tomorrow?'

'If that's the best we can do. But I'd much rather keep her here under observation.'

'But you can't actually *keep* her here.'

'No, I can't. A patient can't be forced to accept treatment, but she'll have to sign a disclaimer.'

Harry put his hand on the door. 'You'd better find one for her to sign, then,' he said. 'Because wild horses, et cetera.'

They went back into the room, where Lin was already standing up.

'Well . . .' Harry began.

She walked over to him. 'Look, Harry,' she said. 'I'm going home now. You can take me there or not, but I'm going home.'

TWENTY-SIX

$\mathscr{F}$OUR YEARS AGO, Lin and Kieran had arrived at the hospital in Liverpool at seven in the evening.

Lin's mother had been put into a geriatric ward. It was a grim place, sectioned off from a corridor, where there was no natural light. As soon as they came out of the lift, they saw the eldest of Lin's brothers, standing at the top of the stairs. He was smoking a cigarette. To Kieran's surprise, he was a broad, fair-haired man: in build, colouring and features somewhat unlike Lin. It was only by her reaction that he knew who it must be. She took a sudden breath and stopped moving. The man turned.

Kieran walked forward with his hand extended. 'Kieran Gallagher,' he said.

The man glanced from Lin to Kieran, then shook his hand. 'Robert Harris. It was you who rang up?'

'Yes. We'd have been here earlier but there was a delay on the motorway. How is your mother?'

Robert Harris was now looking over Kieran's shoulder at Lin. 'She's down there,' he said. 'Second on the right.'

Lin looked away from him. She walked to the door of the ward and peered in. There must have been twenty beds in there, but the nearest was curtained off on two sides, a third side being the back wall, the fourth side adjoining the sister's office. Through the glass wall of this office, four people could be seen around the bed.

Robert had walked in behind Lin and Kieran. 'Only four at a time,' he warned. Kieran looked at the visitors and then back at Robert. 'My wife, and my brother and his wife, and their Mandy,' Robert explained.

At that moment, the curtain parted. A woman looked out, saw Lin, and turned to say something to those behind her. There was a pause, then the curtain was pulled closed. They saw all four people turn and look at them through the sister's office.

Then the woman came out again. She walked up to Lin and looked her over thoroughly from head to foot. 'You remember me, I suppose?' she asked.

'Yes, Sandra,' Lin said.

'I should think you do.' She looked pointedly at Lin's stomach. 'She's got eight nephews and nieces,' she said to Kieran. 'Did she tell you that?'

'Now, Sandra,' Robert said.

'One got married last year. Did she tell you *that*?'

'No,' Kieran told her.

'No, she wouldn't. Too busy at her college.'

Robert, her husband, took Sandra's arm, and tugged her gently to one side. 'Now she's come, let her go in,' he said. He dropped her arm, walked over to the curtains, and went inside. After a moment, the remaining three came out of the cubicle one by one, in a self-conscious line. The other man had a little more of Lin's colouring. His look was far more aggressive. At once Kieran saw the youngest son in him: the petulant little boy, aggrieved and spoiled. He was probably thirty but his expression was that of a child of eight, highly coloured and wide-eyed. Within a foot or so, Kieran could smell alcohol on him. His wife, small and blonde, gripped his arm like a vice. Behind them came a fair-haired girl of about thirteen, who smiled at Lin for a moment, then dropped her eyes.

'This one's pregnant,' Sandra said to them, pointing at Lin.

'For Jesus's sake,' Robert muttered. He gave Lin a push. 'Go on in.'

'Never come to see her mother in five years,' the younger brother hissed at Kieran, as they passed. 'And broke her heart before that.'

Kieran allowed Lin to go in first. After a moment he followed her. She was standing at her mother's bedside, her face utterly white. Then, in the next second, she pressed her hands to her eyes, and slumped down on the bedside chair. He stood at the foot of the bed, staring at her uncomprehendingly. Lin put both arms around her mother's neck.

Kieran stepped forward. He had been about to say it wouldn't be wise to disturb her mother by touching her. Then he realized that there were no machines, no supportive paraphernalia of care, around the bed. In fact, the locker and the walls were bare. The oxygen supply was strapped back to the wall. There were no flowers or cards on show. Lin's mother's hands lay crossed on the neatly stretched sheet, her head in the dead centre of the pillow. Kieran glimpsed a red-haired woman, a florid face with livid, circular patches on the jawline and around the nose and ears. The eyes were closed. A small gold crucifix hung on the neck, just above where Lin had laid her head.

At once, Kieran turned on his heel. Throwing aside the curtain, he looked out into the ward: two lines of bleak-looking beds, some of the occupants asleep, others mumbling to themselves. At the far end, three or four sat in chairs, staring down the ward towards him, their faces blank or preoccupied.

He strode over to the door. The family was standing in the corridor.

'Why didn't you say that she'd died?' he demanded.

Robert shrugged marginally.

'She could have come a week ago,' the younger brother retorted.

'We didn't know a week ago,' Kieran said. 'We only got the letter today. Lin's moved house.' Frustrated anger surged through him. 'We got married just today.'

Sandra gave a grim smile. 'Bit late, aren't you?' she said, her voice flattening out any possible inflection. 'Locking the stable door?'

'We didn't get married just for that reason,' Kieran replied. He looked away from her, back to the two brothers. 'You could have warned her before she went in there.'

'She died only half an hour ago,' Sandra said. She crossed her arms, vengeful fury written in every ounce of her. 'A miss is as good as a mile.'

The younger brother took a step towards him. 'D'you know how many times Mam asked for her?' he said, spittle fringing his thin lips. 'On and on, like a bloody record. She's maybe said three or four words all week. Lindsay, Lindsay—on and bloody on.'

'How could we have known?'

'She would, if she'd bothered to phone her ever. Or write to her.'

Kieran looked back to the curtained cubicle. He could hear Lin's muffled voice.

He went back inside to the bedside, and saw her sitting upright, holding her mother's hand to her face. Lin was sobbing softly and regularly, with a small, hitched, repetitive groan, pressing the cold hand to her face.

Kieran ran fingers through his hair, powerless.

Outside, in the ward, a querulous voice of old age called, high-pitched and plaintive, for the nurse.

TWENTY-SEVEN

$\mathscr{M}$ARK WERTH TRIED ONCE MORE to persuade Lin to stay, but she was having none of it. She stood by the window, holding onto the sill for support, smiling noncommittally at him while he talked. He paused, saw that nothing he was saying was having any effect, and turned back to Harry.

'I told you,' Harry said.

Werth looked again at Lin. 'You must come back in the morning. The scan is at ten o'clock, so you must be here by half past nine,' he said slowly, exactly as a primary-school teacher would explain some maths problem to an eight-year-old.

'I can still understand English,' Lin said.

Werth seemed to admit defeat. 'It's important,' he muttered. 'I haven't finished with you yet.'

Lin was lifting the strap of her handbag across her shoulder so that she could carry it across her body without having to hold it. Werth wrote out an appointment card and gave it to her. 'Half past nine,' he repeated.

They walked to the door, where Werth gave them directions to a service stairway. They took it at a snail's pace, Lin negotiating the steps with prolonged difficulty. They were like two drunks feeling their way in the dark.

Lin started to laugh. 'Oh, hell,' she said under her breath. 'Look at this. They're only stairs.'

Privately horrified at her fragility, Harry tightened his grip on her. 'I told you not to buy street gear,' he said. 'Too pure for you.'

They emerged into the midday sun. Immediately, Lin's hand shot across her eyes.

'Keep hold of my arm,' Harry told her.

'I can walk by myself,' Lin insisted.

'Don't be a silly bitch,' he said.

He had parked his car on the farthest side of the car park, away from the entrance, where even now there was a small knot of people. He did not doubt they had something to do with Lin, so he tried to hurry her.

'My five-mile feet,' she muttered.

'What?'

'Never mind.'

When they reached the car, he unlocked the door and lowered Lin in. She bumped down on the passenger seat with an exhalation of breath that was not quite a moan. He fastened her seatbelt before getting in. As he looked across at her, he doubted she would endure the hour to the Priory. Her face was lightly sheened with sweat, her colour greyish.

'Are you really all right?' he asked.

'What are those plants called,' she asked, 'that you get in a bulb at Christmas?'

'Hyacinths.'

'No, the ones with three big trumpets instead of flowers all on one stalk.'

'Amaryllis.'

'Yes . . .' She laughed briefly. 'I'm fine apart from having an amaryllis on top of my neck.' She mimed her head branching in different, flamboyant directions.

Harry put the car into gear and made for the exit.

As he waited at the junction, he saw a green TR6 pelting towards them. 'Ah, shit,' he muttered.

Lin was leaning back on the headrest, her eyes closed. 'What is it?'

'Shit,' Harry repeated.

The TR6 slewed to a stop right across the hospital entrance, not only blocking it but part of the main road behind. Ben Lazenby got out, dressed in his usual unobtrusive fashion with blue sweat pants, yellow sweater and a gilet emblazoned with a fitness-company logo that he could never possibly live up to. He held out both hands magisterially. Harry wound down his window.

'Is she in there?' Lazenby demanded, poking his head through the open window. 'Lin, sweetheart. Christ, you look like shit!'

'Funny, we were just talking about that,' Harry said.

'Did they discharge you?'

'She discharged herself,' Harry said.

'Hello, Ben,' Lin murmured.

'I want to talk to you,' Lazenby said.

'I wonder why,' Lin said.

'Where are you going?'

'Home,' Lin told him.

Ben shook his head, withdrawing it from the car to give full width to the gesture. 'No, no, you can't do that,' he said. 'Bastards're everywhere—I've just been there.'

Someone behind them blew their horn, and Harry looked in the rear mirror. It was an ambulance, the kind used to ferry outpatients back and forth.

'We can't stop here,' he said.

'Follow my car,' Ben said.

Lin leaned forward. 'I'm going home,' she repeated. 'Nowhere else. *Home*. I want to see Theo.'

'I've just been there, darling. No one home but a lot of vultures camped on your doorstep.'

'Oh, Christ,' Lin muttered, flopping back in the seat.

'Follow me just for ten minutes,' Ben said. 'Just ten minutes.'

In the front seat of Lazenby's car, Harry could see Marianne inspecting her nails, pushing the cuticles back with studied concentration. As Lazenby got in, she looked over at Harry and gave a theatrical, world-weary shrug.

Setting his face, Harry followed the TR6 out of town.

After five or six miles, Lazenby pulled in towards a pub at the roadside.

It stood on its own, on the slope of a long hill, a children's playground on one side, with a grotesque plastic tree in the centre. There was a blackboard propped by the door with nothing written on it. A dog lay in the nearest flowerbed, slumped in sleep as if it had been shot.

All four got out. Ben stood for a moment blowing his nose, passing the used tissues over to Marianne. After three or four of them, he appeared satisfied. Behind his back, she gave him a disgusted face. Ben then threw her the car keys, and she locked up.

Harry took Lin inside and they sat down by the window in a low-ceilinged, brownish room. They were the only customers.

As Ben ordered the drinks, Lin pinched Harry's arm. 'Send him away,' she murmured.

Ben walked back over to them, Marianne carrying the tray behind him.

'Lovely place,' Harry said.

'Chosen for its charm,' Lazenby commented, 'and popularity.'

As they drank, Ben gave Lin a lingering, examining look. She was shielding her face from the glare of sunlight through the window.

'What have you been up to?' he asked.

She shrugged.

'I hear you can raise the dead.'

'Oh, Ben . . .'

'No, no,' he insisted. 'I hear this at ten a.m. on my sickbed—from which I have risen, as you see.'

'Go away,' Lin muttered.

He ignored her. 'Raising the dead?'

'He wasn't dead.'

'Dying, then.'

'I don't know.'

'You don't know if he was dying?' Ben asked. 'I hear on the radio extraordinary things as I drive two hundred miles: mother claiming son cured by TV wife. Speak to me, Lin. What are you doing? Is this the great man's scheme?'

'It has nothing to do with him.'

'Good,' Ben said.

Lin looked up at him. If she was surprised, Harry was not. He had already guessed what was coming next.

'Is it real?' Ben asked. 'No flannel now. Cards down.'

There was silence around the table.

'How long have you had it?'

She said nothing.

'You don't just *get* these things.'

'You think she's psychic?' Harry asked.

They all looked at Lin. When she did not speak, Lazenby carried on.

'There was a man called Harry Edwards,' he said. 'Brilliant, brilliant man. Documented cases. Even cured cancer in the terminal stages. And other lifelong disabilities. As a young man, he worked on the Baghdad to Mosul railway. He started off healing smashed thumbs and abscessed feet. People came to him with lizards impaled on their hands to cure warts, their faces splattered with ink and donkey's blood to heal toothache. Funny beginning for a famous man. A corporal in Twenty-Sixth Cyclist Battalion.'

No one moved.

'But no funnier than being a scriptwriter—the wife of an academic and TV star. Less funny, in fact.'

'I didn't take you for a believer,' Harry said.

'Belief's nothing to do with it,' Ben snapped. 'Coverage—that's to do with it.'

Lin lifted the glass to her lips and took a sip of the mineral water.

'How long have you had it, Lin?' Ben asked. 'I'm serious now. This iron is hot—you strike with it. You understand?'

She still said nothing.

Lazenby turned to Harry. 'You're going to let me in on this thing?' he said.

'There is no thing,' Harry told him.

Ben looked up at the ceiling, as if for help.

'There is no thing,' Harry insisted.

'But there's going to be, right?' Ben said. 'Some time today? I can't see you letting it slip longer than today. You might be Lin's friend but you are also a businessman. A businessman first, if I've got you right—and I think I have.' He leaned forward over the table, looked hard at Lin who was staring down at the floor, and said, 'First come, first served.'

'Look—' said Harry.

'I'm not a healer,' Lin said.

'You are, according to this woman. Have you heard her?'

'I just . . . connected something . . .'

'What?' Ben demanded.

'She keeps talking about connections,' Harry said.

'There was a broken line,' Lin murmured.

Ben looked at Harry.

'Can you *see* this thing?' he then asked her.

She frowned. 'Yes.'

'See it as an actual thing?'

'Yes.'

'Like this glass—this table?'

'Yes.'

'You see a line . . .'

'A kind of current,' Lin said. She hadn't yet met Lazenby's eyes. Her finger traced a dry stain on the wood in front of her. 'I can see an interruption to this current. I can see . . .' She looked up abruptly, past Ben's shoulder, and stopped speaking.

'Are you seeing it now?' he asked.

Marianne leaned forward too, watching Lin's face intently. Irritated at her sudden silence, Ben reached forward and gripped Lin's hand. All at once she smiled broadly.

'What is it?' he said.

Lin started to laugh. 'Your mind's full of food,' she said.

His eyes widened.

'Hungry, hungry, hungry,' she said.

He took his hand away, and her gaze flickered back to the centre of the room.

'Have you always had it?' he repeated.

'Not always.'

'But something before this spell in hospital?'

She looked back at him. 'Not really.'

'Holy shit,' Harry said.

'What kind of thing?' Lazenby asked.

'Not much. Little things. Knowing when people would call. Knowing about sites that Kieran chose.'

'How so?'

'Just a feeling—then confirming it with research.'

'You saw the past?'

'No, no. Just a feeling.'

'*Déjà vu?*'

'Yes, I suppose like that.'

'You never said,' Harry objected.

'No, I never did,' Lin murmured. 'Didn't want to sound stupid.'

'But this is different?' Lazenby asked.

'Yes, this is very different.'

'What else, besides the current?'

'People.'

'Ghosts? Dead people?' Lazenby was almost apoplectic in his excitement.

She smiled. 'Nobody's really dead,' she said. 'They stand around wondering why no one speaks to them. They walk about everywhere . . .'

She raised a hand to her head, rubbing her temple.

Ben tugged at Harry's elbow, getting both of them to their feet. They walked six or seven feet away from the table, where they began a whispered conversation.

'Where's Kieran?'

'I don't know,' Harry said, 'if he's not at home.'

'What's the situation with them?'

'I don't know.'

'For Christ's sake!'

'My guess would be at Ruth's.'

'You see all this?' Ben asked, waving his hand backwards, in Lin's direction. 'This is money you're seeing here.'

'Lin isn't well. This isn't the time.'

'Don't give me that. She's under contract to you.'

'No personal appearances.'

'Well, you'd better rewrite it. And if he's going to desert the series, I want her under seal for *The House*.'

'She has to go back for other tests tomorrow. An MRI scan.'

'Where are you taking her now?'

'Ruth's, I suppose. She wants to see her son.'

'Right . . .' Ben glanced back at Lin. Her eyes were closed, her posture upright. 'If she can do all they say, there's gold in them hills, boy. You know it and so do I. We do film—not live. Mediums fall on their arses live. We do a set of six: *The House* plus. You see it? You see it?'

'Yes,' Harry said.

Ben grinned. 'She gets the vibes—this current—from the places, and she fills in the details . . .'

'Kieran is contracted to the *name* of the programme.'

'Uncontract him. He can't survive without her writing it for him. You know what he did last year—don't tell me he didn't, because I know—he went to the Fact Factory with a proposal for some ditch-water dirge about Roman digs. He wants the funding and the filming for digging up half of Somerset . . . so let him have it. He's negotiating for an American tour, too. Sell his face to the Factory, give him his hole in the ground, let him bury himself. Lin's the talent here.'

'Kieran has a good following.'

'He's got a good face on a boring brain.'

'His books sell.'

Lazenby smiled. 'I bet hers sell better, and so do you. You can keep them both if you act quick enough.'

Harry glanced out of the window at the parched garden. He resented being told his own business, but Lazenby was right. He had already considered the book publication prospects for Lin—but he was not ready to drop Kieran. 'I want to retain them as a team,' he said.

'When they're pulling in different directions?' Ben snorted. 'If he's with Ruth now, you can forget that team. So build them up as separate items. I'm interested in Lin. I've got other people who like Lin. You can do what you like with him.'

Harry did not allow his expression to falter. He knew better than to cross Lazenby, who had his own production company as well as freelancing himself out to others. And he was very good at what he did. Harry looked over at Lin.

'There's nothing really wrong with her,' Ben said.

'Hark the physician.'

'The only thing wrong with Lin is being shackled to that choirboy for too long,' Lazenby said. 'Trust me, I know women. I could have told you this a year ago. All that trouble then was her misery at being Mr Gallagher's ventriloquist.' As Harry was about to interrupt him, Lazenby put up his hand. 'She was an A student at college: straight As—a genius. Did you know that? Until him.'

'I knew that,' Harry said.

'If they split, it's all to the good. You can watch her *go* now—watch her go stratospheric.' Harry said nothing, and Lazenby put an arm around his shoulder. 'Just count me along.'

They began to walk back to the table. 'She doesn't even have to perform miracles of her own,' he added conspiratorially. 'With a headstart like this, you just get her fronting something, you make a few suggestions, sketch a few things in. That's all half of these mystics do anyway. D'you know there's a million dollars on offer in the USA for anyone who can prove contact with the dead? And no one's claimed it yet. But everybody wants to hear about people trying. It's a sick thing. It's a big, sick, populist thing, but bloody good television.'

They were back at the table where Lin was now looking up at Lazenby with a muted, preoccupied expression. Ben leaned down and patted her hand.

As he did so, Lin suddenly grabbed his wrist, and moved her face so that she was within an inch of his ear.

'I see you in pink, Ben,' she whispered, 'playing a harp.'

He stared at her, momentarily aghast.

'Just joking,' she told him.

TWENTY-EIGHT

$\mathscr{R}$UTH CALLED IN AT THE SURGERY AT LUNCHTIME. As she walked down the corridor towards Reception, she could see a figure through the open doors, standing back in the empty centre of the room, looking towards her. She could hear the girls on Reception talking to him, their voices raised in perplexed, polite questions.

'Do you have an appointment at all?'

'How can we help you?'

It was Caroline's son, Martin Devlin.

'Hello,' Ruth said, as she entered the room. 'Are you waiting for me?'

'Yes.'

Ruth studied him carefully. His face had a pinched, exhausted look but he was clean and tidy—very clean, very tidy, as though he had made an effort. He was also very tense, his shoulders square and raised, his mouth set. He was tall but this seemed to underline his youth more than anything, as if he were still a gangly fourteen-year-old.

'What can I help you with?'

'I want to speak to you,' he said. His colour was high.

'OK,' she said. 'Come into my room.'

They walked back along the passage. As Ruth showed him in the door, she glanced at her watch.

'I know what you did,' he said, ignoring her indication of a chair.

'I'm sorry?'

'I know what you did to Mum.'

'I don't understand.'

'When she had the attack,' he said. She saw both his fists were clenched.

'Won't you sit down? Let's talk this through.'

He made a disgusted sound that was almost a laugh. 'Talk?' he said. 'That solves everything.' He looked at the floor, standing motionless. 'That's what *she* says.' It was delivered in a low, even tone that prickled the hairs at the back of Ruth's neck. Under her desk was a panic button that she had never needed to use and which she had objected to even being installed, but she was suddenly acutely aware of it now.

'Look . . .' she said.

He stepped towards her. 'You gave her anistreplase,' he said.

'What?'

'I heard it: anistreplase. And the ambulance men told me.'

'It's routinely given.'

'But you had nothing to check her.'

'Sorry?'

'No machine with you. No *machine*.'

'You mean an ECG?'

'Yes.'

She studied him, wondering where he had learned all this, and why. 'Sit down,' she said, 'please.' To her relief he did so, reluctantly, staring at the arm of her chair instead of into her face.

'Are you feeling better?' she asked.

His head rocked upwards. 'What?'

'Than the other night?'

She had actually meant it as a genuine question, but could see now that it held an unfortunate subtext.

'What's that to do with it?'

'Nothing,' Ruth said. 'How is your mother?'

'Don't you know?'

'Not as of this morning. Have you been to see her?'

'Where do you think I've been?'

The accusatory note was so adolescent that Ruth couldn't help but smile. It was her second mistake.

'Don't you grin at me . . .' Martin said.

'Martin, I'm not grinning at all.'

'Sit there and grin at me—'

'I am *not* grinning.'

'She's in intensive care,' he said. 'She kept arresting . . .'

'I know. I'm sorry.' They had waited together in the hospital at first; Ruth had left him after Caroline was transferred to ITU, once Martin had phoned his uncle and she could be sure that he would not be alone.

'She's got brain damage.'

Ruth had expected this, and said nothing.

'It's your fault,' he said.

'I beg your pardon?'

His gaze was back to the chair, the floor, the desk—anywhere but her face. 'The stupid thing is,' he muttered, 'that she thought the sun shone out of you. *She's a very good doctor.* When Lin Gallagher was always round last year, I got that morning, noon and night. She would always defend you. She'd say what a good doctor you were.'

Ruth was surprised to hear that Caroline had been visited by Lin at her own home, but it hardly shocked her. Lin had been very dependent on her therapist for several months, as was often the way. Ruth had thought of Caroline uncharitably since then, as being the catalyst in bringing the *old* Lin back: that bright, waywardly brilliant, smiling girl. Ruth hated her for it. She didn't want the old Lin back—the Lin that had enchanted Kieran.

Ruth had never known quite what to make of Caroline Devlin. Physically she looked the archetypal counsellor: sandalled feet in summer, wispy Indian skirt, unkempt old-fashioned hair; the duffel coat in winter, the ubiquitous earrings, the long, thin-fingered hands, the soft persistent voice. Ruth had once witnessed her giving a presentation to local GPs, and Caroline knew her stuff. She was undeniably well trained, and also very stubborn, very involved, highly motivated—

something of a perfectionist, driving herself into the ground, taking on far too much.

Ruth could not quite put her finger on her irritation with Caroline. It was something more than just her dislike of the woman's career or her appearance. It was rooted somewhere in last year, when Ruth heard secondhand how Lin felt. She was convinced that Caroline was actively encouraging Lin's childish character traits, as if they were some sort of affirmation instead of the arrant wilfulness of adolescence. Caroline had once met Ruth in the surgery and said, smiling, 'What a lovely girl Lin is.' Her face had then dropped, after realizing Ruth's relationship to her. They had passed on, each with their own reaction.

With this thought of adolescence, her gaze reverted to Martin Devlin.

'And she hated doctors,' Martin was saying. 'That's why she never came about this heart thing.' His hands were clenched so tightly in his lap that the knuckles were now completely white.

'Her ECG here at the surgery was clear,' Ruth said. She was hoping to change the subject a little. 'Her blood cholesterol was high, but there was no family history . . .'

'You should have looked after her,' Martin said.

'I booked her with the specialist,' Ruth said. 'Did she tell you that?'

'That's not what I mean,' he said. 'I'm talking about the other night. You gave her this drug, and I've found out you're not supposed to—not if you don't have something to check with.'

'You called me out when I wasn't on call, Martin.'

'Yeah, that was *her* mistake. Because she trusted you—didn't want anybody else. She was in a temper, she threw things, she screamed at me, and then . . . then she . . .' He screwed his eyes shut. 'Not being on call is nothing to do with it.'

'I'm sorry to correct you, but it's everything to do with it,' Ruth replied quietly. 'Because I wasn't on call, I had no equipment. The portable ECG I would normally carry was in the surgery.'

'Why bloody come, then!'

She smiled: an unconscious reaction because the question was so absurd. 'Because Caroline insisted that I come. Because it was plainly an emergency. Because you had called no one else. Because she was an acquaintance.'

He leaned towards her, fury etched in his face. 'You shouldn't have given that drug when you had no machine. I've asked, so I know about it. You don't give that drug unless you've got the machine to monitor her.'

'Or unless she's about to be admitted to hospital—which was the case.'

'When you gave her that stuff, she wasn't, though, was she? You hadn't called an ambulance.'

'I . . .'

'Had you? *Had* you!'

She looked into his eyes. This was the boy who was so drunk he couldn't register the severity of his mother's attack.

'Let me ask the girls to get us some tea,' she said.

Martin got abruptly to his feet. He stared down at her for a moment, then walked to the window and looked down on the street. 'I've been there all night. Two nights,' he murmured, as though to himself. 'I've been watching her for two nights.'

'Martin,' Ruth said, 'I asked you to call an ambulance when you phoned me at home. By the time I reached you, it still hadn't been called. I then ensured that it was called.'

He said nothing.

'Martin?'

He spoke with his back still turned. 'She was dying, and you told me to ring my own ambulance.'

'That's right. Because by then I was trying to resuscitate her.'

'Look good in a paper, wouldn't it? "Dying woman told, Get your own ambulance".'

'That isn't fair,' Ruth said.

'No,' he retorted. 'She's only fifty-two!'

Ruth's felt her temper rise. 'I think you'd better go,' she said.

The boy rounded on her. 'My time up, is it?'

'I think you'd maybe like to discuss this when you're more in control of yourself.'

He took a sharp breath. 'In control!' he yelled. 'In *control!*'

'I appreciate that you feel—'

'No,' he said, 'you don't know how I feel. You've got no feelings. You don't know the first bloody thing about it.'

'How dare you,' she said.

'No feelings. You're a monster. She's fifty-two, and she'd been to see you, and you'd told her there was nothing wrong with her. You brushed her off.'

'I'd told her nothing of the kind. I took blood tests. I referred her to the consultant. In fact the appointment came through yesterday.' The circularity of the argument was beginning to infuriate her.

He strode over to her and pointed a finger in her face. 'You told her there was nothing wrong with her, you gave her a drug you're not supposed to use, you told us to ring our own ambulance. You're fucking incompetent.'

'Get out,' she said.

'I bloody won't.'

A pulse was pounding behind her eyes. She couldn't bear him to stand in her room a moment longer. Really all she wanted to think about was Kieran. Lin and Kieran. Theo. Getting Lin away from Kieran. Holding on to Theo—the only link that kept Kieran away from her. These pieces of the whole insane jigsaw had been rattling in her head since she had kissed Kieran that morning, and the sensation of his lips was still with her, making the jigsaw puzzle dance and flex and distort in her mind's eye. She was now close, very close, to taking him.

'I haven't time for your reactions just now,' she said.

Mistake. Mistake.

'I'll show you fucking reaction,' he said, 'you supercilious bitch.'

He whirled around. Behind Ruth's chair and desk was a long shelf like a kitchen worktop, with a small sink in it. Above it were more shelves containing her reference books, a couple of houseplants, reps' boxes, sterile packs. He took a pace towards it and, with one hand, swiped the nearest shelf clean. Books and boxes and papers showered down.

The door opened. One of Ruth's partners, Philip Godber, stood on the threshold. He was in his sixties and hardly a match for a teenage boy. Glancing at the chaos, he turned and shouted down the corridor, 'Liz! Get the police!'

'No,' Ruth said. 'It's OK.'

Martin turned round and, with one sudden movement, grabbed her, shoving her backwards until she was up against the wall. One hand was on her shoulder, the other on her throat.

'You listen to me,' he muttered. His mouth was only an inch from hers. 'I'm going to sue you. I'm going to get you struck off, you understand?'

Philip Godber was trying, and failing, to pull the younger man off.

'You stand there,' Martin continued, 'like God almighty, smirking at me . . . You've got no feelings. Mum always said so. She told me, "She's a good doctor, but she's had a sympathy by-pass." She said that, and she was bloody right. You're going to lose your job, you hear me?'

Godber finally succeeded in tugging Martin free. Putting his arm across him, he tried to manoeuvre him out of the door.

'You're going to feel this,' Martin shouted, as he was pulled into the corridor. 'I'm going to make sure, personally! You hear me? This time you're going to *feel* it!'

TWENTY-NINE

$\mathscr{H}$ARRY STOPPED THE CAR FOR PETROL HALFWAY, at a garage high up on the downland in the middle of nowhere.

As he filled the tank, Lin walked to the edge of the forecourt. She leaned on a wooden fence and looked down at the huge scooped field below. The circular line of the hill ran like a vast arm for a quarter of a mile, dotted with scrub hawthorn that could resist the winter winds. Far below, trees appeared as a line of green. Sheep grazed the hill, a huge flock of more than two hundred, but spread out as little discoloured white dots on the landscape. A warm, sweet wind blew off the valley and washed the hilltop like a wave.

Lin closed her eyes.

She had stopped even questioning what was happening to her now. She felt so unbearably tired. As she let go of logic, reason, resistance, the shades of the world altered at will. The voices enclosed her at times, left her alone at other times, but were more claustrophobic than ever when they came. They no longer encircled her but entered her, filling her mind with thoughts of sublime strangeness, a sensation of euphoria, a feeling of being grounded in the roots of life.

Werth had told her that epileptics sometimes felt that they possessed the key to the universe. But she was sure that she was not epileptic. This was not a fleeting sensation; this was conviction that she was part of everything that breathed, and that everything that breathed was part of her. Even blank space rippled with a vibrant code.

The people came to her less insistently now. The crowds had receded, as if marshalled into line by some invisible steward. She saw faint outlines, passing imprints, in certain spaces and rooms: impressions only—spectators who wanted to be noticed or known but who held themselves back. Sometimes their feelings struck her with terrible poignancy. Some of them had accepted their sudden dislocation from life, and turned their yearning attention on those they wanted to reach, but only for seconds. But their agony seemed far away. They were like background music, or wind on a winter night shut out behind glass.

She ought to have felt afraid, but she was not. This had none of the disjointedness, the sense of out-of-place or delusion of a nightmare. She had fallen *into* place, onto the right track. Those that appeared now came specifically for her, with pictures for her. She had begun to understand that she was supposed to listen to them—and only them—and gently press the others to one side.

Of course there were still exceptions. She couldn't control them all, or her response to them. For some reason that was too distant, too peripheral to grasp, Caroline Devlin—and Caroline's kindliness and calm, and her cool, low voice—kept coming into her mind. And then there had been that man as they drove here.

As they had drawn up to traffic lights in a little village—no more than a string of houses, a pub and a tiny shop huddled around a crossroads—she had seen a man running down the side lane to the left of the moving car.

The main road intersected what was no more than a farm road that ran from left to right. She could see him running along, arms pumping, head down.

She had the impression that there was someone or something ahead of him, which he was chasing. As he ran clear of the hedge at the side of the road, the answer became obvious. A dog, a small liver-and-white terrier, hurled itself forward along the road. It looked to be barking, but she heard no sound. The man continued to run heedlessly after it. He was wearing dark breeches, a white collarless shirt. He was no more than thirty. And, as he ran forward into the centre of the main road, he suddenly turned his head.

She saw his expression freeze. Shock and horror distorted his features. In the next split second she felt, rather than saw, a tremendous impact throw him out of the road. She felt him fixed mid-air. Everything around him shuddered. She felt the joints of the day—the hour, the minute of his death—flex.

It was locked to the place. *He* had gone, but the image remained chained to that location. And she picked it up like a radio picking up a dozen transmissions: the road where two tracks had crossed for a thousand years. The echoes of old rains. The man hit by a vehicle whose shape and sound had since been erased. Animals and men and machines constantly re-crossing that point. The faint smudged broadcast of a house that had once stood there.

'What is it?' Harry had asked.

She had blinked. The echoes smoothed back to the traffic lights, the village street.

'Nothing,' she had told him.

She glanced back now and saw Harry wiping the windscreen of the car. If she tried hard, she would be able to hear the vibrations that pressed up to him as neatly and smoothly as a second skin. But she chose not to. Something else scratched at her sight, imposing fragments even on the outline of Harry on the black tarmac forecourt of the garage, the open doors of the little shop with its lazily swinging ice-cream sign.

She turned back to her view of the hill, as she waited.

There were no longer any trees. No hill, no road.

She stood at a window, early in the evening, and looked out at a city street. Opposite her were tall, redbrick Edwardian houses, each with three cream-painted front steps and black iron railings. There was a strip of garden where the roses were dusty.

She had got the number of the place from an ad in a magazine. Irma had given it to her, and encouraged her. Lin had rung the number. She had gone for a first interview. She had seen a doctor: a small

Indian man who had seemed both bored and reproving. The angle of his arms, the spread fingers of his hands, the upright tilt of his head, told her that their business was a necessity but was not of interest to him.

The abortion cost £300, a huge sum of money. Half of it she had already earned at the Hunting Dog; half of it came from Michael. She would have liked not to take anything at all from Michael, but she had no choice. He had given it to her in an envelope, making a big show of patting her hand and ensuring that she put it safely into her handbag. He had told her not to lose it.

The thing that, irrationally, most upset her was that Michael had always claimed he had no money. He lived in a large house with his mother, and he drove a two-year-old car, and he had been on holiday to Spain—while Lin had never been out of the country—but he always claimed that his mother kept him short.

Now, when the time came, he could lay his hands easily on a hundred and fifty pounds—and would have given her the lot. He went to the station and bought her a return ticket to Manchester. A *first-class* ticket. She loathed him more for buying first-class than she could ever say. The ticket collector checked it twice, gazing at her as if she had stolen it. She had sat on that train hating Michael to the roots of her soul.

She had worn a cream jacket that day, short and woolly, the kind of thing she didn't like but had bought from the market because it was cheap and looked "fun", as if she were going on a jaunt or on holiday. She sat all the way there in the silly jacket, pulling at its bulky sleeves, trying to make it longer than it was. When she got off at Manchester, she felt outrageously visible in it; felt that everyone must be looking. She carried a little red-and-white case that, a century before, she had used to carry her only doll around when she was very small. It had held precious possessions, the little rag-faced doll and the doll's over-washed clothes. She had picked it up from the seat and felt it accuse her with the whole innocent force of her childhood.

And now it had the address of the place in it. And three hundred pounds, her pyjamas, her slippers, and a pack of sanitary towels.

When she got to the clinic, she had to wait for a while in a reception area. Five other girls were there, none of them over twenty, and all of them alone. She didn't catch their eyes. All *their* little cases were pushed under their chairs.

She was seen by the surgeon in a panelled consulting room. He had a very fine walnut desk, which she looked at far more than she looked at him. She noticed, from the ring on his hand, that he was married, and there was a photo on his desk of a woman sitting with three children. She had studied those children as he wrote her details in a file.

'How many weeks are you?'

'Twelve.'

'How old are you?'

'Eighteen.'

'Do you live at home?'

'No, in a bed-and-breakfast.'

He had raised an eyebrow. 'Why is that?'

She had paused, ashamed for no good reason. 'My mother threw me out.'

'Threw you out? Because of this?'

'She said I had disgraced her.'

And she had thought of its ironic idiocy, the fury of her mother and brothers, the talk of shame.

'What have I done that you didn't do?' she had demanded. Her mother had slapped her face. 'It was the only time,' Lin protested. 'He raped me . . .'

'You were in his car,' her mother said.

Oh God, the empty street. Running to Irma in her little bedsit. Going to Social Services.

On the doorstep, her brother had said to her, 'This house has been dirty since you came into it.'

Block it out.

Paint it away.

Make the space black.

The surgeon in the clinic asked her to undress. As she went behind the screen, he said, 'Is this your first pregnancy?'

She had sat there frozen, naked from the waist down, a blanket tightly wrapped around her, uncomfortably high up from the ground on a leather couch spread with green paper. She had gazed at the panelling, at the carpeted floor.

'Is this your first pregnancy?' he had repeated.

He had come around the corner of the screen, having taken off his jacket. He was now wearing a pair of surgical gloves. She dare not look at his face, so she looked at the wood panel alongside her, whose edges were caked with polish.

'Would you lie back and relax,' he said.

She couldn't move. She hugged the blanket tighter.

'You must lie back so that I can examine you,' he said.

She began to cry, but she didn't make a sound. She was trying to stay rigid so that her very solidity and stillness would dry the tears up, but they came shamefully pouring down. She stuffed the blanket under her knees, gripped it bunched up in one fist, and wiped her face with the other.

'Don't you want me to examine you?' he asked.

Her mouth wouldn't work without shaking. When she tried to speak, she felt her lips make an ugly shape. The surgeon leaned against the wall, looking weary.

'Would you like to go home?' he said.

'No,' she told him.

'Would you like to think about this a little more?'

'No,' she said.

'You want me to do this operation?'

'Yes.'

'Then, my dear, I must examine you.'

She lay down. He took the blanket away.

'Pull your legs up, and then let your knees fall apart.'

She went away to another place. She looked at the panel, and tried to think whether it had been carved or made by a machine. She tried to think how old it was, how old the house was. He finished, turned away and stripped off the gloves, throwing them into a bin. While she got dressed, he sat at his desk. As she came out from behind the curtain, he gave her a piece of paper and told her to see the nurse outside.

As she had waited for the operation in the private room they had given her, she looked out at the dusty roses and the Edwardian houses.

There was nothing left to cry about, she thought. It was the sensible thing. She was brave to do it on her own. And everything would go back to being how it was before. She would be at university in six weeks, after the summer break. No one would ever know.

She had sat on the bed, her hands pressed flat to her stomach. It was her child. Her first child.

And it would be dead in less than an hour.

A hand settled softly now on her arm.

Lin looked up.

'What is it?' Harry asked. 'What's the matter?'

She gazed at him—back from the clinic bed, from the tall red houses beyond the window, from the sense of oncoming dread.

Looking intently at her, Harry fished a handkerchief from his pocket.

'Use this,' he said. 'It's all right, it's clean.'

She smiled, and wiped her face.

'Why don't you tell me?' he asked. 'I might be able to help.'

She shook her head, gave him back his handkerchief, and walked over to the car.

THIRTY

*R*UTH GOT BACK TO HER FLAT AT TWO O'CLOCK.

As she walked up the stairs, she found Kieran already waiting for her on the landing, and her heart leapt. Theo was sitting on the floor.

'What are you doing here?' she asked, smiling.

'Have you heard?' he asked. 'It's on the news—the bloody regional news!'

'What is?' The temptation to press herself into his arms was intense, but his attention was fixed elsewhere. He was seething with rage, and turned abruptly away from her, as she put her key in the lock and opened the door. They went in and Kieran watched her as she put her bag down.

He lowered his voice. 'I've had to bring Theo here,' he said. 'There are press people all over at the Priory. They were banging on the door, even on the windows. They frightened him to death.'

'I'll give you my spare set of keys,' Ruth said.

In the sitting room she sat down with a thump on the nearest couch. Kieran took Theo into the kitchen for a glass of water. A couple of minutes later, Kieran reappeared.

'What's he doing?' Ruth asked.

'Eating.' It sounded like an aside, an irrelevance to him. 'Was there anything on the radio?'

'I haven't been listening to it.'

He paced to and fro. 'What's this going to do to me?' he asked. 'She's making me a laughing stock.'

Ruth eyed him patiently. 'Kieran, would you like to pour me a drink.'

He looked at her. 'What?'

'A drink. A drink?'

'What sort of drink?'

'A vodka.'

'What for?'

She got up, walked to the cabinet, and fetched it for herself.

'What's the matter?' he asked.

'I'm being sued for malpractice,' she said.

'What?'

She sat down. 'It's just a boy. A boy who refused to call an ambulance. And he claims it's my fault,' she said.

'And he can sue you for that?'

She waved her free hand. 'Oh, it won't get that far,' she said. 'It's just the bloody inconvenience of it all.' The words belied her ragged tone.

'He must be mad.'

'He *is* mad—mad at himself. Looking for someone to blame, that's the problem.' She slammed the glass down, and cursed. 'They never fail to amaze me, the complete irrationality.' She looked up, past Kieran, to the doorway, and suddenly made a visible effort to smooth away her grimace. 'Hello, Theo,' she said, 'how are you?'

The boy walked past them, to the window.

'Go and finish your biscuit in the kitchen,' Kieran said. 'I want to talk to Ruth.'

'I finished,' Theo said. 'I want to go home.'

Kieran took his hand. 'Sit down and watch *Sesame Street.*'

Reluctantly, Theo sat where he was put, his eyes still straying to the window even when the set was switched on.

Kieran went into the kitchen. As Ruth followed, he asked, 'Have you had lunch?'

'No,' she said. 'I'm not hungry. What was on the television?'

He closed the door on Theo so that he wouldn't hear.

'Some woman who claims Lin healed her son.'

Ruth shook her head. 'What on earth is the hospital thinking of?'

'Lin's not in hospital,' Kieran said. 'I just phoned Werth, she discharged herself. Harry's with her.'

'Harry? Where is she now?'

'Coming to see me here.'

Ruth looked at him for a long moment. 'Coming for Theo?'

'Maybe she just wants to see him.' His hand rested on the rim of the coffee mug, into which he had been spooning sugar. 'It's a bloody nuisance. I need to see Caldwell this afternoon. I have an appointment.' He looked up at her. 'You'll have to take Theo somewhere.'

'What do you mean?' she asked. 'I'm on call today.'

'Take him with you.'

'You can't be serious.'

The doorbell rang.

They looked at each other; then heard Theo running for the door. He flung it open.

As they came out of the kitchen, they saw Lin leaning down to scoop Theo up in her arms. Harry stood behind her, in the corridor. Lin walked forward into the sitting room, carrying Theo muffled in her embrace, the boy's head pressed hard into her shoulder. She kissed his downturned head, and sat down on the couch, where both stared delighted into each other's faces.

'Look at you,' Lin murmured. 'All crumbs.'

'I got chocolate doughnut for breakfast.'

'Did you? Wow! What else?'

'Orange squash in a flower cup.'

'He wouldn't eat anything else,' Kieran said from the doorway. He turned back and stared accusingly at Harry. 'What's going on?'

'Lin wanted to see Theo. With all the fuss going on at the hospital, Werth accepted her discharge providing she came back in the morning.'

Ruth had also moved into the sitting room. She smiled at Lin, though Lin didn't raise her eyes. Ruth sat down opposite her.

'How are you feeling?' she asked.

'I'm fine,' Lin said.

'Are you really?'

'Yes.'

'No headache?'

'She has a scan in the morning,' Harry said.

'What kind of scan?'

'MRI.'

'What is that for?' asked Ruth in a cool voice.

There was a silence.

'Would you like a cup of tea?' she said when it was obvious there would be no reply.

'No,' Lin told her. She whispered something in Theo's ear and, grinning, he wriggled down from her lap and ran out of the room. 'We're leaving,' she said.

'Just a minute,' Kieran said.

'Where are you going?' Ruth asked.

For the first time, Lin looked her in the face. 'Home, to the Priory. Unless, of course, you've changed the locks.'

'Don't start being rude,' Kieran said.

Lin looked up at him properly, for the first time too.

'We don't want an argument,' Ruth countered.

'Good,' Lin said. She was still staring at Kieran. 'Will you take us home?'

'She wants to go home,' Ruth mimicked.

Lin glared at her. 'I'm talking to my husband,' she said. She looked back at Kieran. 'What are you doing here?'

'I've nowhere else to go,' he countered, furious. 'Your little display has seen to that.'

'It wasn't a display.'

He was standing within three feet of her, looking down at her, exasperation written over his face. 'I don't understand what's going on with you,' he said. 'First you disappear from home. Then you're sick. Then you discharge yourself. Now this!'

'You wouldn't bring Theo to see me. You forced me to discharge myself,' Lin said. She was shaking and very pale. 'I wanted to see him. That's all I want.'

'You're crazy,' he said.

There was an absolute silence in the room. Lin stood up.

'I'm sorry,' he said. 'I didn't mean that.'

She tried to brush past him.

'I *am* sorry, darling,' he said, catching at her arm.

She flinched from his touch.

'What is it?' he said.

'Don't touch me,' she said.

'Lin . . .'

'I mean it. Please don't touch me.'

They looked at each other. Lin began to cry.

'Lin, darling . . .'

'No,' she whispered. 'No lies. Nothing.'

'What?'

She squeezed her eyes shut. 'I know how you feel,' she whispered. 'I've known it since the other evening at the hospital.'

'Feel about what?'

'Me.' She opened her eyes.

He stared at her. 'I love you,' he protested.

The tears began to fall. 'I've been alone all my life,' she said. 'And nothing has changed. Nothing until Theo.' She wiped her face.

'What are you talking about?'

She looked down at his hand still on her arm. 'I'm talking about you wanting Ruth *and* me, and not loving either of us,' she said softly. A peculiar vibration of tension filled the room. Still staring at his hand, she continued, 'When you touch me, I can feel your thoughts.' She finally raised her eyes to his face. 'You never loved me at all. Not what I would call love,' she said. 'You only love yourself—not even Theo. That's the pity of it . . . the pity of it.'

She began to cry in earnest. He tried to take her in his arms, but she pushed him away. He looked around himself, first at Harry, then at Ruth.

Theo came running back into the room, dragging his coat.

Lin held out her hand to him.

'Hold on a second,' Kieran said. 'You can't just leave like this.' He walked forward, snatching Theo's hand from the direction of Lin, and placing himself between her and the boy. 'You have to go back into hospital tomorrow,' he said. 'What will happen to Theo?'

'He can come with me.'

Ruth made a derisive noise. 'Not into an MRI scanner.'

'Someone will look after him,' Lin said, panic now rapidly climbing into her voice.

'Why not his father, then?' Ruth asked.

'You're not well,' Kieran said.

'I'm all right,' Lin told him.

'No, no,' Ruth murmured.

Lin rounded on her. 'Look,' she said, 'you keep out of this. This is nothing to do with you. This is to do with his father and me.'

'This is to do with a child's welfare,' Ruth countered.

'I'm the one who'll decide that.'

'Are you?'

Lin looked from Ruth to Kieran and back again. 'What do you mean?'

'Sit down,' Kieran said. 'Let's just talk about this for a while.'

Lin resisted his arm, still on hers. 'What's she talking about?'

'Kieran and I will look after Theo,' Ruth said. 'Until you're better.'

'Oh, no,' Lin retorted. 'Oh, no, you won't. You won't!'

'I don't think this is helping the situation,' Harry intervened. Everyone ignored him.

Lin tried to get past Kieran. 'Theo!' she said. 'Come to Mummy.'

'Sit down,' Kieran said firmly.

Lin pushed him in the chest. 'Get out of my way.'

'Lin . . .' Harry interjected.

'Theo!' Lin shouted. The boy tried to extricate himself from Kieran's grasp.

'This won't work,' Kieran said.

'Don't tell me what works and what doesn't,' Lin retorted.

'No one wants to hurt you,' he said.

Lin stopped short. 'Hurt me?' she echoed.

Ruth walked quickly over to Harry, behind Lin's back. 'What is the MRI for?' she demanded.

'I don't know.'

Ruth turned to Kieran. 'Are you going with Lin?' she asked.

'I don't want him,' Lin said almost hysterically. 'I want my son.'

'Are you going with Lin?' Ruth repeated. 'Because if you aren't, Theo must stay here.'

'No, no!' screamed Theo. 'Mummy!'

'This isn't doing anyone any good,' Kieran said desperately. 'Least of all Lin.'

'Don't worry about me,' Lin said angrily.

'Especially with your friend being ill, too,' Ruth said.

Everyone turned to look at her.

'What?' Lin asked.

'Caroline Devlin. She's in ITU.' Ruth looked at the faces which formed a loose semicircle around her. 'Oh, you didn't know?'

'No,' Lin said.

'You really don't know?' Ruth repeated. 'Oh . . . so these voices and so on are not exactly infallible, are they?'

Harry caught Ruth's arm and pulled her backwards, turning him to face her. 'You really are a lovely piece of work, aren't you,' he said.

Ruth did not reply. The merest trace of triumph was in her expression. She looked down at Harry's grip on her arm, and smiled. 'I'm simply thinking of Lin's health. So is Kieran.'

'I've told you—' Lin began.

'I mean your mental health.'

'My . . . ?' Lin wheeled round to Kieran. 'Do you hear what she's saying?'

Kieran stood with his back to them all, pulling at his shirt collar, then biting on his thumbnail.

'Kieran!' Lin said.

'He has to stay here,' he muttered.

'No!' Theo shouted.

Ruth suddenly picked Theo up, barged out of the room, and began to run down the corridor. Theo screamed as if he had been burned. As Lin started after them, they heard the bathroom door slam, and the lock bolt being rammed home. Inside, Theo yelled and sobbed.

Lin ran to the bathroom door. 'Open this!' she shouted. 'Open it!'

Kieran ran after her. 'Lin . . .'

'You planned this!' she said.

'No. No, I didn't. But you're not well enough to look after Theo. You weren't even well enough to leave the hospital. Let me take you back there, where they can look after you.'

'Like last year?' she said.

The two of them froze, their faces within an inch of each other.

'That's not fair,' Kieran murmured.

'Like last year, when she came round and looked after him, and when I came back, he had nightmares for weeks,' Lin said.

'Because *you* had left, not because Ruth was there.'

'How you dared bring her into the house—our house . . .'

'Ruth isn't a monster,' Kieran said.

'Isn't she?' Lin asked. 'Isn't she?'

They looked at each other for a long, fraught moment.

'I do love you,' he said. 'It's true.'

'That's the shame of it,' Lin replied. 'Because you don't—and never have. But I love you.'

Kieran frowned, and put out his hand to steady Lin, who was suddenly swaying where she stood. 'Please . . . sit down,' he told her.

'I'll show you,' she said quietly. 'I'll show you that I'm not insane. I'm not sick. I'm as rational as you are, more rational then you are. I'm more than fit to look after Theo. Better equipped than *she* is. She hasn't got a heart. She's totally selfish. And you want to subject him to that! Can't you see it—can't you see how she is?'

Lin stared into his face, then closed her eyes for a second as if unable to hear what she saw written there. 'No, you can't,' she murmured. She turned away from him. 'There are things that matter more than either of you, and I'll prove it. I'm going to the Priory—I'll be there overnight. That's all. You'll see. I'll show you.' She elbowed her way past him.

Harry stepped forward. Lin turned to him. 'Take me home,' she said.

Harry glanced back at Kieran.

'I've got to stay here with Theo,' Kieran said. 'I must.'

Harry touched Lin's hand briefly. 'What shall I do?' he asked. 'What do you really want?' He hated the way she looked: white, drained, sick.

'Take me home, Harry,' she said brokenly. 'Please, for God's sake.'

THIRTY-ONE

FROM THE WINDOW OF RUTH'S FLAT, Kieran watched Harry's car draw away. He followed its progress down the street, then turned. Ruth had come out from the bathroom and was holding Theo by the hand. The boy stood red-faced, hitching breaths.

'Come here, Theo,' Kieran said, walking towards him and picking him up. The child was like a rigid board in his embrace.

'You shouldn't have done that,' he told Ruth.

'I want to protect him,' she said.

'You're going the wrong way about it,' he replied. He turned his back on her, took Theo to the sitting room and, by a mixture of brute force and cajoling, managed to get Theo's coat on. They came back out into the hall, and Kieran took his car keys from the table.

'Where are you going?' Ruth asked.

'Out,' he told her.

She followed him. 'What are you going to do?' she asked.

He turned to look at her. 'I wouldn't have thought it possible,' he said.

'Thought what was possible?'

'For you to hit below the belt like that.'

'I don't know what you mean,' she said.

'Caroline Devlin,' he said.

She reached out in an attempt to put a hand on his arm, but he stepped away. 'Enough,' he said. 'Just . . . enough.'

'Kieran,' she called, as he went down the stairs. 'Kieran . . .'

As he opened the door to the street, he was met with the warm, billowing air of a spring afternoon. It was past three o'clock, and the primary schools were finished for the day; along the road, mothers and children were coming in their twos and threes. At the gate he let one such group go past: a woman with a child on either hand, listening to some long, involved story from the older girl. She gave Kieran an apologetic smile, then picked up a lurid red-and-green drawing the little one had dropped. He let them go past, eyeing the trio not with envy but with despair.

Kieran crossed the road and went into the park. There was a play area there. At the swings, he let Theo down and gave him a little push in the small of the back. 'Go play,' he said.

Theo didn't move. Instead, he began to cry: a series of long, moaning sobs that would tear any parent's heart. Kieran felt a mixture of rage and impotence wash over him. After a few seconds, he squatted down, took out his handkerchief, and helped wipe his son's face.

'I promise that I'll sort this out,' he said. 'Everything will be all right.'

The look that Theo gave him—a straight glare of crude, closed disbelief—was like a slap in the face. Kieran stood up, and put his boy on the swing seat. They stayed for a while in this desultory duet, Kieran pushing the swing, and Theo sitting in it without making a single sound or movement.

The chestnuts spread broad, tacky-edged leaves above his head. Kieran stared across the other side of the park to Maiden Walk. The route was named for the Iron Age castle a few miles away, the stronghold of the Durotriges who had resisted the Romans. They had fallen, of course: fallen under the advance of time, of a greater power, leaving behind ballista bolts in the spines and skulls of the castle's defenders. Rome had swept in, with its roads and currency and watercourses and stone buildings; with its vetch and flax and vineyards. With ten million sesterces provided by Seneca to make another little Italy.

At the eastern boundary of the park was one of Kieran's favourite places. A tiny portion of the old town wall there had been built fifteen years after the death of Boudicca. Barely ten feet of it now remained, incorporated into the Victorian Hamstone margin. He had brought Lin here once, before they even lived together, and shown her this wall, and found to his bemusement that she knew at least as much about it as he did. She even knew where the cemeteries of the city had been, and the coin hoards, and the fragments of mosaic. Her capacity for knowledge was encyclopaedic. More importantly, it was effortless. She could soak up great skeins of dates, theories and facts, ordering them in her head into her own eclectic categories.

He wondered what theory occupied her now: what outrageous route she was pursuing. He closed his eyes and wished himself out of it, wished himself back two thousand years, to a place where he would feel at home, to a system of belief he'd understood. To a code, to some military convention.

He had been due to see Arthur Caldwell at three; he ought to make a phone call and rearrange the meeting. It was impossible to avoid a meeting. Caldwell's message—left on the Priory answerphone the night before—had all the hallmarks of an ultimatum.

Kieran stopped the momentum of the swing. 'Come on,' he said to Theo, 'let's go and have a cup of tea.'

Theo said nothing.

'Some Coke and a piece of cake?' Kieran asked.

There was still no reply.

'How about a piece of lemon cake with the lemon icing?'

Nothing.

Through the nearest park gate was a public call box. Kieran spoke to Caldwell, who sounded continuingly tetchy, and postponed the meeting till five. Then he and Theo went on to the nearest teashop. Kieran hadn't eaten lunch; he had been too wound up over this unwelcome publicity. As he sat waiting for his order, he reflected that it was lucky no one appeared to know Ruth's address, or connect him with her. Not yet, anyway.

His food was brought, together with a milky coffee. He ate hungrily, his mind continually bouncing back to Lin's stricken, accusing face. Theo played with the icing of his cake, slowly mashing it to a pulp, but not eating it. In despair, Kieran sat back in his chair and watched his son.

Theo was the catalyst that had brought him and Lin together—was that right? He would never know. There had been so many undercurrents then that he had not appreciated. Not appreciated until last year, when the weight of her secret broke Lin's spirit.

Her secret, he thought.

My distance.

After her mother's death, he and Lin had travelled back down south immediately after visiting the hospital. Lin had flatly refused to stay in Liverpool, so they had driven through the night, to arrive back at the Priory at one in the morning. Between leaving the city and arriving home, they had barely exchanged half a dozen words.

He hardly knew what to make of Lin's family. What he could not get over was how different Lin was to them all. It was hard to believe that she was related at all to these sullen men with their broad, flat-planed faces and fair colouring. They were the complete antithesis of her, opposite in every way. Even their voices were not the same. Lin's bore only a slight trace of accent, and was lighter with a quick, self-deprecatory undertone.

He had to wake her up when they reached home. She had climbed out of the car slowly, as if her body ached, but she didn't go inside. On the front steps, she turned abruptly, and, without looking back at him, went around the side of the house.

'Where are you going?' he had called.

'Leave me alone,' she replied. 'I'm OK.'

He went inside, but, halfway up the stairs with the bags, curiosity and concern overcame him. Going out of the back door, he saw her standing far down the garden, past the fence, which she must have climbed over. She was in the field next to the river.

He was seized with a sudden fear. Running down the lawn, he called her name. It was pitch black, and cold, and the ground was slippery. She had moved to the very edge of the water.

'Lin!' he shouted. 'Lin!'

She turned to look at him as he scaled the fence and stumbled over the tussocky paddock.

'What's the matter?' she asked.

He was out of breath. 'What are you doing?'

'Nothing. Just looking.'

He stood there, catching his breath. 'Jesus, Lin.'

'What?'

'I thought . . .' He indicated the river.

She looked at him in puzzlement for a moment, then smiled. 'Oh, Kee.'

He put his arms around her, and kissed her forehead.

'How could I drown in here?' she said. 'It's only three feet deep.'

He said nothing.

The night was still; the wind of the morning had blown itself out. A fog lay in patches all the way along the route of the river, he could see it drifting, a grey ghost above the water, right through the field further back still, towards the village.

'What do you think of me?' she asked.

'Think of you?'

'Staying away from my family.'

'Perhaps you had your reasons,' he said.

'Yes,' she said. 'I had my reasons.' She paused. 'I'm so different to you.'

He had laughed softly. 'Well, perhaps that's the attraction.'

'No, I mean I come from a different background.'

'That doesn't matter,' he said.

'Doesn't it?'

'No.'

'It's effortless with you,' she said. 'You see, I have to make this effort . . . all the time . . .'

'Don't be silly.'

She ran a hand over her forehead, pinching the skin at one temple. 'No, you don't understand what I mean,' she said. 'You see, I never fitted. I've never felt part of anyone.'

She was right. He didn't understand at all. He thought she was tired, overwrought. 'Come back to the house,' he said. 'I'll make a hot drink.'

She made a tugging motion at her hair, the habitual gesture of complexity, of confusion. She did the same sometimes when thinking over mathematical problems. 'I have so many feelings,' she said. 'And I don't know how to . . . how to . . .' She stopped, staring at the ground. 'To be real to you. To me.'

He was totally perplexed. She might as well have been speaking in Swahili for all he understood her.

'She didn't want me. I wasn't real,' she said. 'Just a kind of thing, to be angry with, to blame.'

'Your mother must have been forty when she had you,' he said. 'Perhaps she was too old to be patient.'

'She was forty-two.'

'Well, then.'

'And when I needed her, she . . .' Her voice dropped. 'She turned on me. She beat me with her fists. Her *fists*.'

'Unforgivable,' he said.

She had looked at him. 'Was it?'

'Of course.' But he knew that he had missed something. Something vital had passed by him in the darkness, some revelation she found hard to part with. But it was simply beyond him. His life had always been easy and smooth. He had been brought up by parents who were jolly and uncomplicated. He had never encountered any particular problems, either with women, or money, or school, or work, or with any relationship. He had led, he supposed, a nicely charmed life . . . until he met her. He was always hoping it would come back again, that calm he so valued. Perhaps that was what she meant by his being effortless.

'It would have helped if your father had been there,' he said.

'Either one,' she had murmured.

She had begun to shiver. She leaned down to look at the writhing current of the water, turning over and over, a restless sleeper, on the stony chalk bed. In the summer, there was watercress in this stream. It seemed very far away at the moment.

'She threw me out,' she said. 'I had nowhere to go, except to a friend's. I couldn't believe her hatred. I went back to the house, but she wouldn't let me in. I rang, but she put down the phone. I was nearly eighteen . . .'

'Mothers and daughters often fight,' he had said. To tell the truth, he was very cold, and was trying to think of a way to lighten the mood, and get her back inside. He was also incredibly tired, bone tired, worn out with driving.

'Don't you want to know why?' she asked. 'What caused this . . . fight?'

He had tried to hug her. 'I want you to go to sleep and try not to think about today,' he said.

He felt her stiffen momentarily in his arms.

Then, she had obediently taken his hand, and followed him, over the dark wet grass, into the house.

THIRTY-TWO

*A*s they drove down the hill into the village, Harry looked across at Lin. 'What are we going to say to these media people?' he asked. 'Kieran says they're camped on your steps.'

Lin seemed perfectly calm. 'Do you think there'll be many?'

'I shouldn't think so. After Kieran left, so may some of them. What are they chasing up, anyway? Just a couple of reports on the news. The injured boy's mother might have come across as unhinged—they may be just looking for a denial. We could give them a denial.'

They now were coming down the lane to the Priory. Although the house was surrounded by a high beech hedge and mature trees, the gate which had once spanned the drive had long ago fallen to pieces that were propped in the hedge and now almost covered with shrubbery. So it was no surprise to him to see, as they turned in off the lane, four cars on the drive itself.

'What do I say?' Harry repeated.

They slowed down, and a small knot of people descended on them.

'Lin,' Harry said, 'I don't want you to speak to them.'

She smiled sadly at him. 'You mustn't stop me.' She got out.

'Mrs Gallagher, how are you?' asked a girl, holding a tape recorder to Lin's face.

'I'm fine.'

'Mrs Gallagher, have you heard from Mrs Wells?'

'Sorry, who?'

'Mrs Wells. Her son—'

'Oh, no. But I've only just got home—as you see.'

'Have you got any comment?' asked the man closest to her.

'What does Kieran say?' asked another.

Harry had got out, too. 'Mrs Gallagher is very tired,' he said.

Lin looked at him. 'I'll give a statement,' she said. 'In an hour. I must sit down for a while first.'

'Mrs Gallagher—'

'An hour,' she said. She walked to the front steps. As she did so, she lost her footing a couple of times, just momentarily. Harry opened the door for her, and they went inside.

Lin walked into the sitting room and stared at the evidence of Kieran recently having worked there: a pile of books and papers, in rigid manuscript sequence, lined the large mahogany table by the window. She walked over to them and laid her hand on the first page. Harry saw her wince and rapidly take her hand away.

She turned back to him. 'I'm going to take a shower,' she said.

Harry nodded.

As she passed from the room, she laid her hand briefly on his arm.

He stared after her as she went up the stairs.

She took some time showering, letting the hot water soothe the aching at the top of her neck and across her shoulders. It was the first shower she had taken in three days, having made do in the hospital with a bed bath assisted by the nurses. It felt wonderfully cleansing and freeing to stand by herself, with her eyes closed, under the steady flow of the water, lathering herself with her own fragranced soap. The pleasure of the scent, the sensation of the water on her skin, even the colours of the room were heightened. When she had finished, she opened the window and stood for some time looking out at the trees.

In her second year at college, one of the applied mathematics options had been devoted to the turbulence theory. It was an apparently simple problem that posed impenetrable difficulty, for science couldn't predict the way that water would swirl into a bath, or leaves shake and move in response to wind. It was important to the aircraft industry, in particular, that these movements might be predicted, that a mathematical formula might be found, however lengthy. But the whirling air and revolving water evaded them with their secret, unspecified rhythms. She stared out now at the trees and admired their ability to dance to a higher music than man.

She left the window open, to allow the garden to rush into the room.

When she came downstairs a half-hour later, Harry had brought the remaining three reporters into the sitting room. He had plied them with tea, and they sat balancing their teacups and saucers on their knees.

Lin smiled as she came in the door. She could hear their minds rolling. She sat down with her back to the window.

The girl spoke up first. She introduced herself as Shelley. 'Mrs Gallagher, do you know Mrs Wells?'

'No, I don't.'

'You don't know who she is?'

'No, not at all. Should I?'

The girl smiled. 'Not necessarily. She's the wife of Michael Wells, the printworks man. The company in Bristol.'

'Oh, yes?'

'And you didn't know that?'

'No. Why would I? She was a woman in an ambulance. I don't think I'd know her again, I'm afraid. I hardly saw her.'

One of the men spoke up. 'She says you saved her son's life.'

Lin looked at him. 'What does the hospital say?'

'They don't say anything. They're having a meeting.'

'Oh,' Lin replied. 'That could mean anything, couldn't it?'

'And what do *you* say?' the man asked. 'The men on security told us you were a patient there.'

'Yes, I was.'

'With what?'

'No one seems to know.' She smiled. 'Sorry, I'm not being very helpful. I have another test tomorrow. It was . . . a kind of disorientation . . . I had a terrible pain in my head . . .'

'You were disorientated?'

'Yes.'

'You didn't know what you were doing, then?'

'You mean this morning? Oh yes, I knew what I was doing this morning.'

'And what was that?'

'I heard him. I heard the disconnection,' she said.

All three looked briefly at each other.

'You heard what?' asked the girl.

'The disconnection,' Lin repeated. 'He was . . . it's difficult to explain. He was out of pattern. He wasn't meant to have fallen out of pattern. It wasn't his choice.'

There was a short silence. 'You've lost me,' the girl said.

Lin leaned forward, her elbows on her knees. She spread her hands, gazing down at them. 'We all have a pattern, a kind of blueprint,' she said, slowly. 'It runs through our lives—through everything. We realize it before we come here—'

'Come where?' the nearest man asked.

'Here. Before we're born.'

'We know our lives before we're born?' he repeated incredulously.

She shrugged. 'I suppose so,' she said. 'I just got this . . . sense of a pattern being disturbed. A predetermined pattern. The accident this morning was just that, an accident, not meant to happen. Accidents happen all the time, some of them decided upon, some of them sheer—how can I put it?—interruptions to the scheme, the narrative. He had been pushed out of his line, his choices. I just pushed him back.'

The girl had switched on her tape recorder. 'So you . . . you *heard* him coming, and you *heard* this—'

'Disconnection.'

'You heard this disconnection, and you put it right. You altered it. You changed his injuries, you mean? Is that right?'

'I didn't know what would happen, but I touched him to set

the . . . there's a break in the line, imagine like a break in a monitor line on a machine. It's a matter of reassembling the machine to make the line straight . . .'

All three stared at her. From the doorway, Harry looked at her with a worried, preoccupied expression.

The girl pushed back a wing of hair from her face. 'You . . . healed . . . this boy . . .' she repeated, emphasizing every word.

'*If* I did. I don't say I did. I don't know that I did.'

'When I talked to the hospital manager this morning, he denied that,' the man said.

'Did he?' Lin asked.

The other man spoke. 'Can we just go back to this . . . er, this before-we're-born bit?'

'Yes, OK.'

'Are you a spiritualist?'

'No.'

'A medium? A clairvoyant?'

'No.'

'But you know we come from somewhere . . . ?'

'And we go back to it—yes.'

'What kind of somewhere would that be?'

Lin paused. 'I don't know.'

'Is God in this somewhere?'

'Yes.'

'Right, and you have this hotline to him, do you?'

Lin smiled. 'No, not any more than you do.'

'I'm sorry?'

'Not any more than you do.'

'You mean we can all do this?' the girl asked.

'I should think so. If we concentrated. If we allowed it.'

'Heal people?' the man asked. 'Or travel up and down to God?'

'You don't have to travel up and down,' Lin said, amused. 'You *are* God.'

The girl laughed outright. 'Don't tell him that,' she said.

The first man ignored her. '*I'm* God? People worship me in church every Sunday?'

Lin laughed. 'We've pushed and pulled the picture of God to make it fit religions, but all religions have the same purpose: to connect back. We're all the same spirit, a single . . . no, spirit is too loaded with meaning . . .' she murmured. 'All a single moving force,' she said firmly.

The man gazed at her, then he sat back and began writing.

'So . . . er . . .' the girl interposed. 'We're all God . . . and we can all perform miracles.'

'Yes, I believe we are. We can.'

'Healing miracles.'

'I think we could do anything, see anything, hear anything, if we only tuned in to it.'

'Right,' she said. 'And you're tuned into it.'

'I didn't ask to be,' Lin said. 'It just happened while I was in hospital.'

The man who had been writing evidently could not hold back a grin this time. 'The NHS tuned you into God?'

Lin bit her lip. 'When I was in hospital, I began to see and hear things,' she said.

'What things?'

'I suppose they were dead people. But they're not dead.'

'Dead people aren't dead?'

'No.'

'They're alive?'

'Not exactly. They're alive in another place.'

There was another prolonged, fraught pause.

'And you began seeing them, in hospital?' the girl commented.

'Yes.'

'Can you see anyone now?' she asked.

'No, I . . .'

'What does the hospital say is wrong with you?' the second man demanded abruptly.

'They don't seem to know. It was thought to be meningitis, or perhaps a kind of epilepsy. It could be something else—'

'Something in your brain, you mean?'

'Yes.'

'Would this other test be an MRI scan?'

'Yes.'

'Ah.' He seemed to find this very enlightening.

'It doesn't matter what the hospital says it is,' Lin replied. 'This ability to see has nothing to do with any illness.'

'But I thought you said that it started when you were admitted to hospital?'

'Yes, I . . .'

'But you don't think that's anything to do with it?'

'No.'

He gave her a wry smile that was almost pitying.

'They come and go, do they?' asked the first man.

'Sorry?'

'These dead people you were talking about.'

'I block them out,' Lin told him. 'When I first saw them they were everywhere, all the time, crowding into all the spaces that we think are empty. But I don't see them like that now.'

'So much enlightenment in three days,' the first man commented. It was a mumble to himself.

'So, if I asked you to unblock them, you could see somebody now in this room?' the second man asked.

'Perhaps.'

'And would you do that for us?'

Lin looked from one to the other. 'I don't see the need.'

He nodded, as if confirming something to himself. 'You can't do it when asked.'

'I think I could.'

'If I asked you to?'

'For what reason?'

'If I needed you to do something for me, reach someone for me?'

'Well, I don't know . . .'

'Either it's real or it's not.'

'It is real.'

'Would you reach someone for me?'

Lin gazed at him. 'Is it important?'

'Yes.'

Lin looked down again, briefly, at her hands. 'OK.' Then she stood up.

'Lin, there's no need to do this,' Harry said.

'It's all right.' She smiled at the reporter. 'Would you come over here?' she asked.

He did so. There was a look of frank disbelief on his face—and of contained humour. As he drew level with her, he started to speak, but Lin held up her hands to quiet him. Then she picked up his hand and held it between her own hands.

'Don't tell him anything,' said a woman's voice at Lin's side.

The interjection was so sudden, and so loud, that Lin jumped. She glanced over her shoulder, to gaze into empty space.

'Put his hand down,' the voice continued.

'But he asked me,' Lin objected.

Across the room, Harry began walking towards Lin. The girl and the other man stood up. They had seen her look behind, then squeeze her eyes shut as she spoke.

'I don't care what he asked you.' The woman was much older than Lin, but not elderly. Her voice had a coarse, abrasive quality. There was' a Scottish accent.

'There's a lady here,' Lin said. 'Scottish. She doesn't want me to carry on.'

The man's grip on Lin's hand tightened. 'Ask her name,' he said.

'He wants . . .'

'I hear him.' The last comment seemed thrown away, as if the woman were turning, even moving away from them.

'She's going away,' Lin said.

'What's her name?'

'She won't tell me. She doesn't want me to tell you anything.'

Lin opened her eyes. The man was looking at her intently. His patent scepticism hadn't changed at all.

'What's wrong with me?' he asked Lin. 'Don't listen to her. Tell me.'

Lin was already concentrating on him. It was difficult not to, as his personality was so strong. It came roaring down at her. He was an aggressive man whose finer feelings were deeply buried. She felt stress, like a bright yellow light, colouring him. His whole image was suffused with this ochre stain. He was terribly angry with life, and with another person. She felt this other person sitting helplessly in a chair. The colour that washed over the reporter was echoed in this other, older man. The fingers on the arm of the chair were yellow, the pattern of the brocade of the chair covering was yellow and brown. He was sitting, at this moment, in a chair in a sunlit room, and the light was at such an angle that it was hurting his eyes. But he hadn't the energy to call someone to draw the curtain, and she saw the curtain—free of its loop: a green tassel with a yellow fringe—hanging tantalizingly out of his grasp.

And she felt a circle closing.

His life was ending.

'There's so much yellow,' Lin murmured. 'And it's such a sick colour.' She looked down at their still-linked hands. 'There's nothing wrong with you,' she said. 'It's your father.'

There was a tiny jolt in the man's fingers.

'He has . . . this is linked to his smoking, a chest disease . . . he's at home, very tired. Is he on medication? Everything about him is slurred. His voice is slurred. He's so tired . . .'

She was drifting, just as the man in the chair was drifting in and out of sleep. The pictures of his dreams were lurid, outlined in black like a bad drawing. It was the effect of the morphine.

'Heal him,' the reporter said.

Lin brought herself back to him only with an enormous effort. The others were now grouped around them in a semicircle. The atmosphere was claustrophobically tense.

'I can't do that,' Lin said.

'Why not?'

'I can't. I . . .'

'You healed the boy this morning.'

'I . . .'

'Either you can or you can't.'

Lin shook her head. 'It's nothing to do with me,' she said, distressed. 'The boy's pattern this morning was disrupted. But this man, your father, there's no broken pattern there. He's on the right track, he's completing his task . . .'

'He's got cancer,' the man retorted. He pulled his hand out of her grasp savagely, still staring at her, standing too close. 'He's dying,' he said.

'I know,' she told him. As the man took his hand away, the picture of his father faded rapidly.

'And you can't do a bloody thing about it, can you?'

'No, I can't. This is what he chose for himself.'

The man laughed bitterly. 'Chose for himself? Give me a break. Have you ever seen anyone dying of lung cancer? Have you heard them gasping for breath? Do you think anyone in their right bloody mind would chose to die like that?'

'He chose it for a reason,' Lin said.

'What *reason!*'

She pressed both hands to her eyes. 'I don't know, I don't understand,' she said. 'There's a shape: a course to follow. He chose it for others. There's a lesson to be learned in standing by, witnessing this suffering, and in experiencing the suffering, too . . .'

'What fucking rubbish,' he said. He turned away, strode to the couch, and picked up the papers he had left there. As he turned round, he looked at Lin accusingly. 'You're under some kind of delusion, Mrs Gallagher,' he said. 'And it's a very cruel one.'

'I'm sorry,' she whispered. 'There really isn't anything I can do. It's not up to me.'

He smiled. 'Funny how, when you really need these religious freaks, there's nothing they can do,' he said to the room at large. 'Trust in God . . . ask and it shall be given to you. Faith to move mountains. It's a bloody mockery.' He stuffed the paper into his pocket. Pain was clearly coursing through his face, and he looked down, to hide it. 'My father's been a staunch Roman Catholic all his life,' he said. 'A regular church-goer. He's been a decent bloke. Used to run a taxi firm, and ran free taxis on Sundays for all these old women wanting to go to church, wanting to go to their day clubs even. He was in the Rotary Club, he took kiddies to the seaside in the summer, he was never in the house because he was always out doing this, doing that for other people.' He looked up. 'And now he's got this. He never did anyone any harm, and he's got this. You explain that to me.'

Lin returned his anguished look.

'You can't, can you?' he asked.

'No,' she said. 'But he'll come back.'

'What?' he said. His astonishment drained his colour.

'This is just one life,' Lin murmured, frightened by his expression. 'He'll wait for you, you'll see him again, and then you'll both continue on, to other lives . . .'

In two strides the man was upon her. Harry leapt forward and restrained him with both arms across his chest.

'You've got a nerve, haven't you?' the reporter demanded.

Lin had stepped back, bringing one hand up, expecting to be hit, and shocked when the blow did not materialize. She had seen it, felt its coming force: it was so perfectly formed in the man's mind.

'I'm sorry,' she repeated.

'Sorry! You give me all this crap about living again . . .'

'It's not crap,' she said.

'Yes, it is! It's all crap,' he retorted. 'It's just a sop to make unbearable things palatable. It's just a crutch to lean on, and we shouldn't use it,' he said. 'You know what there is beyond this life? Nothing! Nothing at all! Blackness. The end. Thank you very much and good night. There's no angels, and no blinding light, and no Jesus Christ coming in all his glory to judge the quick and the dead. There's nothing. You live, you die: there's no rhyme or reason to it. D'you know what I saw last week?' he demanded. 'I did a piece on NHS funding, and I went to a baby unit, and I saw a three-day-old child dying because the heart operation she needed wasn't available in that hospital, and they took her to another place, sixty miles away, but she died in the ambulance. You think that's God's merciful plan, do you? You think there's this wonderful reason why they murder sons in front of their fathers in Bosnia, or give children in Chernobyl leukaemia, or have a mother with preschool children develop breast cancer? There's a reason to all that, is there? A plan? *A pattern?*'

Lin had not taken her eyes off him.

All of them looked to her for her reply.

'Yes,' she said finally, 'there is a pattern. We're all linked, and what you do, and what your father does, and what the people you meet do, all affect you. We act, we do things, we help or we don't help, and everything we do acts on other people, and it seems random, but it isn't random at all. There is a meaning . . . there is a greater force . . .'

Harry had dropped his hands, responding to a slackening of the man's anger. The reporter's whole body slumped.

There was silence, and then, in a laboured fashion, the man sighed.

'I feel sorry for you, Mrs Gallagher,' he said. 'I really do.'

He turned to go.

Harry saw that Lin was a ghastly shade of white; there was a faint blue line on her upper lip; her eyes seemed hollowed.

'She's going to faint,' the girl said.

Both she and Harry stepped forward at the same moment.

The two men had met by the door. 'I've seen all I want,' said the first.

While they departed, Lin had been lowered to the sofa; the girl sat embarrassedly at her side.

Harry went to the window, and saw the men getting into their respective cars. He felt badly about the interview: he could guess what they would make of it. When he looked back at Lin, his belief in her was paper-thin. Perhaps she genuinely believed in what she said, but it seemed more likely that she was ill. He should never have allowed her to leave the hospital. He should have gone down to speak to the press and told them it was all a mistake. The hospital people themselves would have backed him up.

Lin opened her eyes.

'Can you tell the future?' the girl asked.

'No,' Lin said, 'I don't think so.'

'Well . . . how do you do this, then? What happens?'

'I have to touch something to get a proper picture.'

'Why?'

Lin smiled; she heaved herself up to a sitting position. 'I don't know.'

The girl looked her over carefully. 'Do you see anything now?'

'No.'

'There's . . . no one around me, for instance?'

'I'm sorry, no. I'm so tired.'

The girl's face seemed to fall. She clicked off the recorder, slipped it into her shoulder bag, and stood up. 'Well, I'll be on my way,' she said. 'Thanks for the show.'

Lin's gaze followed her as she made her way out of the door. Harry escorted the girl to the front door; but she said nothing else. She didn't even look back at him as she walked briskly to her car.

When Harry went back to the sitting room, Lin was in the same position. He sat down next to her.

'They don't believe me, do they?' she asked him. 'No one believes me at all.'

THIRTY-THREE

*I*T HAD HAPPENED A YEAR AGO. Kieran would never forget it. Never.

He had been to a conference. Thank God, sometimes parts of his life followed the old reassuring pattern. He had maintained his post at the university partly because he arranged his alter ego's life in such a way—scheduling his filming and so on—that teaching terms were rarely encroached upon. After absences abroad, filming, he worked evenings, weekends, to catch up. He hadn't taken a holiday in five years, unless his two-and three-week book promotion tours could be called holidays.

That particular week, he had been to Yorkshire. The seminars had been on his old subject: the empires of the Mediterranean. The summer school had been particularly pleasant, based at an adult-education college deep in the heart of the Dales. The weather had been so fine that he had even chaired discussion groups out on the lawns. The next week he was due in New York to deliver a paper, and he had relished the oncoming contrast. He thought of weeks like these as going back to his roots, to his first enthusiastic thirst for knowledge. It had been a peaceful week, good for his self-esteem. After all, he was the famous face guesting for them. Groups parted for his passage, like Moses parting the Red Sea. He came home feeling good.

He had stopped at the college on the way home, parking on Riverside and walking along to the campus. On impulse, he had called into one of the shops. He had wanted to buy something for Lin.

There, at the counter, Ruth had been standing, writing a cheque.

'Hello,' he said.

She had turned, smiled.

They had spoken for a few minutes, then walked out of the shop together. Standing on the pavement, she had asked after Lin.

'Ah, just the same,' he had said.

'Is that good or bad?'

They smiled at each other. At such times he longed for a few hours in Ruth's company. She was so very soothing.

He had kissed her on the cheek. 'Poor old baby,' she murmured. He had put his arm around her, and they walked to her car. They said nothing else, but he had stood on the pavement and watched her pull out into traffic. He had waved goodbye. Afterwards he had spent two hours in college, catching up on paperwork. And then, in the same leisurely fashion, with the same feeling of well-being, he had driven home.

It was seven in the evening when he arrived.

The first thing he noticed as he pushed open the door was a Roman roof finial lying in the hallway. Strange that he registered nothing else at first but the cone-shaped stone fragment with its decorative mock doors and windows, and the bell-shaped peak. He had stared at it, then felt the resistance of the heavy outer door to something lying behind it. He shoved a little, puzzled, and then edged in, pulling his case awkwardly behind him.

The scene that met his eyes was one of devastation.

The finial was only the first in a long, jumbled trail of broken treasures. Lin must have stood either at one end of the hall, or on the stairs, throwing whatever she could find in his study. He saw at once that a few of these items were from the locked glass cabinet behind his desk; the cabinet he'd had made especially to house the more precious things. They weren't valuable in the same way Meissen porcelain or rare silver was valuable, but they were rare.

Kieran had put down his case, shocked beyond words.

Just beyond the finial lay shards of pottery. She had actually bro-ken—*broken*—the four segments of a Roman flanged bowl. Scattered between its sections were his precious tesserae: pieces of a mosaic floor. He had brought those home, illicitly stowed in his pocket, from a dig when he had been eighteen. Their reddish colour was scored into the flagstone floor, as if she had then stamped on them. What made up the greater mess, however, were limestone roof tiles. Each one weighed over eight pounds. Or they had done. These had been flung from a height—undoubtedly this time from the head of the stairs. There were splinters all over the floor, and a couple had cracked completely. The sight of them—they had survived intact for three thousand years, buried under a Wiltshire water meadow, until she got hold of them—made his blood boil.

He had made his way forward, carefully lifting fragments out of his route. At the end nearest the kitchen, he found a little shoulder of black-burnished Purbeck pottery, and a tiny model ploughman and horses—not more than four inches long, and certainly from the first century—which had been cleanly snapped in two.

Kieran was more than angry now; his body shook. It was like coming unexpectedly on the scene of a massacre. As far as he was concerned, the deliberately smashed fragments were as agonizing as broken bodies, cut limbs, severed heads. Shocked to the point of sick-ness, he opened the kitchen door.

Lin was standing with her back to the window, facing the door, a mug of tea in one hand.

'What the hell is all this?' he demanded.

'And what time is this?' she asked.

He looked around him. 'Where's Theo?'

'At Rob McMillan's, sleeping over.'

He walked over to her. 'You did all this?'

She held his gaze. 'I'm standing here thinking what to do next.'

She was extraordinarily still, her face blank.

He gaped at her. 'You're crazy . . . What . . . ?' He itched to hit her. 'Do you know what those things are *worth*? Jesus Christ!'

She looked in a speculative fashion at the mug in her hands.

Then, she hurled it to the floor. He stepped back automatically from the splash of liquid, the shattering of the cup. But she was already in motion, sweeping the worktops clear, knocking everything in reach to the floor. Bread bin, knife rack, spice rack, jugs, tray, sugar and coffee canisters.

'Lin!' he shouted. 'Lin!'

She carried on round the kitchen. When she had finished with the worktops, she began pulling at the chairs.

He tried to catch hold of her. 'Stop it . . . stop it . . .'

She struggled free of him. 'I saw you,' she said.

'Saw me? Saw what? What are you talking about?'

'With Ruth this afternoon.'

'What?'

'I was at Riverside. Theo's been at Rob's all day, so I went to Riverside. I'd been to the library. I saw you.'

'But . . .' For a moment, he couldn't think what she was talking about. He had actually forgotten he had met Ruth at all. 'I didn't see her.'

'You bloody liar.'

'Wait . . . wait a minute. Yes, I did see her. I bumped into her briefly.'

'Don't give me that.'

'I met Ruth in a shop—just a shop, for God's sake. I walked with her to her car. Maybe two minutes, in a fucking *shop* . . . !'

'I saw you kiss her.'

'I . . .' He was so dumbfounded, words failed him. It was all so unutterably stupid.

'And where have you been since?' she said. 'With her!'

'I went into college. I've been working.'

'I don't care where you've been!' she shouted. Then she began to cry.

'Lin . . .'

'Don't touch me.'

'I really only saw her for a moment.'

'I don't care.'

'That's what all this—this *destruction*—that's what it's about? About Ruth? Jesus, Lin!'

'I don't care.' She was standing in the centre of the room with her head in her hands.

'Well, if you don't bloody well care, what have you done this for? What possible bloody purpose!'

She turned away, fumbling for the door handle.

'No you don't,' he said, lurching to grab her arm. 'I want an answer.'

'Leave me alone.'

They were fighting with hands: he, trying to get a grip on her, she twisting her fingers so that he could not. There was a minute of pathetic mime, almost funny in its extremity, a flurry of hands and arms. Inadvertently he scratched her with his watch, a bloody line appearing on her forearm.

'Let me go,' she sobbed.

He finally managed to get a grasp of her, and shook her.

'You've done all this, purposely done all this, just because you think I've been seeing Ruth?'

'You *have* seen Ruth.'

'But only for a second!'

She looked up at him. 'You've been with Ruth. That's why you're late. I'm so sick of it all, Kee.'

'How many times do I have to tell you?' he shouted. 'You think you're sick of it . . . ? How sick do you think I am? Ever since Theo was born, you've never stopped going on about it.'

'And you never stop going on about *her*,' she said.

'What rubbish.'

'Rubbish?' she repeated. 'You never stop comparing me to her.'

'That's not true.'

'It is true,' she said. 'It *is* true. If not straight out, then obliquely. You run your finger along the sills or the table or the inside of the cups, and you look at me and sigh, and you—'

'This is so trivial, I can't believe it,' he said.

'It's not just small things,' she said. 'It's everything. And you criticize the way I am with Theo—'

'I do not.'

'You ask what we've been doing, without ever offering to help with him, and then you never comment. You just look at me as if whatever we've done isn't right, isn't quite correct, isn't what *you* would have done, and yet you never do anything, you ignore him when he speaks to you—you ignore me most of the time. And yet the work I do for the TV series is what you've built yourself up on—'

'Is that what this is all about?' he said. 'You want some sort of credit, is that it? Payment? Credit on the episodes?'

'No, no, no,' she moaned. She clutched at her hair until he thought she would really pull it out by the handful. 'No, I want *you*, I want your love, your attention, I want you here—really here in spirit, not just occasionally in body. I want . . .'

She dissolved into racking sobs.

'Look,' he said. 'You know very well I had a commitment to this summer school. And I have not been with Ruth. God . . .' He searched his mind for some form of reassurance. 'Didn't you see her drive away?'

'No.'

'She did. She drove away. We walked along the pavement, she got into her car, she drove away. That was it. That was all.'

'That's why you're late home,' she repeated.

'It is not. I told you. After that, I went into college. I've been working.'

'Why!'

'What?'

'Why were you working? Why didn't you just come home!'

He held her away from him, staring at her. Then he started to laugh, more in exasperation than anything else. 'Well, which do you want?' he demanded. 'I've been shagging Ruth all afternoon, or I've been working all afternoon. I mean, are you mad at me being with Ruth or mad at me not coming straight home like a good boy? Make up your mind.'

She turned her head away, sobbing afresh. 'I just wanted you to come home,' she said. 'I was looking forward to it.'

'Oh, for Christ's sake, grow up,' he said. He released her. He wrenched open the door, and was met again with the chaos in the hallway. 'What am I going to do with this?' he asked. 'You silly, stupid bitch.'

He felt a blow in the centre of his back. He glanced around, stunned, and with a neat circle of numbness beginning just below his shoulder. To his amazement—and it was amazement more than fear—he saw that she was holding a knife, the small sharp vegetable knife, in her fist. She had picked it up from wherever it had lain at her feet. She was staring at him now, her mouth open, her hand shaking so hard that it described small ragged circles in the air.

Bemused, he felt over his shoulder. Not because it hurt—it didn't hurt in the least—but because he wanted to locate that creeping, crawling numbness. His fingers met with something wet, he took his hand away, and saw that he was bleeding. 'You stabbed me,' he said. It seemed like a joke, an impossibility. He would never have thought her capable of such a thing. He stared at her, dumbly uncomprehending. Her gaze was unfocused. 'You crazy, crazy girl,' he said.

She began to speak in a rambling, hazy, lurching voice.

'I'm so alone here in the daytime,' she said. 'You never come home. You don't talk to me. I can't be Ruth. I don't want to be Ruth. I don't want to live in her house. I want you to love me . . .' She rubbed at her eyes with her free hand, dragging in breath through a dropped-down mouth. She doubled over momentarily, as if this last admission had physically hurt her. 'And I've given up all my work to do yours—and you don't even acknowledge that. You brush over me. You talk to me as if I'm a child. I . . . don't want your bad . . . opinion of me . . .' Her voice broke. 'You would rather work than come home. I want you to help me with Theo. He needs you, too. And I want . . . I just want you to just care a bit, to . . .'

She dropped the knife. 'Oh God,' she whispered. 'I'm so sorry.'

His shoulder was stinging now. It felt hot, as if someone had pressed some flat, scorching surface to his skin. He walked out into the hall, and picked up the phone.

'What are you doing?' she asked. 'I'm sorry. I'm very sorry . . .' She was following him.

With the receiver to his ear, he held out his hand to stop her advance. She halted obediently, sobbing in small monotone notes.

The operator answered.

'Police and ambulance,' he said.

'What are you doing?' Lin asked again.

Kieran gave them his address. He didn't replace the receiver, but sat down heavily on the stairs with it lying in his lap.

'I didn't mean it,' Lin said. She was gazing at him with round, horrified eyes.

He couldn't summon up a single word to say to her. To think that this was the same girl for whom he had given up his comfortable life, his wife . . . that this was the same girl . . . it was inconceivable, unacceptable. This insane girl was the mother of his son. She had forced herself into his life, altered its course. This was the same girl who had danced along the benches, raising her coat hem between each thumb and finger.

But she was no longer his miracle. She was just a crazy girl.

He fell out of love with her in that moment—more quickly than he had fallen in. The magic of the old moments—the heart in his mouth while she swung on the suspension bridge and looked down into the drop, the pleasure at listening to her wayward brilliance—all vanished. It was as if from the first moment of meeting her a taut line had been playing out: his patience, his indulgence of her, his interest in her, playing out straighter and finer and thinner, until it reverberated with tension so tight between them that it became more of a baited hook than love. And he had writhed and pulled backwards, trying to take her with him, until finally the whole line snapped.

There was nothing left. There was not even any physical attraction left; if he were honest, there had not been much since he had witnessed her in labour with Theo. He had never quite managed to successfully eradicate that image of her swollen body, those screams of agony. She had more identity for him now as the mother of his son than as his partner. Every ounce of sexual interest was gone.

She had sat down on the floor, slumped against the wall, never taking her eyes from him. 'Kee,' she repeated, 'I didn't mean it. Don't tell anyone.'

He had rested his head, which suddenly felt extraordinarily heavy, on the newel post of the banisters, and laughed softly.

'I can't believe this,' he muttered.

'Why did you ask for the police?' she said.

'Why do you think?'

'You're not going to tell them I did this, are you? You're not going to tell them that?'

'Why not?'

'Please don't tell them,' she said.

'Did I do this to myself?'

'You could say . . .'

'What? What, exactly?'

'You could say there was a break-in, that . . . someone else was here.' Her voice was desperate.

'Forget it, Lin.'

'But what will happen?'

'I don't give a shit.' He could feel blood easing, like caressing fingers, down his back.

She started to crawl towards him on her hands and knees, across the splintered tiles, the broken pottery. 'Please don't, please don't,' she whimpered.

'Keep away from me,' he warned.

'I'll do anything you want. I'll make it up to you. Don't tell them . . .'

'Get away from me,' he repeated. Her tears fell on his sleeve, on his resting right hand. She was stroking his arm.

'If you don't leave me alone, I'll kill you,' he said.

She laid her head in his lap. He could feel her shaking violently. The touch of her repulsed him.

'I don't know what else to do—to be part of you,' she whispered. 'I've helped you, I've given up my own work, I've stopped my degree, I write your books, you don't acknowledge them—I don't mind that, I really don't mind that; they're your books—but I want to be in your life, for you to feel . . .'

'You've ruined me,' he told her.

She lifted her head and stared at him.

'I had some sort of standing, a position, until you came,' he said.

'I don't understand,' she said.

'I had a reputation which you've taken to pieces,' he told her coldly.

At another time he would have been only too glad to describe to her the exact nature of the change in his academic life. The attitude of colleagues that had altered so subdy: in glances, in facial expressions, during college dinners. He was the freak, the dumb show at the end of the table, the spectre at each feast. He had brought attention to the university, to his subject—and, of course, to the department. But not the right kind of attention. He had become their performer, adding the university's name to the credits following each programme, and they were not able to criticize him for that, but it cast an unappealing pall over him. It was as if he had turned a cheap trick at the college gates, flinging the money into the forecourt and watching it noticed, counted, but not picked up. That was not the role he wanted. He had liked his anonymity to the public, his respect in inner circles. Now he was known everywhere, and given this over-courteous, arm's-length, over-effusive welcome wherever he went.

It was the same with the TV people as it was in the college. He was a star turn, like a performing monkey, a dog dancing on two legs. He didn't . . . and this was the smallest detail but it stung immeasurably . . . he didn't like the way his books looked any more. They used to have smooth dark-green covers, smooth dark-blue covers, the printing small, the lettering discreet. Now his own photograph appeared prominently on them, against an inevitable Mediterranean backdrop. Or worse still, the worst of all, a bloody sword on *Hannibal*, an empty cross and an abandoned crown of thorns on *Christ's Wife*. The publishers described him as 'sensational'. Every time he saw that word, he imagined Ruth's sardonic smile.

'I don't understand,' Lin repeated. Her tone had become pathetic. 'How can I have ruined you?. You're not ruined. I'm the one who's ruined.'

He did not have the energy to laugh at her again. He closed his eyes.

'If you've lost your place in life, I'm sorry,' he heard her say. 'Do you know, we share that? I've never had a place. I learned the meaning of disgust from my mother. She hated to touch me,' she breathed. Lin put both hands up to her face, wiping her eyes furiously with her palms. He turned his head away, retreating, reducing her to a pinprick of light that he could erase with the tip of one finger. As she spoke, he imagined her—behind the luxury of his closed eyes—as a minute shape obscured by the smallest reflex action of his hand.

'She would put on my clothes when I was little,' Lin went on, 'lifting her fingers away quickly if she made any contact with my skin. She bathed me with a look on her face . . . I can't tell you. I look back on it now and realize the fault, but I don't believe it inside,' she confessed.

She looked up, noticing his paleness, willing him to understand. Nothing seemed more important—in those last few seconds before she heard the ambulance arrive on the drive outside, the repeated hammering on the front door—than reaching him. Than meaning something to him. To be more than a shadow, a fantasy, a two-dimensional frame.

'Inside I don't match,' she whispered. 'I don't have anywhere, I'm so lost, and I murdered the only thing that needed me, and I dream about it, Kee, I never told you, I dream of my child screaming and trying to hold on to me while they tear her to pieces, and I need you to let me in, to love me truly, I know you could, I know you could, you could feel something, it would be real, oh God . . .'

She lay down on the floor.

'I murdered my baby,' she whispered.

She lay down full-length, to feel the welcome cold.

Ruth had come to visit Kieran in hospital that same night.

He was lying on his side. No surgery had been necessary; although he had lost a surprising amount of blood, the wound had sliced through and across his flesh rather than deep into it. A year later, he still had the scar, and a curious itching sensation under his skin from time to time. Nothing more.

But that night he didn't know that. He had watched Ruth come in. She sat down at his side.

'Where is she?' he had asked.

'In Fennelwood. She admitted herself for treatment when it was suggested.'

'What did she say?'

'Nothing else. Absolutely nothing at all.'

They looked at each other.

'God, Ruth,' he said, 'this is just absurd.'

She smiled, looking briefly away. She had a habit, when thinking, of averting her gaze as though mentally working out some mildly irritating puzzle.

'What did her GP say?' he asked.

'Postnatal depression.'

'But Theo's nearly three years old!'

'Apparently the GP's been seeing her for over a year. There's some deeper-seated problem: guilt over a termination when she was just eighteen. Since Theo was born, it's got worse.' Ruth delivered this information without a flicker of intonation.

Kieran had lain dumbstruck for a while.

'She won't stay in for ever,' Ruth had murmured.

'I wish I'd never married her—never met her,' he told her. The lights in his room were dim; he was adrift in a sea of medication and quiet, insidious misery. He could not imagine how he was supposed to extricate himself. Then Ruth took his hand.

'So do I,' she said.

'Oh, Ruth,' he murmured.

'Won't you come back to me?' she asked.

'How can I leave Lin when she's in this state? It wouldn't be fair.'

Ruth had looked at him levelly. 'Nothing is fair.'

She leaned down and, in the hazy twilight, kissed his face, his fingers, his wrists. And, as she wrapped her arm around him, he—like an obedient child—had raised his head to return the lingering touch of her lips.

THIRTY-FOUR

Harry spent a sleepless night at the Priory.

Finally, at six a.m., he couldn't stand it any longer and got up from the single bed, crept to the bathroom at the end of the corridor, and took what turned out to be a merely lukewarm shower. Returning to his room, he dressed, then went downstairs.

He had a sick feeling in the pit of his stomach: he could guess what the papers would make of Lin. She would be savaged.

Opening the front door, he went out, down the drive, and out onto the village road, desperate for fresh air and thinking time.

No one was about. It was a greyish morning, humid and still.

He came to the centre of the village, to the ugly hall, and the row of thatched houses looking surgically neat and ordered. For a moment he looked longingly at the pub with its red-and-gold sign and firmly closed doors. Then he crossed over to the telephone box. It was no use delaying. Lin would be furious if he didn't do as she had asked.

Far away in London, the phone rang.

'Hello,' said a man's voice.

'Hello, Geoff. It's Harry. Is he there?'

'Hello, Harry. Good morning, and how are you? What the devil are you up to? He's about to go out. It's location for *Six Of One*, you know.'

'I know. Get him for me, will you?'

'As you desire.' The phone was put down. He heard someone running down a corridor. Then, Michael Shale's voice.

'Harry, you old bugger.'

'Hello, Michael. How's your man?'

'Who? Robert England, Esquire?'

'Yes.'

'Oh, the usual cockney repartee. What can I do for you?'

'*England Expects* this Friday?'

'Yes.'

'Can you fit in another face?'

'Why . . . who is it?'

'Lin Gallagher.'

There was a muttered conversation on the other end. 'Have you seen the papers this morning?'

'No.'

'Look, it's a good prospect for us. And the tennis player and his mother just pulled out last night. But you know that England will rip her to shreds.'

'She insists.'

'They say she's having a breakdown, Harry.'

'Will you book her in?'

'There's no problem booking her in. He'd love it. But don't you remember what he did to that guru headcase? Do you want her to sink without trace?'

'Can you book her in?'

'She's a sweet girl, Harry. Is it for real?'

'Just book her, so I can say it's done.'

There was a silence, then a sigh. 'OK, Harry. He'll be delighted.'

Harry gave him the Priory fax number. In mid-sentence his time on the phone ran out. He replaced the receiver and looked at it hard, thoroughly disgusted with himself.

* * *

Harry and Lin reached the hospital in good time for her appointment. It had been a pleasant enough journey through an early-morning spring landscape.

The secretary showed them straight in, as soon as they arrived.

Werth looked frazzled, tired. 'How are you?' he asked Lin.

She settled into a chair opposite him. 'Headache,' she said.

Harry frowned at her. Only fifteen minutes before, when he asked the same question, she had told him she was perfectly all right.

'How is your walking—your balance?'

'The same.'

'The feeling of disorientation?'

'Better,' she said.

This seemed to surprise him. 'Better?' he echoed. 'Really? How so?'

'I know what it is now.'

He considered her. 'Would this new-found knowledge be the same kind of knowledge I see described in the newspaper today?'

'Yes,' she said. They had stopped to buy several nationals on the way, and Lin's story appeared in two of them.

'I see,' Werth said. 'Would it be fair to say that you now feel convinced you're privy to something not available to the rest of us?'

'Yes,' she said. She was not defensive about it, in fact she seemed extraordinarily relaxed. Even elated.

Werth made a couple of notes on the file in front of him. 'I'd like you to describe this headache in more detail,' he said. 'Where exactly is it?'

Lin gave Harry a look which was very nearly a smile. 'All over.'

'Have you noticed any deterioration in your sight?'

'No.'

'No reduction of vision in one eye rather the other?'

'No.'

'But you've had hallucinations?'

Lin shook her head slowly. 'I don't think so.'

'OK,' Werth conceded, not willing to push her. 'Have you lost any weight over the last few weeks?'

'Maybe a little: three or four pounds.'

He scribbled again, then looked up. 'Well, Lin,' he said, 'you're quite a conundrum.'

'Ain't that the truth,' Harry murmured. Lin now smiled fully at him.

'We have the results of something called an ESR,' said Werth. 'A blood test.'

'Standing for what?' Lin asked.

'The erythrocyte sedimentation rate. It simply measures the rate at which the red blood cells in the blood sink to the bottom of a tube. A raised ESR usually means that there's something abnormal going on.'

'And mine was raised?' she asked.

'Yours was raised,' he confirmed, 'but the X-rays didn't help us much. And the lumbar puncture was clear.'

'So she hasn't had meningitis?' Harry asked.

'No . . . though I tend to think Lin, by a particularly bad stroke of luck, has experienced something perhaps like meningism: a flu-like viral inflammation which looks and feels very like its big brother.'

'Well,' Lin said, 'that's something, anyway.'

'You're still looking?' Harry commented.

'Yes, we're still looking. Because Lin's symptoms are very peculiar.'

'Will you please talk as if I'm here in the room with you,' Lin said.

Werth smiled. 'I'm sorry—common occupational dysfunction.'

'What are you looking for now?' she asked.

'Well, I want to do two tests: an EEG and an MRI scan.'

'The difference being?'

'One *listens* to the brain; one *looks* at it, broadly.'

'Aren't they very expensive?' Lin asked.

'Well, they are; but that doesn't have a bearing.'

'I think it does,' she said, 'as I don't think they're necessary.'

There was a brief silence.

'You don't?' Werth said at last. 'Why's that?'

'Because I know what it is, and it isn't anything physical.'

Harry looked down into his lap, embarrassed for her.

'OK,' Werth said, 'explain that to me.'

'And it isn't psychological.'

'All right . . .'

Lin looked away from him. 'Life has its own policing patterns, despite the randomness of events,' she said.

Werth frowned. 'I'm sorry, I don't understand that.'

251

'Life is a structured system,' Lin said slowly, 'planned and formed by a governing body. Inside that structure, we invent ourselves. We create and learn, we reproduce, we travel, we construct, we die. As does everything else. Everything possesss a consciousness, part of a larger consciousness. Its threads—its energies—run through life. But everything we do isn't part of our main purpose.'

'I'm sorry,' said Werth. 'I really don't follow you.'

'There's only one purpose,' Lin said, 'and that's to recognize the wholeness, the way we're linked—the necessary way we must operate together.'

Werth considered, turning his pen over and over between his fingers. 'Lin,' he said, 'that doesn't help me explain a raised ESR.'

'No, I know,' she said, and then she smiled. 'Although it might. Wow . . . wouldn't that be something, if it did?'

'Go back a little way,' Werth said. Harry had a flash of admiration for the man's patience. 'Do you consider your experiences of the last few days indicate this wholeness, this link? Do they demonstrate an energy flowing through life?'

'Yes,' she said. She seemed inordinately pleased, so much so that she stood up and walked backwards and forwards a few paces, like an excited child, before sitting down again.

'It makes you feel very happy?'

'Yes, it makes me see patterns, makes me feel part of the world. I only have a problem in that no one else can feel it.'

'You mentioned this before: that you couldn't find a sense of belonging or understanding. And now you feel that you have that?'

'Yes, absolutely. I can feel the world thinking.'

'I'm sorry?'

Werth and Harry glanced at each other.

'Thinking, *thinking*,' Lin repeated. 'It thinks all the time. It moves and flows.'

'And you see it?'

'Yes. I see we're all part of a greater scheme.'

'Can you hear it, this energy?'

'Yes.'

'What exactly?'

'Voices in everything,' Lin said.

Werth looked down at his notes momentarily. 'What do they sound like?'

She sighed in exasperation. 'Like an electrical current: a distant humming on a single note. Occasionally the note changes, then drops back again.'

'I've heard other people say that,' Harry interjected. 'I read about it once. It was supposed to mean acute hearing—picking up radio frequency.'

'My hearing's no different to anyone else's,' Lin insisted, 'but I hear other voices—human voices. I can hear people thinking, if I touch them. I hear the living and dead all mixed together, because we *are* mixed, you see? The dead are in a different part of the pattern, but they haven't *gone*, and I can pick them up as easily as I can hear you.' She leaned forward, something like joy in her face. 'Isn't that wonderful?' she asked. 'It all goes around and around. You remember that old song: the music goes round and round, and it comes out here?'

'I remember it,' Harry said. 'But then I'm older than you both.'

Lin laughed. 'It's just like that. *We're* the music. We go round and round, and we come out here. Or there. Or anywhere. And then we go round and round . . .' She lifted her hands, and laughed at the pleasure of it, like seeing a toy revolving and miraculously making sounds. 'It really is fabulous. It's so clever, and it makes such sense. Nothing's ever wasted. We're recycled—everything is.'

'All organized by a higher energy?'

'Yes.'

Werth was writing. 'Have you always had this sense of a personal God?'

'God again,' Harry muttered.

'I'm sorry?' Lin asked.

'Was God always very close and personal to you? Do you see a real personality, hear his voice, and so on?'

Lin laughed briefly. 'No, it's not that. God isn't a face, a name, or a personality.'

'But I see that you think you're in touch with him.'

Lin sighed, helpless in her attempt to describe her sensations. 'Oh, OK, if you like.'

Werth sat looking down at his desk for some seconds. Then he stood up and walked to the far side of the room. 'Would you do a little test for me, Lin?' he asked.

'Yes, OK.'

'Stand up and go to the opposite wall.'

She did so.

'You see that line in the carpet? The join line?'

'Yes.'

'Try walking along that, towards me.'

She set out slowly, placing each foot precisely in front of the other to adhere to the line. Halfway across she stumbled, and righted herself, going back to the line. But her progress after that was erratic at best: wavering away from the line, bracing her feet wider to maintain her balance.

'OK,' Werth said, 'thanks. Sit down again, Lin.'

She sat back in the chair, looking pained, self-critical.

'One of the things we considered, to explain this, was a TIA,' Werth said. 'That's a transient ischaemic attack. It's a stroke-like event that usually goes away after a couple of days.' He smiled at her. 'They simply mean that the blood supply has been cut off by a jamming of one of the smaller arteries in the brain. That part of the brain stops functioning for a while; but then the blood clot disperses, and everything drops back to normal again. These attacks can be quite dramatic. A person might lose the feeling in an arm or a leg, or be unable to speak or understand. We blame platelets—platelets that get bunched up together, fight to get through a reduced entry, and then sort themselves out. The person feels sensation in their leg or arm again, or they can understand again, or they can speak.'

'None of that happened to me,' Lin commented.

'Well . . . no, not quite. But you have an altered feeling in your legs, don't you? In your hands? And you're thinking differently and comprehending the world differently.'

'But better—not worse.'

'Yes . . . yes, OK.'

'So it's not a TIA?' Harry said. 'What else could it be?'

'Well . . . migraine sufferers experience an aura sometimes,' Werth said. 'Euphoria, or flashing lights, or numbness—a sensitivity to light. Women get migraine more than men. Sometimes migraine makes a patient feel that he's grown too big—out of his body—or that his body doesn't quite belong to him, as you've described.'

'Out of his body?' Lin asked.

'Some kind of distortion of the body map inside the head.'

'I see,' she said. 'Would you also get a floating sensation?'

'Perhaps.'

'I see,' she repeated.

'Does that mean anything to you?'

'No,' she replied, but she looked away from him.

'Euphoria?' Harry said.

'Yes,' Werth replied. He didn't look directly at Lin, but Harry did. She had stretched her legs out in front of her, and was scrutinizing them, frowning.

'What else could it be?' Harry asked.

'Epilepsy,' Werth said.

'But she'd already have experienced that. That starts in childhood,' Harry said.

'Yes, usually, but it can start in adulthood too. Temporal-lobe epilepsy causes visual hallucinations. And, rarely, it can cause head-aches. Sometimes, in children, a fit can indicate meningitis. Rarer still, temporal-lobe epilepsy can be *caused* by meningitis, or possibly by a meningism. Which is where all these boundaries between epilepsy, TIAs, meningitis and so on get a bit blurred. You can't really say what you're looking at until the tests are done.'

'There's something else, of course,' Lin said.

'What's that?' Werth asked.

'A tumour,' Lin said. 'Headaches, numbness, hallucinations, epilep-tic fits . . . they can be caused by a brain tumour.'

Werth looked at her carefully, kindly, for a moment before reply-ing. Then he nodded. 'Yes, Lin,' he said. 'Sometimes they can be caused by a tumour.'

* * *

The MRI scanner was located in a different part of the hospital.

They walked there together, a route that took them through the children's department and the Special Care baby unit. It was a glorious morning now, and some of the children waiting for appointments for the ear, nose and throat consultant were playing boisterously in the play area, tumbling over foam blocks.

Harry nudged Lin's arm. 'I'll stay here,' he said.

'You can come with me, if you like,' she said.

'I don't like,' he told her. 'Do you mind? I'd be in the way.'

'Coward,' she said, smiling.

'You saw through me,' he said. 'Sorry.'

She squeezed his arm and walked on.

Werth explained the procedure to Lin as they neared the MRI suite.

'The good thing about this is that it's non-invasive,' he said. 'No probes, no biopsy, no tubes. All you have to do is lie still for a quarter of an hour.'

'And the bad thing?' she asked.

'The bad thing,' he said, opening the door for her, 'is that some people find it a bit claustrophobic. It's a bit like being pushed into a giant cotton reel: once in, you can't get out.' They were now in the reception area. 'Do you think you'll find that a problem?'

'No, I don't think so.'

'Good.'

Werth gave the sister Lin's name. She looked at him twice, evidently a little surprised that he had brought Lin to them himself. Then a light seemed to dawn. The woman looked at Lin with a sympathetic smile.

They all think I'm mad, Lin thought unconcernedly.

Harry sat down on a chair, a little distance from the group of parents patiently waiting their turn.

He watched, envying the freely tumbling children. He didn't think he had ever possessed that ability to let go—even as a child. Right the way through school he had been a fat boy, horribly awkward at games, slow at maths, laughable in art class, appalling at science.

His only interest had been books. Somewhere around the fifth form, however, he had discovered an extraordinary talent. Drafted into the debating society one night as a very late understudy, he found that he could talk.

He found he had the knack of twisting arguments on their head, making little comic asides that won the audience around. He was no humorist, no comedian, but he was quick—and he got to the point without a lot of flannel. When he stepped down from the stage, the English teacher had taken him to one side, patted him on the shoulder and said, 'Marks, you're going to make a great salesman for some lucky corporate giant.'

Harry had known almost instinctively that the man was right. Or, almost right. He knew then he had a gift, but he wasn't going to use it for any company's benefit. If he could be persuasive, he thought, he would use it to make money for himself.

He took fine arts at university. In the evenings he went round the snooker halls and the pubs and the working-men's clubs, and he signed up his first contracts for singers and magicians and comics—most of them dreadful, a handful promising. His break came when one of the snooker players proved to be a nerveless machine at the table.

Harry could still see through people, assess them, rank them. He could smell their potential, and their character faults, sometimes simply by watching their expressions as they waited to go on stage, sometimes by seeing how they related to their partners, to other performers, to the bar staff and cleaners and doormen.

You had to be loved. That was all there was to it.

Perhaps that's what Lin's getting at, Harry thought. Connections. An audience could feel connections: when a comic was with them, laughing at himself, for instance; showing himself perhaps to be a fool, but also the kind of man you would love for a friend. People did laugh at cruelty, but not for very long. They laughed best out of affection.

Harry represented performers—not writers, not academics. He knew Kieran only because the man had camera appeal, though that jaded, slightly superior air was starting to wear thin now. It wasn't yet obvious on screen, but Harry could feel it coming, could see Kieran's future as though displayed in letters twenty feet high. Kieran would become bored with the camera lens; his goals were more internal, more private. Lin, however . . . Lin was emerging, she related to people, she was fun when out of Kieran's shadow. And she had a brain as well as looks. She was the millennium woman, the epitome of girl power. With a mathematical turn of mind, a witty sexy look, a way with words. He could see her as the next thinking man's fantasy.

If she just could get over this.

He looked over at a parent waiting on the row of seats opposite.

The man was reading the *National*. On the third page, Harry knew, in a slot reserved for something shocking and light-hearted, was a photograph of Lin with a cross-page headline:

I am God, says the History Man's wife.

They would ridicule her, for sure.

Pity her, perhaps.

But afterwards . . . afterwards would they love her?

THIRTY-FIVE

$\mathcal{B}$ EFORE HER EVENING SURGERY, Ruth went up to the hospital.

Although the neurology department was housed in the modern wing, ITU was, conversely, in the oldest part: a muddled jumble of buildings closer to the town centre. Parking was a nightmare at the best of times, so Ruth was forced to park on the pavement opposite, and hope that she would not be given a ticket.

Consequently she went inside in a hurry, anxious simply to check on Caroline Devlin's progress with the ward staff. But as she came out of the lift on the fourth floor she spotted Martin Devlin, sitting beneath a huge garish abstract print of depressing blues; his elbows were resting on his knees. As she walked towards him, he looked up.

'Hello, Martin,' Ruth said. She stopped opposite him.

'Hello,' he mumbled grudgingly.

'How long have you been here?'

'An hour.'

'Is your uncle here?'

'Coming later.'

She sat down on the other end of the bench. 'You must be going to university in a month or so,' she said.

'Polytechnic,' he muttered. 'I was going to Polytechnic.'

'But you're still going?'

He looked up at her. 'Why don't you just push off?' he said.

Ruth drew back. 'I came to see how your mother is.'

'What do you care?'

She stood up, hesitating a long moment. 'Do you mind if I go in?'

'Do what you like.'

Glancing back at him, Ruth went on to ITU.

There were only three patients there: Caroline on one side of the ward, an elderly woman and a middle-aged man on the other. The small unit was full of muted sound: the constant buzz and bleep of monitors, the voices of the staff. Alongside the male patient sat a woman in her fifties, her eyes closed.

Ruth studied Caroline. She was hardly recognizable as the woman Ruth had known. Her hair was tied in a plait on her shoulder; her hands lay on the sheet on either side of her. Without make-up, she looked considerably older, her face slightly swollen, and the ventilator tube taped to the side of her mouth. Ruth glanced over at the ward station, where the nurse's shift was in the process of changing.

She was surprised to observe Martin standing directly behind her.

'What I can't understand,' he said in a soft monotonous tone, 'is that . . . you see that woman over there? What is she . . . seventy? Maybe eighty? And there's my mother, fifty-two. She's twenty, thirty years younger than this other woman, and yet she's here . . .'

'Martin,' Ruth said. 'I really did all I could.'

He turned to stare at her. 'That why you came here—to tell me that?'

'No. But I hope you can believe it.'

He looked at the floor.

'It isn't anyone's fault, Martin,' Ruth said. 'An awful lot can be done for coronary patients, but there are a certain proportion who simply die from the first attack, from the first sign.'

'That's just it,' he said. 'She had pain in her chest a lot of times, but she didn't think it was important. She always thought other people were more important.'

Ruth did not reply.

'Is it worth it?' he asked.

'I'm sorry . . . is what worth it?'

He was staring down at his hands. 'Getting involved with everyone. She worried about everyone,' he said. 'I never got it . . . never. Why'd she bother about these people, all these neurotic people? Why did she bother? What use was it?' he continued almost to himself. 'Look where she ended up.'

He glanced up towards his mother. 'She always said you had to be part of other people,' he said. 'That's rubbish, isn't it? What do other people care—what is it to do with them? People don't give a shit—that's what I think. Not really. You have to get on by yourself. By *yourself.*'

Ruth could not think of an answer.

'She always wanted to talk to me, and I just didn't want to talk back,' he said. 'I couldn't stick this talking all the time. I mean, you get on with things by yourself a lot faster. I didn't want her always interfering . . .'

He put his hands to his face, his voice breaking. Ruth looked at the floor and wished fervently that he would not start to cry.

'You must try to be strong,' she said.

He looked up immediately. 'Why?' he said, his face tear-stained and reddening. 'Why must I be strong? I don't want to be fucking strong! I want her back!'

'Yes, I know.'

'You don't know!' he shouted. 'When did you ever care about anyone?'

'I do care,' Ruth said.

'You doctors are all the same. I know what you are.'

The nurse hurried to their side. 'Would you move along the corridor, please, if you want to talk,' she said.

Ruth took Martin's arm. She managed to steer him twenty yards away. 'We do have hearts, like anyone else,' she murmured. 'But if I wept over every patient, where would I be? How could I do my job?'

Martin wrenched his arm away.

'I really do hope . . .'

'Do you?' he demanded. 'Do you bloody hope? Well, ace—because I don't hope. And I don't want you pawing me, and I don't want to be here, and I don't want to hear another fucking bastard's opinion, and I don't want you—and I'm going to see you never keep a straight face over any other corpse you've killed. Never! I'm going to wreck you, all right? Wreck you and your smug bloody life . . .'

Ruth turned and walked away.

She got to the door to the ITU unit, and then to the waiting area outside the lifts, and then she began to run. She ran down the corridor until she reached the women's toilets, where she slammed open the door. She stood staring into the mirror for ten seconds, while her heart banged mercilessly in her throat.

She saw any number of images other than her own. She saw the hot summer ward, that sticky grey cubicle, the mother's wretched face, the face of the consultant paediatrician . . . and she saw an anonymous room where her own hearing took place, one rainy autumn afternoon. *You didn't even consider anaphylactic shock? It never occurred to you?*

Anaphylactic shock. Wasp sting.

No, it had never occurred to her.

She had thought she was seeing a case of child abuse, of possible subdural haematoma. She had been tired that day, weary, defeated, slipping in and out of sleep because she had been on duty for thirty-two hours. Anaphylactic shock? So obvious, obvious, obvious. Obvious to the most junior nurse—but not to her. She had missed it . . .

Accused the parents to their faces.

Never slept properly since. Covered up the guilt and confusion, scraped through, moved area, worked herself into the ground, cauterized any possible emotion, never allowed herself an abandonment to pleasure. Blame and guilt . . . Broken nights . . .

The nausea crawled up her throat and she lost the battle, vomiting into the toilet.

She's a monster.

When did you ever care about anyone?

You've got no feelings.

A monster.

When Ruth had found out, later, that she couldn't have children, she had felt that it was a judgement on her. She had accepted it almost mildly; personal fulfilment seemed like a very dim echo at the bottom of her soul. And then she met Kieran, who cruised through life—without searching for reasons or analysing anyone, Kieran who admired her, admired her resolute calm more than any other quality, and . . .

And then came Lin.

Ruth stood up, wiping her face with a pinched-up bundle of toilet paper.

If she could get him back, the world would not seem so jumbled—not so dangerous. If she had him back, accusations like Martin's would once again roll over her, past her . . .

Monster.

It meant nothing to them, of course. It was just a word said in anger. They couldn't actually believe—sincerely believe—that she was monstrous. She *could* show love. She *could* be loving. She *could* weep and plead. She *could* be desperate and show it . . .

'Oh God,' she whispered.

Ruth dragged herself back to the mirror. She looked old, her skin flaccid and grey, her hair too yellow, over-bleached and stiff with lacquer. She looked at her pale-blue jacket and then, in numbed slow motion, rubbed at flecks of stain with a finger wet from the cold tap.

You are a little oasis of sanity.

Sanity. Sanity?

She glanced back at herself.

Life with Kieran was sanity. Everything else was a caricature.

THIRTY-SIX

$\mathcal{L}$IN FINALLY GOT BACK IN TO SEE WERTH at four o'clock.

The consultant apologized as she sat down. 'Busier than I'd antici-pated,' he explained. 'Is your friend still with you?'

'He's just gone to make a couple of phone calls,' she said. 'I asked him to.'

'Right.'

'He's a nice man,' she said, 'but really this is my business.'

Werth was now considering her file placed in front of him.

'What's the news?' she asked.

He paused a moment before replying. 'There's an aspect to this that's reassuring,' he said finally. 'And that is that there's some explana-tion for what you've been experiencing.' He gave her a small smile.

'Really?' she asked. 'What explanation?'

'There is a small tumour inside the skull—on the meninges.'

There was silence. Then, 'I see,' Lin said. Her expression hardly flickered.

'You haven't had any type of cancer, have you, Lin?' he asked.

She noted the emphasis on her Christian name. 'No, I haven't.'

He remained silent.

'I'd like to know about it,' she said. 'I want to know the details.'

'OK.' He steepled his fingers in front of him, leaning his elbows on the desk. 'The brain is a repository for secondary tumours, but I would guess this is a primary—the only one. We need to operate, but I'm confident in guessing it's benign. Meningioma gets more common as we grow older. Sometimes you can have several there, but they're usually quite separate from each other; they haven't spread as a malignant tumour would.'

'What happens when you operate?'

'We cut a small piece of bone from the skull, and peel the tumour from the meninges. Then we replace the bone.'

'And this . . .' Lin hesitated from using his words. 'This has caused what I've seen and felt this last week?'

'Well, that would be my opinion.'

She smiled. 'You don't sound sure.'

'Your symptoms are curious,' Werth admitted. 'But, then, this tumour is over the temporal lobe, and that's a curious place.' He smiled at her. 'It controls all kinds of functions,' he said. 'Sight, speech, sound, memory, comprehension. The trouble with your symptoms is that they seem all mixed up. If a tumour were in the parietal cortex, for instance, there would be problems with spatial awareness—you wouldn't relate to things on your left-hand side, perhaps. Lesions in the temporal cortex sometimes result in people being able to see something—a tree, a car, their own child—but not to be able to name it until they touch it . . .'

'They know things through touch?' she echoed.

'We all do. But these patients can *only* put a name to them by touching them. Then there are—'

'Do they know any *more* by touching?' she asked.

He paused. 'You mean the kind of things that you say you know through touch.'

'Yes.'

'I haven't heard of it before.'

She frowned.

'The important thing is, the rate of cell death in the area of the tumour will be increased,' he continued. 'Perhaps the images you see are actually retained images being given up as each cell perishes. But I have to say that, although we understand what various areas in the brain do, in some incredible detail, we find it considerably harder to say what the relation between the areas is. How thought relates to knowledge, for instance.' He gave an apologetic shrug, realizing that he was elaborating more than was necessary. 'Whatever that relation, this tumour is in an area you need, so it's vital that we slow the cell death-rate down—that we save the cells from being eaten up. And with a benign tumour, the only way we can do that is by removing it.'

Lin had been looking down at her hands, examining her fingers, massaging the palms. She was smoothing out the ongoing sense of distortion, trying to make them feel a normal size.

'My symptoms are all scrambled,' she murmured. 'They don't conform to where the tumour is. Is that it?'

'Yes and no. Because we don't understand the relation of one part to another enough, it could well be that what you're experiencing is exactly what should be happening. Perhaps the tumour is pressing on a millimetre of structure that represents that unknown, or misunderstood, connection.'

Lin looked away. 'Connections,' she whispered.

'I'm sorry?'

'Nothing . . . nothing,' she said. She got up and walked, very slowly, to the window. 'How long has it been there?' she asked.

'Hard to say.'

'Could it always have been there?'

'It's possible. Meningioma is typically slow-growing.'

'Why would it start causing problems now?'

'Probably because, as you age, it's growing a little larger.'

She was running her index finger slowly along the sill. 'And if it hasn't always been there, why has it appeared now?'

'Again, hard to say. Perhaps you've had a virus. Or it's the site of a head injury.'

'I haven't had a head injury.'

'Then we don't know.'

She turned to look at him, smiling a little. 'You don't know much.'

'No, maybe not. The brain never ceases to amaze me. We understand a lot of its structure, but not all of its processes.'

'For instance?'

He thought. 'Intelligence. Truly intelligent thought is more than calculation, number-crunching or logic. Savants can calculate the expression of fractions as decimals, for instance, to twenty-six, twenty-seven points in a matter of seconds. But they can't make informed decisions about their own lives. They can tell you on what day of the week a certain date fell a hundred years ago, but they can't say when is a good time to cross the street. We can watch the impulses of nerve fibres, the distribution of blood in the brain as a person reads or talks; but we can't forecast creativity, or intuition . . .'

Lin nodded. 'There's something more,' she said, 'than what can be seen, or counted. That's what quantum theories are about. Matter doesn't obey cause-and-effect laws. It leaps. It changes.'

'I don't know a thing about physics,' Werth said.

Lin rested against the windowsill, crossing her arms. 'It's in the same territory you were just covering,' she said, 'that there's a reality which is more than anything quantifiable. A reality operating behind the things we can count, catalogue, see. We are more than the sum of our parts. Something else is happening.'

'I don't know if I go along with that,' Werth said. 'I tend to think that somewhere in the brain there's a place where those tricky, shapeless effects—like love and compassion and pity—are made. It's there in the deep cell structure somewhere. We just can't find it yet.'

'You mean there's a synapse marked "reliability", or "faith", or "aggression"?'

'Oh yes,' he said. 'There's certainly that already. You can fire impulses into a cat's brain and make the animal spit and claw and bare its teeth. You can fabricate fear with an electrical prod. We know about the anatomy of limbic, brain-stem and cortical structures and the neural pathways that connect them to each other. But *how* they function, *why* they function in emotions . . . that we don't know. We infer it. But we don't know it.'

'And you think that one day you will?'

'Oh yes. It's there somewhere.'

'How?'

'In a chemical reaction, maybe. In reactions that we haven't seen or attached significance to. For instance, we know that a transmitter called norepinephrine triggers arousal. If you get too little norepinephrine, you get depressed.'

'And you think there's a chemical like that somewhere that produces intuitive leaps, or intelligent deductions, or artistic beauty?'

'Yes. There must be.'

'You are a good scientist,' she said.

'Thank you.'

'But not a great one,' she said. 'A great one would say that the universe looked more like a thought than a machine.'

'That's your opinion,' Werth said.

'No,' she replied, and she tapped her finger on the side of her head. 'That's what I know.'

'Interesting that you indicate your brain,' he commented, grinning. 'You know it because there's a neural transmission in there telling you.'

'No,' she said, 'I know it because a greater thought moves me. Greater than my own. A greater energy.' She returned to her chair, and sat down. 'Look all you want,' she said. 'Take the brain to pieces and pick over every scrap. You won't find what makes it work. That exists outside, inside—everywhere.'

Werth regarded her for a while in appreciative silence.

'Are you going to pick my brain to pieces, doctor?' she asked.

'No,' he told her. 'We're just going to remove a little bit that doesn't belong there.'

She pursed her lips, considering. 'It *might* belong there,' she said.

'I'm sorry?'

'It might belong there. It might be performing a function.'

'You don't mean the tumour?'

'Yes, that's exactly what I mean.' She smiled. 'Do you know that they say Shostakovich had a splinter of metal in his head—a shell fragment—and that each time he leaned his head to one side he could hear music?'

'Yes,' Werth said, 'I've heard that story. Epileptics can have a musical seizure. The production of music is in the superior temporal convolution, close to the area associated with musicogenic epilepsy.'

'Well,' Lin said, 'I've discovered a kind of music.'

He sat forward, perturbed. 'What do you mean?'

She looked him in the eye. 'You said it yourself. You said that this tumour has caused what I've seen and felt.'

'Yes.'

'Even though it doesn't quite add up.'

'Yes.'

'Then I want to keep it.'

Werth was genuinely shocked. 'You can't possibly be serious.'

'I am. I don't want to lose these feelings.'

'Lin,' he said. 'Perhaps I haven't made myself clear. This tumour could very well be benign, but that doesn't mean it isn't going to hurt you. It simply means that it's self-contained, that it's not a symptom of a another malignancy somewhere else in the body. It doesn't mean, even if benign, that it won't grow more.'

'I don't care,' she said.

'Don't say that without knowing the facts.'

'I don't want to know any more. If there's any danger I'll lose these sensations, I don't want it taken away.'

Werth dropped his voice. It was his way of controlling his temper. 'Lin, if you don't remove a tumour, you'll have greater and more disabling effects,' he said. 'It's only very small now, but it's in a delicate area. You may lose your sight and hearing entirely. Then you'll see and hear nothing—not your son, your family, your books, your home— you'll hear *nothing*, not even your voices.'

She had turned her head away. She put up a hand, to indicate that she wasn't accepting what he said.

'There is no choice here,' he told her.

She flashed him a look. 'Of course there's a choice,' she said. 'And it's mine to make.'

He stared at her. 'You want to chose death over life?'

'It doesn't necessarily mean death,' she said. 'It might just carry on as it is now.'

'Oh,' he said. 'And that's pleasant, is it? This tiredness, these head-aches, the disorientation?'

'No,' she said. 'But it's better than what I had before.'

He ran his hand through his hair, exasperated. 'I don't understand you,' he said. 'Let me tell you, there is no rational choice here. A removal of a benign tumour would let you return to the life you had before.'

'And what makes you think that I want that life?' she asked.

Her reply stunned him. 'What do you mean?'

She paused for some time before she replied to him. There was no confusion in her face, only absolute clarity and calm.

'I don't tell you this for sympathy,' she said. 'I don't want to sound neurotic.' She smiled. 'I've been told that before, and it isn't a good feeling.' She took a long, deep breath. 'I had a very unhappy time as a child,' she said softly. 'That's not so unusual. I'm not going to beat a drum about it. A lot of people have worse times. I was never physically neglected. My mother, in a difficult situation, did a pretty good job, faced with a problem—me,' she said wryly. 'That was her problem—she accepted it, even though it meant admitting a mistake, losing her husband. She was stoical, you see? She thought of it like a judgement, a burden to be carried. She was a religious person. God had given her me to carry, and carry me she did, though it disgusted her.'

She stopped, bit her lip briefly, and then continued.

'I have a great deal to be thankful for,' Lin said. 'I'm intelligent. I always liked to think, to study. It gave me pleasure. I went to univer-sity. I met a man, and married him. I had a child. I know that these are all things that other people long for and perhaps never achieve, and I realize how fortunate that makes me.' She corrected herself slightly: 'How fortunate that makes me in those particular areas.'

He started to speak. She put up her hand to indicate that she hadn't finished.

'But that isn't living, you know,' she said. 'To be grateful that some-thing worse hasn't happened to you isn't living.' She paused briefly. 'You see, Mr Werth, until I had my son I had never been loved. And until this illness I'd never felt that the world was a loving, coherent, living place. I had never been really touched, cherished. And now all that's changed.'

Werth leaned back in his chair, watching her.

'In the first twenty-four hours that I was here,' she continued, 'it was as if everything I'd learned was shuttling together, colliding together, bouncing around my head: images from Kieran's work, from my own work, from the scripts I've been working on, from my life before I met him . . . They say that a dying man sees his life flash before him, don't they? It was a curious feeling. As if my brain were letting off random shots, snapshots of everything it knew or had felt . . .'

'That's quite a typical reaction, you know, Lin.'

'Yes, I realize that,' she said. 'And if that were all I'd felt, I'd accept what you say. But then the world began to be peopled: it was full of faces and sounds. It's stayed that way. Those faces broke through to me in a way that no one else ever has. They need me; I perform a purpose. I'm part of a chain. I have a job to do. I'm a vital part, a needed part.' She smiled slowly.

Werth stood up. He came around the front of the desk and took her hand. 'If what you say is true,' he said, 'it's something more than just the problem in your head.'

'Yes, it is.'

'Then removing the tumour won't affect it. How can it? It's nothing to do with the tumour.'

She considered a moment. 'No, but it's the link,' she murmured, 'don't you see? It's like the door key. It's opened the way. If I have it removed, that might slam the door again.'

'But you just said that the things are greater than ourselves. Greater than our physical parts.'

'Yes, they are. But no one sees them, or senses them, do they? Or very few do. The ones that do, we label religious freaks: hippies, New-Agers, spiritualists. We don't take them seriously for the most part, do we? We treat them like a freak show, a place for the weak to indulge themselves. People feel something . . . they *do* feel something. They recognize goodness, they want happiness, but they don't know the route. It's all so wispy, so amorphous, so intangible. You have to have faith. Faith that the things you believe in are actually real.' Her grip on his fingers tightened. 'But I don't need that faith,' she said. 'Because I've got the proof. I can actually see it and feel it.'

She turned from him and looked at the trees beyond the window, at the long stretches of grass, and paused a moment as if she were listening to them as well as seeing them.

'I can feel the pulse of life in everything I touch,' she murmured. 'I can feel this spirit, this effect, this force moving through the world. I can feel your thoughts, the configurations inside your mind, feel the focus of your interest through your touch. I can feel it as if it had weight and texture, and form . . .'

She turned, and smiled into his face with a transcendent expression of conviction that moved him to intense pity.

'I can't risk losing that now,' she said. 'Could you?'

THIRTY-SEVEN

THE LATE-AFTERNOON SUNLIGHT streamed across Kieran's desk in his room on campus. He had been sitting for some time with the newspapers spread in front of him, looking at them without seeing them.

He had taken Theo to Mrs Sawyer's house in the village. His housekeeper had welcomed the boy with open arms, then asked after Lin, and kept up a constant stream of questions until he got back into his car. Even then, she tapped on the window.

'Shall I give him his tea?'

'Please.'

'What time will you be back?'

They watched Theo run around the back of her house with Mrs Sawyer's grandson in hot pursuit.

'I'll be as quick as I can,' Kieran said. 'Certainly by six or seven.'

But, to tell the truth, he had not been as quick as he could have been. It was something of a relief to be away from Theo's accusing, mute stare of defiance. He could see so much of Lin in that face.

He looked up now and considered the view from his window: the gothic Victorian courtyard with its rosebeds and benches, and the less appealing fourth side of the square where the Sixties additions to the building formed an ugly blue-panelled block. He then glanced around his own room. He had rearranged it recently, throwing out the two couches and the chrome-and-black table and chairs. The one painting that he and Lin had bought together, the loud yellow-and-orange print of African women holding hands in a dancing circle, he had relegated to the corridor. He was back where he had begun—even before Ruth—in a spartan room whose only decoration was books.

He sighed. The print of the newspapers made his head ache—or perhaps it was the content of the articles. He rested his head on one hand and looked at the headlines again.

There was a photograph of Lin and himself. It had been taken three years ago at the launch party for *Carthaginian Kings*, soon after he had been offered the TV series. He remembered how bemused he had felt when he first saw himself on screen. A joke that would not last—a fraud parading as a media face. He was part of that narrow, beloved band, the TV academic—like the TV doctor, the TV biologist, the TV vicar—people of one profession paddling for a while in another. He remembered the party, at a London hotel. Lin had hooted with laughter at the luxury of the rooms the TV company had provided.

'You've made it,' she had said, coming out of the bathroom swaddled in several towels after an hour-long bath. 'Complimentary toothpaste and a view of the park.' She had wanted to go to the launch dressed as Hannibal's Spanish wife; she had even suggested to the publishers that they hire elephants to flank the Covent Garden bookstore.

The PR girls thought she was wonderful, if mad—but Lin had been enjoying herself hugely. Kieran had eventually gone to the shops with her to buy a dress, and, after an argument or two, agreed to the long black design she selected, thinking it safe. He hadn't expected her for a moment to pull the shoulders down and display an acre of cleavage. She had been stick thin, with a round high bosom and round, puppy-fat hips above long legs, a kind of Barbie-doll shape on his arm. There were no real elephants at the store, but there had been twelve-foot-high inflatables bouncing about close to the rooftops in a high wind. The sight of them stopped traffic.

Kieran had become popular overnight—something to elicit condemnation from his colleagues. Ruth, whom he had seen occasionally, treated him as if he had contracted a disfiguring disease and gave him sympathetic smiles of deep sadness. But the picture in the paper . . . this picture resurrected now . . . Lin on his arm, all flesh, throwing back her head and laughing as she tottered on a step and pulled her voluminous skirt out of her way with one free, hip-high hand, was both a sweet and bitter memory.

The same picture was now featured at the top of the newspaper page. And halfway down the same page was a cruel photograph taken of Lin two days ago, evidently as she had stepped out of the car at the Priory. She was dwarfed by an enormous sweater, her legs very thin in black leggings. She looked tired, her eyes ringed, her face pinched. Her smile was weary, no more than tolerant. The caption read: *How the years have taken their toll!*

The article was a full-page interview. GOD IS FEMALE, smirked the headline. *Lin Gallagher, wife of history heartthrob Kieran, declares herself divine*, ran the byline.

There followed a long description of Lin's supposedly privileged lifestyle: the house in the country, the TV husband, totally fictitious figures for the contracts secured on the television series. Then it launched into Lin herself, describing her as a drop-out from university. It claimed that she hadn't been able to stand the pace of her mathematics course, so had since taken to writing the sensationalist scripts of the series. The same unnamed source had said scathingly that these scripts were poorly researched. Worse still, it quoted a family friend as revealing that Lin had always been an embarrassment to him at the university among his own colleagues. It gave a rushed, sketchy account of Lin's illness, and hinted broadly at this being a publicity stunt. Finally, with relish, it ended: *Lin Gallagher has had a little trouble with reality before. Last year she spent two weeks at a psychiatric unit after trashing the family home.*

Where on earth had they got that from? Kieran had never told anyone in the village. He got to his feet suddenly, swept the newspaper up and walked out of the room. The corridors were empty: it was almost six o'clock. He walked around one side of the quad to Caldwell's room, where he knocked on the door.

'Come in,' said a voice.

Arthur Caldwell was lying on a couch under the window. The room smelt of smoke from his untipped cigarettes. He was stretched full-length, propped on half a dozen cushions, with an old-fashioned Photax viewer on his lap. Scattered all around him—on the couch and the low table and the floor—were hundreds of transparencies.

'Come in,' he repeated, seeing Kieran at the door. 'Tell me what this is.' He handed Kieran a slide. Kieran held it up to the light.

'It's Dicket Mead under excavation,' he said.

'No, it isn't,' Caldwell replied.

'The plunge bath is in the foreground. The hot bath's to the left.'

'Hmmm . . . you may be right. And this?'

'Looks like Gadebridge Park.' Kieran lowered the slide. 'Why don't you have them labelled?'

'I shall. They've been left to the faculty. New bequest, from amateur site sleuth.'

'Really?' Kieran held the coloured frame up again.

'D'you want them?'

Kieran didn't answer. He put down the slide, and held up the newspaper.

'Ah,' said Caldwell.

'Arthur, did you speak to these people?'

'I?'

'Do you know who did?'

'Why do you suppose that anyone did?'

'Because there are opinions expressed as being those of the university—or someone here.'

'But that doesn't mean anyone spoke to them, old chap.' Caldwell slotted another slide into the viewer.

'It says that the series is poorly researched.'

'And is it?'

'I do that research myself.'

'Yes, I know that.'

'Did you tell them about Lin's breakdown last year?'

'Surely that was common knowledge?'

'It certainly was not.'

'Then I'm at a loss.'

Kieran stared at him. 'How could you bloody well do that?' he said. 'You know that she's ill.'

'Ill,' Caldwell repeated. 'Yes, I should say so. Tragic.'

'Arthur,' Kieran began.

'I'm listening.' Caldwell squinted at the picture. 'Christ! This one's Brading.'

'Arthur, I want a year off.'

Caldwell looked for another moment at the slide, then switched off the viewer and threw the slide on the floor. He took a pack of cigarettes from his pocket. 'Oh?' he said.

'I've been offered a contract.'

'To do what, exactly?'

'To tour. A lecture circuit.'

'How profitable.'

'It's not for profit, Arthur.'

'No, no,' Caldwell said, drawing on the lighted cigarette. 'It's to get away, I should think, from all this.' He waved his hand at the newspaper. 'And from this wife of yours. I don't blame you.'

Kieran paused. 'No, that isn't the reason,' he said. 'It's to get away from here.'

'Here?' Caldwell raised his eyebrows. 'And why should you want to do that?'

'Because of nonsense like this,' Kieran retorted. 'Because I can never turn my back for a minute in here.'

'What do you mean?'

'Don't be obtuse, Arthur,' Kieran said. 'It's exactly what you've wanted.'

'I? No, not at all.'

'Since my television work began.'

'No, no, why should I? You bring a considerable focus on the department.'

'You've sabotaged me at every step.'

'That's most unfair.'

'Is it? You've hardly supported me.'

'I've allowed you great rein. I'm surprised to hear you say otherwise.'

'Anywhere else would be glad of the publicity.'

Caldwell smiled. 'This kind of publicity?' he asked, nodding at the newspaper.

'This is nothing to do with me.'

'Lin is your wife.' Caldwell swung his legs down from the couch, pinched out the end of the cigarette between finger and thumb, and tossed it towards the ashtray. 'You must do whatever you wish,' he said. 'I'm sure I wouldn't stand in your way.'

Kieran stared at him belligerently. 'That's it?'

'What else do you want?'

'You'll give me a sabbatical?'

Caldwell pursed his lips. 'I can't promise that,' he said. 'This seems like a furtherance of your television career. I suppose it's the USA.'

'It may be.'

Caldwell's face clouded. For the first time, he showed his anger. 'Don't flannel me, Kieran,' he said. 'You've been offered an American tour to accompany the sales of the series to the USA. A package with something called the Fact Factory.'

Kieran said nothing.

'Am I right?'

'Yes.'

'Then kindly don't patronize me.' Caldwell's distaste was now clear.

Kieran looked at him, furious. 'You told the paper about Lin.'

'I said very little.'

'You said she was an embarrassment.'

'So she is.'

'In what way!'

'In this way . . . in the image she has always projected.' Caldwell turned away from Kieran. 'She's not the right kind of person.'

'She's an exceptional talent,' Kieran said.

'That may be—but not an academic talent. She has no discipline.' Caldwell, in the process of picking up the slides, turned back to look at him. 'I'm surprised to hear you defend her,' he said. 'What a marriage it was!'

Kieran stopped. He had surprised himself. Whatever he now felt about Lin, he could not bear to hear her dismissed. What made him so angry was that the root of the disapproval was not in Lin's intellectual abilities at all, but because she didn't possess the correct background. Because of her faint Liverpool accent. Because she had never bothered to humour men like Caldwell.

'Yes,' Kieran said, emotion squeezing his voice to a murmur. 'What a marriage it was.'

He slammed the newspaper down on Caldwell's table and walked out.

Kieran drove slowly home, hearing his own word *was* over and over again. He felt dulled, confused. He went first to the Priory, and, checking that there were no reporters on the step, went inside. The phone was ringing.

Kieran glanced at the clock. It was seven p.m.

'Yes?'

There was a fractional pause. 'Hello, is this Kieran Gallagher?'

'Yes,' Kieran said. He was about to slam the receiver down, assuming it was another newspaper. Just as he took it away from his ear, however, he recognized the voice.

'Mr Gallagher, it's Mark Werth.'

'Hello, Mr Werth.'

'It's about Lin. I saw her this afternoon,' Werth said. 'We took the scan this morning.'

'I see.'

'Mr Gallagher, your wife has a tumour. She needs an operation to remove it. She needs medication before that operation, and someone at hand to care for her.'

Kieran said nothing.

'Are you still there?'

'Yes, I'm still here.'

'Probably I'm breaking confidentiality, but I'm very concerned for her.' 'A tumour . . . ?' Kieran repeated.

'But she refuses to have the operation.'

'What?'

'She refuses the operation.'

'But she can't do that.'

'I'm afraid she has.'

'And this is urgent?'

'She can only get worse.'

'Is it life-threatening?'

'The tumour is almost certainly benign. But, yes, if left to grow, it could result in—'

'Where is she?'

'I don't know.'

'She didn't say where she was going when she left you?'

'No.'

'Was Mr Marks with her?'

'Yes.'

Kieran swore softly under his breath.

'Mr Gallagher, is there any pressure you might be able to bring to bear on your wife to have this operation done?'

'Yes,' Kieran said.

'I should feel much better if I could—'

'Yes, yes, yes,' Kieran said. 'I told you, yes.'

There was a short silence. 'OK,' Werth said. 'Perhaps you would ring me and let me know.'

'All right,' Kieran said. He put the phone down on Werth's goodbye. 'Good God almighty,' he whispered.

He went back out to the car.

He had rung Harry's number at once, but there was no reply.

He drove to Mrs Sawyer's, and knocked on her door. She opened it, still wiping her hands on a tea towel.

'Has Theo been all right?' Kieran asked, looking over her shoulder into the darkness of the house.

'Yes, but . . .'

'Is he ready to go?'

The woman paled. 'But he isn't here,' she said.

Kieran stared at her. 'What do you mean, he isn't here?'

Mrs Sawyer's hand flew to her throat. 'Doctor Carmichael came to fetch him,' she said.

'When?'

'About five o'clock . . . We were just eating tea . . .'

'What did she say?'

'She said that you had asked her to come and collect him because you were going to be held up,' she said. Her eyes ranged over his face. 'Wasn't that right?' she asked. 'Oh God . . .'

'Where did she go?'

'I thought it would be all right . . .'

'Where did she go?' Kieran insisted.

'She didn't say.' Tears had sprung to the woman's eyes. 'She just drove away.'

'And Theo went with her? He just went with her?'

'He cried a little bit. But Dr Carmichael was very nice, she had some chocolate for him, she held his hand all the way to her car, she said—'

Kieran turned on his heel, and ran down the path.

'I'm sorry,' Mrs Sawyer called after him. 'I didn't know. I'm so sorry . . .'

In the car, Kieran picked up his mobile and dialled Ruth's number. It rang unanswered.

THIRTY-EIGHT

*I*T WAS FOUR O'CLOCK when Harry and Lin arrived in London.

Lin had never been to Harry's flat before and was bemused to see, as she stepped over the doorstep, how clean and tidy it was in contrast to Harry himself. They stepped into a single large room with a bare wood floor; on the far left was an open fireplace. To the right was the kitchen. Other doors led off to the bedrooms. The whole of the opposite window faced the river and, even as the evening faded, the room was flooded with light.

Lin walked in, looking around herself with a smile.

'Sit down. You look shattered,' Harry said. 'Let me get you something to drink.'

She obeyed him, positioning herself on a couch which faced a wall completely covered in a display which amazed her.

It was Harry's collection of comics. Over a hundred of them were framed, the rest in plastic-protected volumes on shelves beneath: *Superman, Eagle, Mad.*

'What's that?' she asked, pointing at one.

'It's the Baffler,' said Harry. 'Pretty ugly guy.' He walked to a shelf and picked up a small object. 'Look at this,' he said.

'It's a pig.'

'See the key in it? Watch.' Harry wound the key; the pig tottered forward.

Lin laughed, picking it up and inspecting it. 'Does it do anything else?'

'It grunts. Listen.'

'Not very loud.'

Harry laughed. 'No. It was made ninety years ago. It's too old to learn new tricks.'

Lin shook her head. 'It's wonderful. How long have you been collecting this stuff?'

'Oh, years.' He shrugged, going over to the galley kitchen.

'It casts a new light over you.'

'What sort of light?'

'Fun,' she said.

He pretended to be offended. 'I wasn't fun before?'

She smiled. 'It's a beautiful room, Harry.'

'Thanks,' he said.

'Very original.'

'What did you imagine—lager cans and orange boxes?'

She laughed. 'Yes,' she admitted.

He smiled as he ran the water and filled the kettle. 'What do you want to eat?'

'I'm not really hungry.'

He came out and stood in front of her. 'How are you feeling? Truth now.'

'Shitty.'

'Uh-huh. That's pretty truthful. Do you want some aspirin? Codeine?'

'Yes, please.'

He brought her the tablets and a glass of water, and watched while she swallowed two. 'I'll make an omelette,' he said.

'You cook?'

'I cook. Help yourself to a shower, bed, whatever.'

'Thanks,' she said.

Later, while they were eating, the phone rang.

Harry picked it up.

'It's Kieran,' said the familiar voice. 'Is Lin there?'

Harry half turned away from the table. 'I'm busy just now.'

'Don't sod me about,' came the reply. 'If she is, tell me. It's important, Harry. It's about Theo.'

Harry's heart sank a little. He looked out at the river and hoped that Lin couldn't read his expression. 'Yes,' he said.

'Yes, she's there?'

'That's right.'

There was a long sighing exhalation on the other end. 'Good,' Kieran said. 'I don't suppose Ruth is there too?'

'Who? No.'

'OK . . .'

'Would you like to tell me what this is about?'

'Ruth took Theo from the babysitter this afternoon. I'm trying to find them.'

Harry said nothing.

'Don't tell Lin.'

'I won't,' Harry replied grimly.

'If Ruth should turn up, will you ring me?'

'Yes.'

'Let me speak to Lin now.'

Harry put his hand over the receiver. 'It's Kieran,' he said. 'Do you want to speak to him?'

She held out her hand for the phone.

'Lin,' Kieran said, 'why did you go all that way?'

'Because I wanted to,' she said.

'How are you?'

'All right.'

'Werth rang me. He told me.'

It was Lin's turn to look away from Harry.

'Lin, you mustn't run away from this.'

'I'm not running away.'

'You must have that operation. You can't refuse it,' he said.

She didn't reply.

Frustrated beyond belief, Kieran's grip on the phone tightened. 'Are you listening?' he demanded. 'Lin?'

She hung up.

Harry raised an eyebrow at her. She said nothing. Eventually she pushed the half-finished plate away from her.

'What did he want?' Harry asked.

She shrugged. 'Just to bully me a bit.'

Harry leaned over towards her. 'I want to do some bullying of my own,' he said.

'Oh?'

'I don't want you to do this show.'

'I know,' she said.

'Robbie England isn't what he seems. He can be a miserable son-of-a-bitch.'

'I know,' she repeated.

'But you *don't* know,' Harry said. 'Even his own agent despises him.'

'I've seen his show,' Lin said.

'Then you know what he's capable of,' Harry said. 'OK, most of the time it's all sweetness and light, a few jokes, a couple of weirdos who don't mind being laughed at, a kiddie who can dance and he can do a number with, some paraplegic he can conjure a tear about, raising money for charity—all very high profile. It's all designed to show the world what a good lad he is.'

'And you're going to warn me about the one person every week that he shreds.'

'I am. That last fifteen minutes is designed for just one thing, Lin. It's a live show: very important, very dangerous, very edge-of-the-seat. A big gamble for the TV company. Those last fifteen minutes carry the rest. The whole section there is to root out the hypocrites. He did it with the MP, he did it with that actress and her long-lost daughter—he likes exposés. Robbie tells it like it is. *England Expects . . .*'

'"Every man to do his duty,"' Lin completed. 'I know. I know his regime. Everyone's expected to perform. Ex-chancellors confessing to bounced cheques, vicars with their mistresses, I've seen it.'

'You're in that last segment,' he said.

'OK,' she said.

'It's not bloody OK,' he retorted. 'Lin, I don't want you to do it.'

'I know, but I'm going to.'

'You don't have to. Look, I can get you a couple of good fronting jobs. I know I can. Lazenby wants you to replace Kieran, change the programme a bit. But I can get you better than that, Lin. Leave it with me a while and trust me. If you do this thing tomorrow night, you'll be ruined. Please, Lin.'

She considered him, smiling faintly. 'You don't believe me, do you?' she said.

'It doesn't matter what I believe.'

'It does to me.'

'Look, you could be Jesus himself and England would still destroy you. It's like a bloodsport to him. He enjoys it.'

She said nothing.

'Why are you doing this?' he asked.

'Because it's important.'

'Just to prove something to Kieran?'

'Not just that.'

'What, then?'

'To prove it's real.'

'How can you do that?'

'I don't know,' she admitted.

'You're going to lay on hands or something?'

'I don't know.'

'You've got to have something in mind. You can't just walk out there with nothing in your head. It's like throwing Christians to lions, for God's sake.'

Lin bit her lip. 'I'm sorry you don't believe me,' she said.

'Oh, Lin,' he replied.

She got up, and smiled sadly at him. 'I need to sleep,' she said. 'I know it's early but I want to lie down.'

'Please think about it, if nothing else. Think about it overnight.'

'All right,' she said. 'For you.'

Harry stood up next to her. 'Lin,' he asked. 'What did Werth say this afternoon?'

'I told you, I'm fine.'

'The scan was clear?'

'Yes.'

'He didn't give you any explanation?'

Lin smiled. She stopped, and picked up her plate and cup. 'There was nothing to see. No meningitis, no bleed, nothing. He thought I'd had some kind of virus. There's an inflammation called meningism.'

'And that's what you had?'

'Maybe.'

Harry frowned. 'You'd think they could be more accurate than that.'

She walked towards the kitchen, put the cup on the worktop, and turned to look at him.

'Good night,' she said.

Lin slept for five hours.

She woke at midnight, and saw the reflections of the river on the ceiling of the room.

She had been dreaming.

She sat up and pushed back the covers, not remembering the dream entirely, but with an unnerving sensation of having been a long way off: as if she had been drifting on an isolated current, detached from life. She put her feet to the floor, and was grateful for the contact with something solid and real. She took several deep breaths.

There had been something of Theo in the dream. A sense of loss.

She missed him. Tomorrow, after the programme, she would go back. She would get Theo somehow. She would go back to the Priory, the home he knew. She had no idea what would happen with Kieran. The shock of seeing into his heart was something she could not recover from.

If this was a gift, some sort of second sight, then it was double-edged.

One day she would lose Theo as she had lost Kieran. If only you could keep the pleasure and joy. Keep your loves alive, unchanged, written in stone.

She had once said to Kieran that she wished there were some patented method of bottling Theo's childhood. Then you could uncork the bottle whenever you liked, and relive those irreplaceable moments of surprise and delight and comfort—the first steps, the first jumbled admission of love, the first wobbling twenty yards on an unstabilized bike, the first playground bruise, the first grotesque pink painting, the first picked dandelion . . . the first kiss, the first stodgy playgroup flapjack, the first full-of-water Wellington boot. They would never come again. This was the moment, and it was passing, and it was impossible to catch it and keep it. And all the things that now so irritated her sometimes during the day—the dirty washing, the thumbprints on doors—would one day hold appallingly poignant meaning because they had seemed worthless at the time, and yet in time would ironically become full of value, full of meaning.

Life passed. It grew and changed. That was the essential nature of life. If she had learned anything in the last few days, it was that. And it wasn't a knowledge sitting at the front of her brain. It wasn't known intellectually: it was *felt*. She felt the resonance of that experience, felt its shape and significance in all its detail.

The moments that seemed inconsequential were actually important. Everything was important: all those trivial little moments of life. Just as her life with her son was important in the smallest of ways, so was the remainder of it. Nothing stood still. The trick was to find the voice in the moment as it flowed unstoppably through you.

Lin got up and walked to the window, where she rested her head on the blessedly cold pane.

You'll see and hear nothing . . . nothing, not even your voices.

When Theo grew up, she was going to be very lonely. *Perhaps alone*, she thought. Because perhaps the voices weren't really there. Werth seemed very sure about his diagnosis. He was sure that there was nothing more than the physical. He was sure of rational explanations. He was as wholly convinced of his theory as she was convinced of hers.

She could be wrong, she thought. What if she were wrong? All these thoughts could be phantoms. They could be just the result of pressure on some nameless cell inside her skull.

When Werdi had first told her about the tumour, she had felt numb. He could well have been talking about someone else for all the impact it had made on her. But now, in the dark alone, the thought suddenly filled her with terror. She had a brain tumour: it could end her life. And life, if Werth was to be believed—if the reporter from that paper was to be believed—was just a flash of light in interminable darkness. Like the Anglo-Saxon image of the sparrow flying through a lighted hall, out of night and into night.

That's all there is.

There's nothing else.

She raised her head, wiping tears away.

'Tell me there's something else,' she whispered.

There was nothing for two or three interminable minutes. She had closed her eyes temporarily, felt herself drifting as if falling asleep, and then opened them again. The light flickered around her, and a faint draught blew back the open curtains. And the sensation of water filled the room.

The frame of the picture in which she existed—a woman standing at a window in the dark—dissolved. Her dream came flooding back, sweeping her out of the still frame, picking her up, washing her back on a quick, deep tide.

Water was the liquid thread of her lives.

She was standing on a stone step above a jetty. She was heavy in her body, heavy on her feet. She looked down at herself, and was surprised—but only mildly surprised—to see a yellow robe.

She could hear the waves of the sea below her. The wind was cooling. The water was clear. She was indeed a long way off. She was alive in a dying, warm day in a distant country, and it was perhaps in one of those wheels that Emile had described to her. It was certainly a very long time ago. The light slanted across her face. There was a distinct smell of thyme, and of something else . . . something being cooked in the open, behind the steps, behind the jetty. A smell of smoky oil. She concentrated on the image in front of her.

On the horizon was a single bright star almost touching the sea. Across the bay, in the last oblique light of the day, came a boat through a long, narrow bay of deep water surrounded by low hills. There were no trees, only stone outcrops. Steps were cut in the sandstone, and the ground under her feet was smooth.

She had a building at her back: the library to which she was the doorkeeper. No one was allowed on the jetty or the steps or the smooth stone ledge, but her. She looked down at herself: at fleshy, indulgent hands. She felt the irritating weight of old age, of arthritic wrists and hands and spine. But her mind was fixed on the incoming boat—and the books.

Thoughts echoed in her mind. Fifteen thousand separate scrolls catalogued by the Callimachus system. She was aware of her anxiety shifting between the books and the boat, of a vague premonition of fire spreading from the boat and along the quay towards the library. Fifteen thousand dry, unprotected scrolls . . . the thought flickered like a candle guttering in a breeze. She could hear oars in the mirror-like calm: the soft plash and lift of oars.

Just for a moment, she closed her eyes again.

And when she opened them again, the picture had altered.

She was younger, much younger. The ferocity of youth slammed straight into her mind: insistent, self-centred youth. A feeling of intense identity. She knew at once where she was and who she was. She belonged to the city-kingdom Zarephath. She was female. Zarephath's name rebounded over and over in her mind. She was a daughter of Zarephath in the Phoenician state. She had a piece of glass in her hand, bubbled and dense, a single sand-stained melt from the bottom of the kiln. It was important, vastly important to her. She saw the clay-brick building where she had picked it up. She saw the man who had made it. She saw his other work: beads for jewellery and pressed into frieze . . .

Another life. The patterns changed, became hazy. Brightened.

This is how it is, came a voice. *Not one, but many. Not lost but relived. Over and over and over . . .*

The next life was almost silent . . . there was an interruption in the pattern. The pattern she familiarly felt when in contact with others. This pattern was altered in sound. The world was smothered by silence. *Deaf.* He was deaf. It was all pictures, all visual. Sounds were nothing more than weak vibrations.

The paintings, the pictures were his complete experience . . . he made the birds on the burial friezes. The shape of the tunnel, the shape of the figures—everything determined by single flowing contours. He saw them in his sleep: birds, animals, boats. It was centuries later. It was the sixth year of Mentuhotep II of the Middle Kingdom, although he never saw the face of the god, never the face of his scribes, only the face of the team leader in the half-darkness. In the hours of the afternoon, the heat became unbearable, so he worked at night, from eight until two, and again at dawn. Theirs was a team honoured by their task in the halls of the dead, following the ancient rules of the bands and registers of depiction. He shaped the head of the bird with three strokes; behind him the boy came with the colour. He had that shade of bright turquoise before his eye when he had died suddenly—and without warning—from a failure that he knew was Amun's hand suffocating his heart. They had carried him out into the encroaching dark of the desert valley, and the last thing he saw was the blue bird's eye high in the overhead stars . . .

He passed on, lost his body—rediscovered the other form, luxuriated in it. Listened to the lessons he had learned. Waited for another change, another picture.

And he was not yet twenty.

There were hundreds of others—and they were waiting.

It was a clay-brick alley. The doorposts ahead of them bore the lion's head emblem of the city. It was daybreak and he could hear the other patrols at his back, packed into the narrow entry. It was important to be silent, but it was impossible to be completely silent. Their feet shuffled on the sand. His weapons were heavy. The leather binding of the boot cut into his heel. The sense of waiting was oppressive, the atmosphere charged with fear. Five hundred men held their breath in the city of Baal-shek on the African coast, and he was thinking of his mother, dark and small with an adornment tattoo in henna on her cheekbones. That was his last day. He felt the end rushing up like a wall, the sudden fall of copper-banded iron across his path . . .

Not one but many.

Many lives to live.

White light.

Lazy blue currents.

The river hurled her onwards. She had glimpses of yet more faces. Kaleidoscope years.

She was in a shuttered, claustrophobic shop on a French street. It was the turn of a century. She had a husband and children, and she was depressed and lazy and stupid, and so hot in the airless shop with its calico blinds . . .

A train rattled and swung over tracks. It was dark. From the window she could see orchards in blossom, ghostly acres of blossom . . .

He was in the fields, carrying wood over ground full of flint . . .

He was five years old, and sick and dying . . .

She was dressed in a robe that was too long, with sleeves too long, and she followed another woman up an interminable stair . . .

He was old a thousand years before Christ.

She was young in Bethlehem.

She was bending over a loom, unknotting thin black thread.

He was waiting in line for food.

She was . . .

Suddenly the drift of lives stopped. Lin felt a crushing thud, as if she had been picked up and then dropped. A shudder ran through her, shaking her from head to foot. In a moment of violent descent, she was back somewhere close to the room, and felt Theo—as if she possessed him in body and spirit—inside her, outside her, wrapped around her, so much 'part of' her that the two of them were inseparable. Then he pulled away, and she heard him scream.

Her eyes flew open.

She was back at the window, cold.

Unbearably cold.

She felt her way across the room to the half-open door, and went out into the corridor. The door to Harry's room was closed and the flat was in darkness. She fumbled her way through to the living room and found the phone on the low table by the couch.

She dialled the Priory number.

Nothing . . . nothing. No answer.

Her hand closed to a fist, and she pressed it against the side of her head.

She dialled Ruth's flat.

Nothing.

Finally, she dialled Kieran's mobile.

It rang for only a second. Kieran came on the line.

'It's me,' she said. 'What's the matter with Theo?'

There was fractional pause. 'Just a minute,' he said.

She could hear engine noise, then silence. 'What are you doing?'

'Pulling off the road. I'm in the car.'

'Where is Theo?'

She thought she heard him draw breath. 'He's asleep in the back seat.'

'What are you doing? Where are you going? It's midnight,' she said.

'Nothing . . . nothing. Going home,' Kieran replied.

'You're lying to me.'

'I'm not.'

'Let me speak to him.'

'Look, he's sound asleep. Let me ring you first thing in the morning.'

She couldn't figure out what was wrong; her son's image was right in the centre of her mind, refusing to be pushed aside.

'You're sure he's all right?'

'He's fine.' Kieran's voice was taut.

'Where have you been with him?' she asked.

'Nowhere,' he said.

She let the ridiculous sentence hang in the air for a moment.

'Ruth's,' she said. 'That's what I can feel with you . . . Ruth, Ruth, Ruth . . .'

'Lin . . .' he protested.

She put down the phone, and put her hands over her eyes.

THIRTY-NINE

$\mathscr{K}$IERAN had been experiencing the most fraught evening of his life.

After leaving the village, he had driven to Ruth's flat in town. Taking the stairs two at a time, he got to her door and opened it with his own keys, fully expecting to find Ruth and Theo there, despite her refusal to answer the phone.

But the flat had been in darkness. Switching on the lights in each room, he found no evidence of Theo there. Opening the wardrobes, he found Ruth's suitcases and clothes all apparently still in place. There was no note, no clue to where she had gone. He picked up her phone and rang the surgery, and was rewarded only with a recorded message for emergencies. He riffled through Ruth's telephone book, and rang Dr Godber, who spent a long minute bitterly complaining that Ruth had not turned up for evening surgery. Kieran gave the man his own mobile number with a request that he phone him should he hear of Ruth's whereabouts—or from Ruth herself.

In desperation he rang the Priory again, to hear that same dead empty tone. He speculated wildly that Ruth might have taken Theo to the hospital, perhaps assuming that Lin had gone back there when she could not be found at the Priory. The ward sister answered his call.

'Dr Carmichael?' she repeated, obviously confused. 'And your son? No, I'm sorry . . .'

Then he had rung Harry.

Just for a second he considered telling Lin that Theo was missing; then he realized that it could do no earthly good. Lin was sick enough, worried enough already. What she didn't know about couldn't possibly harm her.

Kieran walked about Ruth's flat in an impotent fury, steeling himself to stay there in case she should suddenly arrive home. Perhaps she had taken Theo to the cinema, or out for a meal? He waited, on a knife edge of anxiety, until the last pub and cinema would have closed.

At last he sat down on the couch, and put his hand out to the phone to call the police. It was half past eleven.

Before he could lift the reciver, it rang.

'Ruth?' he said.

'No,' said an elderly female voice. 'Who is that?'

Christ, he thought. That's all I need: some confused old woman taking up the line.

'You've got a wrong number,' he said.

'Is that Dr Carmichael's flat?'

'Yes. But the doctor isn't on call.'

'I don't want her actually. I wanted Lin Gallagher.'

Kieran stared at the receiver. 'Who is this?'

'My name is Edith Channon. I wanted to speak to Lin.'

'How did you get this number?'

'She left me a list of numbers. This was the second on the list.'

'I'm sorry,' Kieran said, 'I don't know you. This is Lin's husband.'

There was a pause. 'I see,' she said. 'And is Lin there?'

'No, she's in London.'

'London? What on earth is she doing there?'

'I really don't know. Look, if you could just ring back later, I have to make an important call now.'

'Not more important than this one,' came Edith's peremptory reply. 'It's about her little boy.'

Kieran's impatience vanished in an instant. 'Theo?'

'Yes. They were staying in my upstairs flat until Lin went into hospital...'

Light dawned on Kieran at last. 'You're the lady in Hampton. The lady with the doll shop?'

'That's right.'

'Is Theo all right?'

'I beg your pardon?'

'Is Theo all right?'

'I don't think so, dear. No, I don't think so. Is Lin out of hospital?'

'Yes. Look—'

'She ought not to be, you know.'

God, was she never going to shut up?

'Please tell me where Theo is,' Kieran said.

Something in his tone must have struck Edith. He heard sympathy in her reply. 'I will, dear,' she said. 'But I need something of his. There isn't a scrap left in the flat. And I need something . . . a toy, a piece of clothing. A shoe would be rather good.'

'I don't understand,' Kieran said. 'What the hell are you talking about?'

'I'm going to find him,' Edith said, palpably summoning her utmost patience. 'But I can't do it without your help.'

Kieran struggled to hold on to his temper. 'If you know where my son is, tell me,' he said. 'I'm not in the bloody mood for playing games, Mrs Channon. If you don't tell me, I'm ringing the police.'

There was an offended silence, during which he could hear Edith taking a long, deep breath. 'Ring them by all means,' she said, 'and you can tell them whatever you know. I doubt if that's much.'

'It isn't,' Kieran muttered under his breath, 'you mad old witch.'

If she heard him, Edith took no notice.

'And then get in your car and drive over here,' she told him. 'And please don't forget the shoe.'

On his way to Edith's, Lin rang.

Kieran answered the mobile, pulled into a lay-by, heard Lin's barely restrained panic . . . and then the burring of the disconnected line.

For a moment he rested his head on the steering wheel.

'What the bloody hell is going on?' he whispered, before restarting the engine.

FORTY

$\mathcal{R}$UTH HAD BEEN DRIVING FOR HOURS.

She had no clear idea of where she would be taking Theo after she collected him from Mrs Sawyer's house in the village. As she negotiated the long hill out to the main road, he had sat in the back seat, looking helplessly small without a booster cushion, the seat-belt threatening to strangle him. She kept glancing in the mirror, and over her shoulder, to be met with his stony, almost vacant gaze.

Almost at the main road, she stopped the car and took him from the back seat into the front one, alongside herself, where she could see him and be sure that he didn't try to open the door or release the belt. There were no childproof locks or harnesses in her car, and she was afraid he would try to get out while the car was moving.

She couldn't afford to lose him.

He was the most valuable bargaining chip she had. He would get her back to Kieran.

As she bundled him into the seat, he looked accusingly up at her.

'Tea,' he said.

She had taken him from the kitchen table where food was just being served. 'Are you hungry?' she asked.

'Yeth,' he replied, reverting to babyhood and stuffing his thumb in his mouth.

'Where shall we go?' she asked. 'What would you like?'

He didn't answer her. She got back in the car, turned out onto the main road and drove fast and aimlessly north, following the main drag, ignoring the villages and the byroads. The road climbed out of fields and onto downland. Twenty miles further on, she saw a roadside café on a roundabout, a bleak red-and-white sign in the middle of nowhere.

She got out of the car, went inside, carrying him to a table. He pointed out sausages and chips on the menu. She watched him sullenly and slowly devouring his food, trying to spear the sausage, trying to hold the beans on his fork, until light dawned on her and she helped him cut up the meat into pieces. The first time he opened his mouth to the fork she offered to him, his lips trembled as if he were going to cry.

Instead, it was she who cried.

The sobs came rolling up from some hidden, untapped depth. She bunched a paper napkin to her face and tried to stop. Theo put down his fork.

'Eat it,' she ordered. 'Go ahead, eat.'

A waitress came over. 'Is everything all right?'

'Yes,' Ruth said. 'It's nothing . . . hayfever.'

The woman looked at her suspiciously.

'Really,' Ruth said. 'Nothing.'

She stemmed her tears only with the greatest difficulty. Before Theo's plate was clear, she took his hand, walked to the cash desk, left a ten-pound note without ever seeing the bill, and rushed out to the car, where she fastened Theo back into his seat.

'Pee,' Theo said mournfully.

'In a minute,' she said.

It was getting dark. At the junction, she took a right across country.

She travelled on across the Salisbury Plain, ignoring the signs for the cathedral city. The landscape reduced from shadow to complete darkness. To their left stretched the empty downs, haunted by old pathways, prehistoric cursus, and long barrows. Stonehenge emerged for a few seconds, as dusty grey thumbprints in the night, then disap-

peared. Almost at Andover, she turned left, out back into the country, through the isolated airfield villages of the Winterbournes and
Winterslows. She had come in a circle, she realized vaguely. She took
a sudden left, down into narrow lanes, emerging after half an hour on
the outskirts of the New Forest.

Theo was asleep, lolling against the door.

'I'm going to keep you,' she told him. 'We're going to live with
Daddy.' She talked on, letting the words tumble relentlessly out to the
droning of the engine. A green-and-white sign in the roadside verge
announced that she was back in Dorset. She looked at the dashboard
clock: a quarter past twelve.

She had been in the car for more than seven hours.

As she came to a junction, she had to brake sharply to avoid
another car that had oversteered the turning. With the jolt, Theo suddenly woke up. He stared ahead for a second, and then around himself.

'Mummy,' he said.

'Mummy is far away,' Ruth told him.

He began to drum his feet on the seat.

'Don't do that,' she said. 'Sit still.'

'Mummy . . .'

She tried to pat his knee as she drove. 'I'll look after you now,' she
said.

He started to scream, overtaken by discomfort, fear and exhaustion. There was no lead-up to it; it simply began as one high-pitched
protracted yell and veered rapidly upwards to an ear-splitting note.
He pushed his body forward, then fumbled with the belt, hitting it
with his open palms. When that failed, he squirmed downwards,
getting out of the belt by wriggling down into the footwell, where
he forced his body under the parcel shelf and screamed, screamed,
screamed.

The seat where he had been sitting was wet through.

Ruth pulled the car off the road.

She tried pulling on his only visible hand. 'Get out of there, Theo,'
she said. 'Get up.'

He turned his head and sank his teeth into her hand.

She cursed, and slapped him with her other hand: once, twice on the side of his face. She grabbed hold of his collar and shook him, and his head thumped against the hard plastic dashboard.

And, all the time, he screamed.

'Shut up!' She hauled on him, trying to pull him out. His legs flailed wildly, catching her on one elbow, sending a flash of pain up her arm. She shoved him backwards, hard. His head hit the parcel shelf—and the screams stopped suddenly. He slumped to one side.

She stared at him, out of breath, nursing her elbow. 'Now look . . .' she said. 'Look what you've done.'

She sat for another minute or more, staring at him. Then she picked up the mobile, and dialled Kieran's number.

He answered on the second ring.

'It's me,' she said, breathing hard.

'Ruth! Where are you?' A pause. 'Is Theo all right?'

'He's fine.' She opened the car door, and got out. 'Everything's fine.'

'Where are you?'

She looked about herself. High up somewhere: gorse, with trees below. Above her, looking up the slope of land, a tall column against the night sky. Some kind of monument. 'Out,' she said.

'Ruth . . . listen. Out where? Tell me where.'

'Out . . . driving. Out for a ride.'

'Ruth, listen. Let me come and fetch you.'

'Me?'

'Yes . . . you and Theo.'

'Me and Theo.'

'Ruth, please . . .'

She looked over to Theo's side of the car, and saw that his door was now open.

'Where is he?' she murmured.

'What?'

'Where did he go?' she asked, leaning over the bonnet.

'Oh, Jesus Christ,' Kieran muttered. 'Ruth, please listen to me. What's the matter?'

'Are you going home?' she asked.

'Yes,' he said, snatching at a hope. 'Yes, I'll go there. Will you meet me there?'

'Yes,' she murmured. 'Our house.'

A confused pause. Ruth thought that she heard another, softer, voice in the background. 'Yes, that's right, our house,' Kieran agreed.

'Who's with you?' she asked.

'Nobody. Will you go to the Priory now?'

'You never answered my question,' she told him.

'Which question?'

It had begun to rain: a soft, penetrating cloud of rain sweeping over the higher ground. She closed her eyes and let it run down her face.

'Ruth . . . Ruth!'

She put the phone back to her ear.

'Ruth . . . which question?'

'Do you love me?' she asked.

She heard a small, smothered groan. 'Yes, of course.'

'I knew it,' she said. 'And you and I and Theo . . . not Lin . . .'

'Lin is very sick,' Kieran replied. 'She needs an operation.'

'You and me,' Ruth whispered.

'It doesn't matter now. Ruth, put Theo on the line. Is he there?'

'Doesn't matter?' she repeated.

'Let me speak to him.'

'No . . .'

'Can you find him? Put him on.'

'I can't find him,' she said, walking round the front of the car and looking to left and right in the gloom.

'Oh God,' Kieran said.

'It's dark,' Ruth told him.

'For Christ's sake, give me Theo! That's all I want. Theo!'

She looked at the phone.

She lowered it, and stared into the dark.

Monster.

'Ruth? Ruth! . . . Ruth!'

She could see a distant shimmer, far away. The sea. The fleet. She and Kieran used to take walks along that coast. Seatown. Charmouth. Tea in Chideock. Or at Lyme.

Monster.

'Ruth!'

A day in Branscombe, rocky rug beneath, ice-cold sea, flat calm. They swam in the freezing water, on a millpond day. Green and blue, and sand rocks under them. Hand in hand in the water, gasping with the cold.

House in the valley. Garden by the river.

Peaceful, sheltered times.

Cold and sheltered.

Cold inside, always cold—comfortably cold, icy cold.

She was cold now.

'Ruth!'

She looked to the side, up at the tower.

She knew where she was now. Of course she knew.

Hamble monument.

She dimly remembered it: closed for years, recently refurbished. Raised a century ago for a beloved wife.

Open now, though. Open right to the top.

The whole coast must be visible from there.

A beloved wife.

'Ruth!'

She stared at the discarded phone, from which Kieran's voice could still faintly be heard. She looked at the open passenger door and the empty car.

No Theo now.

No Kieran.

No Ruth.

She walked away from the car, across the chalky grass.

FORTY-ONE

$\mathcal{M}$ARK WERTH WAS ALSO AWAKE BEFORE DAWN.

He rolled over in bed and checked the clock: three-thirty. It was very dark. He sat up and looked through the uncurtained window, and saw that it had been raining.

He lived in a small house at the end of a lane. The village was over twenty miles from the hospital: a necessary distance to maintain his sanity. It was not a picturesque setting, although he had been lulled into thinking so when he had first bought the house after seeing it on two consecutive Sundays in spring. It was the last in a terrace, and beyond his garden the lane petered out into a rutted track that linked his village with the next one.

His view was good: pasture and crop and a long wooded hill. The wind blew down the hill, summer and winter, cracking the fascia boards and old cast-iron guttering of the house and, alternately by season, scorching or freezing his irregular attempts at gardening. He was not a good gardener, or cook, or housewife. He forgot to shop, forgot to drain radiators, to fill up the oil tank, clean the oven, or make the bed. He missed being married desperately—his wife had left him ten years before, and they had no children. His life now was filled with work.

He was lonely—especially at three-thirty in the morning.

He got up, knowing by experience that any further sleep would be fitful. He dressed in an old sweatshirt, jogging pants and trainers, went downstairs, made himself coffee, then opened the back door, walking out into the darkness with a full cup.

He went up the long path to the rusty wrought-iron gate, and looked up the lane. It disappeared into the inky green of the hill. He looked back down the row of other houses, and saw a light in one far down by the village main street. He raised his cup to the far dot of light.

The night was cold, and the sky was full of scudding clouds. More rain was coming. There was something intensely intimate in the darkness, as if the night breathed and moved. He thought of Lin Gallagher, wondering where she was.

She had a curious face: it betrayed very little, though it was constantly mobile. Her expressions were rather plastic, as if the merest smile took effort, used more facial muscles than normal. And yet the eyes were a little dead . . . was that correct? Accurate? Perhaps they were not so much dead as self-protective. She reminded him a little of Parkinsonism. There was a rigidity of facial muscles in that, but a random neural firing in the thalamus caused tremor. She was kind of reversed Parkinson's, a mirror Parkinson's. The face moved but the eyes blanked. She was somewhere else inside her head.

He had seen many Parkinson cases. Their suffering was caused by the death of cells in the basal ganglia. There was new work being done in that field, by planting electrodes in the thalamus that overrode the signals from cells deprived of dopamine. This seemed to control tremor, even eradicate it. During the operation to implant the electrodes, the patient remained conscious throughout, so that the surgeon could discover exactly where the implant should be. Then a small generator, activated by a magnet swipe, was placed under the skin of the chest wall.

It had been called the brain pacemaker, and it fascinated him, precisely because it proved to him that the brain was an electrical box—advanced, vastly complicated, delicate beyond measure, but still just a small box of infinitely beautiful electrical parts. He believed what he had told Lin, that feelings were electrical manifestations. He believed there was no life after that electrical connection had been switched off by related systems in the body. Logically there could not possibly be.

He finished his coffee and put the empty cup down on the wall next to him. Yet she had told him that there was something else: a super-system that controlled the lesser single forms, the individual brains. She had told him that, if he only looked, he would see it all around him.

He considered the dark. There were no electrical pylons in this valley, but just beyond the hill a line of them marched all the way to the Bristol Channel. He knew of the mounting evidence that their fields might interfere with human brain activity. He knew that the same studies showed that this influence was greater between the pylons, at a midway point, rather than actually underneath them. He had seen cases that seemed to point to abnormal cell activity as a result of electrical interference—mobile-phone tumours, as someone had called them, close to the ear. Leukaemia in children who slept with their heads close to electrical meters. Nothing definite, nothing absolutely proven, however. He was yet to be convinced.

There were electrical and magnetic fields everywhere. The earth itself was a complex grid of them. Anyone who sat at a computer was bombarded with emissions: light, ultraviolet light, electromagnetic radiation, positive ions. Modern society was an electrical circus: televisions, radios, stereos, air-conditioners, fridges, freezers, cookers, kettles, irons, hairdryers, washing machines. The world couldn't run without its power cables, transformers, substations. Perhaps, when Lin talked of connections, she was actually talking of simple and prosaic physical systems: like the pylons, the cables. He could have accepted that. Even perhaps accepted that the brain responded to them as one electrical cell to another.

But she did not mean that, he knew.

If there was a super-system, an energy greater than themselves, greater than the myriad other electrical systems in the world, where was it located? Its generation would be huge. It would have a source of measurable and overwhelming proportions. But there was no such source. Human beings did not plug into some sort of psychic substation in order to operate. There was nothing that any reasonable human being recognized as the source of their thoughts, other than themselves, their own brains. There was no net site where any superior control could be contacted. Some theories suggested that the world was a single operating machine, but he couldn't see it. No efficient machine regularly destroyed parts of itself, or tolerated beings that were perfectly capable of destroying the whole framework in a single nuclear afternoon. There was no God, no other power. Lin's sensation of significance, that she believed would protect her through her illness, that she believed was so much more valuable than even her own survival, was an illusion. An illusion that would kill her.

He noticed a rim of light just beyond the hill. At first a barely paler shade than the dark, it rapidly changed: first to blue, then white. The trees on the hill became gradually visible. He saw the road going through the centre of this picture, and then disappearing in the woodland. He understood what Lin was getting at; that he was connected to the road, and to the country that lay beyond the road. Because he was standing *here*, at one point along its length, he bore a relation to the road and to every other point along it. And the road bore a relation to the land on either side of it. The field shapes were determined by the road, and vice versa. The positions of the houses were determined by the shape of the fields, the dissection of the roads. That much was obvious. But, if he understood her right, she was saying that the fields could not exist without the road, the road without the houses, the houses without the man, the man without the fields . . . that he was a part of a process of continual regeneration, that without him the whole complex chain of time and effect would fail and alter. That the enormous whole depended upon the microcosmic. The most reverberating event upon inconsequential trivia . . . he watched the sky. Would that colour, that peculiar tone of rose, alter if he had never been here to witness it?

He had sometimes thought of those chains—but not for a long time. It must have been as a teenager, a sixth-form student, when he had last indulged in the kind of conversation that hypothesized on whether Kennedy would have been shot had the car gone a little slower, a little faster; if he had woken earlier; if he had not gone to Dallas at all. Was his death certain, or moulded by detail? Would the plot to kill him have fallen apart because of a series of small alterations?

Werth thought of his own background. Was each birth *meant* to be, or simply an accident? Was each death meant to be? Would he still have been born if his father had married someone else? Lin said *yes*: his soul pursued an organized path.

He knew what he said. He said *no*.

He had no soul. His birth was merely coincidental. In the world as a whole, it had no meaning.

Mark Werth began to smile. He had never understood why people ran after those shapeless notions the way they did. In college he could never work out what the arts students found to write whole essays about. What the hell did it matter if Hamlet loved his mother? Hamlet did not exist. He was a figment of a sixteenth-century imagination. Werth didn't care if Picasso was a cubist, or Luther a visionary. It was all irrelevant.

But numbers, chemicals . . . they were real, they could be forecast. You could write a paper on ribonudeic acid, and it meant something. It moved the world forward a fraction of an inch. It was concrete. It existed.

He picked up the cup, and walked back down the path.

Lin Gallagher existed too—not as an idea or a philosophy, but as a miraculous physical machine that could be repaired.

And, as he put his hand on the door handle, Werth realized that he very much wanted that particular machine to live.

FORTY-TWO

ℋIERAN SAT IN EDITH CHANNON'S LIVING ROOM, staring at the phone.

'She's gone,' he said. 'I heard her put the receiver down . . . she's not answering . . .' He turned to look at the elderly woman.

'Right,' Edith said briskly. 'All the more reason to get cracking.'

'She said Theo wasn't there with her,' he murmured, deeply shocked.

Edith put her hand over his. 'Then we must hurry,' she said.

She had already fetched a large map of the county out of her cupboard, and spread it on the table. Now she brought out a small velvet box. Inside was a pendulum, which she laid carefully beside two rods already sitting on the map.

Kieran stared at her, mystified. 'I don't know what I'm doing here,' he said. 'What the hell am I doing here?'

Edith smoothed out the map. 'You're here to find Theo,' she said. 'Give me his shoe.'

Kieran placed the trainer on the table in front of him. He looked from the shoe to the still-crackling phone.

'She won't answer you,' Edith said. 'Concentrate on your son.'

'I *am* concentrating on my son,' Kieran retorted. He snatched at the phone, and savagely hit the disconnect button. 'I'm ringing the police.'

'To tell them what?'

'What the hell do you think?'

'And where are they meant to look for him?'

Kieran bunched his fists.

Edith picked up the shoe, and closed her eyes. 'I shan't be very long,' she murmured. 'It's a long time since I did this. My father was wonderful at it. He could find anything . . .'

Kieran put his head in his hands.

When he had arrived at Edith's shop, he had been dismayed to see what a run-down street it was situated in. He had stood outside and studied the upper storeys, thinking that this was where Lin had brought Theo. This was where they had lived. Ruth had been right . . . it was a place of dropouts and drug pushers. He had been appalled to think of the desperation she must have felt to come here. The front door had opened, and Edith had ushered him in, double-locking the door after him and setting the alarm.

In shadow, the shop had seemed an eerie place of apparently dis-embodied baby faces. It had sent a shudder down his spine. He had been glad to be ushered into her sitting room behind the shop, until he saw that it too was fantastically cluttered: every conceivable space crammed with ornaments and yet more dolls. The fact that Edith Channon was a collector was blindingly obvious: it looked as if she collected even wrappers and boxes and ribbons. Dolls' clothes were piled around the floor. The few side tables groaned with flowery china, toast-racks, teapots, single eggcups, old ceramic ladles, ivory-handled scissors, Valentines cards . . .

He had had to fight down a sudden claustrophobia.

'Sit down,' Edith had said. 'I've made some tea. Nice and hot and sweet and strong. Drink it up.'

She had been rambling on about Lin, and Lin's voices, as she served, and then his phone had rung. He couldn't get Ruth's strained, faint tone out of his head. He looked down now at Edith's clasped hands.

It was like some awful dream.

Maybe he would wake up soon.

Edith put down Theo's shoe. 'Poor little chap,' she murmured. 'How he loves his mummy.'

Edith picked up the divining rods. She held them out over the map. Nothing happened.

Kieran felt his life draining away into the creased landscape below: the contour lines, the crosses, the junctions, the patches of flat green. He looked at the village names, willing Ruth to rise up out of the stale print page and deliver his son to him.

The rods crossed. Edith looked at the map carefully, and made a pencilled note on a sheet of paper next to her. Then, she turned the map round and started again.

'What are you doing?' Kieran demanded.

'Ssssh,' she said.

He slumped back in his chair, picking up the mobile phone, and switching it from hand to hand.

The rods crossed.

'What is it?' Kieran said.

Edith's fingertip caressed an oblong green area on the map. It was not two miles distant from the Priory.

'That's Hamble Down,' he said.

'Very cold,' Edith murmured. 'Cold and tired. Lost and tired. In the trees where the dogs are.'

'What dogs?' Kieran said.

Edith opened her eyes. 'Did Lin take him here to walk a dog?'

'We haven't got a dog,' he said.

'Someone else's, then. Theo's thinking of a dog.'

Kieran could only stare at her. Perhaps they were both of them mad. That would make a perverted kind of sense. They were both mad—sitting here trying to find a very small boy with two pieces of stick.

'Do people walk dogs in this place?' Edith persisted. 'Lin has taken him here to walk, and there are dogs about.'

Kieran looked down at the map, trying to conjure the Down in his mind's eye. 'I don't know,' he said. 'I'm not often home. I'm very busy.'

It sounded appallingly lame: an admission of guilt.

Edith picked up the pendulum.

It rotated slowly above the map, the crystal glittering reflections in the room's dim light.

'A tower,' Edith said.

'That's right,' Kieran confirmed. 'Hamble Down has a monument. An ugly, squared-off thing with steps to the top.'

Suddenly, Edith gasped.

She dropped the pendulum. One hand was clenched over her heart. 'Oh, dear God,' she whispered. 'The steps.'

'What?' Kieran said, now standing too. 'What steps?'

She stared at him aghast for several seconds.

Then, she snatched up her cardigan from the chair behind her.

'Do you know how to get there?' she said.

'Hamble Down? Yes, of course.'

She came round the table, and gave him a little shove in the small of his back.

'Hurry, then,' she told him. 'Hurry.'

FORTY-THREE

*I*T TOOK THEM TWENTY-FIVE MINUTES to get to Hamble Down.

In any normal circumstances it should have taken forty.

Edith did not appear to be distracted by Kieran's wild driving, or by the screeching of brakes as they took each bend. Fortunately there was very little traffic around, and only one solitary car in front of them, which had pulled over after Kieran's flashing lights and leaning on the horn.

'I'll be arrested for bloody road rage before I get there,' he had muttered.

Edith did not reply. Her eyes were closed, her hands tightly bunched in her lap. Occasionally, she whispered something. On one long stretch of road, Kieran dared to ask his only question of the journey.

'Is he alive?'

'I don't know,' Edith said. 'He's silent.'

They stormed past isolated houses, silent farms, between dark fields. Eventually the road started to rise. They could now see Hamble Down—the tower perched on its hill of heather and gorse—outlined in front of them. The road narrowed to a single-width lane. As he took it at fifty, Kieran prayed that nothing would be coming the other way.

'Here,' Edith said suddenly, as a gravel track appeared as a slash of light in the car's headlights. 'Turn here.'

They were at the top of the hill, under the tower itself. There was a rough car park here for those who came to walk the hills and look at the views towards the coast. As they turned up the last slight gradient, the lights picked out Ruth's car ahead of them. It was empty—with both doors standing wide open.

Kieran killed the engine, and jumped out.

The rain was much heavier now, driving across the exposed hillside. Kieran sprinted forward to the empty car, looked inside and then straightened up, peering into the darkness.

'Is he there?' Edith called, struggling in his wake.

'No,' he said. 'Ruth!' he shouted. 'Theo!'

There was not even an echo.

Edith reached his side and touched his arm. 'The tower,' she said. 'Is he in there?'

'He was.'

Kieran ran over the grass, shielding his eyes against the rain. Just before he reached the tower, he stumbled over the rough ground and staggered forwards. His foot had brushed against something soft lying on the turf. He felt around his feet with his hands—and came into contact with cloth. He continued to run his hands over it, trying to distinguish its shape, waiting for his eyes to accustom themselves to the darkness. Then, he felt hair.

He retracted his hand with a cry. Theo was his first thought.

But it wasn't Theo.

Edith, with more presence of mind than him, had taken the torch from Ruth's car and was coming towards him, a trembling beam of light in the curtain of rain.

'Over here!' he called.

She trained the torch-light on him.

'Shine it on the ground,' he said.

Ruth lay face-down, her soft wool coat bunched around her body, her legs and one foot bare. The other foot wore a shoe with a broken heel. 'Oh, Jesus. No,' he murmured. Afraid of what he might see in her face, he turned her over.

Her eyes were closed. The rain beat down on an expression of complete calm and repose, as if she had fallen asleep. Dust streaked her skin. Tiny shards of gravel were embedded in her forehead. He felt the side of her neck, then her wrist. To his horror, both felt broken.

He looked back over his shoulder, at the looming stone column of the tower.

'What is it?' Edith called, still negotiating the uneven ground.

'Ruth,' he told her. Disbelief blasted him. He withdrew his hand from Ruth's cold face.

As Edith drew level with him, he took the mobile from his pocket, his hand shaking. 'Would you call the police?' he said, passing it to her.

She nodded.

He gazed up at the tower. 'You said steps,' he murmured.

'Yes,' she replied.

He began to run, slipping and staggering on the dark hillside. At the tower's entrance, he saw that the wooden door was open, the lock broken. Inside, it was pitch dark.

'Theo!' he shouted.

His voice soaked into the dark. Groping ahead of him with his hands, he could feel that the steps curved into a spiral. He went forward on hands and knees, the stone scratching his hands. *Make him be here*, he thought. *Make him be alive.*

Thoughts pressed in on him as he fumbled his way upwards.

That he had never been the father he intended to be.

That he had failed his son.

That he should never have gone into the university that afternoon.

He recalled his own low-key, irritated impatience with Theo—the slight relief as he had left him with Mrs Sawyer. He should have stayed with him.

Now he would give anything, anything . . .

'Theo,' he called.

More a prayer than a cry.

'Theo . . .'

He could hear the rain and the wind buffeting the top of the tower. How many steps were there? How many had he climbed already? It felt like hundreds, each one explored first with his fingertips. The incline felt almost vertical. A narrow, black stone box. He gasped for breath as he got to the top. Emerging from the pitch blackness of the stairs, he stepped out, and was shoved sideways by the blast of wind. A four-foot stone wall ringed the platform. The door from the stairs had been opened, and left to crash backwards and forwards. He tried pushing it back, and found that something was stopping it. Half-closing his eyes against the driving rain, he pulled the door towards him.

His son was lying on the ground behind the door, curled into a foetal position.

Kieran dropped to his knees.

He bundled Theo into his arms.

'Wake up,' he whispered. 'Wake up . . .'

FORTY-FOUR

*H*ARRY WAS WORRIED ABOUT LIN.

When he had woken at eight, there was no other sound in the flat and, after pottering about in the kitchen making coffee, while trying to be quiet, he had eventually tapped on her door. When there was no reply, he had opened it a little way and peered in, to see Lin still asleep. He went back into the kitchen and made her a cup of herbal tea. She stirred as he put the cup down beside her and tapped her on the shoulder.

Yet she was still asleep an hour later. Fully dressed now, he paced the floor for a while. At ten he knocked on her bedroom door again, and was rewarded with a sleepy response.

'Ten o'clock,' he said.

'Ok,' she murmured.

She came out of the room wrapped in his old dressing gown, voluminous on her, its raggy white towelling dragging at her heels. He had made fresh tea and toast, and laid it on a table in front of the window.

'I had the strangest dream,' she said, sitting down.

'What about?'

'Ruth . . .'

'Ruth doing what?'

She frowned. 'I can't remember.'

'How are you feeling this morning?'

'Exhausted,' she said, half smiling, half grimacing, 'as you probably gathered.'

They ate and drank in silence for a few minutes, while boats ploughed up and down the choppy grey river outside, and the morning traffic threaded a line along the far bank.

'Have you thought more about it?' Harry asked eventually.

'About what?'

'Doing this programme today?'

She replaced her cup in the saucer. 'I'm still going to do it, Harry.' When he opened his mouth to object, she raised her hand with an expression of annoyance. 'Don't let's go into it all again. I have to do it.'

'There's no *have to* about it.'

'There is.'

Impasse.

'Look,' he said, 'even if you do see these things, hear these things, proving it isn't your responsibility.'

'It is,' she insisted. 'But I don't expect you to understand.'

'I don't,' he admitted.

'You're very much a pragmatist, aren't you?' she said.

'Sorry?'

'What you see is what you get.'

'No,' he replied, 'I like to think I'm open-minded.'

She smiled, leaned back, and put her hand to her head. She traced a finger across her forehead, as if rubbing away an imaginary line.

'Then you must accept—at least the possibility—that there's more to the world than the things you can see,' she said.

Harry leaned forward. 'And this is now your personal mission?'

She started to reply, then stopped. Her hand flew back to her forehead.

'What is it?' he asked.

'Theo,' she said.

'Do you want to ring Kieran?'

'Can I?'

She went to the phone and rang the Priory.

When there was no reply, she next phoned the university. Then Kieran's mobile, which rang and rang interminably, but was not answered.

'Not there,' she murmured. She paused, frowning out at the river. 'When I finish this programme,' she said, 'would you drive me home?'

'Of course,' Harry said.

She turned to him, and gave him a fleeting kiss on the cheek. 'I'm going to get dressed now,' she said.

They were met at the door of the television centre by a very young girl with a very anxious expression.

'Mrs Gallagher?' she asked, holding out her hand. 'How are you?'

'I'm fine, thank you. This is Harry Marks, my agent.'

The girl smiled. 'I'm Lulu. Lulu Friedman.'

'Shout,' said Lin.

'I'm sorry?'

'Shout. *To Sir With Love*. No . . . never mind. Silly joke. Lulu is a singer.'

'Yes,' the girl said warily. 'I know.' She pointed across the echoing foyer towards the lifts. 'Shall we . . . ?'

'Fine,' Lin murmured.

Harry raised his eyebrows at her as they crossed the foyer.

'I'm a tremendous fan of your work,' Lulu said. 'You write scripts for your husband? It's a fantastic series. We all absolutely love it.'

'Thanks,' Lin said.

'Ever such a lot of research and stuff.'

'Yes,' Lin agreed, 'a lot of that stuff.'

They were now standing at the doors of the lifts. Lulu apparently did not possess the ability to stand still. Blonde, small and excruciatingly thin, she wore a pair of dark glasses perched in her bleached, spiky hair. She constantly shifted her weight from one foot to the other, like a dancer warming up backstage.

'Of course, you'll be used to it all,' Lulu said, 'all this fussing about. The magic of TV! Have you met Robbie? He's marvellous. *So* good to his staff. We're just devoted. You have to be devoted, don't you? That's the way shows stick together.'

The lift arrived. Lin stepped in, amused at this breathless team spirit. 'Have you worked here long?' she asked.

'Six months. I did *Party Dogs* before that. With Gabrielle Choux, eleven on Fridays?'

'Oh yes,' Lin said.

'A scream.'

The lift doors closed.

Lin momentarily closed her eyes. Her retention of events seemed to be getting fragmentary. She did not remember the taxi journey, except for the glass partition behind the driver, which did not quite close; she did not remember lunch, although she recalled the decoration on the plate, and seeing Harry's small, square hand around a cup. The rest of the day was somehow drowned.

But Theo's face, seemingly asleep and peaceful, would not go away.

'Have you ever met Robert?' Lulu asked.

Lin opened her eyes. 'Robert?'

'Robbie England.'

'Oh . . . No, I haven't.'

'He doesn't meet people before a show—you realize that? He likes to meet them just on camera. He says it's fresher that way, OK?'

'Yes. That's OK.'

'I'll pop you in make-up, then take you on down to hospitality. I'll be staying with you all through.'

'That isn't necessary,' Harry said. The girl's voice was grating on him.

'It's a house rule—no problem. We stay with our people.'

She was tapping on the lift's steel doorplate, her nails skirting the button for each floor as they proceeded upwards.

'*Restoration*,' murmured a voice.

Not now, Lin thought.

'Floor three,' Lulu announced. 'I ought to walk it, but I never do.' She looked over at Lin. 'Did you drive up all the way from Dorset today?'

'No.' Lin put her hand against her temple briefly. Pain had begun to throb across the left side of her head, down her jaw and into her neck. Her ears and hairline and cheek hurt acutely, blindingly, like a white-hot brand being applied there. Overhead, the ceiling light of the lift fuzzed and flashed once.

Lin could see pictures of clock faces. They were laid out on a smooth-topped bench. She tried to squeeze the image away.

The lift stopped.

'Are we there?' the girl asked herself, puzzled. She was staring at the floor indicator. Floors two and three were lit simultaneously. 'Oh, shit,' she said.

The twin dials of the clock were huge . . . fitted into a building, a church . . . twin dials facing west and east respectively . . . Two dials, both blue with gold Roman numerals. The church was located on a busy street—a shopping street—with two modern doors that opened on sliding runners. Lin thought of Cypriot churches, Greek churches. Once, in Greece, she had seen afternoon prayers conducted in what looked like an open shop-front, curtained, centrally lit, the front wall full of icons . . . but that was not it. This was not a memory of her own.

Time goes out. Time goes out in ripples.

Under the floor of the lift, the shaft plunged down forty feet into silt and gravel. That's all it was . . . silt and gravel where the river had once flowed. Now the water was pushed back into a narrow channel, choked by centuries of its own sand. The gravel lay in thin lenses. Four thousand men had brought the original road from Richborough to the banks of the Thames. It ran . . . west of here . . .

Mark Werth was thinking of someone, a man . . . he was thinking out his problem. He was writing it down. He was using a keyboard: dystonic posturing in epilepsy. He was working in the hospital suite, with his desk turned so that the last faint, dark-gold sun, so dark it was thundery, splashed with dark blue clouds, wouldn't reflect on his computer screen, and he had brought up a document on screen . . . ipsilateral head turn . . . ipsilateral, contralateral . . .

She jolted, and her eyes opened and widened.

Werth was in Kieran's mind. And so was Theo.

The girl next to her was thumping the control panel. 'Come on, for God's sake,' she said. She turned and looked at Lin. 'I hope you aren't claustrophobic.'

Consciously and with a great effort, Lin shut down the roaring screens in her mind, where pictures leapt in high colour: road sections, graphs, clocks. There was something linking this girl with clocks, perhaps her father, perhaps a brother, someone in her past that she had purposely put on one side, shuttering the past behind the present, where it clattered behind the barrier, constantly threatening to undermine her. The hands on those clocks were intimately linked with this same girl's hands . . . Lin pressed and pushed at the words and images, the hands on the dials, the shade of blue, the colour of the river before the silt, the anxiety bridging Werth and Kieran like a brick band, clumsy, heavy to handle . . . she crushed them flat. *Flat, silent.* The confined space of the lift interior came flexing back like a thick, textural colour photocopy that had been rolled into a tight tube and then released. The girl was staring at her.

The lift jolted.

Lulu looked away.

'Thank Christ for that,' she muttered.

The show began at eight.

In the hospital, a hundred miles away, Kieran had not left Theo's side.

Theo had suffered a hairline skull fracture. Kieran had been told it was not serious and that Theo would make a full recovery. But his son hadn't woken at all so far.

'It's a kind of healing,' the nurse had advised him. 'Don't worry. Go home for a little while, and rest.'

But Kieran refused to go.

He had left Theo once too often. He would see him through this, no matter how long it took. He thought of ringing Lin, but didn't know what to say to her. Once Theo came round, he told Edith, who was also still there, he would drive up to London and tell her face to face. In Lin's condition and state of mind, he was frightened of breaking such news to her over the phone. He wanted to be there to make sure she travelled back home with him at once.

He had spent an hour with the police, going over and over the sequence of events involving Ruth. When asked why she had jumped, he had to tell them he didn't know. *Because of him?* Surely not just that. *Work?* Not that either. There was something else, some inner death.

Late in the afternoon, Kieran fell asleep, his head slumping onto Theo's bed, his arms crossed in front of him serving as a pillow. He dozed fitfully, dreamlessly, the sleep of exhaustion, until he was woken by a sensation on his arm.

He raised his head to see Theo's fingers tightening around his wrist—and the little boy's eyes open, staring straight into his.

Lin stood in a corridor waiting to be called.

It was the wrong place to be, but she felt uneasy in the green room. She had walked out into the corridor, and gazed for some time at the river and streets, then turned away from the windows and paced the long passage. Eventually she headed downstairs, using a service stair-way this time. Lulu followed her like a miserable child, cheated of her moment of being depended on. Before their turn in front of the cameras, most other guests did all but cling to her arm, whimpering. 'There's really nothing down here. This isn't the right way. This is all film crew,' she moaned.

'I only want to watch them,' Lin said.

'It isn't allowed.'

'Don't be silly,' Lin said.

Lulu dropped behind her, muttering, 'Bloody hell.' She had unhooked the small mobile from her board and began punching keys.

Lin had stopped outside the studio doors. She could hear the audience laughing inside. Robbie England had a full orchestra, a double set, an audience of two hundred, the biggest studio. And somewhere out there, beyond the hotly lit stage and the tiers of seats and the surrounding dark, were sixteen million viewers, recently increased by virtue of England's own much-publicized divorce and his remarriage to a girl of eighteen. Lin tried to hear his voice.

'Lin!' someone called. She turned.

It was Harry, holding out a phone to her.

'It's Kieran,' he said.

She looked at it, torn with indecision.

'Tell him you can't find me,' she murmured.

'I can't do that,' Harry replied. 'I've told him where we are. He says it's urgent.'

She took the phone reluctantly, and put it to her ear.

'Lin,' Kieran said. 'Lin?'

'I'm here.'

'Thank God. Harry just rang me to say you're still doing England's show. Listen, you mustn't do it because . . .'

She shook her head, and handed the phone back to Harry.

Kieran realized that she had disconnected, and he cursed.

'Isn't she there?' Edith asked.

He turned, and put his arm around her shoulder. 'She won't talk to me. I'll have to drive up to London.'

Edith frowned. 'Be driven, you mean,' she said. 'I'll stay here with Theo.'

'Thanks. OK—be driven.' He started dialling on the mobile again.

'And what are you going to tell Lin when you see her?' Edith asked. 'Besides about Theo?'

'Besides Theo.'

Kieran smiled at her. 'That I believe her, of course.'

FORTY-FIVE

*L*IN WENT ON AIR AT PRECISELY EIGHT FORTY-FIVE.

It was like stepping into a hot electric pool; the lights momentarily blinded her. She needed to walk across part of the set, and then negotiate three steps down, and across to the sofa where Robbie England was waiting with both arms extended, a broad smile pasted over his face.

The applause deafened her. She was aware of the ranked seats beyond the lights, and she could hear—as well as the applause—a sharp rise in conversation. The cameras were following her, like animals stalking her from the shadows. Her entrance took forever, or what seemed like forever. She could barely feel her own feet; they had now lost that sense of being too large, and had simply become free-floating, unwieldy, weightless objects that were capable of tripping her up.

She lowered her head as she reached the three steps, pausing at the top and taking them slowly. But, as she got to the bottom, she tripped.

There was a *frisson* of suspense, a unified intake of breath, and suddenly, to her horror, Robbie England came running forward, yowling. There was no other word for it: he yowled like a cat on a back wall. She had only stumbled and faltered for a second, but he made a tremendous show of pretending to catch her. As she straightened up, he flung

324

himself on the floor, rolling so that he was facing upwards, and yelled, 'Fall on me, Mrs Gallagher! Please fall on me!'

The audience roared. Lin stopped dead. England jumped up and brushed himself down. 'Aw, you spoilsport,' he said. 'Lovely girl like you, denying an old man his few last pleasures.' Laughter rippled through the darkness—Robbie England was barely thirty.

He picked up her hand and kissed it. Lin shadowed her face from the lights with her other hand. Still laughing, he led her to the guest sofas, pretending to wipe sweat from his face. Lin noticed that his fingers merely brushed his forehead under the great pantomime sweeps of his hand; but the man was actually sweating heavily. He plonked himself down with an exaggerated sigh, then immediately scrambled back to his feet.

'I'm forgetting my manners,' he said, gazing at the audience with a mock-humiliated expression. His catch-phrase—when he had first become successful some eight years before—had been *awgawd*, delivered in a thick cockney accent. If anything, the accent was laid on even heavier now, but he had not said *awgawd* on his show for a long time; yet he made the *awgawd* face now, chin pulled down, eyes widened, mouth a tiny little O in his round face.

Lin sat down. She felt his fingers and palm still imprinted on hers. England positioned himself opposite. The applause subsided.

'Well, Mrs Gallagher,' he said, 'how are you?'

'I'm fine,' Lin said. She dared not look out towards the camera—the audience. She looked at Robbie England's round jawline, his camel-coloured suit. He wore a pink T-shirt under the suit. There was a small gold stud in the lobe of one ear. He had blond hair cut very short—almost, but not quite, shaved—and, up close to what had only before been a television image, she realized how alarmingly small he was—more like a child than a man.

The effect was grotesque: he would look vicious without that smile; and she had never seen him without his trademark grin. Whenever his photograph appeared in the newspapers, he was always pulling some kind of face: mock horror, mock surprise, mock lewdness. She had never seen him looking serious, but at the same time, so close to him now, she saw the glitter of savagery in his eye.

In his routines, he made a great play on his diminutive size. 'I need indulging,' he would say. 'My mum never indulged me . . . my wife never indulges me. Here, girls.'—*indulge* me! Indulge him next to you! Go on!'

England's gaze narrowed very slightly. 'We haven't met before, have we?'

'No,' Lin said.

He reached out and vigorously shook her hand. 'Robbie England.' The audience tittered. Lin smiled.

'I've seen your husband,' he said.

'Oh . . . yes.'

'On the box.'

'Yes.'

'Does that history programme—lots of history programmes.'

'Yes.'

'Bit of a professor.'

Lin did not reply. She felt as if the lights were peeling her skin. The salmon pink T-shirt looked semi-fluorescent. She blinked.

'You was at college when you met him?' England said.

'Yes, I was.'

'His pupil, eh?'

'No . . .'

England began singing the Police song, *Don't Stand So Close To Me*. He sang it badly, and began to laugh. 'Like that?' he asked.

Lin hesitated. 'Actually—'

'*Actually . . .*' England snatched the word off her, tipping forward almost out of his chair to grin at the audience. 'I love posh birds, don't you?' he said, then sat back. 'You look different,' he continued.

'From what?' Lin asked.

'From all your pictures. Taken a few years back, mind—that's what it is,' he said, studiedly offhand. 'Now, we all know Kieran—Mr Gallagher. All these girls in the audience know Mr Gallagher. Don't you girls?' he asked his audience.

There was a small riffle of response.

'Speak to Robert!' England roared.

'Yes!' they chorused.

'Yes, we all know Kieran—especially those women up in the third row. Look at them—all catalogue frocks. They know him, and it's not because they like Roman emperors. It's because they like *buttocks*. Own up, girls!'

'Yea . . .' the audience murmured, laughing.

England turned back to Lin. 'Was it passion in the library, love among the ruins, Lin?' She stared at him. 'Where *is* Kieran?' he asked.

Lin floundered for a second. 'He's recording his next series,' she said.

'Oh, is he? I thought he was just keeping his distance.' He turned, as if to shout to someone offstage. 'You've given me duff info here, you silly bint!' He laughed and turned back. 'Are you all right?' he asked.

Lin looked about her.

'You, Lin. Are you all right?'

'Yes,' she said.

'That's good. Now'—he reached behind the sofa—'I know you like reading. You college birds read a lot of books. I know what that's like: I read a book once. Here, look . . .' He brought out a small, folded pile of newspapers. 'I read the papers now instead. And you were in the papers this week, more than one paper, weren't you, Lin?'

She gazed at the tabloid on top, her heart dropping.

'Speak to Robert,' England said.

'Yes,' she replied.

He opened the first newspaper—after glancing twice at the girl on the front page and raising his eyebrows at the audience. 'Here it is,' he said. 'Page three.' He plunged his head into the paper and ruffled the pages, as if in transports of ecstasy. 'No! That's not you,' he exclaimed. 'Blimey! Who *is* that? Never mind. Jesus! No . . . look . . . ah! Page five—that's you.' He dropped the paper into his lap. 'This is all very very interesting, Lin,' he continued. 'It says here you think you're God.'

'I didn't say that,' Lin told him.

England looked at the audience. 'You know, I can believe that,' he said. 'No, listen . . . these reporters, they're bastards. No, they are! I told them I was only interviewing Karen Whittle for charity, and they blew it up out of all proportion . . .'

The audience exploded. Six months before, England had been

caught literally with his trousers around his ankles with a game-show hostess. He raised his hands now in the stock gesture of a fisherman describing an enormous catch. 'Blown up out of all proportion!' he chortled.

Lin glanced back over her shoulder, trying to make out if Harry was standing at the back of the stage.

'Lin,' England said.

'Yes?'

'Are you with us?'

'Yes. I'm sorry.'

'Not in communication for a minute, there, with a higher intelligence of any kind? Not talking to anyone?'

'No, I'm sorry.'

'Tell us about being God, Lin.'

'I didn't say that. I said—'

'Because we would all like to know what it's like. Are there any perks?'

'I said—'

'There must be,' he said. 'Just little things. Bring cream cakes into being with a flick of the wrist. Lie on nice fluffy clouds all day. Flood a few thousand acres for kicks. Live for ever . . . Things like that. Create the blowfly for a laugh. That sort of thing, hmmm?'

A murmur ran through the audience, then drained away into silence. They sensed Robbie England was drawing in for the kill—the usual thrill of his last ten minutes on air.

'Can you see the future?' he asked.

'No,' she said.

'Read my mind?'

'I—'

'Cure cancer?'

'No.'

'You're not God, then, are you?'

'I—'

'Are you?' He leaned forward and pointed at her. 'My mum believes in God,' he said, his voice suddenly dangerously low. 'She believes in Jesus. She goes to church.' He swung his finger over towards the camera with the red light. 'Look straight in that camera and tell her she's got it wrong. That no one actually listens to her praying. There isn't a God up there! He's down here, and married to the man with the tightest arse in Europe. Look in that camera and tell her she's got it wrong.'

Lin stared at him, silent.

'I can understand Kieran not wanting to live with God,' he said. 'Puts him in the shade a bit, poor bloke.' He sat back, looking at her, letting the silence develop. The studio atmosphere hummed with tension.

Lin sat transfixed. England, in contrast, was draped over the sofa, supremely relaxed.

Then he smiled. 'That wasn't very nice,' he said. 'That was a bit below the belt.' He turned to the audience and held up both hands.

'Maybe I've got it round me neck. I'm a bit thick, you know. So you tell us.' He waved his arm at the camera. 'I'm giving you prime time here. You can't get better publicity than that for your new telly series. So . . .' He got up, stepped over to her, and offered her his hand. 'Come with me, Lin.'

She put her hand in his and got to her feet. He pulled her forward.

'Now watch your step,' he said. 'Come on down here . . .' He led her to the front of the set, within ten feet of his audience. For the first time, Lin saw their faces. She felt nothing at all, only a deep gut sensation of fear, so deep and remote that it was hardly real.

Everything else was blank.

Harry was there in the shadows.

Cameras were rolling backwards at the front of the set, so as to capture both Lin's expression and the reaction of the audience.

'Now, all Lin has to do is touch something,' England explained.

'Oh, fucking, fucking hell,' Harry muttered.

'Somebody come down here—anybody want to come down here?' England asked.

Harry turned away. He couldn't watch this. He went back through the gloom, pushed aside the girl standing by the door, and started to head out. Then his attention was caught by a woman in the audience, who had put up her hand.

'You, my love . . .' Robbie England said.

The microphone swung over her.

'Stand up, darling. Come down here.'

The woman did as she was told.

'No, Lin,' Harry whispered. 'She's a plant. He put her there. She's an actress. Lin . . . don't talk to her.'

On the stage, Lin tried to focus. Her sight blurred and cleared, blurred and cleared. The woman had a severe face; she did not smile. England held out his free hand towards her.

'Yes, you come over here and talk to Lin,' he said.

Lin stared at them both, not understanding.

'Go ahead,' England instructed.

'I'm sorry?' Lin asked.

He transferred the woman's hand into her own. 'There you go . . .'

He stepped back, leaving them stranded at the front of the stage under the lights—like some absurd married couple. He strolled off to one side.

'Now, a day or two ago, Lin did a lovely thing,' England announced. 'She touched a person, a boy in an ambulance, and some people say she cured this person. Isn't that a wonderful thing? A miracle. If it's true, you might say. And Lin has asked to come here tonight—I expect, to defend herself. So . . .'

A murmur went through the audience. It was not all in Robbie England's favour. It carried a small, disappointed, embarrassed note: sympathy for the underdog. England registered it, but his smile only became broader. He had expected this.

'No, I'm a fair man—you know that,' he said. 'I've been a bit hard on Lin so far, and she wants to show us this thing is real. So here we go.' He leaned forward to the woman. 'What's your name, love?'

'Andrea,' the woman said.

'Andrea. Lovely. Now . . .'

'I can't do this,' Lin said.

England turned to her. 'Sorry, Lin?'

Lin let the woman's hand drop. 'I can't do this,' she said.

'Can't do what, exactly?'

'I can't do tricks,' Lin said.

'Tricks? I'm not asking you to do tricks, am I?'

'Could I sit down?' she murmured.

'I thought it wasn't a trick,' England persisted. 'Is that what it is, after all, then? A trick? Like a magic trick?'

'No,' Lin said.

'Like David Copperfield? Paul Daniels?'

'No, no . . .'

'What is it then?'

Lin shut her eyes. She felt nothing but a roaring, blinding pain. All the voices, the sounds and images of the last few days had vanished. There was nothing there but one vast, echoing light in which the point of pressure was a white-hot blade. The muscles in her jaw felt slack, uncontrolled. Her right arm began to tremble.

'Tell him Michael is here,' she said.

England glanced behind him to see which camera was operating.

'Michael is here,' Lin repeated.

'Hello, Mike!' England said.

Someone in the front row laughed out loud.

'Shut your mouth, Robbie Donovan,' Lin whispered.

England stopped dead.

'Here comes Robbie Donovan on his bike,' she murmured. 'All the way from Bethnal Green. Such a long way . . .'

England saw the floor manager move forward. He fixed him with a quick look—making a closing, circling motion with his hand, below vision of the camera.

Lin laughed softly. 'And he never give me that money back,' she said a little louder, her voice more guttural. 'That was all I had . . . forty pounds . . . and I was sick for fifteen days, fifteen days in that hospital, and he never came. He only came when I was dead. What fuckin' use was that, boy? You little bastard.'

England's colour was ashen.

Lin turned full circle. Her eyes were still shut. She faced into the far left-hand side of the audience. To her side, the camera reversed quickly to catch her.

'You know that,' Lin said to the silent crowd before her. Her head was turning slowly from side to side, as if to locate a source. 'David? David? Are you here?'

There was complete silence.

'And there is . . . a lady with a red dress . . . her husband is here, he found a dress, a ticket for a dress, to collect . . .'

A man stood up, halfway up the aisle.

'She *is* here. Why did you put the dress away? Take it to the shop and sell it. What use is it now?' she asked.

It had gone beyond pain.

A long, long way beyond pain.

The blade was slowly cutting through the light, unpicking it particle by particle. Lin opened her eyes. She saw the threads of light fall away . . . the colours between . . . the spectrum of lesser lights.

Out of the radiance they came, smoothly free-floating figures, travelling through other senses, other dimensions, corridors of communication that were much more than sound or sight or touch. A hundred frequencies were open to a hundred different minds. Only the human receivers shut down reception. The voices were always there, speaking and rarely being heard. And the force of love transported them backwards and forwards, effortlessly moving—souls never still—through perpetually moving chains of life . . . There were geometric images of intense complexity. Spirals of genetic information . . . so beautiful, so beautiful . . .

'It's real,' Lin murmured.

She opened her arms to catch the light, streaming through the dark.

'It's real,' she repeated.

The fantastic force of it crashed through her. She was standing in its centre, and could hear echo over echo, as though she were standing on the threshold of some enormous hall whose acoustics threw sounds at her over a huge distance. She could hear thousands of voices now: the growing murmur sounding like a gigantic hive of industriously humming bees. She heard rain, she heard the sea drawing over stone and sand, she heard the continual turning and whispering of a countless number of leaves, she heard the light, heard the light refracting, changing. And, just as she did so, the lights overhead that burned with such a fierce glare shorted and flashed, and for a second the whole auditorium was plunged into darkness.

'What the hell!' someone said.

It was Robbie England, somewhere close to her shoulder, speaking in the whispered breath of a frightened child.

Footsteps in the dark.

Almost immediately the lights came back; but the room was filled with noise. There was an ominous, low-pitched drumming. The lights on set were flickering. A musician in the orchestra—off to the far right-hand side—suddenly yelled and leapt to his feet.

'Live cable!' a voice cried.

Thunder filled Lin's head.

'Off air,' someone called. 'Off air yet?'

Footsteps, footsteps.

'Here they are,' Lin murmured.

She tried to see through the blazing white barrier in front of her.

'Here they come,' she said.

As soon as the lights failed, Harry began to run forward.

He tripped over something, staggered, and ran forward again, his hands spread out in front of him. He collided with a piece of furniture, cursed, and swerved to one side. The lights flashed back on, and he found himself centre stage, just above the same steps on which Lin had tripped earlier. For a second, on television screens across the country, several images flashed: a close-up of Robbie England; a blank shot of the empty sofas, and a figure passing in front of them; two or three shots of Lin from separate angles—then a close-up of her face.

Many of the audience were on their feet. There was a deafening rumbling sound of electricity overload. Several people in the centre put their hands over their ears.

Harry was within three or four paces of Lin when England turned to face him. On the younger man's face was a look of complete disorientation. He stared at Harry, as if for support, then turned away, back to the audience.

'Keep your seats, ladies and gents,' he called in a small and unrecognizable voice. 'Please . . .'

Then he suddenly turned back to Lin, who stood stock-still in centre stage. Her eyes were open, looking upwards, her arms still extended in front of her. He held out one hand, and immediately, with a small cry, retracted it. Harry ran forward again, just as England stepped back, shaking his hand. The two men collided.

'She's fucking live,' England murmured. 'Oh God, she's live . . . don't touch her . . . don't touch her . . .'

Lin saw glowing figures materialize twenty, perhaps thirty feet from her.

They were more than beautiful, much more beautiful than the preceding glowing luminosity. They were more beautiful than anything she had ever seen: alight, incandescent, outlined in a glorious living blue that rippled and shook, spreading towards her—covering all those in-between. She felt the audience stand.

'Here they are!' she cried.

Small points of energy—tiny blue balls of phosphorescence—hurled themselves out of the central glare. As though from a tremendous distance, she heard a woman scream. Holding her breath, she stared into the heart of the light.

Just for a moment, she saw Caroline Devlin's face, perfectly clear and smiling, turned towards her. Lin, too, smiled. Her body had ceased to exist: she felt its heaviness drop away, too inefficient, too slow, crumpling to the floor like an encumbering piece of cloth. She was all light now, part of the brilliance exploding around her.

She felt an overwhelming conviction, a sense of complete understanding, of revelation. The world became clear. Simple and clean and clear. All its pretensions and anxieties ceased to exist. There was nothing more important than reunion with that expanding, astounding blue. Nothing mattered at all but the reconnection to the flood, the flood that had brought her so far and was ready to take her back.

The sounds around her faded. Silence enclosed her.

There were two figures in the light.

Lin stood still, knowing at once why they had come and who they were.

Her mother was holding the girl by the hand.

The girl was small, about seven years old. Dark-haired, brown-eyed. Mother and granddaughter smiled. The child hesitated for a moment; but her grandmother laid her hands on her shoulders and gently pushed her forward.

'Lindsay,' her mother said, 'this is your daughter. We called her Elizabeth.'

Lin felt her child move into her grasp. She felt the small hand fold around hers. She felt the warm flesh of her fingers. And more than that. So much more than that.

Joy.

Complete and perfect joy.

FORTY-SIX

$\mathcal{T}$HERE WAS COMPLETE BEDLAM IN THE TELEVISION STUDIO.

Most of the audience was struggling to get out, climbing over seats where aisles and rows were blocked. The lights were on again, the terrible intimidating droning had stopped, but the stage was rapidly filling with technicians. The musicians had left their places: some moving forward, others back towards the exits. Robbie England was standing six feet away from Lin, one hand tucked into his armpit. He said nothing at all, despite being surrounded.

Harry was on his knees beside Lin, who had collapsed on the stage, and lay curled on her side. She was completely white, her body limp and unresponsive.

'What the hell happened?' he demanded to no one in particular.

There was a further disturbance at the back of the stage.

Harry looked up to see Kieran—dishevelled, hollow-eyed, looking like hell—forcing his way through the milling technicians. Seeing Lin on the floor, he ran forward and dropped to his knees at her side, picking up her inert hand. 'She was electrocuted? What caused it?' He glared around him, raising his voice. 'What happened?'

Robbie England was staring down at Lin. With some effort, he lifted his gaze and stared at the group of people gathered around him.

'Did you see that?' he whispered.

'See what?' asked the man nearest him.

England's gaze rested on him for a moment, then he turned to Kieran. 'She was full of electricity,' he said. 'I touched her. There were two people coming down the aisle . . . then she was live . . . I got an electric shock . . .'

Kieran stared at him. 'I'm going to sue your whole bloody set-up,' he snapped.

'It wasn't so bad,' one of the crew said to Robbie England. 'They managed to put the credits up. Maybe there was nothing else to see but a flicker with the lights.' His hand rested on his ear-mike. 'They've given out a voiceover—about an electrical fault. It was just the last ten seconds . . . no problem.'

Kieran stared at Harry. 'I can't feel her pulse.'

He had pressed his fingers against Lin's wrist. There was nothing there: she felt loose, dead. He turned her onto her back, tipped her head back, and lowered his ear to her mouth.

'Is she breathing?' Harry asked.

Kieran did not know for sure. He thought he could feel *something* on his skin. He started shaking, and took a deep, gasping breath, trying to keep himself under control.

'Come back,' he muttered. He put his fingers on Lin's throat.

After what seemed like an age, he felt a butterfly-wing response.

'Get an ambulance!' he shouted over the surrounding din. 'Get an ambulance now!'

Lin was admitted to St Matthew's at nine-twenty. She was rushed straight through Casualty to undergo a CAT scan. Kieran had given them Mark Werth's telephone number, and they in turn phoned it through to the allocated surgeon, now on his way through central London traffic. Kieran and Harry waited in agonized, frozen silence in the corridor, intently watching the outside doors.

Ten minutes later, they were both amazed to see the consultant walking through the lobby at an even, unhurried pace, still speaking into his mobile phone. Under his overcoat, the man wore a dinner jacket. He paused outside the unit door to finish his call, and then turned and shook Kieran's hand.

'Benedict Gray,' he said.

'Kieran—'

'Gallagher. I recognize you, Mr Gallagher. Your wife's neurologist tells me she refused to have treatment.'

'She's got a tumour,' Kieran said bluntly. 'Take it out.'

The consultant smiled, then pushed open the unit door. 'Be with you in just a moment,' he said.

Kieran turned to Harry. 'She's not here,' he said.

Harry frowned. 'What do you mean?'

'She's not in that room. She's not here . . .'

Harry took his arm, and guided him over to the nearest seat. 'She'll be OK,' he murmured.

'I *can't feel* her here,' Kieran repeated. 'She's gone.'

In less than a minute, the consultant came out. He had taken off his overcoat, and motioned Kieran and Harry to follow him as he set off at a brisk pace.

'Is she all right?' Harry asked.

They had now reached a bank of lifts, where the consultant pressed the button for an upper floor. 'No,' he replied. 'There is severe inter-cranial pressure.'

'What does that mean?' Harry asked.

'The brain is being pressed inwards—which causes damage.'

'Can you do anything?' Kieran murmured.

'Yes. We can release the pressure by taking off the top of the skull.'

Kieran blanched.

'This refusing of treatment . . .' Gray continued.

'It's my responsibility,' Kieran said. 'She's my wife, and I don't refuse it. Do whatever you have to.'

The consultant glanced up at the indicator above them. 'It's rather an interesting ethical point,' he said. He pressed the lift button again. 'She specifically did not want any intervention yesterday.'

'She told me that nothing was wrong with her,' Harry said.

Gray glanced at them both in turn, held up one hand and smiled. 'But that was yesterday,' he added. 'That took no account of a worsening condition. And Mr Werth gave no undertaking not to act in the event of such significant deterioration.'

Finally the lift came. Gray stood for a second holding the doors open with his foot. He reached across and put his hand on Kieran's arm. 'We shall do exactly what is needed,' he said, 'but you realize the situation is very serious?'

'Yes,' Kieran replied.

'She's not going to die, though?' Harry asked.

Gray stepped inside the lift. 'When intercranial pressure gets to this stage, every part of the brain is affected.' He paused. 'We have minutes—just minutes.'

'Christ,' Kieran whispered.

'So, we have your permission to go ahead?'

'Yes,' Kieran said. 'Yes, of course. Yes . . .'

The lift doors closed.

Kieran walked numbly away. Harry followed him. They continued aimlessly down the corridor, until they came again into the Casualty reception area.

There was a scattered group of patients: two men sitting alone and apart; a mother with a very small child asleep in her arms. An elderly lady nursing one side of her face, with a younger woman at her side. No one looked up at Kieran and Harry. In the corner a television blared.

Kieran sat down suddenly on the nearest chair, plunging his head into his hands.

'Oh God,' he whispered. 'God help her.'

FORTY-SEVEN

*T*HE SNOW HAD BEEN FALLING ALL NIGHT.

It lay in smooth, unmarked drifts below the hedge, turning the paddock that ran down to the river into an eerie, brilliant cloth, whiter than the sky that lowered into the valley. The river was almost black by contrast, threading in loops past houses, through fields, until it came to the foot of the hill where it scooped a series of spectacular arcs, a lazy scrawl of letters, until it reached the grounds of the Priory.

Here it was subdued into a narrower band. All the old sluice gates in the water meadows stood open: small blackened landmarks in the December snow. Mark Werth stood in the hallway, looking at this monochrome scene through the narrow windows on each side of the door, thinking how hard it was to believe there was anything green under such a covering.

The roads out of the village were all but impassable.

He had come down yesterday, and been ambushed by the weather, a storm that swept quickly over the south of England and closed all but the most major routes. In a landscape like this, where all roads out involved steep hills, you might as well abandon any thought of moving until the farm-sponsored four-wheel-drives forced a way through. He had been out that morning to watch them chugging a path out; but, as fast as they moved on, the snow closed in behind them.

In truth he was not really inclined to go, anyway.

He caught a brief movement further along the drive, and pulled on his coat and gloves. Theo was already hurtling through the dug-out trench of snow. Seeing Mark, he stopped, and scrambled around to point at the woman coming up behind him.

Werth went down to meet her.

It was one of the mothers from the village, out of breath and very red in the face.

'I've lost my own,' she said, laughing. 'They're fighting it out with the Clarks.' She sighed and put her hands on her hips. 'Gosh! It's bloody hard work through this lot.'

Werth looked back at Theo, who was busy pushing a snowball across the lawn, picking up sticks and shreds of dark grass as he rolled.

'Thanks for bringing him.'

'It's no problem. He's been fine.'

'Ready for Christmas?'

'Is anyone?' She smiled. 'Well, I'll be off. Anything you need?'

'No, I don't think so.'

'That's great.' She turned to go. ''Bye now.'

He spent ten minutes helping turn Theo's snowball into a boulder, then took the boy's hand and dragged him indoors. 'You're frozen,' he said. 'You want me to have to tell your dad you turned into a snowman?'

'Yeah,' Theo said, delighted with the idea. Without taking off his outdoor clothes, the boy ran into the sitting room, and launched himself onto the couch.

Lin was sitting there, surrounded by coloured paper strips.

'How're you doing?' Mark asked.

She had held out her arms and Theo wriggled into her lap. 'Hey, you're wet,' she objected. 'Mind the things.'

'I do decorations,' Theo said.

'OK.' She smiled, holding up a short string that she had already glued together. 'So much for your therapy,' she told Werth. 'Look at that. An hour to do twelve of them.'

He smiled back. 'It'll get better.'

Lin had turned back to Theo. 'Take off your . . .'

She paused momentarily, fingering the cloth of his waxed jacket. A spasm of frustration registered in her expression; her eyes trailed past her son's face, trying to find the neural corridor of association that would enable her to recall the word. 'Take that thing off,' she said eventually.

'Its name?' Theo said, unbuttoning the coat.

'Yes, I forget its name.'

'Jacket.'

'Jacket . . . jacket,' she repeated. 'That's the one. Take it off. Hang it up.'

'I'll take it,' Mark Werth said. 'Want some tea?'

'Mmm . . . how is the snow?'

'Stopped falling, but deep now.'

She smiled at him. 'Now we *got* you.'

He laughed. 'I don't mind. It's my week off. Nobody wants me.' He handed her the letters he had taken from the hall table. 'Post finally came.'

She looked at the envelopes, and set them down. Theo snatched up the first, with an airmail stamp. It was addressed to him. Two photographs spilled out as he unfolded the page. He glanced at them, then handed them over to her.

'Hey, look,' Lin said. 'Spaceships.' She read the reverse. 'In Florida.'

Werth sat down, facing her, glancing at Kieran's precise, small handwriting. 'How much longer will he be away?'

'Oh, weeks.'

'He didn't consider coming back for Christmas?'

She smiled. 'Florida for Christmas? Would you?'

Werth glanced at Theo.

'He's promised us a holiday at Easter, somewhere warm,' Lin said.

Werth did not comment.

Theo hauled himself down from the couch and went over to the fire.

'Don't put logs on,' Lin warned him. 'Just look.'

Werth looked towards Theo. 'I'd rather you weren't here on your own,' he said.

'We're not alone,' she told him. 'Mrs Sawyer comes in every day, and the people in the village are superb. And I can walk, make beds, do the whole thing—you know that.'

He returned her smile. 'I know you've defied every instruction to take things slowly,' he said.

'I should damned well think so,' she replied.

He considered her. 'No recurrence at all? You're sure?'

'Nothing.'

'Nothing after the last seizure?'

'Nine weeks ago.'

'You still take the medication?'

'Of course.'

He paused. 'No time losses, no precognitions, no voices?'

'For heaven's sake!'

Her face was such a mixture of expressions, somewhere between exasperation and regret, that he moved over to her side of the couch. 'And you're still determined on college next year?'

'Yes,' she said, with utter conviction. 'The refresher takes three months, and I register in June. The course itself starts in October.'

'If you're sure.'

'I'm sure. After my degree, with any luck, I'll be able to do post-graduate research. That's what I want.'

'What kind of research, do you know?'

She smiled slowly. 'Ah, wait and see.'

He started to pick up the pieces of paper that Theo had inadvertently knocked to the floor. 'And Harry left you alone, finally?'

She laughed. 'Harry wasn't the pain. That was Lazenby. But I won't do TV. I can't anyway. I don't want to scramble words in front of a camera. And that show with Robbie England . . .' She pulled a face, and sighed. 'Still, I said my piece, even if no one seemed to hear it.'

'I'm sure no one thinks any worse of you,' he told her. 'Everyone knows it was the illness. The papers were very sympathetic in the end.'

'It doesn't matter,' she said.

'Still not tempted to take over where Kieran left off?'

'No,' she said. 'I just don't want Kieran's world secondhand. I want my own.'

They paused, watching Theo, who was stretched out full-length on the rug in front of the fire.

'What's Harry doing now?' Werth asked.

'He's found a new supernova: that basketball player turned actor.' She laughed to herself. 'Certainly running rings round poor Harry—but nice profitable ones.'

She picked up a cushion, smoothed it, and hugged it to her chest.

Werth nodded. He stood up, stretched, and walked over to switch on a table lamp. 'I'll get that tea.'

'Might as well make yourself useful, while you're stuck here.'

He gave her a rueful smile and went out.

The dying afternoon drifted on in silence. After a minute or two, Lin got up with some difficulty, and walked to the window, where, after looking out at the snow, she slowly drew the curtains. The room condensed to a cosy glow. Going to the fire, she sat down on the rug next to Theo.

He lay with one hand stretched before him, silhouetting it in front of the flames, waving it to the side, describing circles in the air.

She watched him. Then they both began to listen . . .

For a while neither of them moved.

Mark Werth had turned on the radio in the kitchen. The sound of a recorded play drifted down the hall, filtering through to them in faint, disconnected phrases.

However, they were not listening to that at all.

But to something else.

Theo turned to his mother. 'Are the pretty people coming?' he asked.

She nodded slowly. 'Sssh,' she said. She smiled, and glanced towards the door leading to the kitchen.

Theo grinned, and grasped her hand.

'Lizbeth,' he whispered.

And in the glow of the fire they waited, looking patiently into the shadows.